Praise for
The Secrets B

A *Cleveland Scene* Hot Summer F

BookBub—13 Summer Books to Read

A *WOC Reads* 10 Top Releases

"The novel's plot is wonderfully rich in details of material life, and, though filled with misfortune and cruelty, is, in the end, a heartwarming tale of friendship and courage."

—*Washington Post*

"The women at the heart of this novel inhabit the harsh world of the urban Indian poor, and struggle separately and together for dignity and survival. Thrity Umrigar has written a moving human tale that vividly brings to life both the women and the city of Mumbai." —Salman Rushdie

"*The Secrets Between Us* is a powerful, urgent novel that wields issues of gender and class like a blade. The weight of Bhima's tragic past and her intractable present finds its counterbalance in the most unlikely of characters: Parvati, an elderly homeless woman who is haunted by a history of her own. This intergenerational novel asks hard questions about who we are, who we can become, and what awaits on the other side of our becoming. Thrity Umrigar is known as a bold and generous writer, and *The Secrets Between Us* only further establishes her reputation."

—Wiley Cash, author of *The Last Ballad*

"*The Secrets Between Us* broke me open as thoroughly as any novel I've read in recent years. Bhima and Parvati, two proud, aging women hard-used by life, are as unlikely a pair of heroes as one could imagine, and yet they jump from these pages big and true as life, striving, surviving, learning to hope and even love long past the point where such things have come to seem like a cruel joke. Thrity Umrigar has given us yet another brilliant powerhouse of a novel."

—Ben Fountain, author of *Billy Lynn's Long Halftime Walk*

"Umrigar's writing is vivid and elegant in its specificity, and the story is as resilient as its characters." —*Minneapolis Star Tribune*

"[*The Secrets Between Us*] provides an almost "Siddhartha"-esque experience of sharing a character's spiritual journey, as the plot takes Bhima and Parvati to places where they must question their preconceptions, search their souls and ultimately change."

—*Newsday*

"Picking up *The Space Between Us* first may enlighten readers about Bhima's backstory, but this title easily stands on its own. It chronicles the triumph of women's friendships and fortitude in the face of considerable obstacles—poverty, homophobia, illiteracy, gender discrimination, ageism, and sexual assault. It further displays Umrigar's insights into the deep resilience of the human heart." —*Library Journal* (starred review)

"[Umrigar's] amazing cast is coupled with shining prose and a plot that consistently startles and gratifies. This splendid tale should appeal to all readers with open hearts, regardless of their familiarity with the previous work or the culture of Mumbai."

—*Publishers Weekly*

Praise for *The Space Between Us*

"Umrigar is a skilled storyteller, and her memorable characters will live on for a long time." —*Washington Post*

"With humanity and suspense, novelist Thrity Umrigar tackles love, loyalty, injustice—and survival." —*Marie Claire*

"Heartbreaking. . . . A subtle, elegant analysis of class and power . . . that quietly roars against tyranny." —*Kirkus Reviews*

"Umrigar is a highly skilled storyteller . . . the novel's plot and depth of characterization provide irresistible momentum."

—*Time Out New York*

The Secrets Between Us

ALSO BY THRITY UMRIGAR

FICTION

Everybody's Son

The Story Hour

The World We Found

The Weight of Heaven

If Today Be Sweet

The Space Between Us

Bombay Time

MEMOIR

First Darling of the Morning:

Selected Memories of an Indian Childhood

PICTURE BOOK

When I Carried You in My Belly

The Secrets Between Us

A NOVEL

Thrity Umrigar

HARPER PERENNIAL

NEW YORK • LONDON • TORONTO • SYDNEY • NEW DELHI • AUCKLAND

HARPER PERENNIAL

This book is a work of fiction. References to real people, events, establishments, organizations, or locales are intended only to provide a sense of authenticity, and are used fictitiously. All other characters, and all incidents and dialogue, are drawn from the author's imagination and are not to be construed as real.

A hardcover edition of this book was published in 2018 by HarperCollins Publishers.

P.S.™ is a trademark of HarperCollins Publishers.

HarperCollins books may be purchased for educational, business, or sales promotional use. For information, please e-mail the Special Markets Department at SPsales@harpercollins.com.

FIRST HARPER PERENNIAL EDITION PUBLISHED 2019.

Designed by Leah Carlson-Stanisic

Library of Congress Cataloging-in-Publication Data has been applied for.

ISBN 978-0-06-244221-5 (pbk.)

HB 06.10.2024

To Homai

for countless acts of selfless love

Acknowledgments

I have often thought that it is a pity that the book jacket only carries the name of the author, instead of all the people who help make it possible. I don't mean just the names of the editors and the copy editors and the art designers and the publicity and marketing crew and the countless others at a publishing house who toil in anonymity, though they, of course, are crucial to the production of a book.

I also mean to include the family members who provide unconditional love and who pick up the slack of neglected housework; the friends who offer comfort or celebration, depending on the circumstances; the colleagues who encourage and influence; the pets who sit purring in your lap at midnight, when everyone else is asleep; the children in your life who remind you that this world is unimaginably beautiful and inspire you to create art that reflects that beauty.

And I mean the larger community of writers, whose work inspires and motivates, and the community of readers, without whom there is no book and whose presence at readings or whose encouraging words in an e-mail mean more than they can possibly realize.

Sometimes I wish that books were constructed like movies, in that there would be a scroll of credits at the end of each one. If this book were to list credits, here is a short list of some of the people it would feature:

Homai Umrigar, Eust Kavouras, Gulshan and Rointon Andhyarujina, Judy Griffin, Perveen and Hutokshi Rustomfram, Anne Reid, Barb Hipsman, Diana Bilimoria, Kim Conidi, Kershasp Pundole, Rhonda Kautz, Ilona Urban, Jenny Wilson, Merilee Nelson, Paula Woods, Regina Webb, Dav and Sayuri Pilkey, Mary Hagan, Denise Reynolds, Rick van Every, Vanessa Humphreville, Dave Lucas, Athena Vrettos, Chris Flint, Regina Brett, Mary Grimm, Connie Schultz, Jim Sheeler, Sarah Willis, Loung Ung, Paula McLain, Sara Holbrook, Karen Sandstrom, David Giffels, and so many others.

And, of course, Kulfi and Baklava, my darling feline sweethearts, who have taught me more about character and bravery and the importance of silliness than I could have ever imagined.

Gail Winston, my editor, thank you for your steady, calm presence; Daniel Greenberg, my agent, thank you for your hard work and commitment to my books. Special thanks to Jane Beirn, Lily Lopate, Sofia Groopman, and Mary Gaule for shepherding this book through. Thanks to Jonathan Burnham and Michael Morrison, for their faith in me.

Thank you, all, for being my tribe, my people. In these perilous times, I lean on you more than ever.

The Secrets Between Us

I

I

1

Although it is dawn, in Bhima's heart it is dark.

Even as the first light of the day filters in through the crack where the tin roof meets the horizontal planks of the hovel, she makes no move to get up from the mattress on the mud floor. There is no need. It has been three days since she has carried her meager possessions out of Sera Dubash's house, three long days of being home with her sullen, wounded granddaughter, whose every silence, every unspoken word, is an accusation that Bhima, in her dogged faithfulness to the Dubash household, in her loyalty to the fair-skinned woman who was her mistress for donkey's years, has been wrong, has stupidly spent her life valuing the wrong family over her own. There is no need to wake up this morning because there is no job to go to, no household to manage, no floor to briskly sweep, no pots and pans to scrub until the morning sun twinkles in them, no midmorning cup of tea to share with Serabai. That is, if squatting on the floor and drinking out of the glass reserved for her, while Serabai sits at the table sipping out of her cup of fine china, can be called sharing.

But as she lies awake with her eyes wide open, tracing the morning light as it moves across her shabby one-room hut like a finger moving slowly across the written page, Bhima's heart aches at the thought of those days spent in Serabai's quiet, luxurious apartment, with its air conditioners and ceiling fans, its running water and toilets that flush. And yet, this is not what she has spent the last three days mourning. The loss that is the weight of an elephant, the one that sits heavily on her chest, is the loss of things that are unnamed and unnamable—the pride Serabai used to take in her work; the quiet dignity that she accorded Bhima, so that even when, on occasion, she was annoyed at Bhima's tardiness or some other minor infraction, Serabai wrestled to control her irritation before she spoke; and the familial affection with which Sera's daughter, Dinaz, who had grown up before her eyes, treated her, as if Bhima were a beloved aunt rather than a servant. "Bhima's like family to us," she'd often overheard Serabai say to her friends, and even though Bhima choked a bit on the qualifier, she was smart enough to appreciate the sheer good luck of serving a family this generous, of a mistress who was willing to incur the ridicule and even the outrage of her friends by making such a declaration.

Now, she feels that gratitude curdling into the bitterness that is her true inheritance, her parallel, shadow self. It is as if she had swallowed the seeds of some bitter fruit in childhood and they have borne a tree that grows within her, yielding its bitter harvest time and time again—in the long-ago days following the torturous deaths of her son-in-law and her daughter, Pooja, to AIDS; on the day when her Gopal left her that life-altering letter before absconding with their son, Amit; and the time before that when Gopal's foreman had made her sign a piece of paper that cleaved their family in two.

Perhaps time has dulled these betrayals because when she thinks of them now, it's like watching the ignorant, trusting woman she once was as you would an actress in a movie. But the recent betrayal is a fresh wound, a newly plucked fruit, and it fills her not so much with anger as with shame. Again. It has happened again. And this time, there is no God to blame, no tide of misfortune that tossed her like a coconut onto an indifferent shore. This time, she curses herself for trying to protect Dinaz baby and Serabai from Serabai's son-in-law's poison and instead getting poisoned herself. She should've revealed Viraf's secret the day she discovered it, instead of covering it up and allowing his shame to become hers.

To dislodge the bitter pit at the base of her throat, Bhima rolls to her side and hears the familiar pop in her hip, followed by the second of stinging pain. She waits for the pain to subside and then closes her eyes. After more than sixty years of rising at dawn and stepping into the day, she can sleep in today. Soon, she will have to get a job, but at her age, she knows, it will be difficult. And if Viraf has spread his serpent-poison to the surrounding buildings, if he has fed the lies that he told Serabai to their neighbors and acquaintances, finding another job will be even harder. Bhima looks across the room and sees her granddaughter, Maya, sleeping a few feet away from her. She hears Maya's deep breath and smiles. This is all that remains in her world now, this beautiful, clever-but-stupid girl who allowed herself to bear the serpent's child. Who tried to fight all of them when they asked her to snuff out the child she was carrying. Who even now blazes with anger and spite at the thought of having killed her unborn baby, as if there could have been any other way out for a pregnant girl from the slums, no matter how smart she is in her studies. And this is the thing that worries her—what will she do if Maya continues to refuse to start college again. Or what will she do if Maya wishes to start college again and there is no money.

Bhima grimaces, unable to face the fearful thoughts that the encroaching morning brings. She is an old woman, unequipped to raise a young, beautiful girl-child, an incompetent custodian of someone who has to be guided through college and womanhood and marriage. How will she find a match for Maya when the time comes? In this place of walls as thin as muslin cloth, where rumors and innuendos are a sport and entertainment? Where is Gopal now, when she needs him? But then she reminds herself that Gopal, too, is now an old man, and not the laughing, singing fellow with the crooked smile whom she'd married. She can hardly believe it. Does Gopal's hip shoot bolts of pain, also? Do his knees creak when he walks? Or are his eyes comforted by the green of his brother's fields, a contrast to the mud-browns and crow-blacks of this wretched slum that peck at her eyes daily? Does he breathe in air that is sweet and clean, that doesn't carry the acidic, nostril-burning fumes that blanket this mad city? Despite her anger at him, despite the knife that he stuck in her back that she's been unable to dislodge, she hopes so. For his sake, yes, but also for the sake of Amit, all grown up, whose marriage many years ago she had not been invited to. Amit, the boy who had sucked greedily at her breast, whose fingernails she had cut for the first time, whose tiny body she had washed with a possessiveness that bordered on fury, whose every lie she could see through, whose every secret she knew, Amit, her first and last son, who was cut from the fabric of her body. He was her second self, until the day that he wasn't.

She groans, loudly, and for a minute fears that she's disturbed Maya, but the girl sleeps soundly. She's always been like this, Bhima chuckles to herself. A chit of a girl she used to be, but still she would sleep the sleep of a millionaire—steady, deep, with not a care in the world.

Bhima sighs to herself. No sense in lying here any longer when the sun is hurrying across the sky. Already, the community toilet will be buzzing with flies and people, and she will have to step gingerly to avoid soaking the hem of her sari in the shit and water and piss the slum residents will have left in their wake. The thought of the queue that has surely formed already at the water taps fills Bhima with heaviness, and she rises to her feet. She thinks for a minute of sending Maya to fill their two pots of water today, then changes her mind. Maya is young, and after she marries, a lifetime of toil and drudgery awaits her. For as long as it's possible, let her have her girlhood. Hasn't Bhima slaved for years so that Maya doesn't have to? Today will not be an exception.

She runs her fingers through her scanty hair and then flings open the tin door to their hut and steps outside. Already, the slum is a hive of activity. People walk past her, many carrying pots or buckets of sloshing water. Someone has a transistor radio on; a child flings a stone at a crow sitting on the newly installed electric pole, which only causes the bird to caw louder; two dogs snarl and wrestle with each other in the narrow gully, until an old man kicks at one of them as he passes by. A row of men in their undershirts and lungis sit on their haunches in front of the open gutters, brushing their teeth and spitting into the dank water. Bhima looks up at the sliver of sky and at the lucky sun that is its sole occupant. For a moment, she hates all of it—her neighbors bowing their heads as they pass the makeshift shrine to Krishna that someone has built, the harsh voices of women berating their hung-over husbands, the beady, inquisitive eyes of the unemployed men that follow her as she walks, the loud clangs of the metalsmith who has already started his workday, the piles of broken concrete that dot the landscape, the screaming, laughing children the color and odor of the muck and filth in which they play. All these years she had borne this because she knew that within two hours of waking up she would be making her way to Serabai's tidy, clean, quiet home where she would spend most of her day. Now, there is no respite. The thought of going from house to house begging for work is inexplicable to her. She has no network of friends, no grapevine of fellow servants to call upon. For close to thirty years, hers has been a pinched, severe existence—mornings in the slum, the day at Serabai's, and then home to cook and sleep. Her husband and son are gone, back to the ancestral land that Gopal hailed from. There is no family, other than the pretend family she imagined she had with the Dubashes. There is nothing and nobody to take its place.

Bhima nods to the old woman who lives four houses down from her. When they reach the common bathroom, a large, public room where the women crouch together as they do their business side-by-side, she allows the older woman to go ahead of her. When she follows her in, she keeps her eyes on the floor, as modesty and custom demand.

When she finally gets to the communal tap, there is a line, and by the time it's her turn, the water is down to a trickle so that it takes forever to fill a single bucket. She attempts to fill the second one, then gives up. This is her punishment for sleeping in.

As she reaches her hut, walking slowly to avoid the loss of even a drop of precious water, she is startled by the sight of Maya waiting outside the door. "Beti," she says. "What's wrong? Are you sick?"

In reply, Maya shakes her head impatiently, then gestures toward the door, indicating that she wants Bhima to enter. The young woman silently takes the two buckets from her grandmother and then follows her in. After the brightness of the morning, it takes Bhima's eyes a second to adjust to the darkness of the hut. She gasps when she recognizes the figure sitting cross-legged on the floor. It is Dinaz. Before her visitor can speak, Bhima turns to Maya. "Shameless," she whispers. "Letting Dinaz baby squat on the floor in her condition. Go next door and ask Tara to loan us a chair."

Maya looks insolently at the pregnant woman struggling to her feet and then back at her grandmother. But when she catches the fire in Bhima's eyes, she capitulates and leaves to obey the older woman's command. "Dinaz baby," Bhima breathes. "What brings you here?"

Dinaz smiles, an unexpectedly tentative smile, as if the distance between them has grown in just three days. "You," she says ruefully. "You're the reason I'm here, Bhima," she says. "To beg you to return to work."

Bhima stiffens. She is unsure of what Serabai has told her daughter about why she was let go, or what Dinaz suspects about the serpent she has married and whose child she is carrying. So she waits, wanting to hear what Dinaz has to say.

"Mummy said Viraf accidentally thought you'd . . . stolen . . . taken some cash, Bhima," Dinaz says. "And that you were so offended by that accusation that you quit." She raises her right hand to stop Bhima from interrupting. "Wait. I just came to apologize for Viraf's stupidity. Try and understand, Bhima. He's under so much pressure at work. And with me being pregnant and all. In any case, he's very sorry. Please come back."

Bhima is not sure she can trust herself to speak. But Dinaz's face is so sincere, so innocent, that she must. "Did Viraf babu say he's sorry?"

"Yes." Dinaz's voice wobbles. "That is, not exactly." She attempts a laugh. "You know how men are. Stubborn as oxen. But I'm sure he'll be happy if—"

"And Serabai? What about her?"

There is a long silence. "She doesn't know I've come here," Dinaz says at last. "Neither of them do. I . . . . I just wanted to surprise them." Dinaz tugs at Bhima's sari, much as she used to when she was a little girl. "Come on, na, Bhima. You know how mummy lov . . . how mummy can't do without you. Just come back."

But Bhima hears it all, the space between Dinaz's words. Serabai has not told her daughter what has really happened. How Viraf had accused her falsely of stealing from them, when she would've no more stolen from this family than she would from the donation box at the temple. How, realizing the trap he'd set for her, she'd lashed out with an accusation of her own, this one darker, more powerful than his, because it was true. How she'd accused him of ruining Maya's life, of staining her family honor. How Sera had flinched at her words, seen in them the ashes of her own daughter's happiness. And rather than deal with the truth, the dangerous, life-crushing truth, Sera had sided with her corrupt son-in-law and thrown Bhima out of her home. And now Dinaz stands before her, oblivious of her husband's treachery, Dinaz, who had fought with her parents when they wouldn't let Bhima sit on the furniture that she dusted every day, who, as a child, would insist on taking her meals crouched next to the servant on the floor rather than eat at the table with her parents, Dinaz, who is now heavy with her first child. No, it would remain a secret between them, between her and Serabai, what Viraf had done—impregnated Maya, and then, striking the pose of a concerned but dispassionate well-wisher, planted the thought of an abortion in all their heads. She feels a fresh rush of rage at him for his duplicity.

As if she's read her mind, Dinaz says, "Can't you forgive him, Bhima? You were so fond of Viraf. You used to laugh at all his stupid jokes and all."

True, Bhima wants to say, true. But that was before I learned that he slithers. I was fooled, too, she wants to say, taken in by that handsome face, that forked tongue, that duplicitous smile. Much as you are. But she bites down on her lips until she can taste blood.

Just then, she hears Maya at the door and goes to open it. The girl enters with a metal folding chair and silently sets it on the uneven floor. Even though Bhima is making eyes at her to leave, Maya plants herself solidly on her cotton mattress on the floor. "Please to sit, Dinaz baby," Bhima says. She turns to her granddaughter. "You, chokri," she says. "Run down to the corner store and buy a Coca-Cola." It is Dinaz's favorite drink, she knows.

"No, no, no. No, Bhima, please. It's too early. And, in any case, I'm trying not to drink soft drinks. You know, with the baby and all."

Bhima senses rather than sees Maya scowl at the mention of the baby. Her stomach muscles tense. Don't let the girl say something stupid, she prays. But before she can command Maya to give them some privacy, Dinaz turns to the girl. "Maya," she says. "I was just asking Bhima to swallow her pride and return to work. I mean, sometimes hot words are exchanged among family members, correct? But we must forgive and forget."

Maya turns to look at her grandmother, a look of incredulity on her face, and Bhima makes the slightest motion with her head. She doesn't know, her look says. They lock eyes for a second, and then Maya says in a soft voice, "I can't tell my Ma-ma what to do, Dinaz didi."

Dinaz suddenly looks crushed. "So what are you saying, Bhima?" she says. "That you're definitely not coming back?" Her eyes fill with tears. "After all that we've . . . been through, you're going to quit? Just like that, after all these years?"

Bhima feels her face flush with the effort it takes to quiet the voice that's imprisoned inside her, the voice that wants to scream the truth at the well-dressed woman sitting across from her. But she will not. Mustn't. She loves Dinaz, even loves her unborn child. "Forgive me," she says. "What you ask is impossible."

They sit there quietly, three women, each of them afraid to move, knowing that the slightest movement will let in the outside world and destroy the temporary calm of the bubble that encases them. The silence lengthens, changes shape and texture, goes from peaceful to awkward. Dinaz and Bhima look at each other with love and longing and then look away.

Finally, Dinaz exhales, and the other two realize they, too, have been holding their breath. Maya shifts on her mattress as the spell is broken. Dinaz bends to where her purse is on the floor and rifles through it. She looks at the floor as she speaks. "Mummy was saying yesterday that she owes you money. This month's salary as well as the money you've been saving with her each month." She faces Bhima, who is looking at her openmouthed, wondering how she could've forgotten the small amount she has begged Serabai to withhold from her salary for all these years. A nerve flutters on the right side of her mouth. There will be some money coming in this month, after all.

"Bhima," Dinaz says, a sternness in her voice that makes the older woman pay attention. "Do you know how much you have in savings with Mummy?"

Bhima shakes her head. "Serabai always kept track," she says. "I never asked."

Dinaz gives a short laugh. "That's how blindly you trusted her, huh? The woman whose home you won't step foot in, now?"

Bhima's heart breaks at the bitterness she hears in Dinaz's voice. But again, she wills herself to remain silent, unable to explain, unable to console. It is better this way, she thinks. Let Dinaz walk away from here blaming me instead of Serabai. Let blood remain blood.

"In any case," Dinaz continues briskly, "it was thirty thousand rupees. Quite a good sum."

"Ae, Bhagwan," Bhima and Maya breathe in unison.

Dinaz pulls out a pen and a checkbook. "Mummy was fretting yesterday about how she was going to get the money to you. She was wondering if she could trust our peon to deliver it. But she didn't want to send such a large sum over in cash. And . . . you don't have a bank account?"

Bhima's thoughts are churning, but Dinaz's last question penetrates, and the old shame rises again. "No, baby," she says quietly. "As you know, I don't read or write. My money was always safe with your mother."

"But I do," Maya interjects. Her voice is loud, with a note that Bhima doesn't recognize—Pride? Defiance? Belligerence?

Dinaz doesn't seem to notice. "That's right," she smiles. She bends down and scribbles in her checkbook, then looks directly at Maya. "Here's what I advise," she says. "Go to the bank and open an account. You do not want to cash this check and keep so much money at home."

She rises from her chair and sits on her haunches in front of Bhima, surprisingly nimble given her pregnancy. She lays the check at Bhima's feet. "I've made this out for forty thousand rupees, Bhima," she says.

"But it's only thirty . . ."

"I know. The rest is from me. To . . . thank you for . . ." But here, Dinaz stops, blinking back the tears and then roughly wiping away the errant ones rolling down her cheeks.

Flooded with a dangerous tenderness for Dinaz, Bhima is angry that Maya is here to witness this, is annoyed at the watchful way in which Maya is taking in the scene before her. Go, she wants to yell at her granddaughter. Take your morose face and leave us in peace for a moment. I have known this child sitting in front of me longer than I've known you. I have fed her, washed her clothes, loved her, protected her from her father's temper and her parents' quarrels. But Maya sits there, impassive as a mountain, and Bhima has no choice but to whisper, "Just one minute, Dinaz baby," and scramble to her feet. She crosses the room and goes to the old trunk that houses all the important artifacts of her past. She finds what she's looking for almost immediately, grabs it, and walks swiftly past Maya, half-afraid that her granddaughter will protest. She opens Dinaz's hand in hers and puts the silver rattle in it, ignoring her startled, "Bhima, no. I can't accept this."

"Dinaz baby," she says. "Forgive me. It is but a small gift. My husband bought this silver rattle for my firstborn. Both my children played with it. Maya, too. And now, I want your child to have it."

"Are you sure, Bhima?" Dinaz asks.

"Hundred percent sure. I was planning on gifting it to you the day he was born."

"But you should keep it. For when Maya . . ." Her voice trails away, as she remembers the events of the past year. Behind her, Maya glowers at both of them, but Bhima ignores her.

Dinaz's hand closes around the rattle. "Thank you," she whispers. "I will treasure it."

At the door, Dinaz lingers. "If you two ever need anything . . ."

But now, Bhima is spent, and a cold, dark feeling is spreading within her. Now, she only wishes for Dinaz to be gone. She folds her hands, a gesture at once supplicatory and dismissive. "Thank you," she says.

She pushes open the door for Dinaz, and they step outside. Bhima ignores the curious stares that the neighbors cast at the light-skinned, well-dressed woman beside her, a woman who looks as alien as an astronaut in their part of the city, who lifts the hem of her pants as she walks gingerly down the narrow, rutted streets. The older woman stands outside her hut watching Dinaz's receding back, her eyes stinging from unshed tears, her mouth dry from unspoken words. She waits until Dinaz turns the corner, waves, and disappears from her life.

❀

Maya turns on her as soon as she reenters the hut. "Why didn't you tell her?" she asks immediately.

Bhima pretends to not understand the question. "Tell her what?"

"About her badmash husband. About what he did to me."

The unexpressed anger spikes in her. "And what about what you have done to her?" she spits. "Behaving like a tramp with some poor girl's husband?"

Maya's jaw goes slack, as if her grandmother has punched her in the face. Then, her eyes get narrow and mean. "You are an ignorant woman," she says. "Not even understanding why she came here." She bends down, scoops up the check, and waves it in Bhima's face. "They are not wanting you back, Ma-ma," she says. "She just came here to do her acting-facting. The real reason she came? To give you this money. To buy your silence. Your sweet Dinaz baby? She's very clever. She is knowing everything."

"Shut your mouth," Bhima says savagely. "And lower your voice. Any one of these drunkards around us will come in chup-chap at night and slit our throats if they know we've come into money."

"It's not the people in this basti you have to be afraid of, Ma-ma. It's people like Dinaz and Serabai who have slit your throat."

Bhima closes her eyes, afraid to let her granddaughter know how much her words have hurt her. But Maya is not yet done. "They treat you like a dog, no, worse than a dog. They treat you like an old newspaper, something they read and then throw in the trash box. And still you run after them, Ma-ma. Still you protect their lies and secrets, as if those secrets belong to you. And still you—" here, Maya's voice cracks, "still you give her something that belonged to *my* mother, and therefore belonged to me, as if it was yours to give, as if she is yours to give to. Why, Ma-ma? Why, after all this time are they your family and not me?"

Bhima stands still, eyes closed and afraid to breathe. Maya's words tear at her because she does not know the answer to her granddaughter's questions. The truth is, she had not considered that the rattle belonged to Maya. She is embarrassed and is about to apologize when something strikes her and her eyes fly open. "You are not my family?" she cries. "You stupid, insolent girl. Why do you think I work in their home? To fatten my belly? You think I want to live one extra day on this wretched earth for *my* sake? You wicked girl. You dare say such a shameless thing to me? Everything I do, every drop of sweat I sweat is for you. So that you can go to college. So that my misfortune ends with me. And what do you do instead these past months? Sit at home like a maharani."

Maya opens her mouth to say something, but Bhima raises her hand threateningly. "Chup," she says. "Nothing more for you to say. That rattle I gave away? You don't need it. Because you are not a child anymore, Maya. The only thing you need is an education."

They stand glaring at each other, and then Bhima comes to a swift resolution, her earlier listlessness now dissipated. She reaches out and plucks the check out of the younger woman's hand. "Go get dressed," she commands.

Maya snickers. "Why? You taking me to the Taj Mahal hotel?"

Bhima resists the urge to smack the smugness from Maya's face. "We are going to the bank," she says. "You are going to help your old grandmother open a bank account. I will work ten jobs if I have to. But we are not touching this money. This money is for you to go back to college. And for your future."

2

Her name is Parvati.

Although she doesn't always know it.

Sometimes, in the time it takes to hiccup, the world goes blank and she forgets what she is called and where she is and her place in the world. It is comfortable living in that white space and not having to carry the burden of knowing her name or her history. Then, as she absently fingers the growth on her neck, the world comes into focus again and she knows—she is Parvati, the daughter of a man who sold her for the price of a cow. And in doing so, taught her what she was worth. How long ago this was she no longer remembers, and it isn't because she can't count, because she was one of the few women at the Old Place who could read and write. She simply chooses not to remember. At her age, time has stopped flowing in a linear fashion; rather, it ebbs and swirls, creating a whirlpool at its center that on most days swallows her whole. Her yesterdays have lost their bite; it is her todays that come bearing down with fangs and claws that she has to watch out for.

This morning, Parvati sits cross-legged in the open-air market, her daily supply of six shriveled heads of cauliflower displayed like skulls on the dirty cotton sheet in front of her. She knows that at some point during the day the same handful of customers, almost as impoverished as her, will stop and buy her inventory. Every morning she trudges to her spot on the pavement, carrying the vegetables in a filthy cloth bag that hasn't been washed in two years. She squints at the ferocious sun, which she considers to be her own personal nemesis, spreads out the tablecloth on the sidewalk, then empties the bag so that the round heads of the cauliflowers roll onto it. She had learned many years ago to kill the envy she once felt at the sight of the beautiful produce displayed by her competitors, the gleaming tomatoes, the pearly garlic, the radiant grapefruit and oranges. She has never had the money to increase her inventory so has stopped trying. The twenty rupees a day she earns as profit—and that too, because the man who sells her the cauliflowers charges her a pittance for the produce he would otherwise throw away—covers her fee to sleep on two sheets of cardboard on the landing outside her nephew's apartment and leaves her with a few extra notes.

If she had the energy to examine her life, Parvati would see how thin and nebulous it is—patched together with lies and pity, as if she were one of those cheap kites, built from paper and glue, and falling apart at the slightest gust of wind. The "nephew," for instance, is not a relation at all, but the son of a woman at the Old Place, who, against all odds, still remembers Parvati's kindness toward him when he was a boy. In exchange for fifteen rupees a day and a promise to never reveal his dead mother's past to his wife, he rents her the space. The vegetable wholesaler, too, is a man from the old days, and lets her have the cauliflowers for cheap out of some combination of sympathy and disgust. Every day, one vendor or another feeds the old woman lunch—a banana, maybe, or a small loaf of bread—or sends a leftover piece of fruit home with her. Sometimes, if there is any money left over at the end of the month, she will treat herself to a cup of tea. And on the way to her nephew's home each evening, she stops at a ramshackle restaurant, whose owner empties leftovers from his customers' plates onto a newspaper and hands it to her.

If she is twenty minutes late, he sets the scraps down on the sidewalk for the stray dog that lurks outside the restaurant.

This morning, even the sun cannot hold Parvati's attention. There is a new lump growing on her body, this time at the base of her spine, a painful and inconvenient spot, and one she cannot stroke as absentmindedly as she does the one on her throat. It irritates her, the unfairness of the location. Not once in all these years, has she complained about the growth on her neck, which started as the size of a pomegranate seed decades ago, and then grew to the size of an orange. So much it took away from her—her beauty, her livelihood, even her voice, which is now raspy and harsh, giving her a perpetual sore throat from where it presses on her vocal cords. She has seen its effect on the world around her—the curl of the lip, the averting of the eyes, the occasional gag reflex when someone sees her for the first time. But she has not minded it, has even been thankful, because it was the growth that led her out from the Old Place decades ago. And here, among the querulous vegetable and fruit sellers and fishmongers, it has acted as a talisman of sorts, imbuing her with a dark power that no one wants to cross. It has protected her strip of the pavement, a much-coveted spot at the corner of two streets. Without the deformity, who would she be? An old woman, thin as a stick, with no police protection and few remaining connections in the underworld. But they steer clear of her, even the young goondas who walk around with batons, demanding payments from the other vendors in exchange for their "protection."

"Ae, mausi," a voice says, and she looks up reluctantly, not wanting to waste so much as a breath making idle chitchat on such a hot day. It is Rajeev, the tall, lanky man with the handlebar mustache who delivers groceries to the houses of the rich. Multiple times a day, Rajeev lets a customer fill his large wicker basket with purple brinjals and green lady's fingers and bags of potatoes and onions, balances the basket on his head, and trots beside the shoppers as they make their way home. Parvati has heard Rajeev complain about the flights of stairs he must climb all day long, but even when he complains there's a smile in his voice. She has always distrusted him for that reason, because a man who smiles even as he admits to the harshness of his life is foolish and not someone to respect. Also, he is one of the few people in the market who acknowledges her presence. Always, she wants to shoo him away, like a fly sitting atop her vegetables; always, he somehow gets her to exchange a few words with him.

"Hot day, mausi," he now exclaims. He sets his basket down and then squats in front of her. "Will you take a chai?"

She eyes him suspiciously, unsure if this is a ruse to make her buy him a cup of tea. "It's okay," she says noncommittally.

He looks puzzled for a moment and then smiles broadly. "Arre, mausi, I'm asking if I can buy *you* tea."

She turns away in embarrassment, knowing that he has read her mind. Finally, she looks at him sharply and says, "Why?"

Rajeev bows his head. When he looks up, his eyes are puzzled. There is something else in his eyes also—a flash of understanding, perhaps pity—and Parvati feels her hackles rise. Shameless man, to feel pity for her poverty. If only he knew. What gifts she has had showered upon her, what luxury she had once known. She has eaten at fancy restaurants where he would not be allowed to enter.

Before she can respond, Rajeev gets up with a grunt and walks away, leaving his basket in front of her. She starts to call out to him but sees that he's only headed to the tea shop a few meters away. In a minute he returns with two steaming glasses of tea. Silently, he sets a glass against one of the cauliflowers. "Drink," he says, gesturing with his hand. And when she doesn't, he smiles cajolingly. "Arre, drink, na, mausi. It's tea, not blood."

While she gulps down the sugary beverage, Parvati wonders what Rajeev wants. Maybe it's this spot. People have approached her over the years, even offered to pay her a few hundred rupees for it. But she will never yield it. It's all she has. Without this spot, where would she spend her days? The landing where she sleeps must be vacated by six in the morning, before the other residents begin to leave for work and school. No loitering, her nephew has told her. If I get one complaint from a neighbor, bas, you will have to leave. To appease these neighbors, she sweeps the entire common area in front of their doors each morning. In exchange, they occasionally hand her a used sari, or once, a half-empty bottle of talcum powder.

Rajeev is staring at her with those big, dark eyes. He must've been an owl in a previous birth, Parvati thinks. She flushes, wishing he would look away. She is about to ask him what he wants from her when he speaks. "What's wrong, mausi?" he says. "Your back is paining?"

"What's it to you?" she snaps. She sets down the glass heavily on the stone pavement. "What is it? Business is so slow today that you're swatting flies and watching me?"

Rajeev swallows. "Don't take offense, mausi. I suffer from back pain, too. This job, with all the heavy lifting, is very bad on the body. But I have a good ointment at home. I am only inquiring so I can bring some for you tomorrow."

It occurs to Parvati that if she had had a son, he would be around Rajeev's age. The thought is so unexpected that her eyes fill with tears. But still, suspicion lingers, fighting with the gratitude that seeps into her heart. She bites down on her lip, unsure of what to say to this man who is examining her closely, as if she is some bird from a country he is unfamiliar with.

"Your wife won't care if you share the ointment?" she says, as much to find out if he's married without having to ask.

Rajeev smiles appreciatively, as if he can see through her deviousness. "My wife, mausi? My wife would give her last breath to someone in need. She so kind." He stops, looking at her worriedly. "I don't mean to insult . . ."

She shakes her head. "No. No insult. I understand. You are lucky."

"Mausi. You don't know." He lowers his voice, in order to protect his words from Reshma, the woman vendor sitting next to them who is openly eavesdropping on their conversation. "I used to be a drunkard. Bad drinking problem, mausi. But you believe or not believe, since the day my Radha come into my house, I haven't taken one sip. Not one sip. Just like that, I gave up the moonshine."

Despite herself, Parvati smiles. "That speaks well of you, beta," she says, noticing with a start that she has called him son.

Rajeev doesn't appear to have noticed. "No, mausi. Not of me. Of Radha. We are poor people. But we are having one son. And we are both working hard to make sure he finishes his schooling." He points to the basket. "I climb hundreds of stairs a day, mausi, so that someday my son can ride in a car."

Suddenly, she remembers something. "Have you heard of the poet Aziz?" And when he shakes his head no, Parvati recites:

"I will carry you upon my shoulders, my son
And climb the tallest mountain
So you can behold all the fruit
Of our alive and green valley."

"Wah," Rajeev exclaims. "These words have captured what's in my heart, mausi." But then his face grows thoughtful. "How you are knowing this poetry-foetry?"

Parvati's skin prickles and she regrets letting her guard down. She dismisses his question brusquely. "Everybody knows."

Rajeev lowers his eyes. "I am an uneducated man," he says. "I cannot even sign my own name."

"Sometimes it is better to not even know your own name." She watches as Rajeev's eyes widen at the bitterness in her voice, and is surprised herself. She clamps her mouth shut. She is a cheap woman, bought for the price of a cup of tea. But that is all. She will say no more to this stranger sitting across from her.

As if he has sensed her regret, Rajeev rises to his feet. "Good day, mausi," he says. "Tomorrow I bring the balm for you."

"Don't trouble yourself," she says stiffly, knowing the source of her pain is not a backache.

"No trouble." He smiles and walks away. She follows him with her eyes, watches him kneel and set his basket down to be filled up by the servant of one of the memsahibs from a nearby building. Even from a distance, she can sense the twinge in his back, the pain in his shoulder blades as he straightens up and lifts the basket, balancing it perfectly on his head, holding it in place with barely the tip of his forefinger.

She had not realized that her troubling the thing growing at the base of her spine was so obvious for all to see. She makes a concerted effort to keep her right hand in front of her. At least it's not cancer. This much she knows. Thirty years ago, when the pomegranate seed on her throat had begun to swell and grow, she had been to the doctor and was told it was not cancerous. She knows that its twin, born thirty years apart, will not be cancerous either. But this one is painful because of its location, and sitting all day on the hard pavement does not help.

One of her regular customers stops by and purchases one of the cauliflowers without exchanging barely a word. After he is gone, while she is commanding herself not to let her hand wander to her back, her hand wanders to her back.

One year later . . .

3

It is almost four in the evening by the time Bhima reaches Sunitabai's home. She is late—Mrs. Motorcylewalla, the old lady whose house she cleans each day, had delayed her with her demands that she pay her respects to the prophet Zoroaster before she could leave. When Bhima had swallowed her apprehension and contacted her former employer a year ago, she had hoped that the old lady's mental state had improved, but if anything, her eccentricities had only increased in the intervening years. Last week, for instance, Mrs. Motorcyclewalla would not allow her to use any electricity in the house. Bhima even had to heat the woman's bathwater on the stove because she refused to turn on the electric water heater. She had almost quit that week, her usual irritation at the woman's craziness hardening into rage at the extra work. Now, as she climbs up the four flights of stairs, Bhima thanks God that her second client of the day is hardly ever at home when she arrives. And even when she is, she keeps out of the way, working on her computer while Bhima cleans and prepares her evening meal. Sunitabai has explained to her that she writes for the newspaper—the same newspaper Serabai used to read every morning—and she is often away on business for days at a time. Bhima knows to ring the doorbell of the apartment next door to ask for the key to let her in.

But today, when Vimal Das, the neighbor woman who keeps the key to Sunitabai's apartment, answers the door, she has a funny look on her face. "No need for the key," she says. "Her friend is there. You just ring the doorbell." There is a strange emphasis on the word *friend*, followed by a smirk and a look that Bhima can't decipher.

"Sunitabai is home?" she asks.

"No. But the friend moved in over the weekend." Vimal glares at the door of Sunita's apartment. "This used to be a decent building."

Bhima looks at Vimal sharply as she understands the situation. "The guest is a man?" she says.

Vimal laughs. "Ha. Good one. You could say that, I suppose." Before Bhima can react, she gestures toward the door. "Go. See for yourself. What the world has come to."

Bhima's hand is shaking as she knocks on the door. She will not be alone in the house with a strange man, she resolves. When he answers, she will tell him to please inform Sunitabai that she can no longer work for her.

The door flies open and Bhima gapes. The long-haired woman with the wide smile on her face is not a man at all. Bhima looks back in confusion at Vimal's apartment, but Vimal's door had clicked shut as soon as this one was opened. "Hi," the woman says. "Are you the cook?" Her manner of speaking is different somehow, so that even though she is speaking Hindi, Bhima has a hard time understanding her.

The woman walks into the hallway with the door still ajar, as if she is expecting Bhima to follow. Still trying to reconcile the sinister tone of the neighbor with the innocuous, even friendly manner of the woman, Bhima shuts the door behind her. And gasps. She has been away for only two days, but the apartment is transformed. There are paintings on the formerly bare walls of the living room and two new chairs. Sunitabai's old rocking chair has been moved out to the small balcony; in its place is a wooden contraption holding a half-finished painting of a woman cradling her child. Something about the woman's posture, the bleak isolation of it, strikes a responsive chord within Bhima.

"It looks totally different, right?" The young woman turns around and smiles. "My name is Chitra, by the way. And I already have eaten your bhindi and mutton cutlets. They were fantastic." She makes a thumbs-up gesture for emphasis.

Bhima feels her face flushing at the compliment. Dinaz baby used to praise her cooking, also. As did Serabai, but only to her friends, within Bhima's earshot. Never directly to her.

She must've had a peculiar look on her face because Chitra is looking at her curiously. "Did I say something wrong, didi?"

Bhima blinks, tucking away the past and focusing on the young woman who stands watching her. Didi. The memsahib had called her didi, or older sister, as if they were equals, as if she was not a poor, ignorant woman from the slums. Something opens up in her heart, a flower that blooms, but she crushes it immediately. "My name is Bhima," she says curtly. "You can just call me that, memsahib."

To her surprise, the younger woman looks stricken, as if Bhima's gruff words have landed like a slap. Her mouth twists into a bitter line. "I see. So the neighbors have already poisoned the well." She turns away and then looks back. "Well, I'll leave you to your chores."

And suddenly Bhima gets it—the strange accent, the familiar use of the word *didi*, the offense taken at Bhima's words, which were meant to convey *her* unworthiness but which Chitra mistook for an insult. Of course. The woman has come to them from a foreign land. She was not one of those poor, white-skinned firangis that she used to see when she and Serabai went shopping at Colaba, those impoverished people with their long hair and faded or torn jeans, which always made Bhima feel sorry for them, even though Serabai had tried explaining that this was fashion, not poverty. But despite her dark skin, she was a foreigner, unused to Indian customs. This is why Vimalbai had spoken about her so dismissively. She wants to explain some of this to Chitra, but the woman has already moved into the bedroom.

Shaking her head, Bhima makes her way to the kitchen to perform her first chore—washing the dishes that Sunitabai has left for her overnight. It is her least favorite chore because often, Sunita forgets to rinse those dishes and Bhima must spend the time scraping dried-up food from the bowls and plates before she can wash them. Bhima is fond of Sunita, thinks of her as a young child with her mop of short, curly hair, and the jeans and cotton kurtas she almost always wears. And on the rare occasion that Sunita comes home before Bhima finishes cooking her dinner, she can see the fatigue in that small, sallow face with the oversized glasses. Sunita is always unfailingly polite to her, and best of all, she respects Bhima's solitude, so unlike the querulous presence of Mrs. Motorcyclewalla, who hovers over her and counts the number of shrimp in her curry to make sure that Bhima hasn't popped one in her mouth when her back is turned. But still, sometimes her stomach turns at the sight of those dishes and she feels a spurt of anger at the thoughtlessness of the rich, which, of course, immediately makes her think her conflicted thoughts about the Dubash family.

Now, Bhima enters the kitchen and stops dead. The sink is spotless. And empty. The dishes have been all put away. Bhima frowns, knowing immediately that it is the foreign woman who has taken away her job. She feels a moment's alarm at the thought of being fired, of depending for her income solely on the whims and unpredictability of Mrs. Motorcyclewalla. She marches up to the bedroom, where Chitra sits on an armchair, reading. "The plates," Bhima splutters. "The dishes . . ."

Chitra looks up from her book. "Oh yes. I did them. Less work for you today, Bhima."

Bhima closes her eyes for a split second, fearful of this new threat that has entered her life. How to make this stupid girl understand that what she thinks of as thoughtfulness is thoughtlessness? She hesitates, not trusting herself to speak, and when she does, she does so loudly and slowly, as if speaking to a very young child. "Chitrabai," she says. "You are my memsahib's guest. This is my job, bai. Sunitabai likes dishes to be cleaned one way, only. You please just take rest and don't take tension on your head. Leave the cleaning-fleaning to me."

To her indignation, Chitra laughs. "Ha. That's a joke. Sunita likes her plates to be cleaned in a certain way? She's such a pig she would barely notice the difference."

Even though she has been working for Sunita for less than a year, Bhima bristles. "Sunitabai is very smart," she says, tapping her forehead. "She not saying much, but she sees everything. Do you see how big her ears are? That is the sign of cleverness."

Chitra smiles even more deeply. "Wait till I tell Su that she has big ears. She'll love *that*."

Bhima feels her eyes well with tears of frustration. Is this girl as soft in the head as Mrs. Motorcyclewalla? If not, why does she twist everything that she is saying? Ae, Bhagwan, she prays. Let this chokri leave for her foreign place soon. Two softies-in-the-head I cannot handle.

She is about to leave the room when Chitra rises to her feet, takes a step toward Bhima, and then sits at the edge of the bed. "Bhima," she says, patting the bed. "Come sit here. What's the problem?"

Bhima takes an involuntary step back. This girl is crazy, she is now sure. Even Dinaz baby never asked her to sit on her bed. At least Dinaz was just a child when she used to squat on the floor to eat next to her. By the time she was an adult, Dinaz had learned how to respect the rules. Bhima knows that this is a new jamana, a new age, where many young people act as if they have invented the world. But still, she is shocked. People like her are meant to live in one square, whereas educated, rich people like Chitrabai were born to occupy another one. This is the truth, a natural law. And yet, here she is, patting the bed for her to sit, as if they are two old friends sitting under a mango tree, exchanging giggles and gossip.

Or maybe it is a test. Something to complain to Sunitabai about when she gets home. Look how she has already twisted her compliment about Sunita's intelligence into an insult. This woman is trying to get her fired for sure. But why?

There was a time, Bhima thinks, that this pretty-looking woman could've tricked her. But no more. And so Bhima continues to stand. "No problem, bai," she says evenly. "I am just wanting to do my work." The two women look at each other for a moment and then Bhima adds, "And Sunitabai is not a pig. She is just busy. Important job she is having."

Chitra smiles, and feeling emboldened by that smile, Bhima asks, "What job you are doing?"

"I'm an artist. I paint." She points to a picture above the bed. "That's one of mine."

Bhima nods, pretending to understand. Once again, this woman has confused her. She wants to find out how Chitra earns money. Instead, she has been told that the woman draws pictures, like her daughter, Pooja, used to when she was little. She bites the inside of her lip. This woman's head is an empty pot, and she has nothing to do but sit and read a book in the middle of the day. But she herself is already behind on the day's chores. Bhima spins around abruptly to exit the room and as she does her hip pops so loudly that Chitra's eyes widen with concern. "With your leave," Bhima says and hurries away into the kitchen.

Once there, Bhima opens the fridge to see what food there is.

She eyes the vegetables with disapproval. She has asked Sunita to let her pick up fresh vegetables from the marketplace where she used to shop when she worked for Serabai, but the woman prefers to buy the expensive produce from the vendor who comes to her door each morning. Well, let her waste her money if she so chooses.

She has put the daal to cook and is chopping potatoes when Chitra wanders into the room. "Here, I'll chop the onions for you," she says casually, pulling the knife from the rack before the older woman can answer. She stands next to Bhima in order to share the same chopping board. Bhima stiffens, both in disapproval and in awareness of the sour smell of her late-afternoon sweat. But nothing to do except stand here and let this crazy girl work in this small kitchen when she could be resting in the bedroom. Her wish.

They work in silence for a few minutes, their chopping falling into a synchronized rhythm. Despite herself, Bhima finds her body relaxing in Chitra's silent company. She doesn't think about it often, but it comes to her now, how lonely she is. Other than Maya she has no steady presence in her life. And now that her granddaughter is back in college, they only spend a few hours together in the evening before each of them falls into a heavy sleep. This is what she misses about working for the Dubash household—Viraf's whistling in the shower, his friendly jostling of her, Dinaz's frantic rushing around as she got ready for work, Sera's companionship as the two women sat down to a cup of tea in the suddenly-silent house after Viraf and Dinaz had left for work. Bhima feels a spasm in her heart as she remembers that there is now another member in that house, a baby she would have fussed over, would've helped clean and bathe, whose first steps she would've witnessed with joy, on whose first birthday she would've brought in some homemade sweets, if only . . . She leans heavily on the edge of the kitchen counter for a minute, trying to forget the ignobility of her fall.

"Are you all right, didi?" Chitra asks, and Bhima nods, unable to talk, noticing the use of the familial didi, but not caring to correct her. Let them all call her by whatever name they wanted, what did it matter? Her husband had called her jaan, life itself, but then he'd snuck out of their house like a thief, stealing away her precious son. Her son himself had called her Ma, but he had gotten married and not thought of inviting her to the wedding. Her daughter, Pooja, had called her Ma, too, but she too was gone, preferring to join her husband in death than to stay with her unfortunate mother. Serabai had called her "my Bhima" but had left her behind like a handkerchief one forgot on the train. They were words, just words, and she had heard a million of them in her time spoken in love or in anger, it didn't matter, because eventually all love turned into anger. So let this crazy girl call her older sister. Nobody in this world would ever be stupid enough to believe her.

Now Chitra is reaching for a glass and pouring her ice water from the fridge and urging her to drink it and Bhima feels her eyes sting at this gesture of kindness, even as she registers the great offense that Chitra has committed. "I have my own glass with me, bai," she says, pointing to the small cloth pouch that holds her stainless steel mug and her plate. "I will pour into that."

For the first time, Chitra frowns. "What's wrong with this glass?" she says.

Bhima clucks her tongue impatiently. She doesn't have the time today to educate this girl in basic manners. "This is India, bai," she says. "Servants don't drink from their mistress's cups."

Chitra scoops the chopped onions into a small bowl. "I know this is India, Bhima," she says. "I've lived here most of my life. I was in Australia for only nine years. It's one of the reasons I left Delhi—these stupid customs."

Bhima lowers her head. "These are our customs," she says. "We must respect them."

Chitra's thick hair flies from one side to another as she shakes her head vehemently. "No. No, we mustn't. They are wrong. And it is wrong to perpetuate an unjust system."

Bhima begins to laugh. She only stops when she sees that she has offended Chitra. "Please to forgive, bai," she says. "Your words reminded me of someone I used to work for. She spoke exact-exact like you. Except she was a little girl." The last line comes out more plaintive than she intends.

Chitra gives her a long look. "So Sunita makes you drink out of your own glass?"

"Why khali-pili you blame Sunitabai? She just does what all others do."

"Fair enough." Chitra nods. Then, "What is your salary here?"

Bhima falls silent, unsure of how to answer such a rude question. All she wants to do is cook the meal and hurry home to start her own dinner. She is too tired to figure out what game this memsahib is playing. "You please ask Sunitabai," she says finally. "She tell me not to tell the guest anything." It is not a complete untruth—on the day that Sunita had hired her, she had told her that she was a private person and that if any of her neighbors wanted to know the news they could watch Sky TV. Bhima had nodded appreciatively.

But Chitra has one more surprise for her. "Well, I'm not exactly a guest, Bhima," she says. "I'm living here now."

Bhima almost drops the jar of garam masala she has reached for. "Sunitabai never say," she murmurs.

"I know. She meant to. But she didn't get home in time last week to catch you. Sorry."

The older woman shrugs. "It's your business," she says.

Chitra raises her eyebrow. "And you don't have a problem with it?"

Bhima looks perplexed. "It's her home, bai," she says. "How I can have a problem?"

Chitra opens her mouth, then simply smiles. "Good," she says. She pulls out a pot and says, "Will you take a cup of tea with me, Bhima?"

She knows that the young woman is being friendly, but Bhima doesn't want her in the kitchen anymore. She is already behind on dinner; at this rate, it will be eight o'clock before she can start on her own meal when she gets home. She grabs the pot out of Chitra's hand. "You go relax in the living room, bai," she says. "I will serve you tea. And then I must to start frying the potato patties."

But Chitra doesn't take the hint. "Don't be silly. I'm perfectly capable of making my own tea." She opens the fridge and pulls out a sprig of mint, then measures the water and puts it to boil.

Bhima swallows her resentment. She is getting old, she thinks. There was a time when any gesture of kindness—the young Dinaz joining her on the floor to eat lunch, Serabai slipping a chocolate into her bag to take home to Maya—used to soften her heart with gratitude. Now, kindness or rudeness, love or contempt, it all feels the same to her. She can no longer see Chitra's gesture as anything but inconvenience. Please get out of my kitchen, she wants to yell, but of course, it's not her kitchen.

"You have children, Bhima?" Chitra asks, as she waits for the water to boil, and Bhima freezes. Unlucky woman, she chides herself, that you cannot easily answer the simplest question in the world. "No," she says. "Just a granddaughter. My daughter's daughter."

"Where is your daughter?"

Bhima grits her teeth. "She's dead." And, knowing that Chitra will not be content with this, she adds, "She and my son-in-law both died from the AIDS."

Chitra doesn't extend her sympathies. Instead, she says, "I had a friend who died of AIDS." Bhima gasps. All the people in the AIDS ward in that Delhi hospital had been poor people like her, wasted figures out of a nightmare. How could someone like Chitrabai's friend—educated, wealthy, smart, she is sure—also have died of that same disease?

"He die in Delhi?" she asks.

"What? No. In Australia."

Bhima rubs her forehead. "But this Austala . . . . how you say . . . that's a different muluk, no? How he getting the AIDS there?"

"It's everywhere in the world, Bhima," Chitra says gently. "Don't you know?"

She didn't know. She is nothing but an ignorant, unschooled woman, who signed away her husband's future, who couldn't save either one of her children, who didn't know until this minute that the darkness that swallowed up her beautiful Pooja roamed the whole world. "How old was your friend, beti?" she asks.

If Chitra notices that Bhima has called her *daughter* instead of the usual *bai* or *madam*, she doesn't comment on it. Bhima herself is unaware of the slip, because right now they are tied together by grief, two women generations apart, afraid to know the full weight of the other's loss. Then, Chitra says, "He was twenty-eight," and Bhima wishes she hadn't asked.

She turns away abruptly, blinking back the tears burning in her eyes. She has almost succeeded when she hears herself say, "I am still having a son. But he has left me, also."

"Aw, Bhima, I'm sorry," Chitra says and lays a hand on the bony shoulder, and perhaps it's the realization that no one has ever apologized to her for the loss of Amit or the fact that other than Maya, no human has laid a friendly hand on her in a very long time, but without warning, Bhima loses her battle with her tears. She sobs quietly, facing away from Chitra, the shaking of her shoulders the only indication that she is crying. She understands now what Maya finds unbearable about their life together—not the poverty, not the horror of slum life, but the dreadful isolation. There is no one in their life who worries about them, who asks about their past, who lays a sympathetic hand on them. She and Maya are disposable people, and if they disappeared tomorrow, no one would mourn them or miss them. The thought chills Bhima's heart.

"Maaf karo, didi." Chitra's voice is tentative. "I shouldn't have poked my nose in your business."

Bhima turns around slowly, surprised by this young woman who seems to understand so much and so little. "You did not do anything wrong, child," she says. "You are just reminding me of things that are best left unremembered."

"I know what you mean," Chitra murmurs, as she pours the hot water over a tea bag, and again, Bhima is surprised. She knows from her years spent in Serabai's house that the rich have their problems, too; she well remembers the bruises that Sera's now-dead husband, Feroz, used to leave like tattoos on her pale skin. But close as they were, Serabai never discussed her problems with Bhima, never displayed her bruised heart to her. She is unused to someone like Chitra, the honest way in which she speaks to her.

They both jump as they hear the key turn in the latch. They hear Sunita as she walks into the living room and then comes into the kitchen. "Namaste, Bhima," she says, an embarrassed look on her face. "I see you've met my friend."

Bhima decides it's better for her to come clean. "Dinner is not ready yet, bai," she says in a rush. "What to do, bai? The old lady I work for keep me there longer today. And then I . . ."

"What?" Sunita seems distracted. She turns to face Chitra and

Bhima sees her face soften. "Hi," she whispers and Chitra immediately comes up to her and gives her a peck on the cheek. "Hi, baby. How was your day?"

Sunita flushes visibly. "Fine. I got off a bit early." She eyes Bhima warily. "So . . . everything is okay?"

Bhima nods as she lets out the steam from the pressure cooker. "I finish the dinner fatta-faat, bai." She takes the untouched glass of water from the kitchen counter and offers it to Sunita. "You want me to make you lime water, bai? Or just plain ice water?"

"Bhima. It's okay. I just came home earlier than usual. I'm not even hungry yet." Sunita flashes a look at Chitra. "Can I talk to you for a moment?" she says, and leaves the kitchen with the other woman following in tow.

Alone in the kitchen, Bhima mops her face with the border of her sari. She used to love letting herself into this apartment, performing her chores and leaving before Sunitabai even came home. She had come to value the solitary hours she spent here, flanked as her days were by Mrs. Motorcyclewalla's idiotic chatter at one end and the endless commotion of the slum at the other. But with Chitrabai here now, that short period of relative quiet is about to end. Stupid woman, she berates herself, it wasn't your quiet to enjoy. She begins to mash the daal, even as she puts the rice to boil. Cooking for two people instead of just Sunitabai is also going to take more time. Most evenings, Maya gets home from college around the same time that she does, and tired as she is, Bhima must cook them a meal. She sighs. Sometimes she thinks she was put here on earth to simply chop onions and cilantro, boil rice and daal, wash dishes, and then have the whole cycle begin again. And now the days will be even longer. But still, she reasons with herself, this new Chitrabai seems nice. She cannot say how much longer she can put up with Mrs. Motorcyclewalla's suspicion and madness. Since the last week, the old lady has taken to pulling up a chair into the kitchen and praying from her book while Bhima works, occasionally looking up and glowering at her. Bhima can handle even this, but what she cannot abide is the under-the-breath murmuring of the prayers, recited in an ancient language that neither of them understand. There is something sinister about the murmuring; it reminds Bhima of the mutterings of Serabai's bedridden mother-in-law, who used to provoke equal parts of pity and dread in Bhima each time she went to her apartment to minister to her.

Bhima shakes her head to clear her thoughts. In this past year, she has regretted every occasion when she had been ungrateful to the Dubashes or taken offense at some slight, such as when Serabai would chastise her for being late to work or when Viraf baba would throw in the wash a shirt that he'd worn for a mere twenty minutes. Now, she sees those things for what they were—the small bruisings of life, the happy consequence of working in close quarters with another family. Now, she would give one of her kidneys to have her biggest complaint about Viraf be an extra shirt to wash.

Sunita has come up behind her so quietly that when she says, "Bhima," the older woman jumps so hard that some of the daal spills from the bowl she is holding onto the counter. "God. Sorry," Sunita says.

Bhima mops up the daal up hurriedly. "Yes, bai?"

"We've decided to go out to dinner tonight," Sunita says. "So you can leave now, if you like."

Bhima feels her eyes well with tears. "I swear to God, I did not ask her to clean the dishes, Sunitabai," she says. "I was just a few minutes late coming here and she already washed all of them. If you want, I do them again, bai."

Sunita looks worried. "Are you all right, Bhima? Is there a problem with Chitra?"

Bhima looks at her miserably. "Please don't throw me out, bai," she whispers. "I have a grandchild to feed. I'm an old woman . . ."

"What the . . . ? Bhima. I'm not firing you. In fact, I'm just . . . Chitra said you looked really tired today. So we decided to go out, that's all. To give you a break. You understand? We—we just feel bad. That you work this hard. That's all."

As the air rushes back into her lungs, Bhima feels the weight of her bones. She stands mutely, staring at Sunita, as Chitra strides back into the room. "Go on home, Bhima," she smiles. "Unless you want to join us at dinner?"

Both Bhima and Sunita frown at the outrageousness of that statement, and Chitra looks chastised. "Well, I guess that's a no." She takes a step forward. "In that case, Bhima, let's put the food away. You can finish up tomorrow."

Bhima looks helplessly at Sunita, who notices her discomfort and pushes Chitra out of the kitchen. "Let Bhima do her job," she scolds. She turns back with a grin. "You have to forgive her, Bhima," she says. "She's lived abroad for so long, she's forgotten our customs."

As she leaves the apartment building and steps onto the pavement, carrying her little bundle, Bhima reflects on those words. Chitrabai is not soft in the head, she decides. No, her problem is that she's soft in the heart. She sighs. A few months in Mumbai will straighten Chitrabai out. The soil of this city doesn't allow for the growth of tender, green saplings.

It will take her at least a half hour to reach home. On the way, she stops to pick up a few vegetables and a fistful of rice for tonight's dinner. She hopes that Maya has homework to do because Chitrabai has wrung all the words out of her and she wants to pass the evening in silence. But the sensation of Chitra's comforting, steadying hand on the shoulder follows her home, like the impression of a child's hand pressed in clay.

4

The doodhwalla's arrival tells Parvati that she has overslept. She hears him stomping up the wooden stairs, hears the clanging of the large aluminum container of milk that he drags alongside him. She is rubbing the sleep out of her eyes when he arrives at Meena Swami's flat and rings the doorbell. Although she is covered by the shadows of the stairwell, modesty makes Parvati pull the thin cotton sheet over herself, even as she scrambles to roll off the cardboard sheet and rise to her feet. If she doesn't get to the wholesale market within the next hour, she may be too late to pick up the six cauliflowers that are usually set aside for her.

As she begins to rise, Parvati is assailed by a wave of dizziness and nausea. She sits on her haunches, and waits for the dizzy spell to pass, when, without warning, she vomits. The projectile vomit hits the stone floor and the wall between the two apartments, and even though he is not within its range, the doodhwalla lets out an indignant cry, just as Meena Swami answers her door. "Achoot, achoot," the milkman yells, his lip curling in disgust. "Dirtifying everything early in the morning." He turns toward Meena. "Bai, this used to be a decent building. What for you letting such peoples sleep here? Turning your building into a public toilet, you are."

Parvati opens her mouth to explain, to defend herself, but what shoots out is more vomit. Meena Swami screams in horror.

"Too much," she yells. "This is too much. Even the milkman can see our suffering." Parvati groans, and rests her head on her knees, unable to respond, as Meena Swami holds her nose dramatically. "Who's going to clean up this mess?" she asks. "Not that maharani that your nephew has married."

Parvati raises her head. "I will," she says. "If you just let me sit still for one minute, I will clean everything."

"No," Meena declares. "Enough is enough. This is too much of a nuisance." Still holding her nose with her right hand, she lifts the hem of her sari with her left, and crosses over the puddle of vomit. "I don't care how early it is," she mutters. "Praful has to end this matter once and for all."

"Please, bhenji," Parvati says, raising a tentative hand to stop her. "My nephew is sleeping. Please forgive. I will make everything right."

The doodhwalla clucks his tongue impatiently. "Meenabai," he says. "You wanting the milk or not? Already I am late."

Meena glares at Parvati, her hand on her neighbor's doorbell. She turns back and goes into her apartment, emerges with a bowl. "The usual, bhaiya," she says. "One liter."

Parvati shuts her eyes in thanks at the reprieve. Perhaps Meenabai will take the milk and go inside. She will use the bucket of water she usually uses for her bath to clean up the vomit. "Meenabai," she says weakly. "If I can trouble you for some newspaper, I will start wiping up the floor."

"And where you are planning on throwing the dirty newspaper? Not in my flat."

Parvati wishes she could lie back down and wait for this dizziness to pass. "I'll carry it to the garbage dump, bhenji," she says. "Please, not to trouble yourself. I will manage everything."

Grumbling under her breath, Meena returns with an old newspaper. "And get rid of this foul smell," she says as Parvati nods wordlessly. She has always kept her distance from Meena, ever since the woman created a row when Praful first offered her a place to lay her head. Praful and Meena's husband play cards together once a week, and it is that friendship that had made the man overrule his wife. Parvati sighs as she spreads the newspaper across the floor. There was a time when her life was as solid as the house she had then lived in. That life, too, had come with its share of miseries, but she had not had to worry about where she would rest her head the following night, did not have to listen to the curses and insults of strangers, nor rely on the whims of their charity or compassion. It is not cleaning up her own vomit that she minds—that, she sees as her duty. It is the fact that her future now depends on whether Meena Swami will still be thinking about the incident a half hour from now or whether she will be distracted by the demands of her children and husband; whether Meena's husband will smile or frown at her when he awakens; whether she has ever forgiven him for siding with his friend even when she'd made her displeasure known about Praful's homeless aunt sleeping in their stairwell. This randomness makes her feel like vapor, someone inconsequential and invisible.

She rolls the dirty newspaper into a ball and carries it down the three flights of stairs, dreading running into the butcher or the baker or the newspaper carrier, fearing the open doors of the other residents who will accuse her of fouling up their own entrances and who may join forces with Meena Swami and demand that she be evicted right then and there. She wishes there was something she could offer them in exchange for their silence, but there is nothing, not even a beautiful visage upon which they can rest their eyes. There is just an old woman with brown teeth, tall and gnarly as a tree, with a growth that horrifies the neighbors, terrifies their children, and makes them gossip about curses and divine punishment.

After Parvati throws away the balled-up newspaper, she walks down to where Joseph, a chauffeur for one of the families who live in the new, tall building across the street, is washing a blue Honda City. "You're late today, auntie," Joseph says to her. "Water is all cold-cold." Every morning, Joseph brings down two buckets of hot water from the apartment building to wash the car. He sells one of the buckets to Parvati for half a rupee. Usually, while it is still dark, Parvati carries the bucket over to a deserted compound next to her nephew's building and takes a quick and discreet bath, slipping her hands under the blouse and sari to wash. But today, the water must go to rinse the floor and walls outside Meena Swami's apartment. "I have to take the bucket upstairs today," she mutters. "I will return it as soon as I can."

Joseph turns to face her. The whites of his eyes are yellow and his brow is creased. "What you saying, auntie?" he says. "As it is you are late. My boss is just waiting for me to finish washing the car so I can drive him to work."

"I will return in five minutes," she pleads, sweat building on her face. "Please, it is important."

Joseph frowns. "It will take you five minutes just to reach your building. No, I'm sorry, I cannot help you. As it is if they find out our . . . arrangement . . . I will lose my job. Rich people think everyone is trying to rob them." He shakes his head. "Sorry, auntie. Too risky for me."

Parvati looks around in desperation; she must get rid of the foul smell before more neighbors awake to it. She walks faster, looking for another cleaner who might let her have even a little water. She rounds the corner and spots the two brothers, young men in their late teens. She doesn't know their names, but often when she comes home from the market in the late evening, she has smelled the daru on their breath and heard their taunts and jeers. Today, she forces herself to forget these insults and walks up to the younger of the two. "Beta," she says, "I am having a bit of emergency. Can you spare some water after you've washed the cars?"

The boy's eyes widen, then gleam with mischief. He lets out a giggle. "What will you give us in return?"

She flushes, hears the sexual innuendo in his voice, and refrains from pointing out that she is old enough to be his grandmother. Instead, she says humbly, "Just my ashirvad, beta. Nothing else I am having."

This time, he mocks her openly. "Oi, mausi," he says. "In this day and age, blessings won't even buy an idli."

She looks away, feels the desperation rise within her. "I had an accident today," she says quietly. "I was sick, beta. If I don't clean up my vomit urgently, I will lose the place where I'm staying. They will kick me out, you understand. Only because you couldn't spare me a few drops of water."

The boy stares at her, suddenly serious, then turns helplessly to his brother for advice. The older one, who had been scrubbing the car all this time, comes around now, and peers into her face. He whispers something to his younger brother, then nudges him. The younger one smirks. "We'll give you the water," he says. "On one condition. I want to touch that thing." He points to the growth on Parvati's throat. "My brother says it will bring us good luck."

Parvati swallows her humiliation. They are just two young, ignorant boys, she tells herself. Drunken children, with no education, no real job, no hobbies, nothing but time to create mischief. She forces herself to look into his eyes. "If you wish," she says, and then shuts her own eyes as she feels him rub his fingers, first tentatively, then more firmly round the growth. She only opens them when she hears his triumphant hoot of laughter and hears the other brother say, "You did it, yaar. Saala, no one will believe."

She has known worse violations before, but she is surprised at how deeply this insult has penetrated. All her adult life she has known that she was worth the price of a cow. Now, she is worth the price of half a bucket of tepid water.

She carries the bucket up the stairs before she realizes she has nothing with which to clean the floor. She looks around helplessly, debating whether to ring Praful's doorbell, weighing the odds of his wife answering the door, imagining the put-out look she usually gets on her face when Parvati troubles them for some small thing. Not willing to risk the woman's disdain, she goes to the small cloth bag that holds all her worldly possessions and pulls out the only other sari that she owns. She dips one end of the long garment into the pail and begins to scrub. Her eyes fill with tears of frustration as she does. She knows that she has already foregone a bath today. And now, the sari she will change into tomorrow will smell of vomit, a reminder of the last two years of Rajesh's life, when she spent her days tending to her sick husband as he lay in bed, staring at her without recognition. It wasn't the caregiving that Parvati had minded. It was the physicality of the job she had found ironic, the return to the corporeal aspects of human existence from which her marriage had whisked her away. Parvati finishes the last of the task, stuffs the sari into her bag, and hurries down the stairs. The morning sky is a pale blue by the time she returns the bucket to the brothers, who, now that they have won their macabre dare, seem strangely subdued and avert their eyes from her, their earlier fascination settling into the usual aversion that people feel at the sight of her.

* * *

The straps of Parvati's old leather sandals, hand-me-downs from Praful that are a size too large for her, rub against her ankles, but she barely notices the pain, her feet as leathery as the sandals themselves. As she walks toward the wholesale market to buy her usual wares, her only concern is to get there before the sun begins its daily warfare and to reach her spot at the retail market while the morning is still mellow. There was a time when Parvati loved the feeling of the sun on her face, but that is so long ago that she is unsure if that young woman was her or someone else she dimly remembers.

Nilesh, her supplier, is busy with other customers, and Parvati resigns herself to a long wait. The unwashed sari and the long trudge back to her spot in the market later than usual will be her punishment for her stupidity in dirtying the place where she rests her head. Only animals foul up the place where they sleep, she says to herself with disgust. But then she remembers the suddenness of the vomit, how it erupted out of her mouth like an inopportune word, and she knows there's nothing she could have done differently. As she waits, Parvati allows herself to wonder what caused that vomit. She had not felt sick after last night's dinner, nor had she woken up nauseous or in pain during the night. Abruptly, she remembers the new growth on her body, but she squashes the thought. There is no question of going to a doctor. And the free public hospitals are so bad that there's a rumor in the market that the government runs those to kill poor people rather than to heal them. It is how the government implements its Abolish Poverty campaign, someone had once told her—by getting rid of the poor. No one with any sense or money will step foot in those hospitals, though of course, when they get sick enough or desperate enough, they go. Well, she is neither. Long ago, she had put her life in the hands of God.

Except that she doesn't believe in God, a secret she shares with no one. All around her are people who proclaim their holiness—

Meena Swami goes to the temple each morning, Praful's wife is a staunch devotee of Sai Baba, and Reshma, the woman who sits next to her at the market, makes a daily offering at the Ganpati shrine that someone has carved into a brick wall. But Meena Swami has never said a kind word to her, Praful's wife spat angrily that time when the rains kept her customers away and she was unable to pay her nightly rent, and Parvati has seen Reshma remove her chappals and smack the stray dog who was sniffing her vegetables until the creature limped away. And these are minor infractions, compared to what she had witnessed in the Old Place. No, Parvati knows that what people truly worship are not the imaginary Gods who ride on chariots or float in the sky. What people worship is the flesh, as long as it is young and taut and beautiful; and money, in any state or condition. In all her years, this is the only truth that she has learned.

Nilesh makes eye contact with her and then looks pointedly away, smiling at the buyer in front of him. Parvati flushes. She knows she is the poorest of Nilesh's customers and that the six cauliflowers he lets her have for a pittance is an act of charity. But isn't it also true that if she didn't buy the smallest and stalest of his produce, Nilesh would most likely be throwing it away? What would it cost him to ask her, an old woman, to step to the front of the line, gather her meager wares, and be on her way? There is no hisab-kitab with her, no credit, no accounting, just a simple transaction in exchange for a few atrophied vegetables. She feels a sour taste in her mouth, a combination of shame, resentment, and vomit.

As if he's read her mind, Nilesh sighs dramatically and calls, "Ae, Parvati, come up and take your damn allotment, yaar." As the crowd shifts, Parvati feels a stab of gratitude. She is about to thank him for this reprieve when Nilesh turns to the other customers and says, "What to do, folks? These days even the poorest of people act like they're Sonia Gandhi." The crowd snickers. Parvati wants to protest but thinks better of it. Insults or compliments, taunts or praise, they are just words, no different from the prayers that everybody around her seems to be chanting while they are kicking stray dogs or trying to render old women homeless. That which is real is all that matters, and what's real is the weight of these six cauliflowers that she must now carry to the marketplace to sell.

"You're late," Reshma says in greeting as Parvati unfolds the tablecloth and rolls out her produce. She sniffs her disapproval. "That ignorant oaf stopped by. He was looking for you."

Parvati turns to her, puzzled. "Who was looking for me?"

"That whatshisname. Rajeev."

Before Parvati can respond, Reshma turns away and reaches for her bag. She pulls out a small, half-used tube of ointment and tosses it onto Parvati's tablecloth. "Here," she says. "He left this for you." She lets out a cackle. "Some suitor, you are having. Next time, tell him to buy you sweets." She wrinkles her nose, as she detects a whiff of the vomit clinging to the sari in Parvati's bag. "Or perfume."

Parvati turns her head, not wanting Reshma to see that her insults have stung. It's words, she tells herself. And they are not real.

5

The wailing starts low, tunneling its way from the bowels of the earth, and then it climbs, a black kite soaring higher and higher. At first it is indistinguishable from the other, everyday sounds of misery that circle the basti like satellites: crazed-with-worry mothers loudly berating their idle, unemployed sons; the screams of women protecting their last rupee from their violent, hashish-addicted husbands; the high-pitched squeals of dogs being kicked and maimed by bored children; the vile, steady stream of curses muttered by mothers-in-law toward the women their sons have married; the loud demands of slumlords threatening eviction and moneylenders threatening injury. The wailing synchronizes with the groaning of the slum, until its melody finally begins to separate, becoming its own tune. Rattled old women drop the chapatis they've just baked onto the mud floor, children stop their play, infants begin to cry in solidarity, even the drunks at the bootlegger's shop lower the bottles from their lips. Heads turn to find the source of the wailing, all of them bonded in the knowledge that it could be coming from any one of their huts, and alert to the fact that the intensity of this wailing connotes only one of two things—illness or death.

Bhima shuts her door and then she shuts her ears. It is seven-thirty in the evening; she has just gotten home. She is about to start dinner; after cooking for two different families during the day, all she wants is to feed this girl who is studying under the glow of the single lightbulb in their hut, and then go to bed. It is a small wish, and she thinks that she has earned it.

But the wailing gets louder, like an airplane flying closer and closer toward the ground. Maya looks up from her books with worried eyes and Bhima feels a spurt of anger at this inconvenient distraction. Stop your nuisance, she wants to scream, but just then, knitted into the wailing, she hears her own name. Bhima mausi, the voice cries. Help me. Ae, Ram, help me.

Now, she recognizes the voice. It's her neighbor from the next lane, Bibi, one of the few people in this basti whom Bhima respects. Despite her carefree, devil-may-care persona, Bibi is a hard worker and a devoted mother. Although she is an asthmatic, Bibi works as a maid at a nearby hotel. Her husband, Ram, sells fruit from his own cart. Together, they have built a life whose contours Bhima admires—a neat, well-kept hut with a tiled floor that Ram himself installed last year, a polite, soft-spoken son who goes to school each morning in a clean uniform with polished shoes, a marriage still perfumed by love and respect. Like Bhima, Bibi has not succumbed to the common corruptions and temptations of slum life, has held herself aloof from the gossip and the coarseness and the public displays of dishonorable behavior. But unlike Bhima, Bibi's wit and good humor make her one of the most popular members of the basti, and their neighbors do not seem to hold her success against her. This only makes Bhima admire her more.

And now Bibi is banging at her door, and Bhima has no choice but to get to her feet and open it. She steps out into the alley and is almost knocked over by Bibi, who collapses into her arms. Helplessly, Bhima looks over Bibi's shoulder and the sight makes her mouth go dry—the procession of slum dwellers who have followed Bibi are all grim-faced and silent, even the children, who suck their thumbs in apprehension. The formality in their posture, with none of the usual jeering or shoving or horseplaying, can only mean one thing: death. But whose? Even as she struggles to bear the weight of Bibi, Bhima's mind races—is it a mother or grandmother who has died? A sister living in a village somewhere? Or—Ae, Bhagwan—could something have happened to that little boy of hers, with a face as shiny as those black shoes he wore to school? Bhima shifts a bit in order to ease Bibi off her body. "Beti," she gasps. "Kya hua? What is it?"

In response, the wailing gets louder, and then Bibi says, "Oh, Bhima mausi, they killed him, they killed him," and Bhima's blood runs cold. Who would kill a little schoolboy and why? she wants to scream. She is aware that every mother in this basti has deposited her unrealized hopes into her children because not one woman believes that she will live long enough for her own Age of Darkness to end. It is for their children's sake that the women put up with the bad tempers of bosses, the humiliations and assaults too numerous to count, the arbitrariness of their hirings and firings, the grind of public transportation designed for a city one-third the size of what Mumbai has become. But the killing of little children is not part of this bargain.

But just as she is about to holler her own protest at the cruelty of Gods intent on punishing the same people over and over again, she spots him—the little boy with his neatly parted hair and teary face, staring at his mother's back with his dark, solemn eyes. Bhima's mind whirls—*He's alive, he's alive, look, Bibi, you stupid woman, you are making a mistake*—when Bibi sobs, "Ram, Ram, Ram, how am I to live without you?" and Bhima realizes that the woman is not crying out to the God Ram, but for her husband. "What's wrong?" she gasps. "What happened to Ram?"

"They killed him," Bibi wails. "Mausi, they killed him like a dog in the streets."

Shyam, one of her neighbors, an oily man she has never

trusted, steps forward. "It is true," he says, shaking his head. "Many of the other fruit vendors saw. What the goondas done to him." He lowers his voice, in deference to the widow. "The body is here, Bhima mausi," he says, averting his eyes. "Our men carried it home."

Out of the corner of her eye, Bhima sees Maya standing at the doorway of their hovel, and despite her concern for Bibi, maternal instinct takes over. "Go back inside," she barks, and then, seeing the stubborn jut of Maya's lower lip, "Make Bibi a cup of tea." She turns back to face the crowd gathered in front of her house, unsure of what to do. The sight of Bibi's little boy crying jolts her into resolution. "Bibi," she says, taking the sobbing woman by the chin. "Come in. Bring your son and come in." She opens the door to let the woman and child in before her, but before she can shut it, Shyam has snaked his way in.

Bhima sits on her mattress with Bibi beside her. The younger woman rests her head on Bhima's shoulder and Bhima feels her heart soften. Pooja used to do this when she was sad, she remembers, as she strokes the grieving woman's head. "What happened?" she says to Shyam.

Shyam sits on the floor in front of her, as far away from Ram's widow as he can. When he speaks, his voice is low. "It was those Maharashtra-for-Maharashtrians thugs, mausi," he says. "They're going round the city destroying businesses of non-Maharashtrians. Cabdrivers, vendors, anyone who is a migrant from the North, they're beating up, only."

Bhima shuts her eyes. Kuttas, she thinks, this city is run over by kuttas, mad dogs who move in packs, searching for blood. Muslims killing Hindus, Hindus killing Sikhs, everybody killing Muslims, and now, this new madness unleashed upon those poor, desperate souls who flock to this city from villages in Bihar and UP, searching for jobs. "Mad dogs," she spits, opening her eyes. "Junglees. Nothing they are knowing to do but fight, fight, fight."

Bibi begins to wail again, the sound deafening under the tin roof. "But my Ram was not a fighter, mausi," she says. "We're Mumbai people, fullum-full. Tell me, after spending half our lives here, how can we still be outsiders?"

They all jump when Maya speaks, her face half-turned from the Primus stove she's tending to. "My teacher says in a democracy like India, citizens have a right to live anywhere they want. That right is guaranteed by the Constitution."

Shyam nods, pretending to understand what she has said. "Correct," he says. "Guarantee." He raps on his head with his knuckles. "But in order to understand this, you must have something up here. Hai, na? But these bastards . . ."

Maya places the glass of tea at Bibi's feet and Bhima urges her to take a few sips. Tea is Bhima's solution to everything—grief, loss, hunger, or thirst. She is about to tell Maya to give the little boy a few biscuits when she sees Maya opening the metal tin.

"So what happened?" she asks Shyam again, keeping her voice low.

The man glances nervously at Bibi. "It was a gang, mausi. You know Govind who lives in the next lane? Short fellow, Bengali? He say they came shouting their slogans and destroying all the fruit carts with their lathis, just overturning the carts and beating up anyone who complained. They had a list. They were knowing exact-exact who was Maharashtrian and who were the babus from the North. Govind say he just hide under one of the upside-down carts when the beatings begin. But Ram, he—" He eyes Bibi again. "He fought back. So they kicked and kicked him like a dog. Govind say a policeman was standing right there, laughing. Only when Ram was not moving, the policeman blow his whistle and they run away."

The wailing has given way to a steady sobbing now, so forlorn that Bhima misses the earlier public keening. She wonders why Bibi has sought her out. Bhima is one of the basti's least popular residents, considered a snob because of the way she holds Maya and herself aloof from the daily dramas of slum life. She has never entered Bibi's home; if she has ever known the name of her son, she has forgotten it. Her only association with Bibi is from the line for the water tap each morning, where Bibi will often hold a spot for her, despite the protestations of those behind them. Thinking of that water line, it comes to Bhima now why she's always liked Bibi—unlike most of the slum dwellers, Bibi doesn't have a mouth for gossip. She has never once asked her why she has left Serabai's employ after so many years.

Now, Bhima broaches a delicate subject. "And the body has been brought here?" she asks.

Bibi's eyes grow cloudy. "They brought him to me, mausi," she says. "My Ram is resting in our home."

Bhima nods. "What about the funeral arrangements?" she asks.

The sobbing begins anew. "I cannot. I cannot let my Ram go," Bibi says.

Bhima puts her arm around the woman. "Bibi," she says. "You know the cremation must take place before sunrise. You know that is our custom. Otherwise, the soul . . ."

"I know. I know all that. But my Ram . . ." Bibi lifts her bloodshot eyes to Bhima. "You come with me, mausi. I have no one else in this godforsaken city."

Bhima stares at her, aghast. Don't ask me for this, she thinks. I'll share my last grain of rice with you and your son, but don't ask me to watch another body burn on the funeral pyre. It has been years since I witnessed my own daughter's body eaten by the orange flames, and the smell is still in my nostrils. I will be strong for you, but not this, beti. Don't ask me for this. "I cannot," she gasps. "Maaf karo, Bibi, forgive me. I'm an old lady." She turns helplessly to Shyam, whose face is impassive.

But her refusal has unleashed a panicked wildness in Bibi, who looks around the room in agitation. "What do I do?" she says. "Arre, Bhagwan, what is this darkness that has entered my life?"

Before any of them can reply, Bibi fidgets with the red glass bangles on her arm, then raises the arm and strikes the mud floor repeatedly, until the bangles shatter. Maya lets out a cry at the violence of the gesture, and even though Bhima knows that it is customary for a widow to do this, she is upset at Bibi for choosing to perform this ritual in her home, afraid of her depositing a residue of bad luck into their already hard lives. "Get up, child," she says firmly, gathering up the weeping woman. "I will go with you to the cremation grounds. Now, go home and prepare the body."

When they emerge from the hut, the crowd is still gathered outside. Bibi looks as if she is about to faint, so Bhima enlists the help of two strong-looking women to escort her home. The little boy trails along behind his mother, and Bhima's heart breaks at the sight. Something about his timid posture reminds her of the newly orphaned Maya when she had first brought her with her to Mumbai. She sighs heavily and then reenters her hovel, wanting to catch her breath.

"Ma-ma," Maya says as soon as she enters. "I'll go with Bibi. You stay here."

Bhima growls. "Shut your mouth, you stupid girl," she says. "The only pyre you will ever witness is your old grandmother's."

"Don't say that, Ma-ma," Maya cries, and for a moment, she is that little girl at her mother's sickbed who refused to leave her grandmother's side in the days that followed.

Bhima's outrage softens. "I'm not going anywhere," she says. "My flesh is too bitter and tough for even the fire to enjoy."

"Why did Bibi come to you, Ma-ma?"

"I don't know. Maybe grief attracts grief." Bhima falls silent, struck by a thought. She has never left Maya alone in the slum at night. "Where I'm going to leave you if I go with her for the cremation tonight?" she says. Immediately, she thinks of Serabai, and almost as immediately she is forced to banish that thought.

"I can stay alone one night," Maya says. "I'm not a child, Ma-ma."

"Chup re. This place is a jungle, full of drunken wild beasts." Bhima lowers her voice. "You made a mistake one time, girl. Don't ever repeat it again."

Maya flushes. She opens her mouth to reply and then closes it, and stares at the floor.

Bhima looks at her granddaughter for a minute, then asks, "What time is it?"

"It's getting on eight-thirty, Ma-ma. And we haven't even had dinner yet." Maya's voice is shaking, teary.

Bhima comes to a resolution. "Come on," she says. "Wear your chappals and let's go."

"At this hour? Where to?"

"To the Ashoka. You can eat something there. And I will use their phone to call Sunitabai. If she agrees, you are spending the night there. You can sleep on the floor of her kitchen, then come home in the morning before going to college."

"Ma-ma. Have you gone mad? Why will this Sunitabai say yes? I've never even met her."

Bhima smiles grimly. She is not sure herself. But ever since Chitra baby—yes, she has begun to call her that—has moved in, there is a softening in Sunitabai. Now, when she talks to Bhima she looks at her, instead of like in the old days when Bhima felt like she was writing her newspaper stories even while she was talking to her. Chitra baby almost always works alongside her in the kitchen, asking question after question about her life, and Bhima can tell that she carries some morsel of her answers back to Sunitabai each evening. And so she is willing to risk Sunitabai's refusal rather than leave Maya alone in the slum at night.

Maya grumbles all the way to the restaurant, but once there, she settles into eating a plate of biryani while Bhima uses the phone. It is her good luck that Chitra baby answers and actually seems happy to have been asked. "Do you want us to come pick her up, Bhima?" she asks, as if it is a natural thing for someone like her to walk into the slum at night.

"No, baby," Bhima says bashfully. "We will walk."

"At this hour?" The worry in Chitra's voice makes Bhima flush with pride. "Listen, do one thing. Catch a cab. Tell the driver to honk when you get here and I'll come down and pay him."

If the cab ride isn't enough to impress Maya, Bhima can tell that the girl is taken by the casual friendliness with which the two women greet them. Also, Maya looks comfortable in this modest apartment in a way that she never did in Serabai's much larger and more expensive home. Watching Maya talk to Sunitabai and Chitra, chatting about things Bhima knows nothing about, fills the older woman with awe. So this is what she has bought for her granddaughter. She had thought that her education was merely buying Maya a future job, where she would hold a pen instead of a broom. But it turns out that she had also bought Maya this ease of conversation, this friendly banter, this lapsing into English like rich people do. For the first time since Pooja's death Bhima does not think of her dead daughter with sadness. Instead, she thinks: Look what we made together, Pooja. You, by giving her birth. Me, by giving her a life. From my bare hands and dim wits, I have given your daughter this.

They must've been talking about the circumstances of why Bhima has called them with this unusual request, because Sunitabai is asking her, with that small frown on her face, "Do they know for sure they were targeting Northerners, Bhima? Because if they were, that's a news story."

Bhima folds her hands. "Please forgive me, bai," she says. "I know nothing. We are only repeating what we were told."

There is a short silence, and then Maya says unexpectedly, "I was born in Delhi. So I guess that makes me a foreigner, too."

Chitra lets out a squeal. "You were? Me, too. My whole family is from Delhi." She grins and points to Sunita. "I only moved to this dreadful city because of this one here."

There is a short, awkward silence before Sunita says, "Oh yeah. Because Delhi's such a great city. The rape capital of the world and all."

"Damn. You Mumbaikars are such chauvinists," Chitra responds, as Maya looks from one to the other, as if she is unsure of where her loyalties should lie.

It is late and Bhima stifles a yawn. "If you have some newspaper, bai, please to set it on the floor for my granddaughter," she says politely. "And I have packed a bedsheet for her. I am so grateful to you for this kindness."

Sunita looks pained. "There's no reason for her to sleep on the floor," she mumbles. "We have a second bedroom." She digs into her jeans and pulls out two twenty-rupee notes. "Take a taxi back, Bhima. It's too late for you to be walking home."

Three times during the ceremony Bhima thinks she will pass out. It is all too horrifyingly familiar—the sound of the skull exploding in the flames, the smell of burning flesh and burning wood, the embers of the fire flickering like stars against the black sky, the ritualized chanting of the priests, Bibi's heart-tearing sobs. Does human suffering sound all the same to the ears of the Gods, she wonders? Does that explain their indifference to our misery, this indifference that allows for the murder of a man as good as Ram? If this is so, she thinks, it is correct that a broken woman like herself should be the one holding up the shattered woman standing beside her. If poor Bibi is now entering her own Age of Darkness, who better than Bhima to coach her on how to survive that journey? She feels a moment's anger at the thought. She is still not sure what has brought her to this point, where all she can offer someone like Bibi is a guided tour through misery. She had been a devoted wife but had still ended up letting down her husband; she had been a good mother but had lost both her children; she had been a strict grandmother but still had to preside over the murder of her great-grandchild; she had been a devoted servant and still she had been thrown out from Serabai's house in dishonor. There is a key that would solve these riddles, she thinks, but she can only see it out of the corner of her eyes, hovering near, but out of reach.

Beside her, Bibi moans and the sound is so elemental, so truly an expression of what Bhima's own heart sounds like, that the older woman instinctively puts her arm around the younger. Bibi leans in sideways and Bhima has to dig her feet into the solid earth in order to prop both of them up, the young widow and the old—? But what is she? How to describe a woman whose husband is still alive but dead to her? What do you call a woman who is no longer a wife or a mother, despite the fact that, as far as she knows, both her husband and son are walking the earth a mere five-hour train journey away? Sometimes Bhima catches a glimpse of herself in the full-sized mirror in Mrs. Motorcyclewalla's old armoire, and she stops dead in her tracks, not recognizing the bone-thin, slightly stooped woman with the scanty hair and severe face that looks back at her. Even her large brown eyes have begun to turn a milky gray, giving her a ghostly appearance. The plump, no-nonsense girl that Gopal had wooed and married, the hardworking young mother whose hands moved at the speed of lightning, that woman has disappeared. She glances down at Bibi's tearstained face and wishes there was something she could teach this young woman, some morsel of experience she could feed her to sustain her during the dark days ahead. The only thing she knows without a doubt is that education is what may have saved them, herself and Gopal and Amit, and that even if it means scrubbing pots and pans until the skin comes off her hands, she will make sure that Maya finishes college.

As the priest ends his chanting, the wailing of the mourners begins. Bhima does not join them in this ritual. She barely knew Ram, and what Bibi needs now is not encouragement toward weakness but strength. Being a poor woman, she knows, is the toughest job in the world. So she waits for the wailing to stop and then she mutters, "Strength, beti. Be strong."

Bibi turns tearfully toward her. "How, mausi?" she asks. "How? He was my rock. How do I learn to see the world through my own eyes?"

Bhima falls silent, feeling acutely her own inadequacy. By breathing one breath at a time, she wants to say. By waking up one morning after another. By putting one foot ahead of the next, until your feet recall how to walk again. She remembers again the morning after Gopal had left, how she'd woken up in her new condition—breathing while dead—wishing that the whole world had ended while she slept, because to ask her to step into the still-alive world was a greater insult than the one held in the farewell note that Gopal had left for her.

Now, Bhima ponders Bibi's plaintive question, until the answer comes to her. "Not through your own eyes," she says. "But through his." She points to the little boy hovering beside Bibi.

"Your son has lost his father. Is it your wish that he loses his mother too?"

She knows she has said the right thing by how Bibi's weight shifts away from her. "That's right," Bhima says, nodding her head. "You will learn to stand, beti, so that your son doesn't fall."

"We will go back," Bibi says in a loud, fierce voice to all the mourners. "I will not raise my son in this city, where a man can be killed simply for being from the wrong place."

The other neighbors flock around Bibi and Bhima turns away thankfully. She is tired and she has to be at Mrs. Motorcyclewalla's apartment in a few hours. She takes a few steps away from the crowd and notices a well-dressed man in a white safari suit staring at her. Had he been here all along? She is sure she has never seen him before and he is most certainly not someone from the basti. "Namaste," the man says to her in a low voice. "Are you Bibi's mother?"

Bhima gives a short laugh. "No," she says. "No relations. I am just her neighbor."

"Ah." The man smiles. He looks over her shoulder and then addresses her again. "I'm here on an urgent business matter, mother," he says. "Can you arrange it so that I can speak to the young widow for a minute?"

Bhima eyes the man suspiciously. Her mind flashes back to the foreman at Gopal's factory. Like this stranger, that man had spoken to her with respect. He, too, had a soft voice. Suddenly, she is sure this man wants Bibi to sign a paper that will alter the course of her life. "Wait here," she says in a harsh voice, ignoring the look of surprise on the man's face. "I will bring her."

Bibi is in the middle of the crowd of weeping women. "Beti," Bhima says. "There's a man waiting for you here. Says he has some business for you." She takes in Bibi's tangled hair and sweaty face and knows that in her present condition, Bibi would sign her son over to any stranger who said a kind word to her. "I will come with you," she adds, grabbing Bibi by the wrist and pulling her along.

The man tells Bibi how sorry he is to hear of what has happened to Ram, that he will be filing a police report on their behalf first thing this morning because a grave injustice has been done. He tells her that Ram was a good man, then looks distressed when Bibi begins to cry anew. He pauses, takes a deep breath, then says, "Sister. I have come to talk to you about a time-bound matter."

Bhima tenses, waiting for the stranger to produce a piece of paper and a pen. She will pounce at once, beg Bibi to not sign anything until they have consulted with someone who is not illiterate like them.

Instead, the man says, "I need to talk to you about custard apples."

6

Custard apples.

The godown is filled with the fruit, the air thick with its cloying, sweet smell. Without warning, Bhima's mouth waters at the scent, which she remembers from her childhood. A smile plays on her face as she remembers breaking open the green exterior to reveal the white fruit, then tonguing the sweet, coarse white pulp that clung to each large, polished black seed. She used to spread the seeds on a newspaper, pretending they were pieces of polished gems from which she would make earrings and pendants. Bhima has never been able to afford more than one of these fruits at a time. Never in her life has she seen them in such a vast quantity, stacked on top of each other in a pyramid, the ripe fruit stacked in a separate pile from the unripe ones. To Bhima, this sight is as wondrous as if she were visiting the Taj Mahal for the first time.

Now, Jafferbhai points to one of the piles. "I was telling you about these ones, only," he says to Bibi. "Your husband has paid for these. So, technically, they are belonging to you. You send someone to take them away. You can sell, give away, eat—it's your business."

Bibi swallows and looks at Bhima, her eyes beseeching the older woman to make her case. Bhima nods imperceptibly, then turns toward the fruit merchant. "Jafferbhai," she says. "Many thanks for thinking about Bibi and her son during their time of hardship. But she is a lone woman. What does she know of her husband's business? Very good of you to come and explain." She steals a quick look at the man's impassive face and decides to speak the obvious. "But Jafferbhai. What is poor Bibi going to do with custard apples? As you may be knowing, she works all day at the Kohinoor hotel. What does she know about selling fruit? Please, sahib. Please, you just return the money that Ram gave you and you keep the fruit yourself. This young widow will remain in your debt, sir."

Jafferbhai sighs impatiently. "You're not understanding, mausi," he says through gritted teeth. "That's not the way my business works." His voice turns plaintive. "No other fruit seller would've taken time to come to the funeral to give you a chance to own this fruit. My own employees are saying I'm too softhearted." His eyes harden. "I can give you until tomorrow to come claim the fruit. If you don't want, you don't want. I will sell it to some other vendor at discount price. Case finish." He bows his head and folds in hands before Bibi. "Namaste-ji," he says. "My condolences about your husband. He was a very good man. In his memory, only, I try to help you."

As they exit through the tall iron gates of Jafferbhai's warehouses, the two women walk beside each other in an embarrassed silence, feeling the sting of failure. They are both aware that they have compounded their mistake by taking the day off from their jobs to run this foolhardy errand. Bibi at least has a good excuse—the Kohinoor's hotel manager, who is himself from the North, has sent word that he is sorry for her loss. Bhima knows she has no comparable excuse to offer Mrs. Motorcyclewalla and that the old lady will be relentless in her haranguing tomorrow. She sighs heavily, and immediately Bibi takes her hand in hers. "Forgive me, mausi," she says. "I have cost you a day's wages for no good reason. I shouldn't have asked."

"You did not," Bhima says shortly, in no mood to explain her reason for accompanying a neighbor who is more of an acquaintance than a friend. Except that, out of all the mourners Jafferbhai could have approached at the funeral, he had sought her out. And who better than she to know how the entire scale of life can be upset by one mistake, born out of illiteracy and ignorance? She had not wished that fate on Bibi, not realizing that Jafferbhai was that most unusual species—an honest man.

They have come to the main road and are about to turn right to walk toward the slum when Bhima stops. She looks around for a minute, wanting to get her bearings. "Bibi," she says, as the idea forms in her head. "You go on home. I am needing to be somewhere."

She waits at the corner until she can no longer distinguish Bibi in the crowd, then turns to cross the street. The sun is particularly vile today, and the heat and the smell of exhaust from the vehicles idling at the traffic light make her light-headed for a moment. She steps gingerly down from the curb onto the street, as if dipping her toe in the ocean, but just then a bicyclist going the wrong way almost knocks her down and she mutters a curse and hurries back onto the sidewalk. "Junglees," says the elderly Parsi woman standing beside her. "Savages. No discipline they are having." She peers up at Bhima through her thick glasses. "What I would pay to bring the British back. They'd discipline these idiots in one-two-three." She snaps her fingers for emphasis.

Finally, Bhima manages to cross the intersection, darting between cars that barely slow down for pedestrians, stepping around a legless beggar lying down on a skateboard that he pushes with his hands. Viraf baba used to dread the cripples on skateboards when he drove, she remembers, because it was almost impossible to see them from the car. She shudders at the memory of the gratitude she used to feel anytime he offered her a ride in his air-conditioned car to the marketplace where she is now headed.

She has not been back to this market in over a year, not since the last time she shopped here for Serabai, but it is instantly familiar to her. There is a throng of midmorning shoppers, but she is only looking for one person: Rajeev, the tall, lanky eager-to-please fellow who used to carry the groceries to Serabai's home. If she can persuade Rajeev to give up his regular job for a day tomorrow, they can pick up the custard apples from the godown in the morning, then sell them out of his large wicker basket. Beyond this, Bhima has no plan, not even where they would find a spot for his basket in this busy place where every inch of pavement has been claimed. But Rajeev might know. Then again, Rajeev is dumb—or did she think that only because as the trusted servant of a wealthy Parsi woman, she used to look down upon him? Bhima smiles grimly to herself. Well, look how far she has fallen.

Unable to spot him, Bhima heads to Birla and Sons, the shop where she used to find Rajeev crouched on the sidewalk, smoking a bidi in between his errands. Birlabhai, a portly man who used to chastise her for bargaining with him as if she were spending her own money and not her mistress's, recognizes her immediately. "Bhima behen," he shouts. "How are you? Where have you been?"

Bhima nods her head in greeting but avoids the question. "I'm looking for Rajeev," she says.

"Rajeev? He was here a minute back, only." Birla smacks a young boy who is sitting cross-legged on the floor. "Go find that good-for-nothing Rajeev," he says. "Tell him someone is looking for him."

There are no other customers at Birla's shop, and after the boy has left, Birla looks curiously at her. "So why did you leave us, sister?" he says. "Find better prices elsewhere?"

Bhima utters the first lie that pops into her head. "I work for another mistress now," she says curtly. "Very rich woman. She has her fruits and vegetables delivered from Breach Candy."

"Breach Candy, hah?" The shopkeeper shakes his head. "My son taught me a saying." He says something in English and when Bhima stares at him blankly, he translates: "It means, if a man is a fool, he and his money are quickly separated."

"I work for a woman," Bhima says, not understanding, and Birlabhai clucks his tongue. "Man, woman, a fool is a fool, hai na?" he says impatiently, and Bhima is compelled to nod her assent.

"How is your son?" she asks politely.

"Vikram? He is good, thank God. He got married last February. Girl is from very good family from the California in America. So Vikram is now living there, only." Birla looks at Bhima shifty-eyed. "I looked for you to distribute wedding invitation to, Bhima bhen," he says. "But what to do? You just disappear one day and not come back."

Bhima resists the urge to laugh at this naked lie. She remembers how dismissively he used to talk to her in the old days, when, unlike the other servants, she used to drive a hard bargain, out of a misguided notion that she must handle Serabai's money as frugally as her own. "Your son's good fortune has changed you," she says boldly. "Your happiness shows on your face." Her words are both compliment and insult, and she can see the confusion in Birlabhai's eyes.

"Thank you," he says, and just then a customer appears and he turns away from Bhima to tend to his business. She leans her upper back against the whitewashed wall outside his shop, careful not to let her sari touch the lower half, which is covered with the red streaks of paan juice spat out by passersby. She looks out on the crowded market, anxious to find Rajeev. A second later she spots him, towering over most of the shoppers, hurrying toward her, a big smile on his face. "Mausi," he exclaims as he draws near. "Which God do I thank for this miracle? How are you? Where did you disappear to?"

Bhima smiles thinly, not willing to let Rajeev know how glad she is to see him. "Theek hu," she answers. I am fine. "And you?"

"I'm fightum-fit," he says. "With God's grace."

But when Bhima looks closely, she can see new worry lines on Rajeev's gaunt face. And she notices that his back is more stooped than before. He is a young man—Bhima imagines he is no older than forty-two, but there is a sadness in his eyes that takes her by surprise. "Listen, Rajeev," she says urgently. "I have some work for you . . ."

"Let's go, mausi," he interrupts. "You need delivery to Serabai's?"

She shakes her head impatiently. "No. I am no longer in her employ." She ignores his start of surprise. "This is a different kind of job."

Rajeev smokes a bidi quietly as Bhima explains the situation. When she is done, he looks at her for a long moment and then pulls at his ear. "How many custard apples are there to sell, mausi? How many trips I must make?"

It is a reasonable question, and Bhima is upset at herself for not knowing the answer. "I don't know," she says shortly. "But whatever it is, I will pay you for it."

He swallows. "You are like my mother, mausi," he says. "I don't wish to offend. But what to do? If I earn less money than I do at this job, my wife will not forgive me. We are trying to put a new roof on our home, mausi. Plus I am having a son in college."

Bhima looks away, not wanting him to see the disappointment

in her face. "I understand," she mumbles. It is better this way, she thinks. She doesn't want to get too entangled in Bibi's life because she knows how it will be for Bibi from now on—one misfortune after another, like ants following each other in a row. She tells herself that she is indifferent to this realization. But the hollow feeling in her chest at the thought of failing Bibi tells her otherwise.

"Mausi," Rajeev says timidly. "I have an idea. What if I help you for a few hours tomorrow morning? Let's see what we can do to help the unfortunate widow."

Bhima folds her hands in gratitude. "Shukriya, beta. That would be very good."

"But mausi," Rajeev continues. "If his cart has been destroyed, where are we going to sell the fruit?" He looks around, a worried expression on his face. "No one will allow us to sell near their shop."

"I was thinking we just sell from your basket," Bhima says.

Rajeev laughs. "How we do that, mausi? If I carry the basket on my head, will customer climb on the ladder to inspect the fruit?"

Bhima's eyes fill with tears of frustration. She has not slept much since Bibi had come to her door two evenings ago. "I don't know," she cries. "All I know is there's a man who was killed like a dog in the streets and there's fruit that will rot that he paid for with his blood and sweat." Her vehemence scares her because it belies what she has just told herself about not getting too involved in Bibi's sad story. But Bibi had come to her. To *her.*

"I understand," Rajeev says in a soft voice. "That's why only I agree to help tomorrow morning. But to find the space to sell it, there I cannot help. Forgive me."

Bhima eyes Birlabhai's narrow strip of a shop with envy. Even though the shop is packed with mounds of potatoes and onions, she wonders if there's enough space for her to sell the custard apples. But she knows better than to ask. Birla will ask for so much rent that they will end up owing *him* money.

And then she remembers her. An ugly woman, with a face as shriveled as the cauliflowers she used to sell. With something evil growing from below her jaw. In the old days, Bhima used to hurry past her, because the sight of her, her abject helplessness, the desperate pretense of being able to subsist on the sale of her pathetic wares, used to offend Bhima. And the growth on her neck, which the crazy woman fondled all the time, as if it was prasad from the temple rather than the curse that it was, used to make her furious. She turns toward Rajeev. "There used to be a woman here. Sat at the corner. Had this thing . . ." She expands her fingers, as if she's carrying a cricket ball, and touches her neck.

"Parvati," Rajeev says, nodding vigorously. "She's still there. Same-to-same corner."

"You know her? You can ask her . . . ?"

Rajeev looks bashful. "How I can ask, mausi? This is your business. You ask."

She looks at the man, too embarrassed to tell him she has no idea how much to ask for the fruit, how to calculate its value. How will she know how much to offer Parvati for renting her space?

As if he's read her mind Rajeev says, "She's very poor woman, mausi. You can please offer her forty or fifty rupees."

She considers for a moment and comes to a decision. "Come," she says. "You take me to her."

Bhima scowls.

She had expected the stupid woman to be limp with gratitude

at her offer. Instead, this Parvati is behaving as if she owns all of Mumbai and they've offered her fifty rupees for it. Bhima looks sharply at Rajeev, as if this has been his idea, expecting him to reason with this crazy woman.

Parvati has followed the turn of her head and now, she, too, is glaring at Rajeev. "When you got me the ointment, then only I knew you were trying to trick me," she says. "Working with this woman who thinks she is better than everybody. All these years she was coming and going in this market, ask her if she even take a look at my vegetables."

"My mistress would have killed me if I came home with these rotting vegetables," Bhima hisses. "That's why I never stop before you."

Rajeev looks from one woman to the other. "Arre, arre, so much gussa," he exclaims. "Why for you ladies talking like this? You're both trying to help the other, na?"

They both turn on him at the same time. "Talking to this one here is like talking to someone at a mental hospital," Bhima says, not hiding the disgust in her voice.

"Take your ointment and go," Parvati says. "Trying to steal from an old woman. Did I ever eat your salt that my little space came to poke you in your eye?"

"Mausi, mausi," Rajeev says in a placating voice. "Please. Don't rent your space to her. But keep the ointment. I swear on my father's head, I have no bad intention toward you." He gets up from the ground and looks at Bhima. "Chalo, mausi," he says. "Please come with me."

Bhima glares at Parvati one more time and then walks away. After they've gone a few meters, Rajeev stops. "What time you wanting to go to the godown tomorrow?"

She shrugs. "What for? How we going to sell without a place to display the fruit?"

Rajeev scratches his head. "I don't know. But if the fruit is going to rot anyway, let's see how much we can sell."

Bhima hesitates. "There's one more thing," she says. "How much we should ask for the fruit?"

Rajeev grins in relief. "That's easy, mausi. Today I find out how much others are charging for the custard apples. Whatever price they're asking, we ask for a few rupees less. That way, we get the customer."

Bhima smiles her approval. This Rajeev is smarter than he looks. She looks up at the sky to judge the time. It is much too late to go to Mrs. Motorcyclewalla's house now. She will kill a few hours and then go directly to Sunitabai's house. Yesterday, she had gone to her first job soon after getting home from the cremation grounds and had been so tired by the time she got home in the evening that she and Maya had barely exchanged a few words before she went to bed. Tonight, she would like to go home at a good hour. She turns to look at Rajeev, who is peering anxiously at her. "Is that tea shop still there?" she asks. "The one that serves the vada pav?" The potato patties, served inside buns slathered with green chutney, are Rajeev's favorite snack, she remembers. "Okay, let's go there for a quick lunch. My treat."

Watching Rajeev wolf down the sandwich makes Bhima's heart sting with pity. Once again, she takes in the gauntness of his face, the sinewy leanness of his body. She wishes she had enough money to let this poor man eat to his heart's content, but as it is, she is aware of every rupee that she spends. Last year, there were riots all over the city when the government raised the price of onions. Every year, it seems, the price of food doubles and triples. And even with two jobs, her salary is less than what she was earning at Serabai's. It is only now, now that she is no longer in Serabai's employ, that Bhima realizes how much of her household expenses Sera used to bear: A new sari for her and a new shalwar kameez for Maya at Diwali time. A huge sack of rice and daal gifted for Parsi New Year, along with a box of sweets. Leftovers routinely sent home for her and Maya. And Serabai used to pay for Maya's college tuition and the cost of her books. Bhima can do without new saris and slippers for herself, she can eat a fistful of rice less each week, all to make sure that Maya finishes college. And yet, there is no denying the satisfaction that Bhima feels in watching Rajeev eat that humble sandwich.

"Many thanks, mausi," he now says, wiping his mouth with his sleeve. And then, the cursory, "Next time, I pay."

She lets him salvage his pride by nodding yes. Her mind is already on other things. "So, I come here at seven tomorrow morning," she says. "You will be here?"

"Yes." Rajeev turns to leave, then swings around again. "Mausi?"

"Hah?"

"The widow is very lucky to be having a friend like you." Rajeev smiles shyly. "You try to hide it. But I see it. You having a good heart."

She stands there, unsure of whether to thank him or scold him for his impudence. But his face is open and guileless, like a schoolboy's. Hard to believe that Rajeev is old enough to be the father of a college student.

"Salaam, Rajeev," she says. "I will take your leave now. I have a second housecleaning job to go to."

"Till tomorrow, then, mausi."

"Till tomorrow."

7

Parvati is still muttering to herself as she enters her building that evening, insulted by the impudence of that stuck-up woman, Bhima, and the treachery of that Rajeev, with his big, sad eyes and his pretense of caring. Her cheeks burn with anger as she wonders how long they've been eyeing that little patch of pavement that is the only thing in the world that still belongs to her. It was Malik, a client from the Old Place, who had secured this space for her, Malik with his hard fists and police connections, a tough, muscular guy who had scowled and offered to beat up Rajesh's son in the dark days that had followed her husband's death. When she had refused, he had come up with this idea. In those days, Malik was the underworld king of the neighborhood and he had simply turned out the hawker who used to occupy the spot and given it to her. She had felt sorry for the evicted man, but her desperation did not allow for sympathy. Word had spread that she was under Malik's protection and that, along with the lump, had kept all potential rivals away. Now Malik is long dead, shot to death in a mysterious "police encounter," but word is that his nephew has taken over his business. Unlike Malik, the nephew doesn't walk the neighborhood himself. He has diversified his holdings and Parvati has seen a picture of him in the newspaper, wearing a suit and tie and inaugurating one of his factories. But still, she knows that she is under his protection because she is the only vendor the police don't harass for bribes.

Since the vomiting incident, Parvati has been afraid to eat the leftovers that the restaurant owner saves for her. Unwilling to insult his ego by blaming his food for her accident, she had faked stomach problems earlier today and begged him for a cup of yogurt in exchange for a one-rupee coin. She is weak with hunger but wants to give rest to her stomach even though she has only had a cup of tea and a small loaf of bread all day. She cannot risk any more accidents. Muttering under his breath, the man had pushed the yogurt across the counter, but when she handed him the coin, he pushed it back. "Forget it," he had grumbled. "Consider it an act of charity."

It is dusk by the time Parvati enters the building and rings Praful's doorbell to hand him the night's rent. She prays that he will answer the door, and smiles when her prayer is answered. But just then the door across the hall flies open and there is Meena Swami thundering toward Praful. "Have you told her, ji?" she demands, and Parvati's heart stops beating when she sees the look on Praful's face—guilty, flustered, and, finally, angry.

"Arre, Meena, just wait, na," he says plaintively. "Just now only she rang my bell and bas—you immediately show up. Were you hiding behind closed doors or what, waiting for her come?"

Meena's voice is aggressive. "Meaning what? She's the guilty party and you're blaming me? We are respectable people living here, not . . ."

Now Praful raises his voice. A vein throbs in his forehead. "Go, go," he says, making a dismissive gesture with his hand. "We are all knowing who's respectable in this building. You please keep—"

Meena lets out a shriek. She turns toward her apartment and calls out to her husband. "Oi, ji. Are you hearing this? Your wife's virtue is being insulted and your nose is still buried in your videos?"

Parvati watches in horror as Meena's husband reluctantly comes to his front door and then steps out into the common passage. "What the hell is going on?" he says, looking at his wife with distaste as she tells him about the grave insult she has suffered at the hands of his card game partner.

The two men look at each other. "What is to be done, Praful?" the other man says at last. "I mean, Meena is correct. We cannot have vomiting-fomiting going on in the hallway."

Parvati opens her mouth to explain, to insist that this was a onetime occurrence, but Bhinder Swami gives her a look that makes the words die on her lips. "This woman is a nuisance, yaar," he says to Praful. "I mean, I don't want to bring up this bloody issue at the next building association meeting." He stares in the distance for a moment, then speaks again. "Tell you what. How much does she pay you daily? I'll double that. That way, everyone's happy."

Parvati sees Praful's face whiten at the insult, but just then Meena speaks. "Have you gone mad, ji? Why we should pay to get rid of this problem? We are within our rights . . ."

"Chup re." Bhinder says it softly, but Meena shuts up midsentence. Satisfied, Bhinder turns his attention back to Praful. "So, we have a deal?"

"No." Praful shakes his head vigorously. "You insult me. The money Parvati mausi gives me doesn't even buy my train ticket to work. I . . . she's my relative. She has no one in this world. That's why only we give her shelter."

"Then do it *inside* your home, na, boss?" Bhinder says immediately. There is a coiled, sinister strength to the man that reminds Parvati of Malik. She knows that Praful will not be able to stand up to this man.

She folds her hands in front of the Swamis. "Please," she says, her eyes glittering with tears. "Please seth, please memsahib. I'm a poor woman. I'm all alone in this world. This is my only home. Please take pity."

For a moment she thinks she has succeeded, imagines a softening in Bhinder's eyes. Even when he speaks, his voice is soft, almost regretful. But his words strike fear in her. "This is our home, bai," he says. "Not a homeless shelter. Now, please excuse us." He turns to his wife. "Get inside the house, Meena."

Parvati and Praful look at each other in silence for a long moment after the Swamis shut their door. Then, as if he is unable to face the terror in her eyes, he turns away. "You heard what he said, Parvati mausi. Nothing much I can do."

She stares at him wordlessly. "Praful—" she says at last.

He makes an exasperated sound. "How this has become my problem, I don't even know," he says. "What you want me to do, mausi? You think I am the landlord of the whole building?" He looks behind him furtively. "You know Radhika complains every single day about this arrangement. Says everybody in the building thinks we are beggars, letting you stay in exchange for your money."

"We know that's not the reason why, beta," she says. "I am so much in your debt."

But he is not placated. "I've helped as much as I can, mausi," he says. "You saw how that man talked to me. I have to be able to hold up my head in my community."

She says it softly. "Chotu," she says, slipping into his childhood nickname. "Who first taught you that lesson? To always hold up your head?"

There is a long, stunned silence, and Parvati knows she has gone too far. This is their unspoken agreement—to let the past remain the past—and she has violated it. After a few seconds Praful says, "Stay here," and slips into the apartment, leaving the front door ajar.

Parvati peers in frightfully, half expecting the man to return with a broom with which to beat her. It would serve her right for embarrassing Praful in the way she has. But when he returns, he is not carrying a weapon. Instead, he gives her two pieces of paper. One is a torn sheet with an address written on it. The other is a fifty-rupee note.

"Take this," he says to her, "and go to this address. Ask for Mohan. I will call him to tell him you are coming. He . . . he will give you a cot for tonight. Give him the money."

She stares at him wordlessly, choking on the gratitude she feels at Praful's generosity after the insult she has levied at him but also wrestling with the cold realization that the boy she has known since he was born, the man she calls her nephew, is casting her out from what she had hoped would be her last and final home. "What do I do tomorrow, beta? Where from I get another fifty rupees tomorrow?"

Praful clenches his teeth. "That is not my problem, mausi," he says. "I have done everything that I can do for you. Now, please. Collect your bag and go."

Parvati's eyes flash with anger. "Where are you sending me? What kind of a place is this?"

Praful averts his eyes. "You know what kind of place, mausi." He pulls his lips into a thin smile. "But not to worry. You will be safe there. Your old age will protect you."

It is dark as Parvati searches for Tejpal Mahal. When she finds it, she stands in front of the run-down building, taking in the scaffolding that cages it, the pile of rubble near the front steps, the shrieks and debauched laughter that reach her from the open windows. For a wild moment she contemplates sleeping on the pavement along with the other homeless people, but comes to her senses. She will trust that Praful has not put her in harm's way.

A half hour later she is lying down on a rope cot in a tiny room with thin walls. The sounds she hears from the other rooms make her heart beat rapidly, make her feel like she's never left the Old Place, that Principal is going to burst into this room at any minute and ask her to get ready. She feels a scream start from deep within her at the irony of this situation. Will she never have a say-so in any aspect of her life? she wonders. Does she have no more choice in deciding her own destiny than one of her cauliflowers? Like them, she has been bought and sold, sliced and diced, moved from one corner of the city to another. And Praful, *Praful*, knowing her horror at ending up again in such a place, has still sent her here. She gladly would have slept on the floor of his bathroom than to be here. For this boy, she had purchased a Cadbury éclair every single day out of her meager income at the Old Place. This was the boy who, during thunderstorms, crawled up to sleep next to her, because his own mother was too far gone on the hashish. This was the boy who she took to the movies on her day off and who she walked to school each morning. This is the boy who got out of the Old Place, who didn't become a hit man or a pimp, who worked as a bookkeeper, who married a respectable girl, but who had still sent her here.

She turns onto her side because the cot is digging into the growth at the bottom of her spine. O, ungrateful woman, she chides herself. That boy has spared you from the streets tonight. Show some gratitude, no? At least tonight you will be safe. But what about tomorrow? she thinks. Where does a lone woman go in this bustling city of millions?

And then the answer comes to her: There is no place for her to go but here. And in order to return here, she must pay Mohan thirty rupees a day, an impossible sum. She wonders if Nilesh would allow her to purchase more cauliflowers on credit so that she can earn a greater profit. And perhaps she can cut back even more on monthly expenses like soap and toothpaste? But even as she contemplates the question, she knows that her bare-bones existence will not allow her to cut back too much more. Yes, she decides, tomorrow she will go to Nilesh's place earlier than usual. If he is not too busy, if he doesn't look through her the way he usually does, she will explain her dire situation to him. And if he will not extend credit to her? Her mouth goes dry at the thought. She has only been this frightened once before—on the day she'd arrived at the Old Place.

The solution arrives hours later, just as she's about to fall asleep. She knows what she must do—if she has not chased them away with her anger and disdain, that is.

She must help them sell custard apples.

8

Despite her horror at having spent the night in that disreputable place, Parvati's body hurts less this morning than it usually does after spending the night in the stairwell. For this she is grateful. As she had suspected, Nilesh had refused to give her extra produce on credit, had given her a long, incredulous look before turning away to attend to the next customer. Once again, Parvati has learned her worth—she is not even worthy of a verbal dismissal. Now, she sits in her usual place in the market, and when Rajeev appears at last, she gives him an ingratiating smile. But before she can approach him, Rajeev walks haughtily by and Parvati fights an undertow of regret at having so rudely severed ties with the only person at the market who has been kind to her.

She is about to race after the man when she sees him walking up to Bhima, and her face involuntarily curls up with distaste. For years, this woman Bhima never so much as glanced in her direction. If, once or twice, their eyes met, Bhima would turn her head sharply and look away. The other woman carried herself as if she were better than all the rest of them, as if by working for a rich mistress, she was wealthy herself. Now, Parvati watches as Bhima says something to Rajeev, who trots beside her, his empty wicker basket balanced on his head.

Parvati turns toward Reshma. "Need any help selling today?" she says. "I can help."

Reshma frowns suspiciously. "Are you ill, mausi?" she says. "Or am I looking ill to you? Why for I need help selling my own vegetables?"

Muttering a curse under her breath, Parvati turns away so that Reshma will not see the tears in her eyes. People called Mumbai the city of dreams. All she saw was a noisy, smog-filled, heartless metropolis, a place where the old BEST buses that wheezed down the street seemed to have more heart than the people they transported. As if the city itself has read her thoughts, there is the whine of a drill and the teeth-rattling noise of a jackhammer coming from across the street where the new mall is being built. The fishmongers, who for decades had occupied the land, had been forcibly evicted two years ago, and despite their daily street protests and a court injunction, work on the mall goes on. At first Parvati had been glad, hoping she could go across the street to use the clean indoor toilet facilities, but when she'd mentioned it to Reshma, the younger woman had laughed bitterly. "Arre, mausi, are you mad or what? You think they building a big-shiny mall for us little people to go do our business? In other malls, I've heard they are charging entrance fee, to keep out people like us. And look at this one—like a palace it shines. Who is going to allow you to enter?"

Everywhere Parvati looks these days, the city is shining. New shops selling brand-name clothes and jewelry spring up daily. New, expensive restaurants outside of which young people stand in line to enter. Shops selling fifty flavors of ice cream. Sweetmeat stores that do a roaring business selling barfis and kaju katlis topped with gold leaf. New models of imported cars and more cars on the roads than ever before. Cinema halls that have, she has heard, twelve screens. This new Mumbai hates its old. Every day, old stone buildings are being torn down to make way for tall buildings, thin as pencils, poking up into the sky. Every afternoon, large private tankers come to these new buildings to deliver water because there is not enough public water for the demand. But the biggest change of all, Parvati thinks, is in the people. The Mumbai she has known has never been a gentle, forgiving place. But the old Bombay, the Bombay of Raj Kapoor and Nargis, had a sweetness to it, a childlike innocence. This new Mumbai is fast-paced, coarse, indifferent. She sees that indifference in the frightening blankness in the eyes of the office crowd—whether it steps over a centipede or a homeless person, it's all the same. Nothing slows the crowd down, nothing makes it pause. It is as if everyone in this city is chasing his or her fortune and to get at it, they will stand on and crush the heads of their own mothers. There is only one unforgivable sin in this city, and that is the sin of poverty. Everything else is taken in stride—corruption at the highest and lowest levels, disloyalty, betrayal. In any case, what loyalty can one expect from a city that has surrendered its very name—gone from Bombay to Mumbai—in the flash of an eye? Such a city will consume its poor, parasitic residents the way a big fish swallows up hundreds of little fish, and then cast about, looking for its next prey.

From the belly of the fish, Parvati sits on her little patch of pavement and looks at the world with old, tired eyes.

9

Bhima wipes the sweat off her face with the pallov of her sari. It is midday and they have sold exactly five custard apples. Rajeev was correct—between being chased off by territorial vendors from one spot to another and having no place to set Rajeev's basket down, it is an impossible situation. Her eyes fill with tears of frustration at her own stupidity. Why couldn't she mind her own business? What stupid sense of obligation to Bibi had made her take yet another day off from her own job at Mrs. Motorcyclewalla's home to sell a fruit whose smell she was already beginning to hate? On top of which, she now had to pay Rajeev his day's wages out of her own money. Rather than recovering Bibi's money, she was wasting her own.

As if he has read her mind, Rajeev stoops toward her, clenching and unclenching his right fist. "How much longer you want to do this, mausi?" he says. "I don't want to waste your money. Half a workday still left—I can go back to my regular job."

"And what face do I show to Bibi?" Bhima snaps. She unties the knot on her sari, removes a pinch of the chewing tobacco, and pops it in her mouth. Maya has been lecturing her to stop using the stuff, but right now, Bhima needs its familiar comfort as she confronts the colossal error she has made in poking her nose into her neighbor's business. She looks up at Rajeev. "Don't you know of anyone else in this marketplace who will let us sell from their spot?"

Rajeev shakes his head. "It is not so easy, mausi," he says. "People here will sell you their newborn before they will rent you an inch of space. They are afraid you will claim it as your own."

"Why do I need to claim their filthy space? I just wish to sell the fruit poor Bibi's husband paid for, and bas—I am done." Bhima spits the red tobacco juice on the street. "If only that foolish woman had let us rent her spot, we would've sold these fataafaat and been finished. But no, the maharani prefers to squat all day, playing with that evil growing on her neck."

Rajeev blanches at her words, and Bhima follows his eyes to where Parvati is standing a foot away from them. Her stomach drops. She knows that the older woman has overheard her unfortunate words and opens her mouth to apologize, but Parvati doesn't give her a chance. "I've changed my mind," she says curtly. "You can use my space. But it will cost you fifty-five rupees, not fifty."

Bhima can scarcely believe what she's hearing. She glances at Rajeev and then quickly nods. "It's okay," she agrees.

"One other thing. I want two custard apples. Free."

Bhima nods again.

And so the deal is struck.

Reshma grumbles at the intrusion, but Parvati silences her with a look. They unload a dozen of the fruit onto Parvati's tablecloth, but Reshma bristles with anger when Rajeev tries to set down his large wicker basket. "You and your basket are blocking my customers' view," she hisses. "I'm warning you, if you take one morsel of food away from the mouths of my children, your children will have worms in their mouths."

Bhima turns sternly toward the hysterical woman, but Rajeev's face goes pale at the woman's curse. He has only one child—a son who had battled dysentery throughout his childhood, who, against all odds, is now in college, and upon whose slender shoulders rest Rajeev and his wife's accumulated hopes. The thought of Reshma's curse alighting on Mukesh's beautiful body is enough to make Rajeev shudder. He lifts up the basket immediately. "You sit and sell, mausi," he says to Bhima. "I will keep walking. I'll check back every five-ten minutes, don't worry."

Her lips curling with disgust, Bhima turns her back on Reshma. "Khali-pilli, for no good reason, she's making that poor man walk around in this heat with a topli on his head," she grouses to no one in general.

To her surprise, Parvati clucks her tongue in sympathy. "He's a good boy, that Rajeev."

Bhima eyes her suspiciously, remembering how the woman had berated Rajeev yesterday when they'd approached her for her spot. A little cracked in the head, she decides. Otherwise, who changes their mind like this from one day to the next? But now there's no time to think because she has to tend to her first customer who is holding the fruit in her hand, weighing it, breathing in its aroma. "How much?" the woman asks.

True to his word, Rajeev runs back and forth all afternoon, unloading more of his cargo each time Bhima's supplies run low. To her amazement, Bhima discovers that she is enjoying herself, the back-and-forth with customers, the haggling, the inflating of the price and then softening her stance, the thrill of making a sale. She has been at the other end of this dance all her life, used to love driving a tough bargain because it saved Serabai a few rupees. Now, she realizes that she loves being on this end of the negotiations even more. Rajeev has told her how much the others are asking for the fruit and she has decided to undercut them all. That, and the fact that her fruit is of good quality, is the reason why she is selling out.

At three o'clock she has a visitor, a muscular, light-skinned fellow, who towers over her, scowling. "What's the plan, sister?" he says. "You trying to put the rest of us out of business or what? And where's the permit to be selling at this corner?"

Bhima looks at him nervously, unsure of whether he is bluffing about the permit. But before she can respond, Parvati is on her feet. "You don't have any other job, Rogal? Bullying old women? Talking about permit-fermit? You want to see her permit, you go see Malik's nephew. Then let's see who survives the next day, you or me."

At the mention of Malik's name, the man lowers his eyes. He swallows hard. "Arre, Parvati, why unnecessarily you getting all angryfied? I was just asking . . ."

"You ask-fask on someone else's time," Parvati interrupts.

The man's tone is placating. "Calm down, na. You know I meant no harm."

But Parvati is still scowling. "I know nothing but what I'm seeing with my own two eyes. And what I'm seeing is you still standing in front of my place, driving away my customers."

To Bhima's astonishment, the man turns around and walks away without another word. She turns around to thank Parvati, but the woman is still breathing hard and has such an angry look on her face, she thinks better of it. A moment later, Bhima spots Rajeev and beckons to him to hurry. "Best if you unload the rest of the stuff now, beta," she says to him. "Then we can all go home."

Rajeev stares at her, puzzled. "But mausi," he complains. "There's more of our fruit in the godown. If you say the word, I go now and come back with another full basket."

Bhima shakes her head. "I have my regular job to go to," she says. "Already, I'm going to be late." She sighs, soothed by the thought of being in Sunitabai's cool apartment, a respite from the clamor and heat of this place.

Before Rajeev can respond, Parvati speaks. "If you wish, you can rent this stall again, tomorrow. Until you finish your supply. Same rate as today."

Bhima scratches her head as she considers. "I can't," she says at last. "As it is I've not gone to my morning job in two days. Too much money I am losing. That old Parsi woman I work for is as mean as a mosquito. She will cut from my salary, for sure."

Parvati has not made eye contact with Bhima, but now she looks her fully in the face. "And what about your profit from today? You not counting that?"

Bhima looks at her in confusion. "I pay you," she says. "I pay this one here. And the rest of money I give to Bibi. Where is profit for me?"

The older woman blows her nose on the edge of her sari. Then she looks at Rajeev. "You. Go to that baniya's shop and borrow a paper and pencil. Go and come, quickly."

Rajeev and Bhima look at each other mutely and then stare at Parvati in befuddlement as she writes on the scrap of paper before her. The old familiar shame at her own illiteracy rises in Bhima. If Parvati had turned into a princess before Bhima's disbelieving eyes, she would not have been more stunned. Who would have thought that this old witch, with the ugly fruit growing on her neck, could read and write? Despite herself, Bhima hears herself say, "Your father must have been a great man to have educated a girl. That too, in the old days."

The pencil clatters on the pavement as Parvati sets it down and fixes Bhima a baleful glare. "The pile of dung that was my father," she says, "may he be reincarnated many times over as a cockroach. He had nothing to do with my education."

Bhima stares openmouthed at the woman in front of her. "May God forgive you," she begins, but Parvati stops her with a vigorous shake of her head. "No," she says. "May I forgive Him."

Beside them, Reshma lets out a cackle. "Now you see whom you're dealing with," she says to Bhima. "This woman is . . ."

"Yes," Parvati says softly, staring directly at Bhima. "Now you see." She points toward the piece of paper in her lap. "You still wanting to deal with me?"

Bhima looks to Rajeev for help, but he looks as stunned as she feels. After a moment, she nods. And Parvati resumes her writing.

"How much did the widow's husband pay for his consignment?" she asks at one point, and Bhima tells her. "And how many you bring today?"

"Forty-eight," Bhima says. "Minus the five that are left."

"Two of which belong to me," Parvati says immediately.

Bhima feels the power drain away from herself and toward this woman who is at least ten years older than her. The disdain she has always felt toward Parvati has given way to growing respect and awe. "Yes," she says simply. She glances at Rajeev's tired face, his stooped body. "And two of these belong to him," she says, gratified by the shock of joy she sees on the man's face. "I will take the last one home to my granddaughter."

"It's fine," Parvati says briskly and scribbles some more. After a few moments she stops and sticks the pencil behind her ear, a gesture that Bhima has always associated with educated people. Serabai used to do this, after she made shopping lists for Dinaz and Viraf. If this woman can read and write, what for is she selling these cauliflowers in this wretched marketplace? Bhima wonders. And when she glances at the tablecloth, she gets another shock—the vegetables have disappeared. Somehow in the course of this busy, heady day, Parvati has managed to sell her daily wares.

"Are you listening?" Parvati's plaintive voice breaks through her thoughts. "I'm saying that even after paying the widow her initial investment, you have made yourself a little extra money."

Bhima blinks, unsure of whether to believe this good fortune. She wishes she were somewhere safe and private, where she could count the day's earnings to see whether Parvati is correct. Well, she can request Chitra baby to look over this woman's figures when she gets to her second job. If she ever gets there today.

"Chalo, let's settle up," she says briskly, trying to reclaim some of her lost authority. She counts the money as surreptitiously as she can in the open marketplace. "Here's your share," she says, handing the bills to Parvati. "And this is yours," to Rajeev.

"Shukriya, mausi," Rajeev says, touching his forehead in thanks.

"No, beta. It is I who am in your debt."

She marvels at how Rajeev's face transforms when he smiles. "So, same arrangement again, tomorrow, mausi?" he asks.

Bhima thinks. The choice is between spending the morning sitting next to this clever but blasphemous woman, or listening to the dark mutterings of another crazy old woman who waves her madness like a flag. With its closed windows and her strictures against turning on the lights, Mrs. Motorcyclewalla's musty apartment is as lifeless as a grave. Here, there is the incessant sound of blaring horns and the rumbling of the jackhammers working across the street. "Yes," she says, coming to a decision. "See you at the godown."

After Rajeev is gone, Bhima forces herself to look at Parvati's misbegotten face. "Thank you," she says.

"No mention," Parvati says as she turns away.

Bhima picks up a custard apple, rises to her feet, waits for her hip to pop, and bites her lip against the pain that follows. She feels Parvati's eyes follow her as she makes her way down the winding path of the marketplace and to her second job.

10

Bhima knocks on Bibi's door that evening before entering her own hut. The little boy answers the door and wordlessly lets her in, so that she has no choice but to enter. Bhima has made it a habit to not enter her neighbors' homes because she does not wish to become part of the informal network of slum life. She eschews the small talk and idle gossip and does not partake in the rituals of drop-by visits like her neighbors do, as if they are birds alighting from one wire to another. As best she can, she holds herself aloof, mostly for Maya's sake, but also for her own, as a reminder that unlike many of her neighbors she has known better days, has lived in a small flat in a real building, where she shared a bathroom with just one other family, instead of this communal bathroom they now use, shitting as if they are cattle in a field. All these years she has conducted herself as if she were just a visitor to this basti, and now that Maya is back in college, there is hope that someday her granddaughter will land a job that will carry them out of this place. How realistic this hope is Bhima is not sure—in the old days Serabai would talk about the lack of jobs even among the highly educated—but Bhima clings to it because without hope she may as well be dead. And after all, it costs as much to dream big as to dream small.

But now she is in Bibi's one-room shack with its neat, tiled floor, and an uncharacteristic envy rises in her. There are many rich people in the slum—the bootleggers with their new TV sets and those with political connections who ride around on shiny new motorbikes—but Bhima has never wanted their dishonest wages of sin. She envies Bibi's humble but clean home precisely because it is the house built by two honest and hardworking people, every tile on the floor paid for with their sweat. And so, she smiles warmly when Bibi raises her worried eyes to her and says, "Kya hua, mausi? Any luck?"

"God is great, beti," she says, handing her the money that is rightfully hers. Earlier this afternoon, Chitra baby had gone over Parvati's math and pronounced it correct. Then, she had helped Bhima divide the money into two shares—hers and what she owed Bibi. Chitra had laughed as Bhima had tied the money into two separate knots on her sari. "Did you ever carry a purse, Bhima?" she had asked mischievously.

"Yes," Bhima had answered. "When I was younger. My husband bought one for me, from a man on Chowpatty Beach." She noticed with satisfaction the look of surprise on Chitra's face. And then, before the girl could start with her usual questions, Bhima had shooed her out of the kitchen. She had only known Chitra baby for a month but already she felt comfortable doing so. Otherwise, she would have never asked her to shelter Maya the night of Ram's funeral. Chitra was like a child—there was no sludge, no meanness in her heart.

Bibi's shriek of happiness brings Bhima back into the present. Before she can stop her, Bibi has taken her hand and is kissing it. "O Bhagwan," she breathes. "How can I ever repay your kindness, mausi?"

Bhima hesitates, debating whether to tell Bibi about her share of the money. What is her obligation? she wonders. Does this money also belong to the young widow? She eyes the young boy, looking at her with his solemn face, and comes to a resolution.

Untying the knot, she removes the rest of the money and pushes it into Bibi's hands. "What's this?" Bibi says suspiciously.

Bhima tries to remember how Parvati had described the surplus money. She gropes for the right words, then it comes to her. "We sold the fruit for more money than Ram pay, beti," she says. "That money is the profit. This is also yours by right."

Bibi gets a pained expression on her face. "No, mausi," she says. "These are your earnings. Your reward for your effort. This I cannot touch."

Bhima stares at the younger woman, cut in half between gratitude and obligation. "If Ram had sold the fruit, this is what he would bring home," she says at last.

Bibi's eyes flash around the room. "But Ram is not here," she says. "He did not spend the whole day at the market. You did."

"But beti. Think of the little one. How will you manage . . ."

Bibi folds her hands. "Many thanks, mausi. But this is your money, not ours." She pulls the little boy in front of her and rests a hand on each shoulder. "We now have one less income, mausi. But also, one less mouth to feed, hai na? So, we will manage."

The thickness that forms at the base of Bhima's throat tastes warm and metallic. Sorrow, grief, gratitude, admiration, all gather there, leaving her wordless. The two women look at each other, each humbled and held by the other. "You are an honorable woman, Bibi," Bhima says, as she makes to exit the hut.

Bibi smiles wanly. "Without our honor, who are we, mausi?" she says. "Life has stolen everything else from us. Let's pray it leaves us with our *swaman*."

Bhima is thinking about Bibi's words as she enters her own house and grunts a greeting to her granddaughter. "What time did you get home?" she says after she has poured herself a glass of water.

Maya stretches. "About an hour ago."

Bhima takes in the unlit stove, the flour that has not been kneaded for tonight's meal. "And what have you been doing?"

Maya shrugs. "Relaxing."

Now, Bhima notices the magazine in the corner of the hut. It is a film magazine, she can tell, with the photo of a movie star whose face she has seen on billboards all over town. A thread of anger runs through her, so sharp that she has to fight the urge to remove her slipper and slap Maya's face with it. "Good," she says bitterly. "You relax while your old grandmother slogs all day until her bones break. You can relax on my deathbed, too, you good-for-nothing girl."

Maya's eyes fill with tears. "I work hard at college, too," she yells. "I was happy to get a job. You're the one who is forcing me to finish college."

"Chup. Keep your voice down, you ungrateful girl. Just like these animals around us, you are sounding."

But Maya raises her voice even more. "I *am* an animal. *You* are an animal. Look around you, Ma-ma. Where you thinking we live? At the Taj? We live in the zoo, in this slum. We are no different from anyone else here. You can walk with your head held high as much as you want, but in the end . . ." Maya is sobbing so hard, she is unable to finish.

Bhima stares in shock at her granddaughter. Some days she feels so close to Maya it is as if the girl is a layer of her own skin. Other times, Maya is as unknown as a star. "It's not true, what you say," she says at last. "There is honor—there is even nobility—right here, where we live." She squats on her mattress, then pats it. "Here. Come sit here, next to your Ma-ma. I will tell you a story."

Maya eyes her warily, but as Bhima knows, she cannot resist a story. So she sits next to her grandmother and Bhima tells her about her whole day, including the part about Bibi. But to her disappointment, Maya is not impressed. "So? She just gave you what was yours by right."

Bhima is speechless. Who is this arrogant stranger that she has raised? She opens her mouth to berate the girl again, then stops. She takes in Maya's long, dark hair, the large, innocent eyes, the fleshy lips, the plump, soft hands that have still retained their youthful fat. She is still a girl, she reminds herself. Who has not seen enough of this wicked world to appreciate goodness when she encounters it. But she will. She is Pooja's daughter, after all. The blood of her mother gushes through this girl's good heart. "Come on," she says, smacking Maya lightly on her shoulder. "Go put the rice to boil. Perhaps we will have vegetables with rice tonight instead of rotis."

They eat sitting on their haunches, side-by-side. Bhima scoops a ball of rice with her fingers, mixes it with a little eggplant, and pops it into her mouth. As always, she synchronizes her eating to her granddaughter's, anxious to sweep some of her meal into Maya's plate if the girl is still hungry. She can always make a glass of tea for herself to assuage her own hunger.

"How are Chitra and Sunita?" Maya asks with her mouth full.

Bhima raises her eyebrow. "Arre. You spend one night there and call them by their names? The proper term of respect is *bai*. They are your superiors."

Maya gives her a sidelong glance. "But they only tell me to call them that."

"It's that foreign nonsense that Chitrabai says," Bhima says, aware that she has almost slipped and called the woman Chitra *baby*. "Ignore it."

"She's not a foreigner. She's—"

"She lived in that foreign place so long she forget—"

"It's called Australia, Ma-ma. But that's not why she thinks the way she does."

"Then what?"

Maya eyes her grandmother carefully. "Don't you know, Ma-ma? Chitra and Sunita—they love each other."

"Silly girl. Of course they love each other. They're friends, no?"

Maya swallows her rice before she speaks. "Not like that, Ma-ma. They love each other, like, a woman love a man. Like you loved Gopal dada."

Bhima jumps so violently she knocks her plate, spilling the rice on the floor. "You dirty girl," she scolds. "Mind like a sewer. What filth you speak. This is why I send you to college?"

Maya opens her mouth to speak, but Bhima raises her hand to stop her. "Bas. Enough. Those women take you into their home and this is how you repay them? By telling lies?"

"But Ma-ma . . ."

"Girl. Are you deaf?" Bhima rises, eyes the spilled food. "You clean up this mess."

"Ma-ma," Maya says in her appeasing voice. "I will share my food with you."

But Bhima is headed toward the door. "Not hungry," she says, and it is true. Maya's terrible accusation has looted her hunger. "I am going to the baniya's place," she says. "I need to pick up some sugar." And she is out of the house before the girl can protest.

There is sugar in the house, but Bhima heads toward the grocer's shop anyway. She walks fast, as if to flee her own wicked recollections: The neighbor's caustic comments about Chitra baby the day she'd met her for the first time. Last week, when Chitra had rested her hand on the small of Sunitabai's back while all three of them were in the kitchen. Even at that time, the tenderness of the gesture had registered, but Bhima's mind had blocked out the suspicion that had arisen. But now the images roll into her mind like shots from a movie—the quick, worried look Sunita had cast toward Bhima when Chitra had called her "sweetie," the banter between the two women, the manner in which Chitra's face lit up when Sunita came home earlier than expected, the glances, touches, murmurs that bespoke of an intimacy, a sweetness, that reminded Bhima of—she walks faster, trying to outpace her brain from the conclusion it is racing toward—the sweetness she had enjoyed for years with her Gopal. Bhima stops walking; she cries out loud. It can't be, she thinks. How can two women . . . what would they do . . . Chitra's painting of the naked woman that hangs over their bed . . . maybe the rules of life were different in this Australia . . . but if they were, how were they the rules of life, inviolate? The blood rushes to her head. She had left her precious Maya with those two fallen women. In order to protect her from the wild animals prowling around the slum, she had taken her into the home of these two . . . two what? Unnatural women. Another thought assails her, clangs like a gong in her head. A passerby casts her a curious look and hurries past her, but Bhima barely sees. Instead, she spins around on her heels and hurries home.

She has barely entered the hut and shut the door when she blurts out her question. "Did those two—did they touch you?"

Maya frowns, puzzled. "Touch me?"

Bhima flushes, unable to give voice to the unpleasantness sloshing around her brain. "Did they . . . you know, like that badmash Viraf?"

There is a strange sound, and it takes her a minute to realize that Maya is shaking with laughter. "Ma-ma," she splutters. "Don't take this tension, na. They were nothing but good to me. Treated me like an honored guest. Like a friend."

It is the word *friend* that makes Bhima rush up to Maya and slap her. That, and the backwash of fear at the realization that the world is fraught with dangers she has no name for, that the future she imagines for Maya—graduation from college, a good job, a decent husband, a home far removed from the squalor of their present life—can be toppled over as easily as she had toppled her plate. That everything is an ambush, that there's no one to trust, not even a young woman who spoke with a strange accent but who, with her kind words, had wormed her way into Bhima's heart.

Maya holds her cheek, her mouth slack with shock. "What did I do wrong?" she gasps.

Her stricken grandmother looks back at her, unable to answer the question. It is Chitra she has wanted to strike, she realizes, Chitra with her playfulness, her casual informality, her ever-ready willingness to help in the kitchen. She turns away from the confusion in Maya's eyes. Once again, history has repeated itself. Once again, instead of striking out at the rich who have betrayed her, she has lashed out at her own blood, for no other reason than proximity. She remembers the bitterness with which Maya used to blame her for valuing the Dubash family over her own.

Bhima sighs. The biggest curse of old age is not the pain in her hips or the shedding of her once-full head of hair, she thinks. The true curse is the awareness of how large and sinister and complicated the world truly is. That, and the knowledge of her own ignorance and insignificance in that world. Oftentimes, when she is on the street she looks at the crowd around her and thinks: If she stopped walking, she would still be towed along, like a twig in stormy waters. Everybody in this city seems to have purpose, clarity, a destination. But more and more she feels sluggish and lost. Now there is a new piece of information to digest, to insert into the puzzle of the world, but this one refuses to click into place, unable as she is to reconcile her affection for Chitra baby with the new knowledge of her unnaturalness. Not for the first time, she longs for Gopal to interpret the world for her. Or even Amit, her now-grown son, with his quicksilver intelligence and sharpness. Instead, here she is, left with this trusting girl, who is still a child even though she has expelled a child from her own womb.

Bhima's eyes are wet with tears of contrition. "Forgive me," she says to Maya. "For no reason, I take my gussa out on you. You do nothing wrong, my child." She cradles Maya in her arms.

"It's okay, Ma-ma." Maya's voice is muffled. "I know you are trying to protect me. But Chitra and Sunita are very good people. They don't make me feel stupid, like your Serabai did."

She swallows the immediate retort that gathers on her lips: It is Serabai's charity that paid for your early college, you ungrateful girl. And it is Dinaz's benevolence that continues to pay for it. She remains silent. Let Maya have her bitterness against the Dubash family. It is hard-earned. Her own ambivalence toward the Dubash family is part of the confusion that hovers like fog over her head.

She yawns, and Maya pulls herself away from her and eyes her with concern. "Go to bed, Ma-ma. You look so tired."

She yawns again. "That I am." She crosses the tiny room to her own mattress, then turns back. "But what about your homework, beti? You keep the lantern on, accha? It won't disturb me."

Maya nods. "Okay, Ma-ma."

Bhima has just lain down and is about to roll over to her side when Maya asks, "How was the marketplace today, Ma-ma? You said about the money but not how the day went."

The older woman's mind skips over the entire day—the frustration of the morning, the unexpected rescue by that woman Parvati, her shock when she realized that Parvati was literate. The gratification of earning back Ram's investment and the stunning realization that she herself had earned a profit in doing so.

She realizes that Maya is waiting for an answer. "It was good," she says. "Tiring but good."

But the last thing she remembers before falling asleep was that feeling when the sales picked up and the money flew into her hands. She has no name for that feeling, so new and terrible, like a bird beating its wings inside her chest. And then she knows—it was exhilaration.

11

One day. What a difference one day has made, Bhima marvels. It is only noon and they have already sold more than half of the remaining fruit. She feels a grudging gratitude toward the woman squatting beside her, for the gift of this space, for her kindness in explaining the concept of profit to her. Filled with goodwill, she turns her head to glance at the face that within the span of a day has gone from looking grotesque to ordinary. "Chai peyange?" she asks. Will you take a cup of tea?

Parvati's lip curls with disdain. "No thanks. I don't want to be in your obligation."

Although she knows it is unreasonable of her, Bhima is stung by the hostility she hears in the older woman's voice. Instinctively, she looks around for Rajeev, simple, open-hearted Rajeev, who over the years has happily accepted all her invitations to tea or a plate of vada pav, without pride or reservation. This woman here is a different sort—one step above having to beg for a living, but bristling with pride and prickliness, full of secrets and surprises and sharp corners.

Bhima is about to shrug when she hears herself say, "On the contrary. It is I who am in your obligation."

For the first time today, Parvati looks her in the face. The older woman allows herself a smile so thin it looks like a mere incision. But even this is enough to transform her, and Bhima has a sudden, startling revelation—Parvati must have been beautiful in her youth. Now, she notices the straight nose, the arch of the eyebrow, and below that, the large, beautiful eyes. Her lips part with surprise, and she hears Parvati say sharply, "What are you staring at?"

In response, Bhima reaches for the largest, ripest custard apple and splits it in half. The creamy white pulp on the inside twinkles in the sunlight as she offers half of it to the older woman, who hesitates and then accepts. "This comes out of your share, not mine," Parvati grumbles, even as she scoops a piece inside her mouth, sucking against the black pit to get at the fruit.

"Of course." Bhima smiles. She splits her half again before turning toward Reshma. "Have some," she says, and even though Reshma looks at her with suspicion, she readily accepts.

"Oi, ladies, are you going to enjoy your own produce or sell me some, also?" a male customer complains, and Bhima puts her own share down on a piece of newspaper to tend to him.

"You bargain well," Parvati says after he leaves.

"I learned. The mistress I used to work for, I guarded her money as carefully as if it was mine."

Parvati looks at her curiously. "You no longer work for her, then?"

Bhima feels the familiar shame at the memory. "No," she says.

"Let go, were you?" She says it softly, but Bhima jumps as if she has been prodded.

"Did that Rajeev open his big mouth to you?" she says. "Just wait till he comes back. Poking his nose in . . ."

"Behenji. Please stop. Rajeev has said nothing."

"Then who?"

Parvati sighs. "Look around you, sister. What do you see? A market of nawabs and princesses? No. We are all discarded people. Husbands, children, parents, bosses—someone or the other has betrayed us. Do I speak the truth or not?"

Yes, but in my case it is person after person, Bhima thinks. Have all these people here endured as much loss as I have?

"I take your silence as assent," Parvati says, and Bhima hates her for her astuteness.

"Where did you learn to read and write?" she asks, wanting to change the subject.

Parvati looks at her for a long time. Then she says, "A woman taught me. We used to call her Principal."

"You went to school?"

"You could say that. But it was the kind of school no parent should agree to place their child in."

Bhima frowns, frustrated with Parvati's habit of talking in riddles. She is about to ask another question when one of Parvati's usual customers shows up to buy a cauliflower. She is a homeless woman who lives on the street with her three children, all of whom beg for a living. Parvati raises her hand in greeting. "Kaise hai?" she asks, and the woman replies with a weary, "Still alive, sister."

Unable to bear the pathetic sight of the few coins dropping from the woman's hand into Parvati's, Bhima turns away. In any case, she has two new customers, one of whom buys half a dozen custard apples from her, after much haggling over the price.

"I know her," Parvati says after the woman leaves. "Works for a rich woman who lives in one of those new buildings on Forest Road. Acts like it is her own money she's spending, instead of her owner's."

"I told you. I used to do the same."

Parvati spits her contempt onto the pavement. "Then you were as big a fool as she." She raises her hand to prevent Bhima from protesting. "We poor people? We should have only one loyalty in the world. And that's to other poor people. Anything else is foolishness. Anything else is suicide."

Bhima stares at her, unable to muster a counterargument. "Serabai was good to me," she finally mutters.

"Good to you? Didn't you just say she discarded you like a flat tire?"

"My granddaughter feels the same way you do," Bhima says. "Always berating me for my loyalty to Serabai's family."

"Then your granddaughter is smarter than you."

For the first time, Bhima smiles a genuine smile. "That she is. Going to college, she is. Top student."

Parvati's eyes light up with interest. "Accha? Really? Then may all your hard work be fruitful, sister."

Bhima nods, too overcome to speak.

"What is her name? Your granddaughter?"

"Maya."

"That is a fine name. And where is her grandfather, may I ask?"

The question grazes at Bhima's skin. "Gone," she says shortly. "All gone. Maya's parents, too."

She expects sympathy, a tsk-tsk, a clucking of the tongue. Instead she gets, "Just as well. The less people to love, the better off you are."

Bhima's face flushes with anger. "What kind of a woman are you?" she says. "Are you a woman at all, that you talk in this manner?"

Parvati smiles. "You're right, sister. I'm not a woman at all." She tears a small piece of the newspaper that the custard apples are piled onto and holds it up. "I am like this paper. People can write on me, spit on me, tear me up, it makes no difference. One strong gust of wind and—" she releases the scrap of paper—"bas, I'm gone. And no one will even know that I was here."

A lonely, reciprocal feeling rises within Bhima. Harsh as Parvati's words are, they join hands with her own thoughts. What had the older woman called them? Discarded people. Parvati has simply given words to the melody that Bhima has hummed for a long time.

"Mausi, I'm hungry." Rajeev's plaintive voice startles both women. The man bends his knees into a squat and lowers the basket onto the sidewalk. "Jafferbhai says this is the last of the consignment."

Bhima stares at him in wonder. "After this lot we have recovered what Ram paid? This is the entire stock?"

"Yes, mausi."

Bhima raises her eyes to the sky. "Thank God. I will fulfill my promise to Bibi."

Rajeev beams. "Shall we get some lunch, mausi?" he says after a moment.

Bhima peels off a few notes. "Buy what you want," she tells him. "Bring back something for me. And for this one here, also."

"You will still owe me my rent money, lunch or no lunch," Parvati says promptly, and Bhima and Rajeev exchange an amused glance.

"Yes, yes, bhenji," Bhima says, still reveling in her good fortune. "Nobody is cutting your share, don't worry."

From the manner in which Parvati's hands shake as she unwraps the newspaper bag that holds the two samosas, Bhima realizes that the woman is starving. The afternoon sun beats relentlessly on their heads as they eat, and she shudders at the thought of Parvati sitting below it day after day. Unlike Rajeev, who wolfs down his food, Parvati tries to refrain from doing so, and for the second time in two days, the word *swamani*, honorable, forms in Bhima's mind.

By two in the afternoon, they have sold out almost their entire stock. This time, Bhima holds back six of the fruit and divides it equally among the three of them. And when she hands Parvati her day's rent, she is surprised at the feeling of regret that wells up within her at the thought of not seeing the old woman again. "Thank you," she says. "You have earned a young widow's blessings with your generosity."

"People's blessings have never helped me," Parvati says. "It is only their curses that have come true." She lets out a mirthless cackle.

As Bhima stares at the woman, puzzled by her incessant need to be disagreeable, Rajeev comes up and takes her by the elbow. "Come on, mausi," he says. "I will walk you to the corner."

Bhima shakes her head as they walk, her earlier goodwill toward Parvati's self-respect curdling into irritation at her false pride. "Not two paise to her name but too much *gamand*," she mutters to Rajeev.

"It's all she has, mausi," Rajeev says quietly. "Don't you see? Her pride is what is holding her together."

Bhima peers up at Rajeev's guileless face. Where does it come from, this ability to see the best in others? she wonders. Could it be that like Parvati, this Rajeev, too, has depths to him of which she is unaware? Bhima looks around the crowded street, and for a moment she sees it—each human body a mystery, cradling a thousand secrets, like the wiring that is hidden behind plastered walls. She feels dizzy at the thought.

When they reach the corner, Bhima smiles at Rajeev. "You have worked hard these past two days," she says. "For this, I am in your debt."

Rajeev grins broadly, and Bhima has a quick sense of what he must've looked like at age seven. "For you, Bhima mausi, I will drop everything to help," he says, and Bhima basks in the warmth of his words. "Besides, it was fun, eh, mausi? It made me feel like—like, I was more than just a donkey, carrying other people's loads."

She nods. "I know. It was hard work, but it was good." Then, to lighten the mood, she adds, "Perhaps we can both get jobs working at that new mall when it opens."

Rajeev scratches the back of his neck. "And what would we do there, mausi? Such places are not meant for people like us."

She feels a sudden urge to show off, to tell him that she's been inside expensive hotels and stores with Serabai, but she resists. "Chalo," she says, after a minute. "I must be off to my afternoon job."

"And I must go back to being a donkey again."

Bhima is halfway to Sunitabai's house before she remembers the entire conversation from the night before. A feeling of revulsion rises in her again. There is no way she can face Chitra baby, with her incessant prattle, her questions about Maya, her offers to make tea for Bhima while she cooks, not after what Maya has revealed to her. A lethargy comes over her. She has already cancelled on Mrs. Motorcyclewalla today. She will not go to her second job either. Maybe by tomorrow she will be able to face Chitra again. Yes, tomorrow she will go, but she also will look for another job, working for a decent family with a proper husband and wife. Today, she will instead go home and prepare an extra something for Maya out of the day's earnings.

The loose change jingles inside Bhima's sari as she walks toward the slum. It is only as she is entering the basti that the thought comes to her: the money she has earned yesterday and today are the first wages she has ever earned doing anything besides domestic work. With a lift in her step, she walks down the dank by-lane that leads to her hut.

12

The music of the dancing girls is exceptionally loud tonight, and Parvati twists and turns in her cot, unable to sleep. When she had first arrived at the Old Place as a terrified twelve-year-old, the woman they called Principal had tested her ability to sing and dance. But Parvati was the daughter of peasants, and after a few sessions, Masterji had shaken his head and declared that the new girl had no discernable talent. Principal's lips had thinned then, in that disapproving manner that Parvati was already beginning to recognize, but the woman had recovered soon enough.

"This little calf will yet yield milk," she had whispered, cupping her hand under the young girl's chin to raise her face.

For two years, she had used Parvati as bait. Every evening she would dress the young girl up, put kohl to her eyelashes to accentuate the shape of her eyes, color her pubescent lips with red lipstick, fit her into a tight-fitting blouse and choli that displayed her growing breasts and narrow hips. Parvati would line up on the balcony of the three-story house that Principal ran, along with the brightly painted older women, and cower inwardly as the hungry, lustful eyes of the men would ravage her. But if one of those men so much as touched her face or arm, there was Principal, spitting her rage, banishing them from the house for a week, until they had learned their punishment. Soon, the men learned that Parvati was for display only. Many of them, longing for the day the young virginal girl would be placed on the market, would wonder how much it would cost for them to be the one to break her in. They would take out their pent-up frustrations by fucking the older prostitutes, but in the meantime, the price for Parvati kept rising. And since the girl was consuming milk and rice and meat and wearing the good clothes that Principal bought for her, and since she had shown no ability to be a dancing girl, there had to be other ways in which she earned her keep while being groomed for the right man. The girl was adept at housework, but soon Principal discovered that the beautiful face hid an intelligent mind. Any dumb cow could scour the pots and pans and sweep the rooms; Principal needed a sidekick in managing the accounts of an increasingly prosperous business. She nurtured Parvati's aptitude for numbers, and began to teach her to read and write. The girl worked hard, in the dim hope that her bookkeeping services would prove indispensable enough to spare her the fate that had befallen the other women in the house.

Parvati never did find out what Anand Pandit, the businessman who finally bought her virginity, paid for her. A few times, Principal alluded to the fact that her asking price had been about twenty-four times the price she had paid for Parvati. Despite the two years she had spent being demystified about the mysteries of sex, of being around men who were still zippering up when they left the room and women who slept with their breasts hanging out of their blouses, nothing had prepared her for Anand Pandit's brutal use of her during the six hours he had rented her. She had emerged from the room bleeding, glassy-eyed, and shell-shocked, oblivious to the catcalls and whistles of the other women, who had resented having to ply their trade while Parvati had lived like a china doll for two whole years. Now she was one of them, and they celebrated her fall.

What none of them had anticipated was the fact that Anand Pandit would fancy himself in love with her, a girl thirty years younger than himself. He lost all interest in patronizing the nachwalis, the dancing girls, who were a large part of Principal's income. He barely looked at the other, more experienced prostitutes. Instead, he "booked" Parvati for himself all day on Saturdays and on Tuesday and Thursday evenings. Once, when one of the other girls let slip that Principal was entertaining the prospect of showing Parvati to some other rich patrons, he flew into a mad rage, berating Principal for violating her word that he had exclusive use of the girl. Parvati watched in numb wonder as Principal talked to him in an appeasing tone she seldom used with anyone else. After he had left, Principal shook her head. "A mad kutta," she said. "He has gone lost his head with you, the poor fellow. Only one thing to be done when a dog goes mad."

"You're going to kill him?" Parvati asked, half hoping that the answer would be yes.

Principal frowned absently. "Kill him? Girl, what rubbish you speak. Why would I kill my golden goose? No. I just have to direct his dick someplace else. Just long enough for him to forget your scent."

She was true to her word. Six months later, another girl from the hinterlands arrived. This one was not beautiful, but what she lacked in beauty, she made up in age. She was ten years old. Within a week, Anand Pandit had attached himself to her like a tick.

After all these decades, Parvati still remembers the screams from the room when Anand had had his way with the child for the first time. She had almost rushed into the room, wanting to offer herself instead to the debauched man, but Principal had gripped her arm tightly. "You crazy girl," she had hissed. "I kept my word to you. This is what you wanted, na? Now why are you lusting after him?"

She had stared at the woman, aghast at being so misunderstood, unable to speak because her ears were being assaulted by the child's whimpering, transfixed by the knowledge that the little girl's fate was her fault. "Come now," Principal continued. "Jealousy doesn't become you. I will get you someone better, who will pay ten times more for you than that fucker."

Above the drone of the sarod and the thum-thum of the ankle bracelets from the dancer in the next room, Parvati hears that long-ago screaming, again. She shifts in her bed to escape the sound, but it is inside her head now, and that terrible brew of relief and responsibility that she felt more than a half century ago is choking her again tonight. It was guilt that had made her befriend that ten-year-old child, Nandini. Nandini, who years later would give birth to Praful, the boy she raised like a nephew, especially as Nandini receded more and more from their blighted world, fading like the smoke that she emitted from her hashish pipe.

O stupid woman, go to sleep, Parvati scolds herself. What use remembering all this old stuff? Principal was dead, as was Nandini. What had happened to the Old Place, she has no idea, although she wishes it has burnt to the ground. That much she will always be grateful to Rajesh for, for getting her out of there.

But look where I have ended up, she thinks. Despite my efforts, I am resting my head in a room that's a paper-thin wall away from the life I thought I was leaving behind. Other people have lives that appear to unfold in straight lines, delineations of past, present, and future. What paap did I commit in my past lives to deserve this?

Parvati sighs. She has earned enough money the last two days to ensure a few more nights in this place. And Mohan has given her a cot to sleep on and a bucket of warm water for indoor bathing—luxuries, compared to how she has lived for the last several years. But even as she feels a swell of gratitude, fear follows on its heels. Where does a lone woman in a city of eighteen million go when the money runs out?

13

The cursing and berating begins as soon as Bhima enters Mrs. Motorcyclewalla's apartment. And the body odor tells Bhima the woman has not bathed in at least two days.

"Stupid ghadheri," the woman screams. "Not showing up for work just like that. You eat my salt and this is how you repay me? Shameless."

"Sorry, bai," Bhima lies. "I had a funeral to go to."

"Whose funeral? Your own? I will create your funeral if you do this no-show business again. Next time, I will pour kerosene on you and light you up like Guy Fawkes."

You know she's mad, Bhima says to herself. She doesn't know what she's saying. Let her run on, like a steam engine. She will soon deplete herself. But despite herself, she feels a pinch of fear. This woman is mad enough to carry out her threats.

"Sorry, bai," she says again. "I give you extra time today, accha?"

But Mrs. Motorcyclewalla is not appeased. "I want you to clean the whole house today, top to bottom," she orders. "Wash the walls, clean the tops of the ceiling fans."

Bhima eyes her carefully. "You know that's not my work, bai," she says. "If you like, I can contact Balraj for you. But he did full house cleaning for you last month, only."

The woman emits a scream so piercing, it makes Bhima's eardrums thrum. "Bas. I've had enough of your laziness. You do what I'm asking you to do. Understand? Otherwise, I will burn this flat down." With a sudden movement, she rushes to the front door and bolts it. "You are not leaving until all the work is done. You are not leaving until I say you can go."

Mrs. Motorcyclewalla has one daughter, but she lives in Pune. The woman is busy with her own family, and Bhima has always tried to spare the woman from hearing about her mother's shenanigans. But now Bhima wonders if it is time for the daughter to visit Mumbai. She has never seen the old lady so out of control. "Okay, bai," she says. "Don't take so much tension. You go sit and watch TV. I will do all the cleaning."

Mrs. Motorcyclewalla gets a triumphant look on her face. "Good. You are the servant. You must listen to me," she says, and then marches into the living room.

Relieved, Bhima enters the kitchen. And gasps. All the pots and pans are out of their drawers and on the floor. The entire silverware drawer has been emptied out. A huge stack of dirty dishes awaits her in the sink. Bhima wants to go into the living room and slap the stupid woman. Is her life not hard enough that the spiteful, thoughtless kook has created more work for her? It would serve her right if she just put all the pots and silverware back in place without washing them first. But tempting as the thought is, Bhima knows she won't do that, which means everything has to be rinsed and washed.

She groans as she hears footsteps coming into the kitchen. The next second Mrs. Motorcyclewalla enters the kitchen and lets out a shriek. "Ahura Mazda Khodai," she says, putting a hand on each cheek. "Bhima, what have you done? Why this badmashi? You eat my salt . . ."

"Bai," Bhima yells. "The kitchen was in this condition when I walk in. Why you khali-pilli blaming me for what you do?"

"You stand in my kitchen and lie to my face?" Mrs. Motorcyclewalla has a look in her eyes that scares Bhima. Spittle gathers at the corners of her mouth. She looks around the room wildly. "You stand a few feet away from the portrait of our Lord Zoroaster and you lie in His presence? Come. Put your hands on His picture and beg His forgiveness."

What do I care about your God, Bhima thinks to herself. She herself is a Hindu, believing in her own Gods. Every day she swallows her distaste and pretends to bow her head before the large portrait in the kitchen, in an attempt to placate her mistress. But today, something in her rebels at the charade. "Please, you go watch TV, bai," she says. "I will straighten everything out."

Mrs. Motorcyclewalla bellows, making Bhima drop the fork she has just picked up from the floor. "Besharam. I gave you an order." Her voice is thick with rage, speckled with madness. "Bow your head and beg His forgiveness for your sin."

Bhima takes two steps toward the portrait and then stops. "No, bai," she says quietly. "That I will not do."

Mrs. Motorcyclewalla's pale cheeks are blotched red. "Then get out. Get out of my house and don't let me see your shadow again."

Bhima looks at her, unsure of how to handle the situation. "Why you are starting all this nonsense, bai?" she implores.

The woman lets out an ear-piercing scream. "I told you. Get out. Otherwise I'm calling the police." In another minute, Bhima knows, a neighbor will bang on the door. And if it is her word against the hysterical woman's, she has no illusions about whom they will believe. "What about my pay?" she begins, but the look on Mrs. Motorcyclewalla's face is her answer. She walks past the woman, careful not to accidentally brush against her for fear of triggering another round of false accusations. She unlocks the bolt at the front door and then looks back, willing her mistress back into sanity. But as she hears Mrs. Motorcyclewalla's agitated breathing, she knows the woman is too far gone, and in the moment before she pulls the front door shut after her, Bhima feels as if she is abandoning a wild animal in its cage. Her absence seems to have precipitated Mrs. Motorcyclewalla's descent into madness.

Even before Bhima crosses the foyer of the building and emerges onto the street, the memory of the last time she had been ignobly cast out from a job is upon her. It is not an identical situation, she knows: this time, there is a feeling of relief, as if she is escaping with her life, whereas leaving Serabai's home was akin to leaving one of her arms behind. But the shock at this abrupt turn of fortune, the horror of a false accusation, the lack of control over her own fate, is achingly familiar. As are the tears pooling in her eyes, and the sense of exile, the terror of sudden unemployment. This time, there will be no Dinaz appearing at her doorstep with an unexpected check; this time she will forego the salary she has earned. Mrs. Motorcyclewalla's daughter will soon have bigger concerns to deal with than whether her mother has paid the wages due to Bhima. Maya is back in college, and without this second income, expenses will have to be cut even further. Even with two jobs she has had to dip into the savings that Dinaz had delivered to her. Without the extra money Serabai used to slip into her hands, Bhima can barely make ends meet, and just last week she had seen Maya darn the same tear in her blouse a second time. The girl is frugal, but sometimes Maya talks about the girls from college asking her to join them for a movie and how she always declines. Shame, sour as vinegar, rises in Bhima then, and her mind casts about for ways to spend even less money on herself—no sugar in her tea, one less chapati to eat at dinner.

Now, her mind sifts through the names of other servants she could approach to find out if someone is looking for a housecleaner. Her stomach turns at the thought of interrogations, the speculative looks, the outright caustic remarks she will have to face. Why had she lost a second job in less than two years? they will want to know. And what will she say? She herself is in a state of shock over how this morning has unfolded. She had thought of asking for leave for the days she had spent at the marketplace, but she knew the old witch never would have granted it. Still, it was wrong to stay away without any explanations. But that is not exactly why she has lost this job. Some screw that was holding Mrs. Motorcyclewalla's sanity in place had come loose during her absence.

It had all been a mistake. Bhima curses her extravagance at having treated Parvati and Rajeev to lunch yesterday and the distribution of the custard apples. Perhaps she should not have returned all of Ram's money to Bibi? She chastises herself as she avoids the potholes on Mumbai's broken streets, shutting her ears to the noise of construction that seems to be going on in every inch of this city. Charity, compassion, and generosity are not luxuries people like her can afford. How had she forgotten this?

But then, a wave of resistance rises within her. If she has truly been brought so low that she has to second-guess the simple act of sharing a fruit with a woman even more destitute than she, then why not relinquish all claims to human society? She may as well join the pack of stray dogs that lives just outside the slum, who snarl and wrestle each other over a bone. Bhima remembers what her father, a humble mail carrier, used to say: "Beti, a grain of rice will double in your stomach if you share it with another." How mortified he would be to read her uncharitable thoughts.

Bhima comes to an abrupt halt. A woman runs into her, knocking her shoulder and glaring at her as she makes her way around. Bhima barely notices, focused as she is on the idea that's forming in her head. Just thinking about it makes her heart race.

Then, she begins to walk toward the bus that she will take to Maya's college.

As she enters the campus, Bhima remembers the last time she was here. That mission—when she had falsely accused one of Maya's classmates of being the father of Maya's child—had turned out to be a fool's errand, and perhaps this one will, too. Bhima prays that she will not humiliate herself with what she is planning to do.

From the time she was seven years old, Bhima has held a broom or a mop or a scouring pad every day of her life. Her hands are as rough as that pad, her arms as thin and hard as those mop handles. She is tired of working as a domestic, having to learn the tempo and rhythms of a new home, the quirks and eccentricities of another mistress. Instead, she wishes to spend the rest of her days in the dumb, easy companionship of fruit and vegetables. And yes, she wants to feel again that exhilarating feeling of making a sale, of driving a hard bargain with a customer, of being able to treat a destitute woman and a hard-working man to lunch. Of knowing that she is worth more than simply the speed of her hands, the sinewy muscles of her legs, the bend of her back. Of employing other parts of herself—her intellect, her ability to size up a customer, her deftness at closing a sale. Already, she knows the rudimentary concept of making a profit—without Bibi to pay, surely there will be more?

There is a throng of students outside the college, some sitting on the marble steps, others milling around the turbaned man selling bowls of pyali, the mouthwatering mix of spicy chickpeas and potatoes. Amid the shrieking laughter of the girls and the loud, boisterous voices of the boys, Bhima feels intimidated, out of her element. She marvels at how Maya navigates the distance between this joyful cacophony of youthful exuberance and the grim, dark solitude of their home life together. She feels a renewed appreciation for how stoically Maya bears her burdens, how few demands she makes on her grandmother.

She has failed Maya. How passively she has accepted her worth; how dumbly she had believed that the only thing she was good for was housework. But all this time, this ever-changing city had shouted out a different truth to her—from the skyscrapers that rose from the rubble of the old, demolished buildings, to the new prosperity of erstwhile bank clerks and postal workers who were now millionaires. Even in the slum, there is a rumbling of discontent to which Bhima had shut her ears. Now, eyeing the well-dressed students who are Maya's classmates, Bhima knows: Maya deserves better.

She is about to approach one of these young people when she spots her granddaughter. There she is, in the middle of a group of giggling girls, a bowl of pyali in her hands. Maya's head is tossed back as she laughs; she has released her long black hair from the demure braid in which she ties it when she leaves home each morning. Bhima's breath catches. Maya looks—Bhima gropes around for the right word—modern. Educated. Confident. Not at all like the sullen, awkward girl who sits across from her in their hut each evening. This Maya is ready to take her place in the new Mumbai.

Now that she has seen her, Bhima is hesitant to approach her, for fear of embarrassing her granddaughter. She is aware of what an anomaly she is among these bright, cheerful students; she, with her severe face and brown, broken teeth. She stands at a distance, willing Maya to look in her direction, content to allow her granddaughter to not acknowledge her presence. After a few moments, Maya looks her way, blinks her eyes as if she's seen a phantom, and then gasps. She sets down her half-eaten bowl and hurries up to her grandmother. "What happened, Ma-ma?" she breathes. "What is wrong?"

Bhima smiles. "No. Be at ease, beti. Nothing bad."

"Then why are you here?" Already Maya has begun to walk away from the knot of students, and Bhima follows.

"I'm sorry. I should have waited until evening. I just had this foolish thought—"

"Ma-ma. What is it?"

Bhima swallows. "I need to go to the bank. To take some money out. I came here because the bank will close before you come home."

"What for?" Ever since Maya has helped Bhima open the account, she has made herself responsible for every withdrawal. "And why are you not at your job?"

Bhima searches Maya's face. "Beti," she says. "I have an idea. But is there some way you can miss your afternoon class and go with me to the bank? I will explain on the way."

Bhima is nervous to be carrying so much money, but Maya puts the hundred-rupee bundles in her bag as if she does this every day. Once again, Bhima marvels at the change—Maya in the world is different from the girl at home. It is now two p.m., and Bhima longs for a cup of tea. "Shall we sit?" she says, pointing to an Udupi restaurant.

Maya glances at her watch. "You going to Sunita's house soon, no?"

Bhima falls silent, remembering her earlier indecision about whether to return to that job. But that was before she lost her morning job. She stares at a spot over Maya's shoulder. "How often do I get to be out during the day with my granddaughter?" she says evasively. "No work for me today."

"Ma-ma." Maya's voice is worried. "What is it?"

How to explain to this girl how ignorant she feels at not having guessed what the neighbor was hinting and what was under her nose? "They are indecent women," she says at last. "I am not wanting to encourage their badness."

Maya laughs, a loose, public laugh that makes Bhima want to instinctively shush her. "Indecent? Why? Because they are loving each other?"

"Chup re, chokri," Bhima says crossly. "You are too young to understand these things."

Maya's lips twist. "I aborted my own child. Do not tell me I'm too young to understand."

"Chokri. You . . . Don't. It's immoral."

Maya stops walking. "Was it immoral what that man did to me, Ma-ma?" she asks softly.

"Of course. If you have to ask . . ."

"Then why did you continue to work in that house, Ma-ma?" Maya asks.

Bhima stares at her, stunned. "I don't know," she whispers at last. A sob rises in her throat as she remembers riding in Viraf's air-conditioned car even after Maya had broken the news to her, how the words with which to confront him had died like burnt leaves on her lips, smoky and withered. She had once loved Viraf, but everything about him had also intimidated her—his soft-as-cream voice, his spotless clothes, his handsome, light-skinned face, the indecipherable English music that he played on the stereo. Bhima is struck by a thought—Chitra baby, too, is educated, but she treats Bhima as a respected aunt, rather than as a servant.

Maya touches her wrist, shaking her out of her thoughts. "Go to work, Ma-ma," she says.

Bhima thinks for another moment, then makes up her mind.

"I want to go to the market before Jafferbhai leaves," she says. "But let's find a phone and call Chitrabai first. I will tell her I will come to work tomorrow, for sure."

Maya accompanies her to the wholesale market, and Bhima is glad for her presence. Jafferbhai is openly skeptical as Bhima describes how she has managed to sell all of Ram's inventory. "Arre, wah," he says mockingly. "Here I have seasoned vendors who don't sell out their entire supply. But you did?"

Bhima flushes, but before she can speak, Maya does. "My Ma-ma never lies," she snaps. "Anyway, believe her or don't believe, makes no difference to us. If you're not interested, she can take her business elsewhere."

"Maya," Bhima exclaims, but Jafferbhai is smiling. "I hope when I am a grandfather someday, I will be lucky enough to have my grandchild defend me like this." His eyes twinkle. "What do you say, little memsahib? How much inventory should I sell to your Ma-ma to begin with?"

But here, Maya looks her age again, and turns uncertainly toward her grandmother. Bhima furrows her brow. Could she sell twice the amount of produce that she had sold in one day? And beyond custard apples, what else should she purchase? She has no idea. Suddenly, she longs for Parvati to be by her side. Then she scoffs at herself. How desperate she is, to wish for the help of a miserable old woman who herself sells only six cauliflowers a day. With her business acumen, why doesn't she sell dozens more? Is there something that she, Bhima, is not thinking of, some large and dangerous pithole she is about to fall into? She shivers at the thought of making a fatal mistake, a mistake born out of illiteracy and unworldliness. What is she doing here, at all?

"Bhimaji," Jafferbhai says. "Maaf karo, but I don't have all day to chitchat. Now, you buying something or what?"

"Yes." Bhima finds her voice. "Rajeev will come tomorrow

morning for pickup." She places an order, fighting the feeling of unreality that grips her. But when it's time to pay, the moment is all too real, and Bhima watches with fear and regret as Maya opens her bag and counts the money. For a moment she wants to call the whole thing off, but then she remembers the dispiriting trudge down the flight of stairs from Mrs. Motorcyclewalla's flat, and knows that she cannot return to such unpredictability. If she continues to sell fruit at the rate she did the past two days, and if Sunitabai doesn't fire her tomorrow, she should be fine. Of course, she has made an awful assumption—that Rajeev will continue to work for her and that that sourpuss woman, whose tongue can scorch like a lick of fire, will continue renting them her precious space. After she and Maya take their leave, she turns toward her granddaughter. "One more stop," she says. "To the marketplace. I have to set up things for tomorrow."

"Shouldn't you have done that first?"

Bhima smacks her hand into her forehead. "Yes. But I'm an ignorant woman. I'm doing everything back-to-front."

Maya squeezes her hand. "Ma-ma," she says. "Why are you taking on all this headache? So many people are looking for servants. Why you don't just get another job?"

Bhima stands staring at her granddaughter, blinking in the sunlight. Suddenly, it is clear to her, the difference between herself and Parvati. It is not the woman's utter impoverishment that distinguishes them. No, what separates them is that Parvati has no one to love. Whereas she has Maya.

"You," she says simply. "You are the reason. If my hard work puts an extra grain of sugar in your tea, an extra stitch of clothing on your body, if it buys you one more pen or textbook, then I will sacrifice my very heart for you."

Maya's nose reddens. "Thank you, Ma-ma," she whispers. "I love you, too."

It is a new thing, this saying of *I love you* out loud, Bhima knows. In her time, nobody said such vulgar things to each other. Movie stars did, of course, a chorus of catcalls and whistles erupting from the men in the cheap seats, after every such on-screen declaration. And rich people like Serabai said it, to Dinaz. But she would've jumped down a well before saying such embarrassing words to Gopal. And he would've looked at her as if she were running a fever if she had. Because there was no need. What tied her to Gopal, what ties her to Maya, is a rope built from muscle and bone, and not from a thin string of empty words. Maya is of her time and generation and needs this verbal comfort, but Bhima is unable to provide it to her. Instead, she puts her arm around the girl's shoulder and gruffly draws her close. In this manner, they walk from the wholesale to the retail market.

14

Halfway through this busy selling day, Bhima looks over and sees a shadow of pain cross Parvati's face. It lasts as long as the blink of an eye, but she catches it—the biting of the inner cheek, the furrowing of the brow, the action that causes it—the old woman is touching a spot at the base of her spine. "What is it?" Bhima asks, and Parvati scowls. "Nothing," she says loudly, jerking her hand away from behind her.

Bhima flushes at the woman's unforgivable rudeness. She places a large pinch of chewing tobacco in her mouth, grinds down on it, and looks away. Her eyes search for another customer, and she forces herself to do what the other vendors do incessantly—call out to passersby to hawk her wares. Beside her, Parvati snorts. "First two days, I thought you'd never learn," she says. "Now, you can yell with the best of them. Keep it up and they'll mistake you for a fisherwoman."

"I have a young mouth to feed at home," Bhima snaps, tired of this crabby woman at her side. "So I do whatever I have to do."

"Do, do," Parvati says, shaking her head. "Whatever you have to do, you must do."

But her tone is so dismissive that Bhima is irritated. "Some of us are blessed with children to look after," she says.

Parvati's head jerks up at the insult. But she recovers immediately. "I never considered them blessings," she says. The cloudy eyes search Bhima's face, like a vulture looking for the softest place to peck. "Which is why I killed two, three, four of them. While they were still inside me."

Bhima's hands tremble. She wishes to rise from this strip of pavement, fling the rent money into this monstrous woman's lap, and leave without ever having to see her unfortunate face again. "May God strike you," she breathes.

Parvati laughs. "Sister, your wish is fifty years too late. God has already struck me—over and over again. But here I sit."

There is not a hint of self-pity in the woman's voice. Instead, there is defiance, as if God is an adversary she has beaten. Bhima stares at her openmouthed. She has never met a man as strong as Parvati, let alone a woman.

All morning long, whenever she is between customers, Bhima notices Parvati's hand slipping absently to the spot at the bottom of her spine. The woman shifts from one buttock to another, and Bhima can tell that sitting on the hard pavement is making the pain worse. Finally, unable to bear it, she gets up abruptly. "Watch for me," she says, and before Parvati can reply, she walks away. She heads directly to Mehta & Sons, a general store where she used to purchase cleaning supplies for the Dubash household, and buys a small plastic stool. "For you," she says, when she returns to her spot. "Hard to sit on the ground all day long."

"You use it, old woman," Parvati says promptly. "You need it more than I do."

Overhearing the exchange, Reshma cackles. "You can't do anything nice for her," she says to Bhima, as if Parvati is not present. "This one's heart is as tough as leather."

"As is your pussy," Parvati says, and the other two women gasp.

"Bai," Bhima cries. "Show some shame. It's only out of respect for your age that I . . ."

"Respect for my age? Or respect for this spot upon which you're making your money?"

Bhima looks away. She is gratified to see Rajeev huffing his way toward her, carrying another basket full of fruit to replenish her stock. "Is there more after this?" she asks, and the man shakes his head no. "Nahi, mausi," he says. "Jafferbhai said this is the last. He even gave you a few extra, to fill out the basket."

"I should go to this Jafferbhai," Parvati mutters. "My supplier will not even give me an extra fingernail." Bhima and Rajeev exchange a look, both of them picturing a distributor like Jafferbhai dealing with someone like Parvati. Bhima knows the only reason the man is selling to her is because of the odd circumstances in which they had met.

But now, Bhima is struck by another thought. "What is the time?" she asks.

"Almost two in the afternoon, mausi. And today, I've not even taken lunch," Rajeev says.

Bhima stares at him, willing him to see what she is thinking. "And we are almost sold out?"

But Rajeev's immediate concern is food. "I can go get us something, mausi," he says, waiting, until Bhima feels compelled to take out a note and hand it to him.

The two women watch him bound away, and Parvati says, "He's a bewakoof, that one. Good-natured but a fool. All he's good for is working like a mule."

Eyeing the woman's six unsold cauliflowers, Bhima bites down the sharp retort that has come to her lips. But Parvati follows her eyes and laughs. "Yes, yes, say what you're thinking. Who am I to be judging Rajeev?"

"Why you don't buy more stock?" Bhima demands. "Since you are so good with the hisab-kitab, knowing how to keep track of money . . ."

"And where from I get the money to buy more?" Parvati says, and for a split second Bhima sees it—the terror, the hand-to-mouth existence, the cuts sustained from living on the edge. But then, the usual hostility enters Parvati's eyes. "And like you say, I have no mouths to feed. Bas, I can live a bindas, carefree life."

"Forgive me," Bhima says quietly. "I was wrong to . . ."

"No. You spoke the truth, sister. Why apologize for this?"

Rajeev returns with six vada pavs. The three of them spread out the newspaper they are wrapped in and begin to eat. But before they can take a bite, Reshma sniffs, "Wah, mausi. Last two-three days you are eating rich-rich food." She turns to Bhima. "Usually, one of us does charity and feeds her lunch."

Parvati stiffens at the word *charity*, but before Bhima can chastise Reshma, there is a shout. "Chal, chup," Rajeev thunders. "This woman is needing nobody's charity. If you lucky enough to feed her, it is a blessing on your head, only."

There is a stunned silence, and then Reshma emits a small giggle. "Pagal," she says. "All three of you are having yogurt for brains. Good you found one another."

Bhima suddenly sees them as Reshma must—two old women in different stages of disrepair, and a valiant but foolish man, each of them trying to better their meager lives. Looking at the other two, she feels a new, astonishing sensation—responsibility. All her life, she has simply followed orders. Every day someone had told her what meals to prepare, what masalas to grind, which rooms to sweep first, which clothes to iron. She has never borne responsibility for anyone else's livelihood. But Rajeev has thrown in his lot with hers, and she has to guarantee him a certain daily income. And Parvati has agreed to let Bhima rent her space for at least a month, which means she must get her money, too. How did this happen? Bhima marvels. Until recently, she had only one responsibility in the world—Maya. Now, she has two more mouths to feed. And God help her, she likes the feeling.

Is it wrong, what she is doing, building her good fortune on

Bibi's misfortune? Guilt pokes her in the ribs. But then she thinks, how does it help Bibi, my unhappiness? Does it bring her husband back? Do my tears add a rupee to her income? Would my unemployment fill her belly? No, Bhima thinks, it is better this way. Menfolks like Rajeev can perhaps find their way in this world. But this proud woman beside her, as raw as shaved wood? Bhima senses that she desperately needs the money she gets from renting her spot to them. Although Parvati will die before admitting this.

"Two-three days of earnings and she thinks she's rich as a neta's wife." Reshma continues her mutterings. She glares at Parvati. "But wait until this woman cheats you out of your space. Then you will be an ordinary bhikhari again, begging for food."

Before either of the other two can speak, Bhima raises a placating hand. "Arre, sister, we are all trying to survive. Hai, na? Why unnecessarily you are saying these wicked things?" She reaches for one of the sandwiches, tightening her stomach to control its growling. "Please. Share this with us. It will be my honor."

Reshma's lips thin into a smile. "Shukriya," she says as she takes the sandwich. Noticing Rajeev's eyes glittering with hatred for the woman, Bhima gives him a warning look. Between the heat of the boiling sun, the noise of the marketplace, and the quarreling Reshma, she cannot handle any more stress. The man chews silently, his jaw muscle working hard, as he swallows his food along with the unspoken words.

Parvati saves one of her sandwiches for later. Bhima debates whether to set aside a banana for her, but just then a customer stops by and buys all eight of the remaining bananas, as well as a dozen oranges. The man, who is dressed in a beige polyester safari suit, turns to Rajeev. "You are knowing where Sunshine Apartments is located?" Rajeev nods. "Good, good," the man continues. "If I buy the rest of the fruits and vegetables here, can you run them over to that address? Will it all fit in that topli of yours?"

Bhima speaks before Rajeev can. "Yes," she says. "We can make it all fit."

The man gives Rajeev directions. "My brother will be home," he says. "Tell him I'll be there within the hour."

But even after Rajeev leaves, the man lingers. "Good quality you have here," he says. "Better than anyone else in the market. Where you buy it from?"

Bhima opens her mouth to answer but is intercepted by Parvati, who pinches her hard on the thigh, then turns to the customer. "We are honored you like our product, seth," she says. "But where we get it from is our affair."

Bhima is horrified by Parvati's rudeness, but to her surprise, the man laughs appreciatively. "I understand." He pulls on his lower lip for a minute, making a demonstration of the fact that he is thinking. "Tell you what," he says at last. "I am a caterer. I do catering from home for small parties. If I buy from you at least four to five times a week, how much discount you can give me?"

Again, Parvati intercepts. "How much you buy?"

The man shrugs. "Hard to say. It will depend on the size of my catering order."

Bhima looks from one to the other, glad to have Parvati's expertise. But then she remembers—when she shopped for Serabai, she always got a discount when she bought a dozen of something. "We give discount if you buy a dozen," she says.

The man barely glances at her. "Yes, of course," he says dismissively, before continuing to talk to Parvati. "But how much?"

"We give five percent discount on every dozen," Parvati says, without consulting with Bhima.

"That's not enough—"

"Wait, seth. If you buy at least a dozen of four different items, we give you another two percent on the whole order. Theek hai?"

The man shakes his head. "I will have to think about it."

"Well, don't think too long, seth. Because every time you place a bulk order, you must let us know one day before, only. That way, we will get your merchandise for sure. And you must put twenty percent deposit to guarantee your order."

Bhima gasps, stunned by Parvati's impudence. But to her astonishment, the man nods and pulls out his wallet again. "Theek hai. You have a piece of paper? I can tell you what I'm needing for tomorrow."

After he leaves, Bhima turns to look at Parvati in wonder. If the old woman had turned into the goddess Kali before her eyes, she wouldn't have been more surprised. "You are a jadoogar," she says. How else to explain the inexplicable fact that a perfect stranger had handed them a few hundred rupees in exchange for a mere promise?

Parvati's mouth twists into a smile. "Yes. Only one last trick left for me to do. To make myself disappear." But despite the bitterness in her voice, Bhima can tell she is pleased with herself.

"Thank you for your help," Bhima says humbly. "I am in your debt."

"Debt-febt, nothing," Parvati says. "On your sale to this customer, I charge you one percent." And when Bhima looks worried, she adds, "Don't worry. There's still a good-proper profit for you."

Bhima feels as if she's been tossed onto unchartered waters with a single, broken-down raft. That raft is Parvati, and she is reluctant to climb aboard, suspicious and distrusting, but there is no other option. And so, she nods her assent. "Okay," she says. And then, "You please do today's hisab-kitab. We will settle up and then I must leave for my next job." She pulls out a little notebook and pencil she had purchased on her way to the wholesale market this morning. "Here. You write in here." If Maya is not busy with schoolwork tonight, she will ask her to look over Parvati's figures.

When Parvati is done, she looks up, an astonished expression on her face. She leans in, to prevent Reshma from overhearing her words. "Wah, bhenji," she says. "If you sell in this manner, you will not have to work the second job soon."

Bhima looks at her wordlessly. Is this woman telling the truth? Or is she setting a trap in which to catch her? But the bundle of notes tucked under the spread tablecloth is proof of the day's earnings. She looks down the street for Rajeev to appear before she leaves, debating whether to give him a few extra rupees for running this last delivery.

"Have you been hearing a word I'm saying?" Parvati's plaintive voice reaches her ears.

"Maaf karo, sister," she says. "I was lost in my thoughts."

"I was saying that if you keep selling at this rate, God willing, you must ask that distributor of yours to give you on credit. Why for you paying cash?"

"I don't follow . . ."

"Oi, you head of sawdust. Your money is in the bank, na? So why you must pay that man every time you buy? If he is extending you credit, you pay him once a month or once a week. In the meantime, your money in the bank is collecting interest. Understand?"

Bhima nods. "Yes," she says.

Parvati exhales sharply. "You go home and talk to that granddaughter of yours," she says. "She is as bright as her grandmother is dim. She will tell you what I'm advising is one hundred percent correct."

Involuntarily, Bhima's eyes wander to the six unsold cauliflowers. Parvati seems to read the unspoken question in those eyes. "Don't worry about me," she says. "Same people will come and buy. They are just late today."

"And for this you sit all day baking in the sun, sister?"

Parvati shrugs. "At least the sky provides a roof over my head."

How many layers of hell are there? Bhima wonders. Each evening when she enters the slum, she feels as if she's in the jaws of hell. But suddenly she is thankful for her hut, with its tin roof, for the shelter it provides. For the first time, she thinks of the basti as home. "Are you . . . where do you live, sister?" she asks, wanting to know, not wanting to know.

The older woman averts her eyes. "I used to stay in my nephew's building until recently only," she says. Bhima waits, expecting Parvati to finish her sentence, but after a few minutes, understands that there will be no more information. She has come to realize something about Parvati—harsh words will not hurt her, but pity will singe her. And so, Bhima sighs and stands up, and as always, her hip pops.

"What does the doctor sahib say about that?" Parvati asks, pointing, but now it's Bhima's turn to be secretive. She shrugs noncommittally. "Accha. I'll take your leave," she says. "God willing, I see you tomorrow."

"Bye-bye," Parvati says in English and turns away.

15

As she rings the doorbell, Bhima braces herself for a flood of recriminations for having stayed away from the job. But Chitra flings the door open on the first ring, beams at her in the usual way, and exclaims, "Ah, Bhima. I'm so glad you're here. I've been waiting for you. I need your help today."

Even Serabai was tight-lipped if she missed a few days of work. Bhima looks curiously at this crazy chokri as she enters. What kind of a mistress is this? Someone who doesn't complain or chastise a servant for tardiness or absence? "You take it out from my salary, bai," she says, but Chitra just blinks at her. "What?"

"For missing work. What to do, bai, I . . ."

Chitra makes a dismissive sound. "Forget it. It's no big deal."

They walk into the living room, and Bhima gasps. The room is covered with streamers and balloons. A large silver banner runs the length of one wall. She turns to Chitra with wondrous eyes. "It's Su's birthday," the younger woman says. "I just wanted to surprise her. Do you like it?"

Bhima is unsure what touches her more—the fact that this girl has gone through all this trouble for her friend or the fact that she is asking her opinion. She smiles. "Sunitabai will be very happy," she says.

"Good, good." Chitra rubs her hands together, a gesture that suddenly reminds Bhima of Amit, when he'd come home to find that his mother had made carrot halva, his favorite dessert.

She laughs out loud at the memory, and also at this silly, sweet child's obvious glee. Chitra is looking at her closely, a strange expression on her face, and Bhima covers her laughing mouth with her hand. "What is it, Chitra baby?" she says.

"Nothing. It's just that . . . I've never seen you laugh before. You should do it more often. It suits your face."

"My granddaughter always saying same-same words to me."

"She's a bright girl, your Maya. How is she? How are her studies?"

"Good, thank God."

"If she ever needs a quiet place to study, tell her she's always welcome here. I know Sunita won't mind. I'll fix her dinner or whatever. Okay? You tell her it's an open invitation."

Bhima smiles shyly. "It's not your duty to serve her, baby. It is our duty to serve you. We are eating your salt."

To her astonishment, Chitra laughs. "Oh, Bhima. Surely you don't believe this mumbo-jumbo." She scratches the tip of her nose. "What salt? What duty? We pay you, yes, but you work in return, no? So we are as much in your obligation as you are to us. In fact, we eat *your* salt, you could say."

Bhima is scandalized. What is this Australia place, that has built a girl like this? "How you talk, Chitra baby. If your neighbors hear you, they will kill both you and me."

Chitra's lips twist with bitterness. "Oh they want to kill me, all right," she says under her breath. Then, she brightens. "But Bhima, come on. We have to go shopping."

Bhima looks at her, confused. "Bai, I got work to do," she says. "The house hasn't been cleaned in two days, plus I need to cook, no?"

"No, no. I've done everything," Chitra says briskly. "And I've made dinner for tonight. But I still have to go pick up the cake and wine. Parking is so difficult at Kookies, I need you to run in and pick up the stuff while I wait in the car, okay? So can we go? Su's promised me she'll come home early, so we don't have much time."

As soon as Bhima enters Chitra's air-conditioned car, it comes back to her, that last car ride with Viraf. How had she borne it, riding next to the devil with an angel's face, the man who had plotted the murder of his own child? Bhima sits up with a jerk as a thought strikes her—could it all have turned out differently if she had told Serabai his scandalous secret, told it calmly, and made her understand the great injustice that had been done to her family? Could they have defanged him together? But . . . but Dinaz had been pregnant. Dinaz, who was the first child she had loved outside of her own. Dinaz, who looked at Viraf as if he were a piece of the moon. Was there any way to destroy him without destroying her? There wasn't. In those awful days, when life and death had entered their lives almost simultaneously, she had felt even more dumb and helpless than she normally does.

Dimly, Bhima registers something warm on her arm and realizes that Chitra is patting it. "Everything okay?" the girl asks gently. "Shall I stop and get you a lime water? Or something else to drink?"

She shakes her head, letting the past click back into place before answering. "I'm okay, bai. I just was thinking of something."

"Well, that thought must come with nails attached to it. Because you looked like you'd swallowed a fistful of them."

Bhima does not reply but looks out the window instead. They drive in silence, until Chitra pulls up in front of Kookies. The younger woman points out the bakery and the adjacent wine store to Bhima, then lets her out. She has already paid for the cake; now she hands the older woman a piece of paper with the brand of the wine she wants and a wad of notes. "The cake is under Agarwal," she says, and this is how Bhima learns Chitra's surname. "I'll go and come quickly-quickly," she says, and hurries out of the car because already there is someone furiously blowing his horn behind them. "If I have to circle around and come back, don't worry," Chitra calls after her. "Just wait here."

Bhima goes into the wine shop first, such a contrast to the dark, dirty bar where Gopal had drunk away their future. This store is well lit, the bottles beautifully displayed, and a well-dressed man is behind the counter, instead of the hairy bootlegger in his white undershirt and lungi. "Yes?" the man says in English. "Can I help you?"

Suddenly tongue-tied, Bhima hands him the note. "Ah," the man says, nodding in understanding. "Your master told you to pick up?"

Confused, Bhima stares at the man, who turns away from the counter, then whirls around again to ask, "You want it warm or chilled?"

Chitra baby hadn't said. "I'm not sure," Bhima starts to say. Viraf baba used to bring beer home that he would set in the fridge to chill. But he bought it how? Thanda or garam? She doesn't know. And is this wine the same as beer? The only time Bhima had ever tasted beer was at a wedding and it was warm. She had hated it.

"Well?"

"Thanda," Bhima says, making up her mind. Cold.

"Okay," the man shrugs. "That will be ten rupees extra." And now Bhima is sure that the man is cheating her, but it is too late to argue.

She falls in love with the cake store. There are white and pink and chocolate-colored cakes there, some of them shaped like cars and houses and fairies. Maya, with her sweet tooth, would love this store. After the cake has been put into a pretty pink box, she lingers, then points to the smallest round cake and asks, "How much?" and blanches when the salesman tells her. He laughs openly at her reaction, and then points to a single pastry. "You buy this, madam. Only twenty-five rupees."

Even that is an astronomical price, but the laughter that lingers in the man's eyes makes her flush and say, "Accha. Give me one piece." And then she is disappointed to find that he drops the pastry into a small bag instead of a pretty cake box.

She pays, then steps out into the street. She spots Chitra's car immediately, and when she reaches it, Chitra leans over and opens the door for her. "Just place these in the back seat," she says and Bhima does, before getting into the passenger seat. Almost immediately she hands over the change to Chitra, but the woman is focused on merging with traffic and waves her off. "Later, Bhima," she says. "Or, you can set it down here in the cup holder, if you like."

"You please count, baby," Bhima says.

"Why? I'm sure it's correct."

"No. Please. You count." Bhima's voice is stronger than she'd intended, and Chitra gives her a curious look. "Okay. If you insist, I will later. But I trust you, you know."

There once was a time when such words would've warmed her heart. Now, they make her apprehensive. "Trust-fust is okay, Chitra baby," she says. "But later on, I want no problems."

Chitra stiffens. "Why should there be a problem?" she says coldly. For the first time since she's met this young woman, Bhima feels as though Chitra is annoyed at her. "I'm sorry, memsahib," she says. "If I say something wrong, please forgive me."

Chitra pats her lightly on her knee. "Relax," she says. "You're fine."

No mistress she's ever worked for has touched her as casually as Chitra does. Does this young girl not realize that she lives in a slum, where dirty water flows right past her home? Bhima remembers that Chitra had once told her that when she was a college student she used to volunteer at a slum to teach little children how to read and write. Could it be that Chitra is so free with her because she is an unnatural woman? Maybe women like her have different customs? Maybe they don't believe in the superiority of their caste? But then, Sunitabai is not like this. She is always polite and pays her on time each month, but Sunitabai keeps a proper distance from her. With Sunitabai, Bhima does not have to doubt who is mistress and who is servant. But this impulsive girl next to her treats her as if they are equals.

Chitra glances at her. "What's that?" she asks, pointing toward the pastry bag that Bhima is clutching. Bhima opens it to show her. "Something I purchased for Maya," she says. "I pay for it from my own money," she adds.

Chitra smacks her forehead. "I am so thoughtless," she says. "I should've given you money to buy a cake for yourself. Shall we go back?"

"Baby." Bhima's voice is loud, as if she is tutoring a particularly slow student. "Why for you should buy me anything? You pay my salary, no? That is enough."

Chitra grins at her. "You're a strange one, Bhima."

No, Bhima thinks. It is you that is strange. Even Serabai, who used to always give Bhima chocolates and sweets for Maya, never offered to buy a full cake for her.

Miraculously, there is a parking spot in front of the apartment building, and Chitra grabs it. Together, the two women climb the flight of stairs to the flat, Chitra insisting on grabbing the heavier bag from Bhima. They are at the second-floor landing when they run into Vimal Das coming down the stairs. Chitra stands aside to make room for her next-door neighbor, who does not acknowledge her presence. If Chitra notices, she doesn't react. "Hi, Vimal," she says as the woman brushes past her. In response, the woman looks at her, her face exhibiting a fury that takes Bhima's breath away. And then, deliberately, slowly, she spits. The wad misses Chitra's feet only because she jerks back. Bhima looks at the younger woman, who seems transfixed in place, her eyes wide with incomprehension. "What the hell? Oh my God. Did you really just . . . ?"

"You dare use God's name? After you come into this respectable building and soil it with your presence?" Vimal hisses. "Don't you dare say hi to me again. We are respectable people living here. You want to live your filthy life, you go live in the slum with this one here." She looks at the cake box that Bhima is carrying and her upper lip curls. "There you can have a hundred girlfriends and sit and eat cake all day long."

Now, Chitra's eyes are blazing. "'This one here' has a name. And you're right. I'd rather spend time with someone like Bhima than all you so-called respectable people."

"Then, go. Go. Get out. Take your vileness elsewhere."

"I will remind you that Sunita owns her apartment, Vimal," Chitra says. "We have as much right to be here as anyone else."

"At the next building association meeting, I will ask for a resolution," the older woman says. "Then we'll see."

Chitra laughs, a wild, bitter sound. "A resolution saying what? Listen, Su's best friend is a real estate lawyer. We know our rights. We're not going anywhere. Just get that into your head."

"Yes, yes, we all know that whore of yours is a big-shot journalist," Vimal yells. "We are looking into sending a letter to the editor . . ."

Chitra's face grows pale. "What did you call her?" She takes one step closer to Vimal, who shrieks dramatically. An apartment door flies opens and a head pokes out. It is Mehroo Sethna. Years ago, Bhima had worked for the woman for a week when her own servant had gone to her village for a holiday. "Vimal? What's happening?"

"This degenerate is attacking me."

"Bai," Bhima's voice rings out. "Why khali-pilli you telling lies? Chitra baby has done nothing. You please, just continue with where you're going."

"Do you see?" Vimal says to Mehroo. "What things have come to? Where a slum dweller can order around a homeowner in her own building? How this woman—or man, or whatever she is—has corrupted even the servants?"

Mehroo Sethna wrinkles her nose. "Just live and let live, Vimal," she says. "Why do you have to make everything that happens in the building your business?"

Vimal looks indignant. "This only is why this country is going to the dogs," she mutters. "Jao. All of you can go to hell," she says, waving her hand dismissively as she begins to descend the stairs. Bhima breathes a sigh of relief. They wait until the woman is gone, and then Chitra turns toward Mehroo. "Thank you," she whispers. But Mehroo simply shakes her head and shuts the door.

They walk up the flight of stairs in silence, and when they enter the apartment, Chitra wordlessly opens the fridge and sets the bottle of wine in it. "What shall I do with the cake, baby?" Bhima asks, but Chitra doesn't answer. When Bhima looks at her, she sees that Chitra's eyes and nose are red. "I'm going to take a short nap, Bhima," she manages to say, and then she goes into the bedroom, shutting the door behind her.

In order to organize her own emotions, Bhima looks around for something to do. Chitra baby has already cooked dinner and the dirty dishes have all been washed and put away. Bhima picks up the broom and begins to sweep the living room, her mind whirling. Nothing that Vimalbai said is different from what she herself has thought about Chitra and Sunitabai. And yet, the hurt on Chitra baby's face is a scar on her own heart. How is it that she could hear the ugliness in Vimal's words but not in her own uncharitable thoughts? She had even considered giving up the job until Maya had talked her out of it. Bhima knows that it is not common, this women loving women, but it is also not common to have an educated, rich woman like Chitra treat a servant as kindly as she does. Why does she like one kind of uncommon and not the other? And suddenly Bhima understands, what Maya had said about feeling more comfortable with the two young women than she ever did at Serabai's home. She remembers the years of physical abuse that Serabai's husband had inflicted on her and how she had told no one, not her parents nor her friends. Only, she, Bhima, knew why Serabai wore long sleeves in the summer. Only she managed to get her mistress up when Serabai took to bed for days after a beating. And yet, the world had considered Feroz seth to be an important and respectable man. All of Serabai's friends used to talk about how lucky she was and what a good husband she had. Bhima would hear their chatter when they came over for a party and could scarcely control herself from rushing in to expose the man and his violence. To unmask him, the way Serabai could never do. And then the bile rises in her throat as she has another thought: Those same people probably tell Dinaz baby the same thing now; how lucky she is to have married a handsome, decent man like Viraf. Vimal would've loved having Viraf for a neighbor. And yet, how could she blame them? Even in the Ramayana it was so: Demons never looked like demons, but came to earth disguised as humans. But Bhima knows: Every shiny object has a dark underside. Chitra baby and Sunitabai are not being blamed for the fact that they are two women sharing a love; it is for the fact that they are not hiding it.

When Chitra emerges from the bedroom an hour later, she has changed into a new outfit. She smiles wanly at Bhima and then busies herself in the kitchen, frying up golden raisins and almonds to garnish the pullao she has made for the birthday celebration. Bhima studies her surreptitiously, flushed with a new awareness of the younger woman. What she had thought of as childishness was strength; Chitra's treatment of her was deliberate, a resolve to not inflict on others the kind of pain she herself had known. How many other times had this woman stood up to the kind of insults that Vimal had levied against her? Bhima had assumed that wealth and education protected people from other people's insults; now she wondered if this was truly so. She wants to ask Chitra a hundred questions but is limited by her ability to formulate her thoughts. But something has changed, and now there is a protective instinct to shield this tender young woman from shrews like Vimal.

Chitra turns to her, a shy smile on her lips. "I have a request to make of you, Bhima. Please don't mention a word of what happened today to Sunita. I don't want to upset her. She's . . . very sensitive like that."

And then Bhima sees it—the quiver of the lower lip, the tentativeness in Chitra's eyes, the slight flush of the cheeks—and she knows. Chitra baby doesn't know how to navigate life's meanness any better than she does. There is no protection against people like Vimal, just as there is no protection against snakes like Viraf. Life is fraught with danger, betrayal, cruelty. Which is all the more reason to cherish the moments of kindness, of connection, of sweetness—the pat on the knee, the offer to buy her a cake.

"Just forget it, baby," she says. "That woman is a witch. What for you bothering your head with her evil? You just mind your own business and live your life."

Chitra's eyes brim with tears. "Thank you, Bhima," she whispers. And then, before she can respond, Chitra takes two steps toward her and takes her hand in both of hers. "Thank you," she says again.

Something about the way Chitra looks at her reminds her of Maya. And as if she has read her mind, Chitra says, "She's lucky. Maya is. To have someone like you to protect her."

A cavern opens up in Bhima as she hears the wistfulness in Chitra's voice. "Are all your people in Delhi?" she asks. "Are none of your relations here?"

Chitra makes a wry face. "Su's my only family in Bombay." And then, improbably, she adds, "And you. The two of you."

The words are out of her mouth before she can take them back. "How we can be family, baby? You must be of Brahmin caste, I am lower caste."

"Do you know most religions don't have a caste system, Bhima? The Christians don't, the Muslims don't. So how do they form families?"

She blinks in incomprehension. "How they know, then?"

"Know what?"

"How to live. Who to marry."

Chitra chuckles. "They just do. They follow their heart."

Out of the blue Bhima remembers Gopal's dogged, single-minded pursuit of her and an involuntary smile forms on her lips.

"Ah, Bhima. I see you know what I'm talking about."

She feels herself blush. "My husband . . . he was . . ." She stops, unable to convey to this young woman the circuitous paths of her life.

"Is he dead, Bhima?"

It is a simple enough question but impossible to answer. "What to say, baby?" she says at last. "He is living, but our marriage is dead. He killed it when he left me and returned to his ancestral village with our son."

"Oh, God." She can hear the concern in Chitra's voice. "How long ago was this?"

But the old familiar shame is upon her. After all these years, the dishonor is still overwhelming because everybody knows that when a man leaves his wife, it is the woman's fault. Chitra will not judge her but the sting of her pity will be almost as unbearable. And so, Bhima simply lowers her head. "Let it go, Chitra baby," she says. "Let the past remain the past. Today is a happy day. Why we should darken it with sad stories?"

Chitra watches her for a beat and then exhales. "You're right. Today *is* a happy day. And I still have to wrap Su's gift. You want to see it?"

Despite herself, Bhima smiles. She has never met a grown woman as effervescent as Chitra. "If you like," she says.

"It's in here." Chitra takes Bhima's hand and pulls her into the bedroom. Bhima marvels at how soft her hand is, like Maya's. They make their way to the closet, and Chitra riffles through the hung clothes and then pulls out a package wrapped in newspaper. She sets it on the bed and unwraps it.

Bhima gasps. It is Sunita's face, sketched in black and white, staring back at them. There is the slight frown that is permanently etched on the woman's brow. A smile hovers uncertainly on the thin lips. And the eyes in the painting are Sunita's eyes, but there is an expression in them that transforms the face, making it more real than a photograph, as if Chitra has looked beyond skin and flesh and bone and into Sunita's spirit. "You make this picture, Chitra baby?" she asks, and when Chitra nods, she is awed again. In capturing the essence of Sunita's soul, Chitra has revealed something deep about herself.

"Think she'll like it?" Chitra asks, and Bhima stares at her wordlessly. After she and Gopal had been married for six months, her husband had taken her to a photo studio where a man had taken many-many pictures of them, out of which Gopal had selected three. At that time, Bhima had chastised her new husband for wasting his money so foolishly, but over the years, the photos had become her most cherished possessions. "She will," she replies. "She will keep it as a remembrance, forever."

"Good." Chitra smiles, and then she pushes Bhima lightly. "Accha. You go finish up and then you're free to leave early. I just need a few minutes to gift wrap this."

Before Bhima leaves, she removes two of the three oranges she had saved for Maya and leaves them on the kitchen counter. "A small gift for Sunitabai," she says shyly. It is rare that she shares something she's saved for Maya with someone else, but today's exchange with Vimal has shaken her, made her feel a strange solidarity with these two young women and their solitary life together. Besides, she thinks, as she makes her way home later that evening, perhaps the extra income from working at the market will permit her to feel like a human being again. If, after all these years of labor, she cannot even share two pieces of fruit with someone as nice as Chitra baby, then for sure her time on this earth has been a failure.

16

Even though Rajesh has been dead for over twenty-seven years, Parvati is unsure as to whether she ever loved her husband. If she did, it was probably in the last two years of his life when he lay in bed dribbling saliva and helpless as a baby, following her with his eyes as she crossed the bedroom of their tiny apartment, or swallowing the food that she would mash for him.

She had first met him when she was thirty-two, at the peak of her powers, her beauty, and ability to please a man making her more valuable than any of Principal's other girls. Unlike the others, her eyes were not dull from smoking hashish, her teeth were not decayed from smoking bidis or chewing tobacco. Even after two decades spent in the brothel, she still retained some of the robustness, the musculature, of the farm girl she had once been. Indeed, despite the three abortions she'd had by the time Rajesh came calling, as well as the gonorrhea she'd contracted at least half a dozen times, she was one of the few women at Principal's home who had not been run ragged and spectral by the demands of her job. Two things had saved her from that fate: her beauty, which made Principal reluctant to hand her over to every client who wanted her, and her aptitude for keeping the woman's books. As Principal grew obese, gorging herself on goat biryani and parathas fried in ghee, she found herself relying more and more on Parvati to do the bookkeeping.

Ordinarily, Principal never would have rented out Parvati to someone as lowly as Rajesh but would have preserved her for the businessmen and the rich college boys who blew their fathers' money on girls and booze. But Rajesh was a police inspector, and the brothel fell within his precinct. He showed up there on his first week on the job, asked to be given a tour of the place, and when it ended, pointed his nightstick at Parvati. "I'll take this one," he said simply, as if choosing a pineapple at the market, and Principal had no choice but to acquiesce.

Tonight, Parvati sits at the edge of the bed in her room in Mohan's place, and goes through the cloth bag that holds all her worldly possessions. She digs to the bottom until she finds what she is looking for—a blue plastic hair clip. Rajesh had brought it to her the second time he'd come. She had pretended to be grateful, but accustomed as she was to the lavish gifts given to her by her regulars, she had planned on throwing it into the trash as soon as the stupid man left. But she hadn't. The clip had remained on her dresser, and the next time he came, she put it in her hair. And was amused by how gratified he looked. He was gentler with her this time than the first two times, and soon it became a ritual for her to clip her hair when he visited. Principal was pleased with this development because despite the weekly bribes and the free use of the girls and the liquor by his constables, the previous inspector hadn't always looked the other way. Under Rajesh there would be no sudden raids, no publicity-generating arrests during election season.

Parvati fingers the clip in her hand. There is something malevolent about this trick that destiny has played on her. Despite her strenuous efforts to escape her life in the brothel, she has ended up in yet another house of disrepute. She fears that she will end her life in this place, so similar to the place that had ended her childhood. The hair clip feels like a talisman, a reminder of the irrefutability of destiny. She is not even sure why she has carried it around all this time.

Except that Rajesh was the first to discover the pomegranate seed growing at the base of her chin. They had been lying in bed one afternoon and he had his arm around her, one finger idly stroking her cheek. The finger wandered to her chin, stopped, then felt around. "Kya hua?" he said. What happened?

"What?"

"Over here. What is this?"

She touched the spot where his finger lay. "I don't know." She shrugged. "It's nothing. Doesn't hurt. It'll go away."

But it didn't. Slowly, almost imperceptibly, it grew. At first, no one could see it. But Rajesh knew it was there and kept an eye on it. "It's growing bigger," he said one day. "I think tumko cancer ho gaya. Have you gone to the doctor?"

"I have no time for a doctor-foctor," she said dismissively. "It's just a pimple. It will go away."

"I will pay," he said quietly. "I will talk to your madam about giving you a day off."

At the memory of this, Parvati digs through her cloth bag again. She pulls out a small metal photo frame with a picture of Rajesh in his police uniform and stares at it for a few moments, hoping to feel a wellspring of love for the man who got her out from under Principal's thumb. But if there ever was love, it had dried up in the drought years that followed. Instead she feels a curl of gratitude for those early years of kindness. Rajesh became more and more territorial, arguing with Principal about ruining Parvati's youth and health by pimping her out to too many men. Even after the doctor said that the growth was non-cancerous, he continued to advocate for her, and when Principal's avarice proved greater than her fear of him, Rajesh played his trump card. Late one evening two of his constables, regulars themselves, swooped into the place and arrested Principal herself, their faces impassive in the face of her threats and curses. Two days in the lockup with no charges brought against her and no access to a lawyer made Principal realize who she was up against. Parvati never found out what words were exchanged between Principal and Rajesh, but after she was released, there was a new arrangement. Now, Parvati had only two duties—to comfort Rajesh and be his exclusively, and to help with the books.

Over the years, their relationship changed. Now, Rajesh would show up at the end of his work shift and say, "Get ready. There's a new film I want to see," and off they'd go, Principal and the other girls glowering behind their backs. He would take her for a snack and mango kulfi at Chowpatty after the movie, then drop her off on his motorcycle. Somewhere around this time, Parvati remembers, he took to referring to her as his girlfriend.

Taking over the accounting for Principal also gave her some say-so in the running of the brothel. Parvati knew that everybody assumed that she was siphoning off enough money each week to, say, allow herself to buy Camay soap and foreign-made nail polish from the smugglers at Flora Fountain, or to order an extra Limca or a plate of chicken biryani. But she didn't. What she did instead was buy a chocolate every day for Praful. And use her influence to convince Principal to give a night off to his mother when she was in a particularly bad way. And badger the older woman to be the first one in the red-light district to offer free condoms to their clients, although so few of the men used them that Principal berated Parvati for wasting her money. "No man with any izzat, any honor, will use this if he doesn't have to," she lectured. "Stupid you are, for not knowing this."

Ten years after Rajesh first claimed her, Parvati's life had fallen into a routine. During those years, Rajesh had been transferred twice to nearby precincts, but somehow his influence over Principal had not waned. There was also the fact that during that decade, the pomegranate seed had grown into an orange, and Parvati had gone from being the most desirable woman in the brothel to the most contemptible. Early on, she had encouraged the rumors and the superstition that ran rampant among the men who flocked to Principal's place. It didn't matter if the clients were illiterate taxi drivers or educated college boys—they all believed in the efficacy of curses. Parvati used this to her advantage, until their fever for her left their eyes. Rajesh alone seemed unaffected by the growth, possibly because he had first touched it when it was a seedling and also because he had heard with his own ears the doctor pronounce it a freakish, benign tumor, with no risk of infection to anyone else.

And yet. It wasn't always gratitude that Parvati felt toward Rajesh. Sometimes, before she had time to check her emotions, she bristled at the proprietary tone he took with her. And she resented him calling her his girlfriend. Who was he to give her that designation, for which he seemed to expect gratitude? What kind of a girlfriend was this, who had to acquiesce to all of his demands but never was allowed to make one of her own? What would happen if, one day, when he showed up to take her for an outing, she refused?

Then there was the fact that Rajesh was a full eighteen years older than her. With a face as long as a white pumpkin and a ridiculous-looking mustache, he looked like a nawab from a hundred years ago. Everything about him was stiff and starched, as if he had sprouted from the uniform he wore. It embarrassed Parvati to have this man dote on her, claim her, call her his girlfriend. At one time or another, all of Principal's girls had held the fantasy of some man—a boyish, gentle man with a face like the young Rishi Kapoor—falling in love with them and taking them away from this place. Parvati had even seen it happen, once or twice. But here she was, stuck for the last ten years with an older, stern-faced man, who expected her to be grateful for the outings and inexpensive gifts he occasionally bought her.

"Kutta," Parvati now spits. Dog. But even as she says the word she remembers how it was never that simple. Rajesh was increasingly talking about his retirement from the police force and how he'd promised his wife that they would retire in Pune. "I will miss you," he would say, and Parvati would smile, half hoping for and half dreading the inevitable parting with the man who had spared her the worst degradations of her profession for almost ten years.

And then, seven months before his retirement, Rajesh's wife took ill with dengue fever. She was dead three days later.

Perhaps she had loved him on the night he'd come to her a few days after the funeral, Parvati now thinks. That night, she had consoled a Rajesh she'd never encountered before, as he nestled into her like a wounded animal. In all their years together, Rajesh had barely mentioned his wife, had never uttered her name, and only referred to her as "the mother of my son." But now he spoke of his Usha, how she made the best upma in the world, how well she had managed their finances and run their household all these years. The paradox hits Parvati only now, all these years later—if she had ever loved Rajesh, it was on the night that he had spoken of his affection for his wife. At that time, she had only wondered whether the dead woman had known of her existence during the last decade of her life; and how and why she had tolerated her husband's visits to a prostitute.

Parvati rolls to her side on the rope bed and pulls the thin cotton sheet up to her ears as if to block out the chattering voices of the past. For so many years, she has treated the past like a condemned house she is no longer allowed to step into. But these days it creeps up on her, triggered by the glassy laughter of the dancing women, the thud of the tabla music as familiar as her heartbeat, even the smell of the fried foods that the girls eat in between customers, taking her back to the fetid heat and smells of Principal's house. She has put so many miles between herself and that brothel, first by marrying Rajesh and later, by being on her own, and yet, here she is, protected only by her old age from the goings-on just outside this room. There is no God. Or, if He exists, it is simply to torment His human creations.

She still recalls her stunned silence when Rajesh had approached her a few months after his wife's passing and proposed marriage. "She will never let me go," she'd said at last, meaning Principal, of course, and Rajesh had stiffened, his professional pride hurt.

"She will, if she wants this bleddy place to remain open," he'd said. "You forget. I am still a police inspector. I have not retired yet."

"You don't know Principal," she'd replied, unsure if she was simply avoiding his proposal. "She will put up a fight."

Rajesh had looked at her sadly. "I'm only saying this because you're forcing me to, janu. But your market is down. For one thing, you're no longer young, hai na? And then, with that thing growing under your chin . . ." He stopped. There was no reason for him to complete his sentence.

Still, Parvati had remained silent until Rajesh's eyes flashed with impatience. "Not too many men would offer a woman like you a respectable life, Parvati," he said. "I'm offering you a good home, among decent people. Any woman in your place would be sobbing with gratitude. Or are you so fallen that you cannot be rehabilitated?"

Parvati looked up at the challenge in his words. "You go speak to her. See what she says."

"Arre, wah. You act as if she owns you . . ."

"Doesn't she? She purchased me . . ."

"Even if she did, you have repaid her a thousand times over. How many men a night did you . . ."

"If you are to be my husband, you cannot talk to me like this. About what I did with other men, before you. Ever. You understand? Promise me."

He smiled appeasingly. "Accha, accha, what for you getting all angry? Okay, baba, I promise."

Parvati groans. If she ever added up the number of people who had broken their promises to her over the years, she could build a ladder to the moon. Best to leave the past where it belonged and fall asleep. It would be morning soon enough.

17

Because it is not enough that the tyrant sun beats upon them all day long, baking their flesh as they squat in the open marketplace

Because it is not enough that the incessant jackhammering across the street is so jarring that they can feel its vibration long after they leave the market

Because it is not enough that Bhima was jolted out of a fitful sleep at predawn by the sounds of one of her neighbors beating his unfortunate wife

Because it is not enough that as Parvati left her room this morning a strange man wearing only a pair of shorts stood on the balcony and leered suggestively at her, making her chest tighten with fear

Because it is not enough that Rajeev's wife has the pneumonia and they still owe the doctor sahib four hundred rupees from the last time she was sick

Because it is not enough that Rajeev's son is pressuring his father to ask for more money from his new, strange job of carting Bhima's groceries around

Because it is not enough that both Parvati and Bhima have tossed and turned all night long to escape the ghosts from the past that still haunt them so

Because it is not enough that both women are glued together in this tiny spot in hell, bound by their need and mutual contempt for one another

Because it is not enough that after faithfully buying her produce every day from Jafferbhai, he had laughed in her face this morning when Bhima had broached the subject of credit

Because it is not enough that Jafferbhai's insult still burns and has made Bhima even less tolerant of Parvati's incessant rubbing of that nasty thing growing under her face

Because it is not enough that Parvati immediately picks up on Bhima's distaste and this makes her even more crotchety than usual

Because it is not enough that there's a rumor that the displaced fishmongers are planning on protesting the opening of the mall, thereby disrupting all the other businesses

Because it is not enough that there has been an unexpectedly sharp hike in Maya's college tuition

Because it is not enough that despite the higher income Bhima still feels insecure, held hostage to Parvati's whims and moods

Because life is not hellish enough, and money is not tight enough, and their fears are not fearful enough

Suddenly and without warning it begins to rain.

The monsoons have arrived.

18

Business has been cut in half.

Bhima is sick with worry. The largess that she had felt toward Parvati and Rajeev has soured into resentment. She is especially annoyed at Parvati because despite the torrential rain, the old woman still sells all six of her cauliflowers each day. Now, she waits until Parvati's third customer of the day—a bedraggled, skeletal woman who is soaking wet—leaves and then turns toward her. "What I don't understand," she says, as if continuing a conversation, "is where do the customers go during monsoon season? They still have to eat, no?"

Parvati talks to the air. "Some people are having eyes, but still they are blind." She looks at Bhima condescendingly. "Look around, sister. See these pucca shops with walls and floors and roofs? Why should they buy from you when they can buy from a real shop?"

Bhima tugs at the plastic tarp that Rajeev has set up for them to sit under. "But those shops charge more," she says.

Parvati lets out a cackle. "Nahi. Those crooked baniyas are smart. On days like this, they give extra-special pricing. Just to steal business away from small people like you." She fingers the lump absently. "Besides, tell the truth. When you were shopping for your mistress on a wet day like today, did you mind paying extra to stay out of the rain?"

Bhima flushes. It is true. Even though she guarded Serabai's money, she used to pay asking price from the shopkeepers on miserable days like this one.

Despite his raincoat, Rajeev's hair is matted down on his forehead and water runs down his face as he hurries toward them. "You needing me to go pick up more of our produce, mausi?" he pants.

Bhima gestures toward the unsold fruit. "What for? First we have to sell all this, no?" She avoids looking him in the face. "If a customer wants you to do a home delivery, you are free to do so today. Business is bad here." It wounds her to say this to him after the selfless service he has provided her. In fact, for the past three days she has continued paying Rajeev his daily rate. But now, she must stop. She is here to do business, not charity, and every morsel she puts into Rajeev's mouth, she takes out of Maya's. Still, she will miss the exhilarating feeling of paying Rajeev more money than he used to make at his old job. Unlike the sourpuss woman sitting to her left, Rajeev is always grateful.

Rajeev's face falls as he understands her meaning. But he merely replies, "Theek hai, mausi. I will check in with you a little later."

A half hour later, she is still mulling over what Parvati has said about the advantage the shopkeepers have over pavement vendors like her. She waits until it is time for lunch, and sure enough, there's Rajeev trotting up to them like a pet dog expecting to be fed. She considers telling both her companions that they must start paying for their own lunch, but at the last minute, she reconsiders. Instead, she says, "You bring back something to eat and stay here until I return. Can you manage?" Even though she doesn't ask, she knows that Parvati will intervene if Rajeev, sweet as a sparrow and dumb as a pigeon, makes a mistake. "I will just go and come," she says, snapping her fingers. "Accha?"

She braces herself for some caustic comment from Parvati,

but the older woman merely looks at her with raised eyebrows as Bhima grabs the day's earnings from under the tablecloth and hurries away.

There are three customers ahead of her when she gets to Birlabhai's onion and potato shop, and Bhima uses that time to survey the premises. The shop itself is filled to the brim with Birla's own stock. But the shop has an overhang, and there is space under it for her to sell her fruit. Will Birla agree to rent out this tiny area to her? And if so, how much should she offer? The low sum she pays Parvati each day will offend him, she knows. But how much is fair? Bhima feels a twinge of guilt at the thought of abandoning the older woman, but guilt is a luxury she cannot afford. She is not here to save the world.

"Ah, hello, Bhima bhen," Birla finally says. "How many kilos you need?"

She sneaks a quick look around her and speaks in a low voice. "Nothing I need to buy," she says. "I'm here to discuss another matter."

Birla gives her a curious look and waits. "Yes?"

"You may have heard. I am now selling fruits in the market." She grimaces. "Business was good. But these rains are killing me. So I was wondering how much you will charge to let me set up my place outside your shop."

She is not done, but already Birla is crisscrossing his hands in front of his chest, to prevent her from continuing. "No, no, no, bhen," he says. "Ask me for anything, but not this, please. My dear departed father always teach me—Give a hungry person a roti but don't loan a homeless person a home. Sorry. I'm not interested."

"But I will pay you . . ."

"Bhima bhen. Don't take this the wrong way. But we've been in this location for over sixty years. In that time, we have been approached by people who drive Mercedes cars and can buy and sell small folks like you and me a million times over. But my rule stands. No rental-fental. I don't need that headache."

As if to stress his words, there is a loud clap of thunder, and they both jump. Birla smiles ruefully and turns away. "I am sorry," he says.

Bhima stares at the shopkeeper for a moment and then turns back and heads to her spot. She is soaked by the time she climbs back under the tarp. "You smell like a wet dog," Parvati says in greeting, then shuts up as Bhima glares at her. The two women sit in a huddled, miserable silence.

"Where did that Rajeev disappear to?" Bhima asks after a few minutes.

Parvati shrugs. "He had a delivery. So I tell him to go. As it is, we only having one customer. Your money is under the sheet."

"Thanks," Bhima says shortly.

"So, he said no to you?" Parvati asks.

"Who?"

"Who else? The shopkeeper you went to see."

Bhima's eyes are blazing. "Nothing is private in this wretched place. Who told you?"

Parvati laughs. "Nobody told me. I explain to you why you have no customers and a little later you rush off, like you are having to do urgent soo-soo. I can see what's below my nose."

Bhima's hands itch with the desire to slap the woman's smug face. "Some of us want to better ourselves," she hisses spitefully. "Not all of us are lazy, happy selling six cauliflowers a day."

Parvati looks at her intently. "For unfortunates like us, there is no bettering ourselves. You can try all you want, sister. But you end up where you started. This much I know."

Her words echo what Bhima already believes and so it is hard to argue. But then she hears herself say, "I don't have that luxury.

Of admitting defeat. I have a granddaughter to educate and to marry off."

To her great surprise, Parvati nods. "Sahi baat hai. You are correct. That is the biggest difference between us."

Bhima's eyes fill with tears at this unexpected softening. "It's all for her," she splutters. "I . . . So that she can have a better life than . . ."

Parvati pats Bhima's wrist with her own bony hand. Twice. "Sister. No need to explain. I understand." She is quiet for a few minutes and then she says, "Let me see what I can do. To get you a better spot. Covered."

Bhima doesn't try to hide her skepticism. If Parvati can help her, she thinks, why hasn't she helped herself all these years?

"Who did you approach? That rascal Birla?"

"Yes."

"That was your mistake. He is too fat and prosperous to care. You need to find someone whose business is not so strong. Understand?"

Bhima's eyes search Parvati's face, but the older woman's visage is inscrutable. "How you so clever?" she says.

Parvati emits a low hoot. "Clever? Sister, I'm so clever that I spend my days killing flies at this market. And then going home to a place that can be shut in a police raid at any—" She catches herself, clamps one hand over her mouth, and stares at the pavement.

Bhima's mind is whirling, but she looks away, pretends to have not heard. She lets a moment pass, and then says, "Who should I approach, then?"

"I don't know. Let me make inquires."

She is about to profess her gratitude when Parvati intercepts her. "Of course, I will take a finder's fee from you. To make up for my loss of income."

Bhima has no choice but to nod her assent.

19

His name is Vishnu and he owns a small, nondescript shop not too far from where Parvati has her spot. Bhima has walked past it daily, but the shop must be as unassuming as its owner because she has never noticed it. Unlike the other shopkeepers, Vishnu doesn't call out to passersby but waits for them to come to him. That is his first mistake. The second, Bhima notices, is that he is a painfully shy young man and has a disconcerting habit of looking over the shoulder of the person he is talking to. She has been selling fruit for only two months, but already she has learned the importance of eye contact, of salesmanship. This Vishnu possesses none of that.

But he is a tough bargainer. Instead of a flat rental fee, he wishes to claim a percentage of her daily earnings. Bhima stares at him, unsure of whether to agree or disagree. She wishes Parvati were here to help her, but the older woman is back at their usual spot. As it is, Bhima feels she may have no choice but to agree to this young man's terms. The rains have been so heavy the past two days that yesterday their whole street was flooded, and she was unable to sell anything. Jafferbhai has agreed to hold her produce for her in the warehouse for an extra day, but Bhima knows she needs to move quickly. Besides, Vishnu has a corner store, one end of it abutting a wall that she can lean against all day. "You please wait," she says to him. "I will come back in fifteen minutes, only."

Parvati scowls as Bhima tells her what Vishnu has offered. "In a way, it's better," she says. "But on a good day, you will pay him a lot more. Accha, do one thing. Tell him no more than three percent."

Bhima sighs, loathe to give away three percent of her hard-earned money. Watching her, Parvati shakes her head. "Don't think small like a mouse. This location will bring new customers to you." She groans as she rises to her feet. "Chalo, I'll go with you. I've known that Vishnu for donkey's years. He thinks he's a big shot now. I'll set him right."

Bhima watches in wonder as Parvati and Vishnu go back and forth. They both scribble numbers on a notepad, they each raise their voices and call out numbers. Finally, Vishnu's voice rings out. "Three percent," he says, smacking his hand on his counter. "Final offer. Lower than that, I will not go. Take or leave."

Parvati chews on her lower lip. She turns slowly to Bhima, stares at her mournfully. "I've failed you, sister," she says. "I know it's a hardship for you, but what to do? This here Vishnu drives a hard bargain. Well, today is an auspicious day. My advice is you agree to pay him three percent."

Bhima is bewildered. "But that's what we . . ."

"Sister." Parvati is blinking furiously. "Don't argue so much. Just say yes."

"Yes but—"

"Then the matter is settled." Parvati gives Bhima a quick wink before turning back to the shopkeeper. "Vishnu beta. Do this old widow a favor and get someone to wash and paint the wall before she starts. It stinks of urine and is covered with paan stains. Bad for the business."

"What to do, auntie? People see a wall and think it's a urinal, only. I paint today, they deface it tomorrow."

Parvati smiles. "Do one thing. Get the painter to paint some pictures of saints and Gods. A few Lord Krishnas, a few Sai Babas should do the trick. No one will piss on a saint."

Vishnu blinks, his mouth agape at such casual blasphemy. But he nods his agreement. "Accha, auntie. Give me one-two days."

Bhima casts Parvati a sideways look as the two women walk away from Vishnu's shop. She can tell that Parvati is pleased with herself. "You should be in the politics," she says at last. "In my whole life I have never known someone like you."

Parvati points one finger to the heavens. "Destiny," she says. "Kismet." Then she whirls around and points the same finger at Bhima. "You will still owe me full payment until the end of the month."

20

Parvati was right. The new location has attracted new customers. Rich people, servants, everyone is grateful to be out of the rain for a minute, to be able to hold a mango or custard apple in their hand, weighing it or smelling it without getting soaking wet. For the last two weeks Bhima has made it a point to continue buying lunch for Parvati, but if she is grateful, she doesn't say. Sometimes, if the rains are heavy, Parvati seeks shelter under the overhang where Rajeev and Bhima squat and eat their lunch, her mouth moving dully as a cow's as she munches on her sandwich. Bhima forces herself to ignore how often the woman's hand moves involuntarily to her backside, how, in between bites, she sets her sandwich down and rubs the spot in a rapid, circular motion. Once or twice, Rajeev has made a sympathetic sound, asked if the ointment he had given her was effective, but Parvati has silenced him with a curt, "Everything's fine." And every morning, as Bhima passes the spot where Parvati sits huddled under the tarp, she fights the pang of guilt that she feels at having left her former partner behind.

But for the most part, Bhima is content. Her days have fallen into their own rhythm. Rajeev is a reliable and affable assistant, and she thrills each time she has a repeat customer. Vishnu, too, has proven to be a good landlord. Each afternoon before she leaves for Chitra's home, she cleans the space she is occupying, careful to give him no reason to be unhappy with her. At home, too, things are better—she has started looking around their tiny hut and wondering if they could afford a few new things. The kerosene stove she cooks on, for instance, is twenty-two years old. Surely she can afford a new one. And perhaps, after a decent interval, she could approach Bibi and find out the cost of putting down a tiled floor, as she and Ram had done. Even fantasizing about these things makes Bhima feel better. All her life she has earned just enough to put one foot in front of the other. Just yesterday, she had slipped a ten-rupee note into Maya's hand, and the girl's start of surprise had warmed Bhima's heart. Always, she had believed that it was enough, the getting by. But it turns out that her heart is no different from Serabai's or Chitra's—she remembers how pleased Serabai would look when they went shopping together and Serabai found a blouse or scarf she thought Dinaz would like. Or Chitra baby's delight when she surprised Sunita with a book or a bracelet. She had thought it belonged only to the rich, this pleasure in giving. But she had needed that same satisfaction also.

The displaced fishmongers do not show up at the grand opening of the mall, as everyone had feared. That day goes off without incident, although, thanks to the presence of a movie star Bhima has never heard of at the ribbon-cutting ceremony, the traffic is even more hellacious than usual. Loud film music blares onto the street from makeshift speakers and a string of long, black cars follow one another to the entrance, garlanded in roses, as if this were a wedding party. Bhima turns away in disgust, having no interest in the antics of the rich. Today, security is so tight that the police will not allow her to cross the street to begin her trek to Sunitabai's house. She mutters curses at all of them as she walks the extra distance—at the no-name movie star, the Chief Minister who is rumored to attend the opening, the stupid traffic policeman who has redirected her, the anonymous builders of the mall, whose marbled exterior and pristine glass windows are a taunt, and only reflect back to her the smallness of her life.

The trouble comes a week later. Bhima has just completed a sale when she hears it—the roar of the mob, followed by shattering of glass. She looks across the street and blinks. Where did they all come from, this group of men and women who are pelting the mall with rocks, prying at the marble with their hands? She knows at once that this is the anticipated protest by the fish vendors. On her side of the street, people have stopped to stare at the protesters, their mouths agape. For a few minutes the tableaux remains the same—the rioters working at demonic speed to destroy the mall and the bystanders across the street standing motionless, transfixed. And then a new sound enters, the ominous wails of police sirens as the Jeeps arrive and dozens of policemen descend upon the fishmongers. From across the street Bhima can hear the whisk-whisk of the policemen's bamboo lathis as they shiver in the air for a second before landing indiscriminately on the heads and limbs of the rioters. Like rats chased out of their nests, the vendors run helter-skelter away from the lathis and across the street, running toward the vegetable and fruit market. The police follow, and now there is no getting away. Bhima watches as a policeman trips over a stack of limes. Furious, the man spins around and indiscriminately beats the vendor who is in a crouch. Bhima cries out as blood spouts from the man's head, watches as the policeman kicks him before turning his baton on someone else. She herself is only a few feet away from it all, but Vishnu's shop and the adjacent wall act as a kind of protection, and she hugs against the wall, as if to render herself invisible. But the next second she remembers that Parvati is out there, sitting miserably under her tarp, Parvati, old, frail but tenacious, not one to back away from a fight. "Auntie, get in here," Vishnu screams, holding out his hand at the entrance of his shop, but instead of grabbing his hand, she turns around and runs into the street toward her old spot. People are rushing by her, screaming, and the sound they make is like the high-pitched whistle of the wind during a storm. But still she runs the other way, and then she sees her—Parvati, standing in the middle of the melee, with her hands on her hips, leaning forward just a little bit, as if she is about to lecture someone. Parvati, the only still point in a turbulent sea, and despite the danger, despite the chaos, Bhima notices the expression on Parvati's face. It is bemusement. And the absolute absence of fear. And maybe it is the anger that Bhima feels at such arrogance that makes her grab the older woman's hand more roughly than she should and give it a yank. "Come," she yells, and Parvati follows, without struggle or protest, matching her pace with Bhima's, and Bhima has the strangest feeling that Parvati was simply waiting for her to come find her.

Vishnu is in the process of lowering the metal shutters when they reach the shop. "Come on, hurry up," he screams, bending low to help them climb the three stone steps that lead them inside. "My fruit," Bhima begins to say, but is silenced by the look that Vishnu gives her. "Your brains will look like mango pulp if one of those officers lands a lathi on your head," he mutters as he lowers the shutter, locking them in.

"For no good reason you dragged me here," Parvati says. "I was fine in my spot. No one was bothering me."

Before Bhima can react, Vishnu lets out a disbelieving guffaw. "Kamaal hai," he says. "Unbelievable. Most people would be kissing this woman's feet," he scolds. "What a risk she took, going out there. Instead, you are complaining."

For once, Parvati looks chastised. "Thank you," she says, but

Bhima knows it is for Vishnu's benefit and turns pointedly away. She herself doesn't know what made her go out in search of this dour woman with the face of a jackfruit. And then her heart clenches with fear. Rajeev. Where is he? He's the one she should've gone looking for, not this ungrateful heap of dung.

"Don't worry about Rajeev," Parvati says just then. "He hasn't returned from the delivery you sent him on. So he should be fine." And then she smiles, a thin, triumphant smile, as if she knows that Bhima is unnerved by her ability to read her mind.

Despite the ceiling fan, it is hot in the shop. All four of them look at each other when they hear a series of piercing whistles, followed by a fresh round of screaming. "The kuttas are beating those poor people good-proper," the assistant mutters.

Vishnu frowns. "What business those fishermen are having destroying private property?" he says. "That mall is the pride and joy of this neighborhood."

"You can't feed pride and joy to a hungry baby," Parvati says. "What are those fish vendors supposed to do now? This is the only life they are knowing."

"Good point, auntie," Vishnu says. "But what to do? This is the new India. People will sell their grandmothers if the price is right."

Parvati's head jerks up, a look on her face that chills Bhima's heart. "If that's so, then the new India is no different from the old India. Money was king then, and it is king now."

"Sahi bat hai." Vishnu nods vigorously. "You speak the truth, auntie."

They all fall silent, and Bhima sneaks a look at Parvati. What accounts for this bitterness? Parvati can read and write. Why then is she so powerless? Who has hurt her so? The tendril of a thought drifts through Bhima's mind—something the woman had recently let slip about a police raid, something about hating her own father—but it is driven out by a fresh, urgent one. "What time is it?" she gasps. "I have to go to my next job. My bai will be waiting."

"Arre, auntie, have you gone mad? Are you not hearing the commotion outside? You better just stay here chup-chap."

She feels teary at the thought of missing another day's work. Chitra baby is so good to her—she doesn't want to abuse her goodness. But Vishnu is correct. "Do you have a phone?" she asks. "I will call her and tell her I'll be late."

"Auntie, in what jamana do you live? Don't you have a mobile?"

Bhima remains silent, and after a minute, Vishnu pulls out his phone. "Here. Use this."

"I can pay—"

"Forget it. Just make it quick."

Chitra doesn't sound a bit angry, just worried. "Are you sure you're safe, Bhima?" she says. "Do you want me to try and get down there?"

"Baby," she says sharply. "You please don't come here. It is not safe. I will try to come later and cook dinner."

After she returns the phone to Vishnu, he says, "You're a businesswoman now. You need to have a mobile." He stares at her for a second and adds, "Give one to that deliveryman of yours, also. That way, you will do more business."

"What I need a phone for at my age?"

Vishnu shrugs. "You think about it. My nephew sells Vodafone. I can get you a good discount."

"That way you can talk to your Maya, also," Parvati pipes up, and Bhima feels a rush of irritation. Who told this old woman to defile Maya's name by using it?

"Why she needs a phone?"

Parvati lets out a cackle. "You go home and ask her. All young people these days are having a mobile."

Can she afford to buy Maya a phone? Bhima's mind is awhirl. Will it be possible with this new location, she wonders, to have a little extra? What would that feel like, to not worry over every single purchase?

It is then that she notices, for the first time, the white cloth bag at the foot of Parvati's chair: the leftover cauliflowers. In the midst of a riot, the older woman had the presence of mind to save her inventory. Whereas she, dumb cow that she is, had abandoned her business to rush to the aid of a woman whom the Gods themselves probably couldn't strike down. Bhima feels a grudging admiration for Parvati. Even as there is much to despise in Parvati, there is much to admire.

When the thought first crosses Bhima's mind, it is so unpleasant that she flicks it off, like a spider on her skin. But it crawls back: If she wishes to be successful, she will need the help of this irritating, querulous woman sitting across from her. She must humble herself and ask Parvati to join her in her new business.

21

As she leaves the market and trudges home, Parvati is smiling to herself despite the fact that she is carrying two unsold cauliflowers. She remembers the feel of Bhima's trembling, sweaty hand in hers as the woman had pulled her to safety. She had not realized it, how much she missed the touch of another's hand. And the woman had run through a riot to come find her. Which meant there was still some decency left in this sad world. She has been wrong about this woman, Bhima. All these years she had thought she was gamandi, a snob. But now she understands—what she had thought of as unjustified pride was simply self-defense.

The police had cleared the street after today's riot, sent all of the vendors packing. It is much too early to return to that awful room, and the rains have held off today. Surely there is someplace for her to pass the time. She briefly contemplates going to the cinema hall, but she knows better. A single woman going to a film, even a woman as old as she, will attract unwanted attention from the young men who fill the seats of the darkened theater. In the old days, she and Rajesh used to go to the movies often. Even after he had retired, her husband still retained enough influence that he never had to purchase those tickets, the managers grateful for his years of turning a blind eye to the black marketeers who scalped tickets before every movie show.

The sun is out for the first time in days, and Parvati feels it following her as she walks aimlessly, unsure of where to go to kill the hours. Then she has an idea—ever since she's arrived at Tejpal Mahal, she has been curious about the Old Place, wondering who runs it now and how the dilapidated building has withstood the storms of time. Never before has she had the inclination to find out, but today, she feels an intense desire to know. She has no idea what she will do when she gets there, but she hopes to find proof that her stay at Tejpal Mahal is a trick of fate and not a defect of character.

After all this time, she knows exactly which bus will take her there. She stands at the bus stop along with a throng of people—she can still recall a Mumbai where people used to stand in line, but those days are long gone—and when the bus arrives, allows herself to be swept inside by the current of the crowd. Her heart pounds hard for a few seconds; it has been years since she's ridden the bus, years since she's interrupted the circuit of marketplace to home and home to marketplace to travel anywhere else, and the fear of being pushed aside by the mob, or of falling from the ledge of the open-door BEST bus, is intense. But then she is in and digging into her white bag for the small purse in which she keeps her money. The conductor looks at her as if she is insane when she offers him a few rupees for her ticket—it turns out that the fares have gone up considerably since the last time she rode the bus.

She knows she has a ten-minute walk from the stop where she disembarks to the Old Place, and she takes her time, knowing that the longer this journey takes, the more she can delay her return to the despised Tejpal Mahal. She smiles mirthlessly at the irony—the longer she spends on this visit to the old brothel, the less time she will have to spend at the present one. As she walks, she remembers the days when she used to take these same streets with Rajesh, back when his ardor for her allowed her to mask her indifference toward him. They would walk down this street after a movie or dinner, and even though she hated the weight of his hand on her slender shoulder, she was grateful for breathing fresh air, for getting out of the stifling, stale atmosphere of the brothel, for escaping for a few hours the petty jealousies, the cheap perfume, the same-same jokes, the snide remarks of the other girls, that mostly marked her days. Even though Parvati knew she had simply traded Principal's domination for Rajesh's possessiveness, it still felt good to escape the narrowness of her life for a few hours—to lose herself in the love triangles and melodramas of the giant figures on the cinema screen, to walk down these free streets and hear the peals of laughter of the college girls, the enticements of the shopkeepers, and the ringing of the temple bells. And for this she was grateful to Rajesh, and if that gratitude sometimes felt like love, well, that benefited both her and the older, married man who had claimed her as his girlfriend. In the darkened movie theaters, in the packed trains and buses, he used to finger her, aroused by the anonymity of public places, emboldened by his own audacity. And she bore it, unable to move his prying fingers away, unable to make the claims of virtue or even ordinary decency that any other woman could.

Parvati stumbles, then rights herself. For a moment she hesitates, wonders if she has the strength to face that building that still haunts her dreams. Principal is dead, she knows, killed in a train derailment. Most of the other girls are probably dead as well, some undoubtedly victims to tuberculosis or typhoid or the STDs that ran unchecked through the place. Even during her time there, several of the Old Place girls had hung themselves or ingested rat poison or had gone missing and were later found stabbed to death or drowned. Neither was it unheard of for a girl to simply disappear, along with her regular client. Principal would swear for days, complaining about the ungrateful girl and the loss of income, swearing that the dead or missing girls were a conspiracy to bankrupt her. After everything that she'd done for them.

Rajesh had spared her any such fate by taking her out of there. And that too, taking her out not as his mistress but as his wife. Parvati had heard of other men, of course, who had lost their hearts to the women they fucked, and married them. But such men were usually low-class themselves—truck drivers and rag-pickers, men used to living a lonely, nomadic existence with not too many prying family members. It was practically unheard of for someone of Rajesh's stature to marry a whore, to bestow his good name upon her, to enshrine her in his ownership flat, located in a modest but good building. It helped that Rajesh was recently retired—there would be no superior officer who would raise his eyebrows or require an explanation. Other than a son and daughter-in-law who lived in Pune, he had no family. His dead wife's family, aghast that he was remarrying within a year of having lit his wife's funeral pyre, denounced him and broke off all ties. In his own way, for the first time in his life, Rajesh was also free. And the first thing he did with that freedom was to ask Parvati to marry him.

Parvati pinches at the orange at the base of her chin as she walks. If only she had understood his reasons for asking her, she thinks, she would not have wasted one moment being flattered by his proposal, would've turned him down. But then another thought hits her—could she have refused? Or would Principal, still intimidated by Rajesh's ability to shut her down, have sold her to him? Already, her value to Principal had declined. As for doing the books, some of the newer girls knew how to read and write. How difficult would it have been for one of them to take over?

Is it possible, Parvati wonders, for a human being to be sold twice during one lifetime? First by her father and then by Principal? But even as she asks the question she knows the answer—in this pitiless world, a human being can be bought and sold not once, not twice, but a million times over. In this country, human life has as much value as this stone she is kicking down the street.

Lost in her thoughts, Parvati gives the stone a savage kick, and the motion makes her rubber chappal slip from her foot and fly a short distance. She hurries to retrieve it, hoping that nobody has seen. But in this city of a million busybodies, of course someone has, a teenage boy who laughs out loud. Parvati flushes and ignores him, slipping her foot back into the slipper. Serves you right, old woman, she scolds herself. Walking down the street kicking stones as if you are a carefree teenager.

Would it have been possible, she wonders, that despite not being in love with Rajesh, they could've had a good life together, one based on respect and kindness? She had never known a prostitute to whom sex was important, and she herself had come to think of the act as an odd, mechanical thing, something a male body did to a female body, sometimes painful, sometimes not. Whenever she read one of those stupid women's magazine articles on how to entice a man or how to be a dutiful wife, she fought the urge to throw the magazine across the room. Parvati felt nothing but contempt for those young, naive virginal women from good families, lining up to enter the marriage market, which, to her jaded eyes, seemed more dishonest than the red-light market. At least men paid *her*, rather than the so-called respectable families who paid lavish dowries to have their daughters taken off their hands. She did not wish to trade places with them, found their deference to their husbands, fathers, and brothers to be hypocritical, saw it as a survival tactic deployed by women in a world ruled by men. If the deer lives in the same jungle alongside the tiger, the deer must learn to flatter, praise, and obey the tiger. That's how Parvati thought of marriage—an arrangement between a doe and a tiger.

Still, in the early days of their marriage, she was hopeful, her distaste for Rajesh—for his sagging breasts, his paunch, the gray hair growing out of his nostrils and ears—tempered by her gratitude for getting her out of the Old Place. The marriage certificate, the red sindoor in the parting of her hair, meant nothing to her, though he didn't understand this. But after decades spent in a noisy, public place with a wraparound balcony and children running in and out of every room, she was thankful for the quiet of their one-bedroom flat. In her new home, no strange man leered at her when she came out of the bath dressed in only her choli and petticoat. She could spend hours in the kitchen listening to her cassette tape of Mukesh songs while she cooked and Rajesh watched TV. And until he ordered her to stop wasting his money, she bought four roses to put in a plastic vase every two days. Just walking down to the small market near their building and shopping for groceries, and then returning home with the small bundle of flowers, tasted like freedom to her.

When did the troubles begin? Parvati asks herself, then shakes her head because the answer has always been as hard to reach as a cloud in the sky. Did it start with Rajesh's realization that Parvati was a poor housekeeper? That she barely knew how to cook? She remembers the first, disastrous meal she had made for him—a fried chicken that was golden on the outside and red and raw on the inside. He had taken one look at it and flung the plate across the room, leaving her to sweep up the shards. But this was still in the early days, and after a few minutes he had apologized and ordered some food from the cheap Muslim restaurant around the corner from them. Still, Parvati had known that she was in trouble then. There was no one to turn to for cooking tips—no trusted friend she'd grown up with, no wise mother, no exasperated-but-helpful mother-in-law, no shaking-her-head-and-laughing sister. There was only this long-faced man, whose motives and expectations were not yet clear to her. Except that he expected her to cook his meals. And wash his clothes. And clean his home. And seemed dissatisfied with her efforts.

Two months after they were wed, there had been a knock at their door. She opened it to see a thin-lipped young man standing there. "Yes?" she said.

"Is my father at home?"

Parvati's face lit up with understanding. "You must be Rahul. Please, come in."

She could see his eyes wander to the tumor, but Rahul's face was expressionless. "I'll wait. You just let my father know I'm here."

Was she imagining the hostility in his voice? Perhaps he was upset with his father for remarrying? She awoke her husband from his armchair, and Rajesh hurried to the front door, while Parvati retreated to the kitchen. "Come in, son," she heard Rajesh say. "Why you are standing there like a stranger? This is your house, na?"

She couldn't hear either man for a few minutes. Then, she heard Rahul say, "Will not tolerate it," but couldn't catch Rajesh's muttered reply. A few seconds later, she heard the word *randi*, and Parvati froze. Whore. So Rahul knew of her past. No wonder he had stood stiff as a corpse at their door. Now, she could hear the men arguing and talking over one another. She heard the words *your grandchild*, then *shamed*, then *randi* again, and, finally, *disgraced the whole family*.

"Lower your voice," Rajesh said. But he had raised his own voice to say it.

Parvati stepped out of the kitchen. "Please," she said, folding her hands before Rajesh's son. "Please, beta, do not be angry with your father for my mistakes. Try and understand . . ."

A muscle twitched in Rahul's jaw as he pointedly looked away. "This is between father and son," he said. "Do not interfere in our business."

"Rahul," Rajesh said loudly. "Bas. Enough of this. I won't tolerate this. Like or don't like, this is your new mother."

Parvati flinched at the same moment that Rahul did, knowing it was the wrong thing to say. Usha had been dead for less than a year, and how could she be mother to a boy she'd never met? "Don't." Rahul's voice was raw. "Don't you dare compare my mother to this . . . this . . . thing." He looked at both of them, his eyes speckled with hatred. "Have you lost your senses, old man? It wasn't enough for you to just fuck this gold digger? What jadoo did she do to make you marry her?"

Parvati closed her eyes. So this was the respectable world. These were the decent, God-fearing people. In all her days in the brothel, no one had spoken to her as disrespectfully as this mouse.

Both men were staring at her openmouthed, and she realized she had said this out loud. Her hand flew to her mouth. "Maaf karo," she apologized. And before Rahul could answer, she hurried back to the kitchen.

A moment later, she heard the sound of a slamming door. She waited a few minutes before joining Rajesh in the living room. Her husband sat in his armchair, holding his head in his hands. When he finally looked up at her, his eyes were bloodshot. And in those eyes was something she'd never seen before. Regret.

She has been going around in circles for the past ten minutes. First of all, the name of the street has changed, from its short English name to a long, unpronounceable one. All over Mumbai they've been doing this—even Victoria Terminus, the most famous and beautiful building in Bombay, has been renamed after the great Marathi warrior Shivaji. Still, Parvati is fairly sure that this is the street, recognizes the round corner building that used to house a bakery and now houses a Sony electronics store. She feels disoriented, as if the characters in a familiar story have been replaced by new ones. Even the tall coconut trees that stood in the compound across the street are gone. And instead of the squat, three-story building where she had spent so much of her life, there stands a pencil-thin skyscraper. She cranes her neck back to look, but the tumor makes it hard to stretch her neck and the top of the building is lost to her.

Could this be? That the Old Place is really gone? Broken up into bits, razed to the ground? All of its miseries, its dark secrets, its perversions, gone? Turned into rubble? What does it mean that the place that destroyed her is now itself destroyed, and yet, she remains? What does she do with this old body that still stands in witness, when there is nothing to testify against? Parvati looks around her in bewilderment, even reaches out to stop a man hurrying by, before checking herself. What would she ask? Whether once, not too long ago—or was it a long, long time ago?—a house of ill repute stood here? Who would know? Who would answer truthfully? Who would admit to knowing, to participating in the evil that happened within its four walls?

As if in answer, she hears a squeal of laughter and watches two young schoolgirls in uniforms and pigtails run down the marble steps of the skyscraper and into the street. Their maids follow. "Careful, baby," one of them shouts. "You wait for us by the taxi stand, okay?"

Parvati follows the two girls with her eyes until they round the corner and disappear. And without warning, tears roll down her cheeks. How did he do it? How did he sell his only daughter in order to feed his own stomach? And why had Ma allowed it?

Why did she not kill herself and her daughter to prevent such a travesty? She was twelve, a young peasant girl who knew nothing of the world. And suddenly, she *feels* that girl inside the wizened shell of her body, feels the well-oiled joints inside her own creaky ones, feels the smoothness of the girl's muscles inside of her stringy ones, feels the innocence behind her jaded eyes, the trusting, open heart that beats beneath her barb-wired organ. That girl is alive.

Stop your craziness, stupid woman, Parvati berates herself. Get out of this rich neighborhood before someone calls the police. Muttering to yourself in the middle of the street, pretending that you are young. If a thousand new buildings sprout from the spot where the Old Place stood and if these buildings grow tall enough to touch the face of God, so what? It still won't change the fact that the Old Place existed. Or the fact that the Old Place will never die, that it will simply change addresses and rise up elsewhere. In fact, you are renting a room in one such place. And that's the hard truth you must live with the rest of your days.

Her heart sinks at the thought of returning to Tejpal Mahal, but Parvati also knows that she has no more business on this unrecognizable street. She gives the new building one last look and begins the dispiriting trudge home.

22

"Why you so quiet tonight, Ma-ma? Are you still scared after what happened today?"

Bhima forces herself to concentrate on Maya. "No. I'm all right. Just a little tired."

"At least you saved all the fruit," Maya says, pointing to where the unsold fruit sits in the corner, still in Rajeev's basket. He had been good enough to drop it off for her at the end of the day.

"Yes," Bhima says. "It is good."

"And Chitra was not angry about you being a no-show?"

Bhima feels a flash of irritation. Why all these questions? The truth is she is still shaken by the memory of the bleeding man and the sound the lathis made as they struck human flesh. Tonight, their small hut feels oppressive to her, and she longs to fling open their door and let in the night air. But that, she will never do. She is not one of those common slum women who leave their doors open all the time, subjecting themselves to lewd comments and leering eyes. Besides, an open door is an invitation to flies and mosquitoes and the smoke from a hundred wood-burning stoves. Better to remain in here and tolerate the questions of this inquisitive girl.

"So Rajeev uncle is fine?" Maya asks, and Bhima clucks her tongue. "Yes. I told you. Don't you have your homework tonight, chokri?"

Maya yawns. "I'm done." She pauses and then asks, "And that other lady? Parvati? Is she unhurt?"

Bhima's eyes narrow. "You only meet her one time. Why are you worrying about her?"

"I liked her. She reminded me of you."

Bhima looks indignant. "Of me? Kya matlab? Meaning what?"

"Nothing. Just that she's tough from the outside. Like you." Maya lets out a giggle. "Like those custard apples you sell. Rough on the outside. Sweet and soft inside."

Bhima smacks Maya lightly on the head. "Stupid girl. Knowing nothing, you are. That old woman is a witch." She hesitates. "But I was thinking of asking her. To join my business. What you think?"

Maya shrugs. "If you need help with accounts and all, Ma-ma, I told you. I can help you."

"No. You have only one job. And that's to get good marks in college. I can manage. Besides, this woman is knowing more than numbers. She knows how to talk to people, how to bargain, everything." She sees that Maya is hurt and pulls her close to her. "But if I am needing extra help, I come to you. Okay?"

Maya rests her head on her grandma's shoulders. "I will always help you, Ma-ma."

"I know, beta," Bhima says, stroking Maya's lush hair. And it is true. In a world where nothing is as it appears, this young girl's goodness and love is something she can count on.

23

It is one in the afternoon and Rajeev has given her several plaintive glances. At last, Bhima digs into her purse and unfolds a solitary bill for him. "Go get yourself lunch today."

"What about you and her?"

"You don't worry about us today. We are having something to discuss. We will manage."

Rajeev opens his mouth, but Bhima shakes her finger at him. "Go now," she says, turning away from him.

After the man leaves, Bhima gestures toward Vishnu's young assistant. "Ae, beta," she says. "I am taking a lunch today. Fifteen-twenty minutes, tops, I'll be away. Can you manage?"

The boy looks at her uncertainly. "Only if I am not having any customers of my own," he says. "Vishnu bhai is out today, also."

Bhima nods. "I know. I will not be gone long."

Parvati is haggling with a customer Bhima doesn't recognize when she reaches her. She waits impatiently for the transaction to conclude, and when the woman walks away without buying, Bhima feels a sense of relief. Parvati looks up at her with a raised eyebrow. "To what do we have this honor?"

Bhima gazes at her silently. Is it her imagination, or does Parvati look even more thin than usual? How old must the woman be? Bhima doesn't know her own age, but Serabai had guessed that she is sixty plus seven years of age. This woman must be at least eight years more.

"I was going to the Udupi restaurant at the corner," she says. "I was hoping you would join me."

Parvati sighs. "What you needing from me now?"

Bhima controls her temper. "Behenji," she says. "It is true I wish to talk with you. But let us do it over hot tea and idlis." She glances toward where Reshma sits. "Away from listening ears and wagging tongues."

For a minute she thinks Parvati will refuse, but then the woman rises and the two of them make their way to the nearby restaurant.

"I am in your debt for buying lunch daily," Parvati says after they place their order. "But no need to do this. You have enough mouths to feed. That Rajeev alone has a mouth the size of a watermelon."

Bhima laughs out loud at the image, and Parvati allows herself a half smile. "It is true," Bhima says. "That man eats like a buffalo."

"But you didn't bring me here to speak of Rajeev."

"Correct," Bhima says. Just then the waiter arrives with their glasses of water, and she waits until he leaves. But before she can speak, Parvati interrupts her. "Before you ask, the answer is no. I am not giving up my space to you. Ours was a temporary arrangement."

"It was. And so it shall remain. But my offer is different—I wish for you to join *me*. In my business. By the grace of God, business is good." Bhima looks away, knowing she won't be able to bear the gloating in Parvati's eyes at what she is about to say. "But sister. I am an illiterate. And I am needing someone who can keep the books, do the hisab-kitab."

Parvati is silent for so long that Bhima forces herself to raise her eyes. There is no gloating on the older woman's face. Instead, she sits plucking at her lower lip, a thoughtful look on her face, and Bhima suddenly feels hopeful. "Will you consider what I am asking?" she asks.

Parvati is silent as the waiter sets their food on the table. "What terms do you offer me?" she asks after he is gone.

"You please say, sister." Bhima has already humbled herself before this woman; she is ready to defer to her.

"I will still buy and sell my own vegetables, daily," Parvati says fiercely. "This new arrangement may work, not work, we don't know. I am not giving up my livelihood."

"Yes, of course."

"And I am holding on to my spot. We will store our surplus there. That way, Rajeev doesn't have to go back and forth to the wholesale market. We can use him more for home deliveries."

"But how does he carry more . . ."

"Simple. He takes a tempo every morning to bring the whole day's produce at one time, only."

Bhima's eyes widen. "Tempo costing money . . ."

"We will recover it. As I say, we will use Rajeev for home delivery. Personal service."

"And what if someone steals from . . ."

Parvati clicks her tongue. "Let them try. You leave that to me."

Bhima's mouth is dry with fear. This woman sounds as if she has thought about this for months. If she swindles her, will she even know it?

As if she's read her mind, Parvati says, "I'm many things, sister. But I'm not a liar. Or a thief."

Bhima flushes. "Of course. I didn't think . . . But why you willing to help me?"

"Who says I am helping you? I'm helping myself." Parvati is silent for a moment before she says, "If I believed in God, I would say it was God who brought you here. Today of all days."

"Meaning?"

"Meaning that yesterday I learned a new lesson. That the past doesn't exist. People say that all the time, of course. But yesterday, I see proof with my own eyes. It just disappears, like that." She snaps her fingers. "So then what's left?"

Bhima blinks, trying to follow along. To her, the past is more real than the present. She is debating whether to contradict Parvati when the older woman thunders, "I asked, what's left?"

"I don't know," Bhima says in a bewildered voice.

"The present, that's what," Parvati says triumphantly. "And for that reason only, I will join your business."

Bhima lowers her voice. "Ah, yes, but you see, behenji, for me, my every thought is for my Maya. It's for her sake I want to do well. For her, I . . ."

"Sister. I swear on my mother's head. I am not a cheater. I know you are having a big responsibility."

Aware that her fifteen minutes are up, Bhima tries to catch the waiter's eye for the bill. "Accha, then," she says. "Time to . . ."

But something is disturbing Parvati today. "I couldn't even find the address I was looking for," she mutters. "The very name of the street had changed. And in place of the building was a new one. The old one, gone. Like waking up from a dream."

"True, true," Bhima says, nodding her head vigorously, even though she has no idea what the woman is going on about.

Parvati bangs her hand on the table so hard that the water in Bhima's glass jumps. "You are not hearing me," she says. "What I'm telling you is it's all changing. The whole city is unrecognizable. You know why? Because it is dying and being born, dying and being born again. And people are getting rich, sister. And so, we, too, must die. And be reborn."

Bhima curses her misfortune. Once again, her luck has turned sour. The woman before her has gone pagal, totally mad. Maybe a lathi did land on her head yesterday, when she was standing proud as a queen in the middle of the riot. She eyes Parvati cautiously. "Chalo, behen," she says. "We will pay at the counter. We can talk some other time."

She watches the light go out of Parvati's eyes. "You not understanding a word I'm saying," she says. "You think I'm mad." She stares at Bhima's impassive face, then shrugs. "Think what you must. But do you wish for my help or not?"

Reluctantly, Bhima says yes, more out of awkwardness than conviction. She pays, and her heart is heavy as they walk back.

"Listen," Parvati says, as they reach her spot. "With your permission, I will go with Rajeev to the wholesale market tomorrow. It is time your supplier start giving you goods on credit. And I can find out about which tempo service is reliable."

"No," Bhima says. "For now, ji, please you just help with the accounts. Maybe in a few months, I approach Jafferbhai."

Parvati gives her a hard look but acquiesces. "Whatever you wish." She squats on the ground and then calls after Bhima. "One more thing." She waits until Bhima turns around, then rises to her feet and draws close so that Reshma will not overhear them. "One more idea. You cook in people's homes, correct? Tomorrow, you please come with some good-and-tasty recipes. Make sure they use lots of onions and potatoes. And cauliflowers. That way, we make your stall and Vishnu's a one-stop shopping for customers."

"I don't have time to tell recipe to each customer. Besides, my business is mostly fruit."

Parvati hits her forehead in frustration. "Baap re. Who said anything about telling them recipes? We will make Xerox copies to give out. You speak them to me and I will write them down."

"But what for? Everyone having their own ways of cooking."

"Exactly. But we must make them change what they use. Whatever we are selling, they must buy that day. So if we get cabbage cheap from your distributor, we give them cabbage recipe. Understand? And if you increase Vishnu's business, then you ask him to take less of a fee."

Bhima stands there with her mouth agape. "Who taught you all these things?" she asks at last.

Parvati shrugs. "Nobody." And then she smiles bashfully, showing her broken teeth.

Bhima smiles back, suddenly reassured. "Accha, I'll take your leave," she says after a few minutes. "Till tomorrow, sister."

Parvati nods. "Tomorrow we start," she says. "You mark my words, I will make your stall the most popular one in the marketplace within two months."

II

One year later . . .

24

Parvati is unwell. For days Bhima has tried to ignore this truth, afraid of what it means. But it is unmistakable: the woman's face is even more sallow, the cheeks more sunken. Sometimes, in the middle of a conversation, Parvati stops and her eyes go glassy and Bhima knows that she's waiting out the pain that shoots through the base of her spine. These days, Parvati rubs that spot more often than she does the thing on her neck.

"That's it," Bhima says. "Bas, no more arguing. You take the money and go see the doctor."

"And what is the doctor going to do? Will he hand me the poison that I will beg him for?"

Bhima turns away with a frown. "Like a madwoman you talk, sometimes."

Parvati laughs, cups Bhima's chin, and turns her face back toward her. "Arre, baba, why you're taking so much tension? I'm not going to leave you high and dry. I told you, na. I'm not dying until your Maya finishes her college."

"Why must you always talk about dying-fying? None of us gets to go until God is ready for us."

Parvati slaps her knee. "That only is what I'm saying. You think God is ready to face my judgment?"

"Arre, wah. You will judge God? Instead of Him judging you?"

"Of course. Who is He to judge me? What crime did I ever do

against Him? And what crimes He has committed against me are too many to count."

"Be careful, sister. God will punish you for this idle talk."

Parvati's face turns serious. "Hasn't He been punishing me every day of my life? What more can He do to me?"

Bhima turns away again so the older woman cannot see the tears that suddenly sting her eyes. In the year since Parvati has been working alongside her, she has learned a few things about this woman's bleak existence. A much older husband who is dead but whose memory arouses none of the sweetness that Gopal's memory arouses in her. Once or twice Parvati has alluded in an oblique way to the beatings she suffered at the man's hands and confided that after his stroke, he spent the last years of his life shitting and pissing in bed. "Those years were the happiest in my life, sister. He just lay there, mute as a broken radio," Parvati once said, but by this time Bhima knew that the older woman often said outrageous things just for effect.

As for Parvati's life before her marriage, Bhima knows little. Ask her a direct question and Parvati turned to brick. Or, she would give a nonsensical answer that would set Bhima's teeth on edge. "Why do you carry so many secrets?" she'd once snapped.

Parvati had given her an intense look. "Because without my secrets I am nothing."

Now, Bhima says, "Accha, if you won't go to the doctor, I will go to the temple and pray for your good health."

Parvati shrugs. After a minute she asks, "So how many apples and strawberries you wanting me to set aside for your party?"

Bhima looks at her with worried eyes. "How to guess, sister? That chokri Chitra is touched in the head. For all I know she will invite five or ten homeless people to celebrate her birthday."

Parvati laughs. "Why you say that?"

"Have you ever heard of a mistress inviting their servant to a birthday party? Now, if she is wanting me to come and serve her guests, that's my duty. But to go as one of the guests? And she looked like she going to cry when I say no. That's why only I must go. Maya, too."

"It's good for Maya. To get to know these influential folks."

"I know. But . . ."

"But-fut, nothing. You go. Let someone take care of you for once." Parvati scowls. "Why you are so afraid of these rich people? I'm telling you, in the dark, the cocks of rich men look no different than those of the poor."

Bhima covers her ears. "Baap re baap. What filth you speak. Whoever heard of a woman with a mouth like a sewer?"

"Theek hai." Parvati shrugs. "Listen, don't listen, I don't care. But go to the party." She reaches out and pinches Bhima on the wrist. "And eat until your stomach is full. All skin and bone you're becoming."

Bhima laughs, shaking her head, wise to Parvati's tactics by now. "I tell you to go to the doctor and you . . ."

"Sister. I told you. It's between me and God now. And God will win. The bastard always does."

Bhima goes to remove her slippers as soon as they enter Sunita's house, but Maya squeezes her hand. "Ma-ma, don't," she mutters, and Bhima realizes that despite putting up a nonchalant front, Maya is as nervous as she is.

"Wow, Maya," Chitra beams, as she takes Maya's hand in hers. "I love your outfit." She moves to hug Bhima, and the older woman stiffens at this breach. Instead, she hands over the fruit basket to Chitra. "For your birthday," she says. "A small gift."

"Thank you," Chitra says. "Come, come in." She takes them into the living room where two well-dressed women are chatting with Sunita. "Hey, Ferzin and Binny. These are our friends Bhima and Maya."

The two women look up and smile. "Hello," they say.

"Namaste-ji," Bhima says.

"How are you, Bhima?" Sunita asks quietly, a bemused look on her face. It is the same expression she wore the day Chitra had invited Bhima, as if Chitra is a child whose whims she indulges. Even though Bhima had agreed with Sunita's unspoken disapproval on the day of the invitation, she now feels an uncharacteristic spurt of resentment. It is this anger that makes her stay in the living room rather than offer to help in the kitchen. She is about to squat on the floor when Maya pinches her discreetly and guides her to the chair. "Sit here, Ma-ma," she says in a tight voice. "A hard chair will be good for your back." She herself sits on the couch next to her grandmother.

"What do you do, Maya?" Ferzin asks, and Bhima listens with pride and amazement as Maya talks to the strangers in a matter-of-fact manner, with none of the deference that she herself feels around important people. Bhima can tell that these are important people from how tall the women sit, their good clothes, the perfume that lingers on them, the fact that they speak mostly in English.

The woman they call Binny turns toward her. "And you are Maya's grandmother?" she asks, and Bhima nods.

"I see. And—how do you know Su and Chitra?"

Maya, who has overheard the question, cuts herself off midsentence and gives Bhima a quick look. "My Ma-ma is a businesswoman. She owns a fruit and vegetable stand at Ambedkar market. You are knowing where it is?"

Bhima almost laughs out loud at Maya's caginess, but the two women don't notice. "Not really," Binny says. "Our driver does all of our grocery shopping."

"Then you must have him try our products," Maya says. Bhima wonders if she is the only one who hears the tightness in Maya's voice. But the next second she hears Sunita's gentle voice change the subject. "So, Maya is one of the best students in her college. Isn't that so, Maya?"

Chitra drifts back into the living room, her face flushed from the heat of the stove. "What will you drink, mausi?" she asks, and Bhima tenses, waiting for the other guests to register that this silly girl has just called her aunt. But the two women are deep in conversation with Maya, and she says, "Just some water, baby."

"Okay," Chitra says. "You relax. I'll bring it to you." And she returns a moment later with a Coke for Maya and coconut water for Bhima. "Try this, mausi," she says. "Better for you in this heat." She sets the tray on the coffee table and then plops down on the floor in front of Bhima, resting her elbow on the older woman's knee. "You sit here," Bhima protests, trying to rise from the chair, but Chitra smiles. "I'm fine. I've got to get up in a minute, anyway."

The others are chatting away in English and Chitra clears her throat. "Hey, why don't we make this an English-free zone tonight? That way, everyone can participate. And I'll get a chance to improve my Hindi."

Su raises her eyebrows. "I thought you Delhi folks spoke the purest Hindi," she teases. "Whereas we uncouth Mumbai folks bastardize it."

"Arre, don't start your Delhi-versus-Mumbai fightum-fighting, yaar," Maya says, in a tone so familiar that Bhima is about to scold her when she realizes that all four women are laughing at her remark. How is this possible? she marvels. Maya has only met Sunita and Chitra a handful of times and already she behaves as if she is one of them. One of *them*. The words are an ache in her heart. Maya is all she has in this world. What if she ever . . .

"Bhima." Chitra's voice interrupts her thoughts. "Will you come taste the bhindi for me? Tell me if something is missing?" And with that, Bhima rises.

In the kitchen, Chitra rests her hands on Bhima's shoulders. "Are you all right in there?" she whispers. "Not feeling too uncomfortable?" And when Bhima shakes her head, she continues, "I invited Binny and Ferzin at the last minute. I thought maybe they'll be able to help Maya find a job when she's done with college."

"I'm grateful to you for thinking of . . ."

"Of course. Maya's a friend." She gives Bhima's shoulders a quick squeeze before dropping her arms.

Serabai would've undoubtedly helped Maya find a job, also. But Bhima can't imagine her old mistress throwing a party to do so. "God bless your parents for having a daughter like you, baby," she says fervently. "I give thanks to them."

Chitra gives a short laugh. "Oh, they wouldn't agree with you." She says it lightly, but Bhima sees the flicker of pain in her eyes before she turns away, and understands exactly what Chitra is alluding to. She takes Chitra's hand in hers. "Their misfortune," she says deliberately. "Their bad naseeb. For not knowing what a gem they are having."

Chitra's nose turns rust-colored and her lower lip quivers. "Thanks, Bhima," she says.

"Bad luck to cry on your birthday." Bhima gives Chitra a push. "Baby. You please go rejoin your guests. I will do everything here."

"Oh, no. I didn't invite you here to work. You are—"

"Chitra. You please go. Enjoy. All of you can talk happily in the English. Please. I am comfortable here."

She and Chitra serve dinner together, and Bhima is stunned by the number of dishes. She is no stranger to a bountiful table—

whenever Serabai and Feroz entertained at home, there was enough food to feed the whole neighborhood—but it dawns on her that Chitra has cooked or ordered dishes that are her favorites. As if to confirm her suspicion, Chitra leans toward her and says, "I made the bhindi especially for you, Bhima. Hope you like it."

Maya is seated between her and Ferzin, and halfway through the dinner, over the sound of the other voices, Bhima hears her granddaughter say, "I always wanted to be a lawyer. That was my dream." Bhima stops chewing, a puzzled look on her face. "What did you say, chokri?" she asks.

The girl glances at her impatiently. "Nothing. I was talking to Ferzin, only. She is a lawyer."

How could this be? This woman across from her looks so high-class and decent. Bhima has heard that all lawyers are crooks and scoundrels. "Chup re," she says to Maya. "Don't talk rubbish."

There is a sudden silence at the table as the five of them stare at her, and then Maya lets out a giggle. "That's why only I never say anything to her," she says triumphantly. "My Ma-ma thinks every lawyer is a thief."

Bhima turns scarlet, but Ferzin smiles. "And she's right—most of the time." She turns toward Bhima. "I practice labor law, ji. Which means I protect the rights of working people. Whereas this one here—" she gestures toward Binny, who grins sheepishly, "she works for the big shots—the big industrial houses."

Bhima finds herself wishing Parvati were here. Somehow, in the past year, Parvati has become her interpreter to the world, cutting up information into tiny slices that she can digest and comprehend. "Accha?" she says vaguely.

"I want to be lawyer like you," Maya says loudly. "So that what injustice happened to my Ma-ma and Dada can never happen to someone else."

Again, Bhima makes to shush Maya, but it is too late. "What

happened?" Ferzin asks, her eyes resting warmly on Bhima. And Bhima has no choice but to tell the story of Gopal's work accident and how the crooked foreman had tricked her into placing her thumb impression on the contract that freed the company from any liability.

"Wow," Ferzin says when she's done. "How long ago was this?"

Bhima's eyes are cloudy as she looks into Ferzin's face. "This was a long time ago, bai," she says.

"And how is your husband now?" Ferzin asks gently. Bhima falls silent, her eyes downcast, and it falls upon Maya to say, "My Dada moved back to his home village. He took my Amit uncle with him. Many-many years back. Before I was even born."

There is a short, sympathetic silence before Binny says, "Well, if you're willing to work really hard, Maya, we can certainly help you. If you're serious about becoming a lawyer, I mean."

Bhima watches as Maya's face lights up and then falls again. "Thank you," she says at last. "But I will need to get a job after graduation."

"Chokri," Bhima interrupts. "I don't know anything about becoming a lawyer. But if that is what you want to do, I will work ten jobs. No need for you to get a job after graduation."

"And no need for you to work ten jobs either, Bhima," Binny says, smiling. "I'm sure we can all pitch in. If Maya goes to Government Law College, the fees are not that much."

Bhima's head bobs with gratitude as Chitra claps her hands. "Now this is what I call a great birthday," she says. She reaches for the okra and spoons more of it onto Bhima's plate. "Eat," she says, and even though Bhima protests, she does. "You give me the recipe, please, Chitra baby," she says in between bites, and Chitra nods. "Do you guys know what Bhima does at her vegetable stall?" she tells the others. "She hands out written recipes to her customers. Pretty ingenious, eh?"

Binny groans. "Share a few with us, Bhima. We are both such awful cooks."

"You tell me what you want," Bhima says at once. "I will cook for you. You both are Parsi, no?" And when they nod, "You are liking dhansak? Sali boti? I know all Parsi dishes."

"No kidding. How?"

Bhima gives Maya a quick look. "I used to work for a Parsi lady," she mumbles, wishing she hadn't brought up the issue, dreading the question she knows is coming.

"Really? Who?"

"Sera Dubash," she says dully.

"Oh, my God. You know Dinaz?"

"Yes, of course. I saw her grow up before my eyes." All the time aware of Maya's eyes boring into her.

"So you quit to start your own business?"

Bhima hesitates, unsure of what to tell. But before she can respond, Maya says, "My grandma is so happy with her new life. Better pay, you know?" and the others nod. But Chitra is looking at Bhima curiously. After a moment she says, "Okay. Let me clear the table and then we'll have dessert." And Bhima is grateful that she allows her to help with taking the dirty dishes into the kitchen.

"Everything all right?" Chitra asks, and Bhima nods, even though she can tell that Chitra is not fooled.

The strawberry cake is like nothing she has ever tasted. It is light as a cloud, sweet as rain. Her thoughts go to Rajeev and Parvati. Have they ever tasted anything this good? She swallows and then turns to Binny. "I come cook for you, bai. In exchange for you helping my Maya."

Binny gives an embarrassed laugh. "Oh, you don't have to do that, Bhima. If Maya decides to study law, we'll help in any way we can."

Bhima smacks her granddaughter's hand. "You hear this? For the next six months, you are to keep your nose in your books. Don't look up once. You need to get the best marks."

"Ow, Ma-ma. What you hitting me for? I'm already the best student in my class." Maya addresses her, but Bhima can see her eyes wandering toward the other women and knows that she wants to impress them.

"Look to your feet," she instructs. "Otherwise you'll give yourself the evil eye."

Maya grins. "My grandmother is superstitious," she says. The others chuckle, and even though Bhima knows the joke is at her expense, she doesn't mind. She remembers what Parvati had said to her earlier today about introducing Maya to important people. How is it that every piece of advice that Parvati has given her has improved her life when the woman has flopped at bettering her own? But then, she thinks, surely Parvati's life has improved a great deal, too, in this past year. Just last week the woman had come to work wearing a new blue sari. And she has replaced her old chappals. By the grace of God, their business is doing well enough to provide for both of them. Rajeev, too.

Perhaps, she thinks, it is finally their time. Now, at long last, it is their time.

25

It happens so suddenly that there is no time to prepare. One minute Parvati is laughing at something Bhima says, whereas in the next second she covers her mouth, moves a few meters away from the folding table they have recently purchased, and throws up. The first projectile misses their customer by inches, and the woman squeals, pinches her nose dramatically, and then scuttles away. Somehow, Parvati manages to turn toward the wall, and the next round of vomit hits the wall so hard, it flies back onto her sari. Bhima gags at the sight, but then she blinks rapidly because nestled within the yellow-green vomit, right across the picture of one of the saints, is an unmistakable streak of red. Blood. She hurries over to where Parvati is weakly lowering herself onto the ground, holds her up from the waist, and half drags her away from sitting in her own mess. The woman's thin hands are clammy to touch. Bhima is dimly aware of the fact that Vishnu is shouting at them, but all she can think is one incessant thought: *Parvati is sick. Parvati is very sick.*

Bhima looks around frantically. "Get her a cold drink," she yells. "And pull up the chair for her."

Vishnu looks annoyed but slaps his assistant on the thigh. "Move. Go next door and get a Limca," he orders. And he himself hurries down the stone steps with the folding chair.

"Maaf karo, maaf karo," Parvati is whimpering. "This is so bad for our business."

"Forget the business," Bhima says. "You tell me. What is wrong?"

Parvati wipes her mouth with the side of her sari. "God only knows. Must be something I ate yesterday."

Bhima looks at her in disbelief. "And that is making you sick today? All these hours later?" She knows that Parvati never eats breakfast. "Tell me the truth, sister. What is wrong with you?"

Parvati struggles to retain her authority. "Arre, Bhagwan. A woman cannot simply be sick without getting the third degree?" But her voice is weak, and Bhima sees through the posturing. She stares silently at the older woman, cold with anger, shaking with disappointment. More than a year of working side-by-side and still Parvati is as secretive as ever.

She sees Vishnu's assistant hurrying toward them, an open bottle of Limca in his hand. She takes it from him and says, "Go get me a bucket of soap water, beta. I need to wash this wall."

The boy frowns. "Didi, such work is beneath you." He chews on an extra drinking straw. "That sweeper woman was still in the market. I saw her cleaning out the latrines. She will stop by here when she is done."

Bhima heaves a sigh of relief. "I will give you a tip later. Many thanks."

"No problem, didi," he says in English as he heads back into the store.

"Here," Bhima says, holding out the bottle to Parvati. "Drink this. It will settle your stomach."

Parvati takes a small sip, then stops. "I can't," she says. "My mouth is still tasting of vomit."

A slight breeze blows and the smell almost makes Bhima gag again. Parvati's sari is speckled with vomit. There is no way she can spend all day beside her. "Sister," she ventures. "Why not go home today? Get washed. Get some rest."

Parvati looks at a point just past Bhima's shoulder. "I cannot," she says at last. "The place where I stay only allows me to go there to sleep. Otherwise, the room is occupied."

Bhima frowns and is about to ask what kind of a place wouldn't allow a sick woman to return to her own room, when the answer comes to her. Soon after she had met Parvati, the woman had made some reference to a police raid. Now she understands what she had meant. She stares at the frail, elderly woman before her as her brain formulates the unthinkable: Is it possible that Parvati rents a room in a brothel? All this time, even as their business has grown, even as she has taken pride in her growing ability to provide for others, this woman who has weathered both sun and rain alongside her, who is the brains behind their success, has been going home each and every day to . . . to . . . ? Bhima feels the bile rise to her mouth, and for a moment she thinks it's her turn to be sick. How can it be? she asks herself. Can there be so many levels of hell? All these years she had thought that she was on the bottom rung—a wife who wasn't a wife, a widow who wasn't a widow, a mother who had no children, a woman whose home was not much better than a bird's nest haphazardly strung together. But now she feels positively blessed. To have a home. And to have someone to share that home with.

She feels a sudden, indiscriminate anger, although she's unsure of its target—the Gods who toy with women like her and Parvati for their own amusement, this cruel city that begets so many poor people that it cannot take care of them, or at her own obtuseness. "Come on," she snaps, coming to a decision. "Get up. We will get you washed up."

"The latrine is too dirty . . ." Parvati begins.

"Who said anything about the latrine?"

They cross the street hand in hand, Parvati meekly following Bhima, who smiles grimly. If she needed proof that Parvati is not well, here it is, in this meek acquiescence. Parvati walks with her head down, does not look up until they are at the entrance of the mall. They have barely taken two steps toward the spotless glass doors when they hear a whistle. "Ae, ae, ae," says the chowkidar as he races toward them. "Where do you two madams think you are going?"

"We are needing to use the bathroom," Bhima says shortly.

"As is half of Mumbai." The man sneers at them. "Go use the public latrines. This place is not meant for you."

Bhima flushes. "This mall is a public facility, correct?"

"Correct. But not for women like you."

"Shameless boy. Show respect for your elders."

The man smacks his thigh in frustration. "Arre, why you're making trouble? Is this your father's house that you can foul up the bathroom and then leave without buying anything?"

Parvati groans. "Ask him how much he needs to let us in," she says in a whisper loud enough for the man to hear. But instead of being insulted, he merely smiles. "The old lady is smarter than you."

"How much?" Bhima says.

The watchman scratches his beard. "One hundred rupees and you can stay in all day for all I care."

"Give him fifty," Parvati says. "He can take it or leave it."

The man glares at her, but when Bhima offers him the money, he quickly grabs and pockets it. "Have a nice day," he says in English.

Bhima mutters under her breath as the glass doors slide open for them to enter. It is nearing the end of the month, and she has to settle with the baker, the doodhwalla, and the grocer. Maya had told her just yesterday that she needed a new textbook. She needs to watch her money, not spend her days offering bribes to corrupt watchmen.

A blast of sweet, cool air hits them, and both women shiver

and lean into each other. They feel the air dry the sweat on their bodies, and in another moment they are seduced, by the exquisite beauty of the marbled floor they are afraid to walk on, by the jeweled twinkle of the shops they pass. Several of the shopkeepers stand at the entrances of their stores, ready to welcome customers with promises of discounts on luxury goods, but not one of them makes eye contact with the two women who obviously have no business being here.

"Arre, Ram," Bhima breathes, gazing up at a huge chandelier. "I had no idea this building was so big. How we going to find the bathroom?"

"I'll look for the signs," Parvati says. Her voice is hoarse, strained, and Bhima looks at her with concern. "Can you walk?" she asks.

"I'm walking, no? So why ask a stupid question?"

At one time, she would've been insulted. Now, Bhima simply shrugs it off as Parvati being Parvati. Is it because the woman has no one to care for her that she has become so gruff? Or is it because she is so gruff that she has no one to take care of her? Bhima shakes her head, not knowing the answer. But whereas once she felt nothing but exasperation for her business partner, now affection has taken root between them. Now, she has learned to look past Parvati's rude demeanor and words and appreciate the fine mind and good heart that lie beneath.

It is tempting to stop at the windows of all the stores they pass—Bhima is particularly struck by a red embroidered kurta that Maya would love—but Parvati's sari needs to be washed. As they look for the bathroom, Bhima asks hesitantly, "What happened, sister? And has this happened before?"

"No," Parvati says. "It was just heatstroke."

Bhima remembers the scarlet streak. "But . . . I think there was blood on the wall along with . . ."

"Don't talk nonsense. It was probably a streak of paan that someone had spat out. In fact, I think I saw that yesterday."

Bhima nods. After a minute she asks, "And, how is that spot on your back? The one that is always paining you?"

Parvati stops walking. "Did you get your doctor's license in between selling brinjals and spinach? Or is there another reason you're being so nosy?"

This time, Bhima doesn't bother to hide her irritation. "No wonder you don't have anyone," she says. "Always pushing everyone away."

For a split second, Parvati looks stricken. Then she smiles a slow, strange smile and puts her arm around Bhima. "Why, sister," she says softly. "I have you, na?"

Bhima's throat burns. "Maaf karo," she says. "I didn't mean what I said."

Parvati chuckles. "Let me teach you something. Never seek forgiveness for speaking the truth. And here—left turn for the bathrooms."

Bhima wets paper towels and wipes down the front of Parvati's sari. As she bends to clean the border of her sari, she feels the older woman's hand lightly stroke the top of her head. "I wish you had been my blood sister," Parvati says. "Perhaps my life would've turned out differently."

The compliment is so unexpected that it is hard for Bhima to talk. "Do you have sisters of your own?" she asks at last.

"Nahi. Just three brothers. I was the oldest."

"And where are they now?"

"In hell, I hope. Along with the old boodha. Their father."

Bhima blanches, remembering her own beloved father. "Wasn't he also your father?"

"Yes. My misfortune."

Bhima throws away the dirty towels. "Why do you always talk about your pitaji so disrespectful?"

"Because I cannot kill him. So I have to content myself with cursing him." She looks around. "Shall we leave? God knows how many errors that stupid boy has already made while we were away."

They use the toilets before they exit, grateful that even in this fancy place, there are two stalls with Indian-style toilets and not seats that they must sit on. As they make their way back out, trying to find the entrance, they make a wrong turn and the smell of food assails them. In response, Bhima's stomach lets out a long, loud rumble. She remembers how the watchman had sneered at them and tried to stop them from entering because he knew they couldn't afford any of the shiny, beautiful things sold at the mall. But . . . surely they can afford a cup of tea? Maybe some hot-pot vegetable fritters to accompany the tea? Visions of the fifty rupees she has wasted paying off that corrupt watchman dance before her, but she turns away from them. She may never be inside such a fancy building again. And maybe food in such a good place will restore Parvati and settle her stomach? It will be hard to justify such an unforgivable expense, and she knows she will regret it later. But. To sit a little longer in this blessed air, which smells like perfume and feels like ice on her flesh. To rest on the cushioned chairs and eat at a table, instead of sitting on their haunches in the open marketplace. To not be pestered by flies and beggars as they eat lunch.

Bhima comes to a decision. "We will take lunch here today," she says.

Parvati frowns. "Have you gone mad or what? You having any idea how much they're charging? For one cup of tea here we can drink for a whole week."

She almost allows herself be persuaded by Parvati's argument. But she also knows that she needs this indulgence. That she needs to feel that she's more than a beast of burden. And so she tugs at Parvati. "It's okay. I will pay. Let us enjoy this cool for a little longer."

"What about the stall?"

Bhima fights down the apprehension she feels. "We will work harder when we return. Just a cup of tea and something to eat."

And so they sit. Instead of tea, they get lassis, the cold yogurt drink trickling thick and sweet down their throats. Instead of fritters they get potato chips, long, fingerlike strips of deep-fried potato. And they split a masala dosa, the thin crepe crispy and browned. The cost is astonishing, and they can barely look at each other as Bhima pays. As they sit down with the meal, they glance at each other, like nervous children who have done something daring, but once they begin to eat, the price seems worth it.

Watching Parvati slurp the last of the white, frothy drink, Bhima registers a deep pleasure, feels something being knit in her chest. Without warning, her mind flashes to Gopal in the days after the industrial accident—bitter, unemployed Gopal, sitting at home all day, stripped of his role as the family breadwinner. Bhima knows she is not responsible for Parvati; the woman sitting across from her is not blood. Yet she is astonished at the pleasure it gives her to treat her to this expensive lunch. In the old days, when she, Gopal, and their young daughter, Pooja, were all working, she remembers how she used to buy sweets for neighbors in their old building at Diwali time, how she would drop a coin in the hands of the beggars she would pass on her way to work, how she would buy Amit a small top when he did well in school.

"Lost in your thoughts, sister?" Parvati comments, and Bhima shakes her head. "Just remembering my son," she says.

"He must be a grown man now. What news do you get of him? Is he married? A father?"

In her mind, Amit is still nine, the age he was when Gopal stole him away from her. But Bhima knows that time is a devious adversary. "Hah," she nods. "He is married. I got a notice from them after the wedding took place. But we were not invited. And if he has children, I do not know."

"Arre wah." Parvati's voice is indignant. "How can that be? You may be a grandmother five times over, for all you know."

"I don't know," Bhima repeats. "Though life in the village is a hard one, sister. My husband's plot of land is small. And he is missing three fingers. So feeding many extra mouths would be hard."

"I know." Parvati falls quiet, lost in her own thoughts. "What about when your chokri finishes college? You will not inform her grandfather?"

Bhima feels the heat rise in her cheeks. "What for? What kind of grandfather doesn't know of his granddaughter's existence? Or his own daughter's death?"

Shock cracks Parvati's usual impassive face. "Hai, Ram. He doesn't know?"

"My Pooja was a proud girl. No, it was me alone with her and her husband in that Delhi hospital. They died within a week of each other."

"Car accident?"

"AIDS."

Parvati's eyes narrow. "AIDS? What did your daughter do?"

"Nothing." Bhima can hear how defensive she sounds. "My daughter was blameless. Her . . . it was her husband who bring that demon illness home. To her."

Parvati shuts her eyes, and when she opens them they are bright with an emotion that Bhima cannot identify. "I know about the AIDS."

Bhima nods. "Now everybody knowing about the AIDS. But in those days . . ."

The older woman continues looking at her, her eyes searching Bhima's face. "Of course, when I was in the trade, it was not present. I was long gone by that time, thanks to my husband."

"Your vegetable trade?" Bhima says, puzzled.

"No, sister. I'm talking about before. Years before. The red-light business."

Bhima blinks. Looks away. Blinks again. "Meaning what?" she says at last, barely able to breathe due to the hammering of her heart.

"Meaning I was a whore. Meaning that when I was even younger than your Maya, my father sold me to the woman who became my madam."

The sweetness of the yogurt drink suddenly makes Bhima want to gag. The dosa feels oily and heavy in her stomach. What is this woman saying to her? Could she be so stupid, so ignorant that she has spent the last year in the company of a fallen woman? She, Bhima, who has not so much as looked at another man since her husband left her? She, who has taught her granddaughter to walk with downcast eyes, to not dress or laugh or talk in a manner that would attract the attention of those mawalis in the slum? Of course, Maya had slipped once, but that sin is nothing like what this strange woman seems to be confessing to her.

"What are you saying?" she gasps, looking for a way to end this meal and leave.

But Parvati's eyes are unforgiving, have her pinned. "I am saying that I have known many, many women die from mistakes made by men. That is what I'm saying."

"No father . . . No father would do what you say. It is not good, blaming others for . . ."

Parvati emits a loud snort. "It's too bad you cannot read.

Otherwise you'd see for yourself what the newspapers say." Her eyes are hard, milky marbles. "Every day fathers get their daughters married off to men thirty years older. Or to men who are cripples or imbeciles, or deaf and mute. Why? To pay a smaller dowry. Every day fathers kill girls who have been raped by the men in their village. Why? Because the girl has stained the family name by getting raped. Honor killings, they call them. No father would do what mine do? Wake up, sister. Look around. Right now, probably half the men here have fucked their sisters. Or their daughters. Or betrayed their wives."

"Enough." Bhima covers her ears with her hands. "What is the matter with you, that you talk such filth? No respectable woman talks in this manner."

"Respectable woman? You say that as if that's worth something. What did being respectable ever get you? Did it pay a single debt for you? Did it keep your husband? Bring your Amit back?"

"Don't. I won't have my son's name on your tongue."

Parvati smiles viciously. "If you don't want to know the truth about my miserable life, sister, why then are you always poking your nose into my affairs? Always asking this and that."

"Is this why you couldn't go home today? Because you live in a brothel?"

"Sister. Listen carefully because I will only say this once. I am no longer in the trade. I left it many years ago because of this," Parvati gestures to the growth below her face, "and because the man who married me needed a housekeeper." For a startling moment Parvati looks as if she might cry, but she doesn't. "My current situation is not my doing. The boy who I considered my nephew abandoned me. And the only place I can afford is my present home. That is the place I go to rest my head."

Suddenly, Bhima sees it. Sees how hard Parvati is trying. It is all a façade, an act—the toughness, the cynicism, the insults to her father. What sits before her is a scared, broken human being, a woman with even less control over her life than herself. Once again, she feels deeply grateful for Maya, who anchors her days. But unlike her, nothing ties Parvati to this earth.

"Do you—did you—have children?"

Parvati looks at her unblinkingly. "Sister. It is better you don't ask me this question."

Now Bhima remembers an earlier, offhand reference to multiple abortions, and a hole opens up in her chest. "Did he—did your father—really . . . ?"

Parvati bows her head. "He did."

They sit in a worn-out silence, too exhausted to speak. When Parvati finally looks up, she is crying. And as if the tears have oiled her tongue, she begins to tell her story.

It begins with an illness. Her mother is sick. There is no money for a doctor, but when the Christian doctor visits for a few weeks of free clinic, her father takes his wife. The man prescribes a medicine they cannot afford. And so they decide to wait out whatever this illness is that makes her sweat and shiver on the hottest days, that leaves her mouth dry no matter how much water she drinks, that makes her turn away from the sight of food. After a few days, it appears she is getting better, but then, the symptoms come back.

Mother used to work construction, could balance a metal tub filled with bricks or stones onto her head and carry it around the job site. A strong woman, the muscles on her thin upper arms hard as pebbles, who worked all day under the punishing sun without complaint. A severe, silent presence at home but a good mother and a blessed companion to her peasant husband. Every morning they left home soon after dawn, she, to walk to her job site; he, to dig the inhospitable soil of his little patch of land and coax it to yield potatoes and carrots. His one pride and joy was the cow he owned, whose milk he sold, feeding the surplus to his four children. It was a mild-tempered beast whose every rib showed, and he worshipped that animal. The cow was the difference between starvation and existence. Parvati, the eldest, would stay home and watch the other three children. If the parcel of land her father tilled had been large enough, she would've been expected to help, but as it was, she was more useful at home, to mind the others.

He was a tall, bony man, her father, with a pensive face and dark hair that fell across his forehead. When she was a child, Parvati's favorite game was to push his hair back, only to watch it flop down again. She thought it was magic, how that happened, something that her father was doing to entertain her. He would laugh along with her, and even their mother would let a small smile play on her lips.

The loss of the mother's income is calamity enough, but then comes the drought. The soil turns dusty and large veins crack its surface, making it look diseased. Breaking up this dry soil with a hoe is like hitting concrete. The father lies awake at night, waiting for the welcome sound of the first raindrop hitting the metal roof. He and Parvati stand outside their hut looking up anxiously to a sky that has turned its back on them. Their lips are as chapped and dry as the soil they stand on. As the temperatures rise, so does their anxiety. The mood at home becomes grim, the silences longer. There is no money coming in. There are no crops to sell. The drought has even affected the cow's output of milk. One day, Parvati suggests to her father that he beat the cow in order to get her to yield more milk, and before he can check himself, he angrily thumps his daughter on her back so hard, she stumbles forward. "Stupid girl," he says before turning away. She hates the cow then, the dumb, vacuous beast that her father clearly favors over her.

A few weeks go by. They now understand. There will be no rains this year. They are on their own. No God, no government, no landlord is going to help them. They are going to slowly starve to death. The father briefly contemplates the cost of buying enough rat poison to kill his whole family. He cannot afford it. There is no money, no money, no money.

Parvati has noticed that every time she looks up from her chores, her father is staring at her. Some times he absently strokes his chin as he looks at her. Her mother is now just a small pile of clothes and bones in the corner. The baby is too exhausted to even cry. The other two boys fidget and pinch and claw at each other, in misery and boredom. No one bothers to stop them anymore. Parvati and her father are only aware of each other's existence; something charged and electric runs between them. She doesn't know what it is. But he looks at her. Looks at her. Looks at her.

The following week, he takes her to the train station. While they are waiting on the platform, he tells her. It is between selling the cow and selling her. And he has made his decision. He begs her to understand. To forgive. If he sells the cow, their only source of nourishment is gone. He needs the cow. She is a beautiful child, his daughter. He is getting good money for her. Her sale will keep her whole family alive, does she understand? He is a father, a husband, the head of the household. He has a responsibility toward all of them, not just her. She is a girl and he would've had to marry her off soon, anyway. And where was the money for the dowry going to come from? This way, his three sons will have a chance. To eat. To live. To be strong. Would she dare stand in the way of this? Because of her selfishness? The man who is to meet them here is taking her to Bombay. Bombay! Home of the film stars. Who knows? She may get to meet Raj Kapoor or one of his handsome brothers. One day she will thank her old father for this opportunity. What, beta? Does your mother know, you ask? I'm not sure. Perhaps her mother's intuition tells her something. But I believe she thinks we are at the marketplace. Though truth be told, she will be relieved, too. Maybe, out of the money I will get, I can buy her some good-proper medicine. Wouldn't you like that, for your ma to get well? And what do you want here, anyway, chokri? What can we offer you except worry and grief and pain? Now come on, wipe your face. The man will think he is purchasing a water fountain instead of a girl, if you don't stop. Why can't we water our fields with our tears instead of rain? Ae, Bhagwan, why didn't You make it so? We'd all be rich if that were the case.

And so it happens. They are met by a fat man with oily hair and a belly that dribbles like a basketball under his shirt. He looks at her up and down, up and down, and then his red, paan-stained lips crease into a smile. "Theek hai," he says, giving her father the thumbs-up. He opens his wallet, takes out a few bills. Her father protests even as the sound of the approaching train drowns out his words. The man pulls out a few more bills. As soon as the train comes to a stop, he tries to push her up the steps and into the compartment. She screams, turns around, and clings to her father. "Forgive me, my child," her father says. "Try to understand." She feels a yank on her arm, and the pain is so acute, it makes her light-headed. "Come on," the man says, not slacking his grip. "No time for this drama-frama." He bundles her into the train just as it gets moving, then blocks the door. She tries frantically to look out of the window at her statue-still father, but the car is crowded and she can barely see. Still, she gets a final glimpse of him standing motionless, one hand raised, as he watches the departing train, his eyes shedding the monsoons that never came that year.

Bhima hates the air-conditioning now. Perhaps that is what makes her shiver as she looks into Parvati's eyes, which have gone opaque, flat. They sit there, looking at each other, the last of the dosa cold and untouched. Bhima knows she should say something, something comforting and false, but her mind is blank. Perhaps it is best to say nothing, because only silence can honor the enormity of what Parvati has confided in her. Words are pretty butterflies that seduce and flit away, words lie and betray—who knows this better than she? No, the only way to honor Parvati is with silence. But as they sit, Bhima's anger gathers, like seaweed at the water's edge, and finally she has something to say: "A million curses are not enough for what your father did to you."

Something flickers in Parvati's dead eyes, a small light. But she says nothing. Then, after a long silence, "So now you know. All my secrets."

How to pour everything she feels into the thin, feeble vessel of language? Bhima feels a storm gather in her chest, feels something dark and foreboding enter her blood. "Were they miserable years, sister?" she hears herself ask. "The years you spent in that place?"

Parvati shrugs. "No worse than the years I spent being a slave to one man. My husband. What I wish is that instead of talking about love and marriage, he had told me straightum-straight what he required. A cook, a housecleaner, and someone to fuck."

Bhima flinches at the crude word. But she does not chastise the older woman. Parvati has earned this cynicism. She sighs. The glossiness of the mall suddenly feels oppressive to her. "Chalo, sister," she says. "Let's go back to our little stall. Whatever little hope there is for us in this life rests there."

Parvati nods, begins to rise, then sits back down. She covers Bhima's hand in hers. "I . . . I . . . No one has ever heard my full story," she says. When her chin wobbles, so does the growth below it. "I hope I have not dishonored myself in your eyes." And before Bhima can respond, "Because, believe or don't believe, sister, your good opinion matters to me."

"Whatever dishonor there is, the stain is not on you."

Parvati nods. "Thank you."

The stare at each other for another moment and then rise. On their way out, Parvati holds Bhima by the crook of her arm. They walk in this manner, like two schoolgirls, toward the exit sign. They are almost out the door when Bhima hears someone call her name.

26

Bhima recognizes the voice calling her name before she even turns around. Still, for a second after she spins around, she doesn't spot Serabai. She lets out a small cry when she does, her hand flying to her mouth. Because next to her old mistress is a little boy, holding Serabai with one hand, sucking his thumb with the other.

She frees herself from Parvati's hold and rushes toward the woman and the boy, and when she reaches them, she gasps. This is not Serabai but a ghostly version of the woman she hasn't seen in two years. This Serabai has dark circles around her eyes and the skin sags on her face, which is framed by graying hair. It isn't even the fact that Serabai has aged. It is something else, some defeated quality in the stoop of her shoulders, the slight hunch of her back. Bhima knows she is staring, and in order not to, she bends from the waist and says, "Ae, Bhagwan. Is this beautiful boy my Dinaz's . . . Is this . . .?"

Sera smiles. "This is Darius. Dar, this is Bhima, our old servant. Say hello."

In response, Darius hides behind his grandmother's dress and peers out at Bhima. "He's shy around strangers," Sera says apologetically. Bhima nods but registers two things—Serabai has labeled her a stranger. And she has introduced her as her servant. Her mind flashes to Chitra's birthday party where Chitra had introduced her as a friend.

As if to atone, Sera touches Bhima's shoulder. "How are you, Bhima?" she asks quietly. "I miss you so much."

Bhima turns around, and before she can say a word, Parvati gives her a nod. "I'll go mind the stall," she calls. "You come when you are done."

"Accha, thanks."

Sera glances at Parvati as she walks out the glass doors, then faces Bhima again. "Stall?"

"We—I own a fruit and vegetable stall, bai. Just outside of Vishnu Brothers. Not too far from here."

"Really? Since how long?"

"More than a year back I started it." Bhima looks at her carefully. "I used some of the money you sent to us with Dinaz. Every day I give thanks to you for my new livelihood."

Sera looks embarrassed. "I didn't," she says. "I only mentioned that you'd left your savings with me. Of course, I planned to get it to you. But Dinaz took it upon herself to drop it off."

There is an awkward silence as Bhima tries to remember the details of Dinaz's visit. "I think she said that you . . ."

"Probably. But that's Dinaz for you." The two women exchange a knowing smile. "How's Maya?" Sera asks.

"She's good, bai. Almost finishing with the college." Bhima hesitates for a moment, not wanting to attract attention from some troublemaking God who happens to be flying by. "She say she's going to study law, bai. We have some friends who are helping her."

She notes with satisfaction the look of surprise on Sera's face. "Really? But can you afford . . . I mean, she will have to delay getting a job for a few more years."

This time, she abandons all attempts at humility. "That's okay, bai. By the grace of God, I can afford it. Business is good."

"I see." Sera studies her. "You've changed, Bhima. I—I can't say how. But you're different."

"And you, bai? How are you?" It is the gentlest of queries, but Sera blanches and breaks off eye contact with Bhima.

"Good," she says finally. "I am good." She makes a rueful face and runs her fingers lightly over her torso. "As you can see."

"But you don't *look* good, bai."

Sera gives a startled laugh. "This is what I miss about you, Bhima. Your brutal honesty."

"Who you have working for you now, bai?"

"Let's see if I can remember the latest one's name, even." Sera rolls her eyes. "I think we've had about eight servants since you left."

Bhima knows it's cruel, but the words slip out of her. "I did not leave, bai. You forced me out."

Sera flashes her a quick look, then stares at her feet. "Fair enough." She chews on her lower lip, then nods repeatedly to herself, as if trying to gather up her courage. "I had no choice," she whispers. "After what you said. About Viraf."

Bhima digs her slippers into the floor, to stand her ground. "I said nothing that wasn't the truth."

Now, finally, Sera looks up. "That is precisely what made what you said so dangerous. The truth. Don't you understand?"

They stand looking deeply at one another. The chatter and noise around them fades away so that Bhima feels it is only the two of them alone at the mall. The moments tick by. For two years Bhima has wondered what Serabai knew and whom she had believed. And now, on this day of revelations, she has her answer. "Why?" she croaks at last. "How could you . . ."

"How could I? Because I had to. I had no choice." Sera's eyes flash with anger. "My daughter was pregnant. Remember?" A vein throbs on the side of her right eye. "What would you do? If someone told you something that would destroy Maya? If they handed you a grenade that you knew would blow up her life?

Would you use it? Or would you throw yourself on it in order to save her?"

"But bai . . ."

"No, Bhima. I did the only thing I could. And I don't expect you to understand." She points to her grandson. "I did it for his sake. And for Dinaz's. And don't think you're the only one who has suffered. I have suffered, too. I have sacrificed, also."

"What have you sacrificed, bai?" Bhima asks dully, remembering those dreadful days of working at Mrs. Motorcyclewalla's home.

"What have I sacrificed, Bhima? You dare to ask me this? I have sacrificed you. *You*. I have lost you. You knew me better than any of my friends. You knew what went on within those four walls better than my own parents. Even now, every afternoon when I have tea alone, I think of you. How we used to talk. That's what I gave up. For my daughter's sake."

And suddenly, Bhima can see it, the price that Serabai has paid for keeping Viraf baba's dark secret. It is in her eyes, the twist of her mouth, the bend of her head. "You never . . . Dinaz baby never . . . they are happy?"

Sera glances quickly at Darius, but the boy is clearly distracted by the noise and lights of the mall. "They have their ups and downs. Sometimes I think that Dinaz suspects something. In any case, she's not blind. She can see that I'm . . . reserved around him. In the beginning I'm sure she thought it was because I was angry at him for falsely accusing you of stealing the cash. But Dinaz is not a fool. She . . ." Sera breaks off abruptly. "I don't know. The atmosphere at home is not right. You took all the brightness out of my house when you left, Bhima."

Bhima pulls the pallov of her sari around her. She is shivering again. "Dinaz baby must never know," she says abruptly. "You are one hundred percent correct about this, Serabai."

Sera speaks in such a low monotone that Bhima is not sure if her former mistress has even heard her. "One time, only one time I came close to threatening him." She raises her head at the memory. "You remember you sent a rattle for Darius with Dinaz? Viraf was all upset about it. Refused to have his son play with it. So I pulled him aside. I didn't even have to say much. I just said that this was a gift from you. And that I wanted my grandson to value it. Bas, he got all thanda after that. Must have seen something in my eyes."

Bhima has a startling thought: Nothing she has endured in the dark days following her unceremonious dismissal from Serabai's employ can match the hell that her mistress has undergone. A lump forms in her throat. "Jaane do, bai," she says. "Let it go. He's your family relations. My Maya is safe. Nothing good to be gained from remembering what he did."

"He destroyed us," Sera whispers. "And he destroyed his own child. Every time I look at my Darius, I think . . ." Her eyes dart from side to side and for a second there is a look in them that chills Bhima's blood.

"Serabai," she says sternly. "You have a beautiful grandson. It is your duty to remain healthy for his sake."

Sera laughs. "Life is strange," she says. "Everything is topsy-turvy." She makes a visible effort and pulls herself together. She reaches into her purse and removes her wallet. But even before she can take out the notes, Bhima is shaking her head. "No, no, no, bai," she says. "There's no need. We are doing well, by the grace of God."

Sera looks taken aback. Her hand hovers uselessly for a moment. Then, she recovers and says, "Buy something from me for Maya for her graduation. I will have no way of finding out."

Bhima hesitates, loath to offend the woman who has been so good to her over the years, but unwilling to accept her charity.

She is not even sure if she will mention this unexpected encounter to Maya. Already, Serabai's confession from a few moments ago is beginning to feel like a dream. "I will let you know when she finishes college, bai," she says. "I will send word to you with Mrs. Sethna's servant. Accha?"

As the insult behind her refusal becomes obvious to Sera, she flushes, nods, and places her wallet back into her purse. After a second, her head tilts back, and she is once again the proud, dignified woman Bhima has always known. "Well. Please give Maya our best wishes," she says stiffly.

Bhima feels a wave of self-chastisement. Why did she have to go and hurt poor Serabai, after she had just exposed her raw heart to her? "Thank you, bai," she says. "God has heard my prayers and put you in my path today."

She can tell that Sera is now in a rush to get away. "Stay well, Bhima. I may come visit your stall one of these days."

Bhima bows her head. "It would be my pleasure." She bends to pat Darius's head. "And may God bless your little one. Exactly like you, he is looking."

They walk out the mall doors together, and just as they are about to part, Bhima turns around. "Bai. From my end, there is no more bitterness. I . . . I understand now why you behave the way you do. We—Maya and I—bear you no ill will. So, please, you also forgive yourself, bai."

She hears Sera's sharp intake of breath and fears that she has offended her. But then, the woman smiles. "You are a natural-born healer, Bhima. You always have been. I am lucky to have known you."

And then, with a little wave of her hand, Sera walks away, little Darius trotting beside her. And Bhima stands still, watching them, feeling like the luckiest and most unlucky woman in the world.

27

"Who was she?" Parvati asks when she returns to the stall, and when she answers, nods. "Hah. I thought so. I could tell from how stuck-up she looked that this was your Serabai."

"She's not stuck-up. Not at all," Bhima says reflexively before realizing that Parvati is being kind and showing her solidarity. She forces a smile. "She has her own problems, sister. Just like the rest of us."

Parvati snorts. "When you don't have to worry about where you will rest your head at night, other problems become easier."

Her words jolt Bhima out of the fog she's been in ever since she had said goodbye to Sera. "How are you feeling?" she asks sharply. "Still feeling the nausea?"

Parvati waves her away. "Didn't you see me eat like an ox? Can a sick woman eat like that?"

No, but a hungry woman can, Bhima thinks, and the thought is a burn to her skin. "You come to our house after you finish here tonight," she says. "Whatever food we eat, you share with us."

"No. I told you, I'm fine."

Bhima waits on a customer, who buys two cabbages and a pomegranate from her. Before leaving the woman says, "That recipe you gave for the saag aloo, the other day? My husband ate so much, he was fully fed-up. And he ate the leftovers for breakfast the next morning. Too good, yaar."

"Shukriya," Bhima says. "I can tell you how to prepare the cabbage, if you like."

The woman smiles. "Arre, you forgot. Already you've given the recipe. That's why only I'm buying the cabbage today. I'm preparing it tonight."

"You know what they say," Parvati says. "The way to a man's heart is through his stomach." There is something so lewd in the way she says it that the customer gives a startled laugh, exchanging a look with Bhima, who only rolls her eyes.

"Yes, yes. Well, bye-bye."

As soon as the woman leaves, Bhima faces Parvati again. "Nobody said you're not fine. I'm just inviting you to my home. If we are too lowly for you to accept, that's understandable."

Parvati narrows her eyes. "Don't talk rubbish." She plays with the lump on her throat as she thinks. "You don't need to feel sorry for me. This road that I'm on, I've chosen for myself. I prefer to be alone. I can move faster that way. No one to tie me down."

"Sister. All you do is go from the market to that . . . that place where you sleep. You are moving faster to go where, exactly?"

Parvati falls silent, and Bhima is sorry for her cruel words. Why is she hurting this old woman who has already been so hurt by the world? But before she can apologize, Parvati speaks over her. "What time I should come? When will you get home from your other job?"

Bhima smiles. "You come by seven. I will rush home as soon as I'm done." She tears a piece of paper from her notebook. "Here. I give you exact directions. You please take down."

As Parvati writes, she grumbles, "Why you still working the second job? You making enough money here, no, to do some aaram when you get home?"

"I like my bais," Bhima says simply. "They are both good to

me. Chitra baby, especially, she never treats me like a servant. And she is helping my Maya in her studies."

"What's the other's name?"

"Sunita."

Parvati nods. "And they are funny, correct?" she says knowingly.

Bhima shakes her head in confusion. "Funny?"

"One is a male?"

She understands immediately what Parvati is insinuating. It is no different from what Vimal had said to her on the first day she'd met Chitra. A strong protectiveness rises in her. "No one is a male," she hisses. "They are both women, like us. And they are kind to each other like no menfolk was ever kind to us."

To her surprise, Parvati nods. "Agree. I meant no insult. In my time, I've seen many like them. Some of the women in the Old Place were like that. It was the only comfort in their lives."

Bhima doesn't realize she's been holding her breath. Now, she exhales. "They suffer," she says. "This one neighbor called Sunitabai a—a very bad name." She stops, silenced by a thought. "Parvati. Do all human beings keep secrets from one another? Today you tell me about your life. And then, ten minutes later, I run into Serabai. And she—she is being killed by the secret she is keeping. And Chitra baby says her own father and mother don't know that she moved to Mumbai for Sunitabai. Why do we all walk around like this, hiding from one another?"

Parvati's thumb circles the lump in a fast motion as she ponders the question. "It isn't the words we speak that make us who we are. Or even the deeds we do. It is the secrets buried in our hearts." She looks sharply at Bhima. "People think that the ocean is made up of waves and things that float on top. But they forget—the ocean is also what lies at the bottom, all the broken things stuck in the sand. That, too, is the ocean."

"I don't follow," Bhima says, not understanding how they've gotten from Chitra to the ocean.

Parvati clicks her tongue impatiently. "It doesn't matter, sister. Too much thinking is bad for health. Now come on, let us sell a few more carrots and brinjals. This is who we are, not poets or philosophers."

When Chitra opens the door to let Bhima in, she can tell that the younger woman is working. It is not Chitra's paint-stained T-shirt that gives it away; it is that faraway look on the woman's face that Bhima has come to recognize. Also, the strained manner in which she speaks, as if doing anything other than painting is an effort.

"Hi," she now says. "I'm working in the bedroom. If possible, don't disturb. Okay?"

"You go do your painting, baby," Bhima says. "I will take care of everything." Chitra nods and without another word disappears.

Fifteen minutes later there is a yell, the slamming of the bedroom door, and then Chitra is in the kitchen. "It's no use. I can't paint today to save my life. Just one of those days, you know?" And Bhima nods, although she has no idea what she's agreeing to. She still doesn't understand how a grown woman, one as filled with life and energy as Chitra, can stay home day after day, doing nothing but painting pictures, as if she were five years old. And yet, every so often, Chitra talks about selling one of her pictures. Bhima imagines her squatting on a sidewalk selling her wares, like the hawkers at Flora Fountain sell their plastic soap dishes and combs.

"Why you always painting such sad-dark things, baby?" she now says, trying to be helpful. "You paint something pretty, na, like a parrot or a flower." For the past three weeks, Chitra has been painting the same picture, of a skinny beggar woman sheltering an infant. Who will buy such a picture? Bhima thinks. All you have to do is go down the street to see a hundred such unfortunate women. Why she needs to make a picture of them?

Chitra stares at Bhima as if she hasn't heard a word. Then, she takes the spoon out of Bhima's hands and sets it down, while also turning off the stove. Bhima yelps. "What you doing, Chitra baby? Rice needs to cook, na?"

"Come," Chitra says. She drags Bhima out of the kitchen and into the living room, where she pushes Bhima onto a chair and leans her forward until her hands rest on the coffee table. "Can you stay like this?" she says, arranging Bhima's hands. "Just a minute, I'll be right back with my notebook."

For the next two hours, she sketches Bhima's hands. Often, just as they are beginning to cramp, Chitra rearranges them. Spreads the fingers. Rests them flat. Has Bhima make a fist. Bhima feels a growing impatience. Is this why this crazy girl is in love with another woman? Because she is a little mad? As much as she loves Chitra, there is so much she doesn't understand. Who is going to cook their dinner if she's sitting here wasting both their time?

As if she's read her mind, Chitra laughs. "Bhima, relax, yaar. I'll get you out of here on time. Are your hands hurting? You need a break?"

"Baby. I'm still having to cook and clean. So if you're done with this, I need to start on the housework."

"Don't worry about the cooking. Su's at a work party tonight, so it's just me. I'll eat leftovers." She thinks for a moment, then asks, "Or, do you want to eat with me tonight? We can go get Maya?"

She is no longer taken aback by Chitra's impulsiveness. "Forgive me, Chitra baby," she says. "I am actually having a guest of my own tonight. I will need to go home and cook."

"Oh? Who?"

"The woman who helps me in my business. Parvati is her good name." Bhima hesitates, unsure of how much more to say. "She is having no relations of her own. And she was sick today. So I ask her to come eat with us tonight."

"That's great. Can I come too?"

Bhima gives an embarrassed laugh and covers her mouth at the outrageousness of the request. "Baby. My house is at Gharib slum colony. How can someone like you come?"

Chitra gives her a puzzled look. "What do you mean?"

"My house is not fit for you." Bhima's face burns with shame. "We . . . we are not even having . . . it is one room, only. And no AC."

Chitra is quiet for a moment. Then she says, "If you don't mind having me, Bhima, I'd love to see where you live."

Bhima feels a moment's dread at the thought of walking down the narrow, filthy alley with Chitra. She sees the murky water in the open drains, hears the buzz of the flies and mosquitoes, pictures the openly curious stares that will follow them home. But then, another picture comes into her head—the four of them sitting perched on the two mattresses, eating together in companionable silence. Or better yet, she making sure Parvati gets enough to eat, while Chitra talks to Maya about schoolwork and other important things with which she cannot help her grandchild. They are lonely, she and Maya, in that little dimly lit hut. Night after night, they follow the same routine—cooking, a little conversation while eating, and then Maya opening her books while Bhima sweeps the little room and gets ready for bed. Surely it will be good to have this bright-eyed girl in their home. "If you are sure?" she asks, and Chitra squeals. "Let me go change," she says. "We'll ride together."

In the car, Bhima continues to fret. "Where are we going to leave your car?" she says. "Those slum children are animals—they will scratch the paint or steal your wipers. Just out of spite."

But Chitra waves off her concerns. "Don't worry so much. That can happen anywhere in the city." She thinks for a moment. "You know the Marriott? Big hotel not too far from your area? I'll valet park. We can walk it up from there."

"Good idea." But now something else troubles Bhima. There are only two metal plates at home and no forks and spoons because she and Maya eat with their hands. And then the idea comes to her, and it is as if a weight has dropped off her shoulders: They will order food from Mughal Kitchen, the Grade 1 restaurant outside the basti. She will pay for all of it. That way, she doesn't have to rush to cook. And best of all, she will request extra plates and a fork and spoon for Chitra from the restaurant. She wonders if Parvati will actually show up and hopes that she will not be upset to see another guest.

Even though Chitra has slipped into a nondescript shalwar kameez outfit, her effect on the slum dwellers is electric. Everything about her—the cut of her clothes, the way her hair is styled, the elegance of her sandals, the gingerly way she walks through the basti—marks her as an outsider. As they walk, a crowd of children begin to follow them, pushing and shoving each other for a better look at this stranger in their midst. Chitra carries on a steady, friendly conversation with the urchins, but Bhima's face is tight with embarrassment. And that embarrassment turns to fury at the sight of one of the louts openly staring at them and licking his lips. Looking at Chitra, the man rubs his crotch suggestively. A scarlet-faced Bhima turns toward Chitra, wanting her to avert her eyes from such indecency, but Chitra looks coolly at the man and stares directly at his hand. At first, the man seems thrilled at her response, but when Chitra keeps staring impassively at him, the man mutters an obscenity and moves away. Chitra nods to herself, a slight movement that only Bhima catches. She feels a new sense of respect for the younger woman. How she has crushed him, like an insect under the foot.

The first thing Bhima notices when they arrive at her home is that the front door is open. It takes her a second to recognize the strange sound that wafts her way. It is laughter. Parvati is saying something in her low, guttural voice, and Maya is laughing. Bhima bends her head and enters first. "Ah, Ma-ma," Maya says guiltily, stopping midlaugh. "We were just chitchatting."

Bhima smiles at Parvati. "Welcome, sister." She turns toward the door. "We are having another guest, also. Please, come in."

"Chitra. Oh my God, I'm so happy to see you." Maya scrambles to her feet and gives her a hug. Bhima is shocked by this easy familiarity, is about to scold her granddaughter for forgetting her place, when she sees Chitra returning the hug. "I came to see you," she says.

"Chitra baby, this here is Parvati."

"Namaste-ji," Chitra says.

"Hello," Parvati replies in English.

Bhima looks around. "Let me go borrow a chair for you, baby," she says, but before she can move, Chitra plops herself down on Maya's mattress. "Don't bother. I'm fine right here."

Maya lets out a laugh, and hearing it, Bhima feels a tug at her heart that's equal parts joy and regret. How happy it makes Maya to see a face other than her old grandmother's. She moves toward the door and steps out. "Chalo, shoo," she yells at the children still gathered outside. "This is not a cinema hall for you to gawk. Jao, go home."

"Shall we start supper, Ma-ma?" Maya asks when she comes in and shuts the door behind her.

Bhima crooks her finger at her. "Come here." She moves to a corner, unties the knot of her sari, and hands the cash to Maya. "Go to Mughal Kitchen," she whispers. "You pick whatever dishes you think they will like. Make sure they give extra plates and forks. Then come straight home, understand?"

"What guss-puss are you two doing, ji?" Parvati calls.

"Bhima." Chitra gets to her feet. "What are you doing?" She looks at the money in Maya's hands. "If you are not cooking, this has to be my treat. I was the one who invited myself, remember?"

"Chitra baby. You please make yourself comfortable. You are our guest tonight."

"Yes, but—"

"Please, baby. It is the first time you have honored us. Do not insult us."

"Arre, jaane do. Leave it be," Parvati says, startling all of them. "During all this fightum-fighting over who will pay, we could've killed and skinned three chickens."

Maya giggles, Chitra grins, and Bhima gives a sigh of relief. "Go beta," she says.

"Okay. Like that only, I will go and come," Maya says.

"And be careful. And keep your eyes down. Don't look at anyone, left or right."

Maya sighs theatrically. "Yes, yes, Ma-ma." She pulls a face and looks at Chitra. "Same lecture every day."

"Arre, besharam." Bhima raises her hand in mock anger. But she is smiling.

"Shall I go with you?" Chitra offers, but Bhima shakes her head no. "You relax, baby. Just now only you have come."

"Nice girl," Parvati says after Maya leaves. "Found a boy for her, yet?"

"What?" Chitra says. "She's just a kid. She's not even done with college."

Parvati acts like she hasn't heard. "What about that Rajeev's son? He stopped by the market the other evening. Polite, handsome boy."

Chitra looks from one of them to the other. "You wouldn't do that, would you, Bhima? Marry Maya off?"

Bhima smiles at the distress she hears in Chitra's voice. "One thing you should know about this one here," she says as she pokes at Parvati with her toes, "is she is a first-class trouble master. Best to let everything go in one ear and out the other."

"Arre, wah," Parvati says. "What a thing to say."

Chitra grins. "How do you two know each other? Are you childhood friends or what?"

Parvati lets out a loud snort. "Arre, beti, until two years ago, this one here wouldn't even acknowledge my existence. Mrs. Nose-in-the-Air, I used to call her."

"Meaning?"

"Meaning, even now she doesn't like me." The laughter in Parvati's voice removes the edge from her words. "It's just her need that makes her keep me around."

Bhima rolls her eyes. "Bewakoof," she says to no one in particular. "Yogurt-for-brains."

Parvati chuckles. Then she says, "And where is your missus tonight?"

Chitra looks taken aback. "My missus?"

"Hah. Bhima says you have a missus."

"Parvati. Chup. Keep your trap shut," Bhima scolds. She turns to face Chitra. "Please don't take offense, baby. I told you, this woman here is pagal."

Chitra licks her lips nervously, then looks Parvati dead in the eye. "She will be happy to know you inquired about her. She is at a business dinner. Otherwise, you could have called her my missus to her face."

Parvati raises an eyebrow appreciatively. "This one here is a firecracker," she says to Bhima.

"Any other personal questions you want to ask?" Chitra says.

Parvati has the grace to look embarrassed. "I am having no quarrel with you and your type."

"Good. Because I have no quarrel with your type, either."

It is an innocent remark, a simple parry and thrust, but Parvati gasps and swings around. "What did you tell her about me?" she asks Bhima, who is dumbfounded by the direction the conversation has taken.

"Nothing. I have said nothing."

"Parvatiji," Chitra says. "Relax, yaar. The only thing I know about you is that you were sick earlier today. I was just joking back with you."

Parvati exhales slowly. "Theek hai," she says. "I'm sorry."

"No, *I'm* sorry. That you were sick," Chitra says smoothly. "How are you feeling now?"

"A little tired." Parvati fakes a yawn. "I should be making my way home, sister."

Bhima is about to protest when Maya walks in, carrying bags of food. "I am so hungry," she says loudly, and they all chuckle as the atmosphere in the room rights itself.

Bhima gasps inwardly at the amount of food the girl has purchased. "Are others joining us for dinner?" Chitra says drily, and Maya shakes her head. "Just us," she says happily. "Just us."

All four of them sit on their haunches on the edge of the mattress and eat with their plates on the floor. Despite the cutlery Maya has brought, Chitra eats with her hands like the rest of them, though Bhima can tell she is inexperienced at doing so. "I like your floor tile, Bhima," Chitra says after a few moments. "Is it new?"

Bhima glances at Maya, who is choking with pride. "Thank

you," the girl says. "We buy it from one of our neighbors. He is working for a contractor."

Despite the solitary overhead light in the hut, Maya now reaches to light one of the two oil lamps. "I use this to read after Ma-ma goes to sleep," she tells Chitra.

"You study under the light of the oil lamp?"

Maya nods, and Chitra smiles ruefully. "And yet you're first in your class. Good thing your classmates don't know. Otherwise, they'd all study under oil lamps."

Bhima can see Maya flush at the compliment. She feels Parvati's eyes on the girl, also. "Not just smart but beautiful, too," the old woman says, and now Maya can't take it anymore. "Stoppit, all of you," she says, shaking her body like a wet dog, as if to cast off their caresses.

The others laugh. "I like being here," Chitra says suddenly. "It feels—safe."

Bhima gives a start of surprise. In all her years of living in the basti, she has never thought of it as safe. But as she looks at the four of them in this room, the light of the lamps casting their shadows on the walls, she thinks she knows what Chitra means.

Out of the corner of her eye, she sees Parvati reaching for more of the biryani and feels a deep satisfaction. How is it possible to have this much feeling for someone who is not a relation? As she watches her, Parvati is gripped by one of those painful spasms that seem to be emitting from her lower back more and more frequently. When she sees that the spasm has passed, she whispers, "Everything all right, sister?"

"Of course."

Soon after they finish dinner and wash up, Parvati rises. "Accha, I will take my leave," she says. "It is getting late."

"I'll drop you home," Chitra says immediately. "Where do you live?"

Parvati freezes. "Nearby, only," she mutters vaguely.

"Good. My car is not too far away. No need for you to walk alone at night."

Bhima exchanges a look with Parvati. "You don't have to trouble her to take you to your door," she says. "Just have her drop you off at the end of your street."

Parvati stares back at Bhima, then gives in. "As you wish."

Chitra leans in to hug Bhima, who stiffens by habit and then offers a lukewarm hug back. "Thanks for a wonderful evening," the girl says. "Ready?" she asks Parvati, then takes her by the elbow and the old woman throws Bhima a dumbfounded look before she allows herself to be led out of the house and toward the main road.

When it is just the two of them again, the little room feels empty, still holding the ghosts of their laughter. As Bhima readies for bed, she hears Maya say, "After I become a lawyer and get a job, we will throw such parties every week."

"What were you and Chitra baby whispering nonstop in the corner?"

Maya shakes her head. "Just girl talk, Ma-ma. You wouldn't understand." And she is so earnest that Bhima chokes back her laughter.

"Chalo. I'm off to bed," she says. She turns over her pillow and something falls out—three bills of a hundred rupees each. Three hundred rupees. Chitra baby has left the money to pay for everybody's dinner. Even as she is grateful for the girl's generosity, Bhima feels a thread of disappointment undercut her gratitude. Wasn't it just earlier today that Serabai had tried to force money on her? She shakes her head. She has begun to think of herself as a successful businesswoman. But truly rich women, like Serabai and Chitra, still see her as someone who needs their help.

28

Three weeks later she is grateful for the extra three hundred rupees. It will help pay for Parvati's medicines at the government hospital.

It is not the same hospital that had treated Gopal after his industrial accident, and for this Bhima is grateful. After all these years, the memory of that episode—the indifference of the nurses, the callousness of the doctors, her own clammy fear upon finding a delirious Gopal drenched in sweat and three fingers gone, lying on sheets stained with blood and pus—still burns like acid.

Bhima sits on the hard, wooden bench beside Parvati, who had fainted this morning during a conversation with a customer, simply dropped like a stone, hitting her head on the steps leading to Vishnu's shop. Bhima, who was less than a foot away from her, had been unable to prevent the fall. She had cradled the old woman's head in her lap, willing Parvati to open her eyes, even while fighting the terror that she was dead. After a few awful minutes, Parvati had finally come to, dazed and disoriented at first but then looking around with growing awareness. She had insisted she was fine, that she had been affected by sunstroke, but Bhima had had enough. She had called Rajeev over and asked him to take over because she was taking Parvati to the government hospital.

Waiting for Parvati to be seen by a doctor, Bhima feels as if she's fighting on two fronts—one, with the ghosts of the past: the nurse who had told her that Gopal had an infection, the harried doctor who had withheld the antibiotics, until Serabai's late husband, Feroz, had bullied the doctor into submission—and two, with the woman who fumes and grumbles beside her. "Whole day we are wasting," Parvati says. "As if we are having no kaam-dhandha. Sitting here like nawabs while our produce rots in the sun."

"Rajeev is there. He will manage."

Parvati hoots in derision. "That limp piece of lettuce? For all we know, he's giving money to the customers instead of taking."

Bhima's face is tight with anxiety and anger. "Why you must fight me on everything? Twice in one month something bad has happened to you, hai na?"

"Sister, I'm an old woman. A little bit of trouble here and there is to be expected, no?"

Bhima looks her squarely in the eye. "And this pain you are having nonstop in your back? That is also a little problem, only? All day long you sit rubbing it."

"Pshaw. It's nothing. Whatever this lump is below my face, it's now on my back. Years ago, the doctor tell me it's nothing."

"Years ago, when?"

Parvati thinks. "Before I was married. Maybe when I was forty?" She falls silent, shocked at her own words. "Hai Ram. How can that be? So long ago. But I still remember the doctor's face?"

"You see?" Bhima says. "Now just sit here chup-chap until they call us."

The doctor is a short, bearded man with an impatient manner. He makes Parvati lie down so he can examine her, but when he asks her to lie on her back, she cannot. He lowers her sari to investigate why, and Bhima gasps when she sees it—a fat, dark, ugly mass. The doctor looks up to meet her eyes. He frowns, shakes his head. "We need to aspirate this," he says. "I am admitting you tonight."

"No need," Parvati says immediately.

The doctor gnashes his teeth. "Okay, I'm telling you straight—don't waste my time. Okay? A hundred more patients are outside waiting to see me. If you come to hospital, you must follow what I say. Understand? I have no time for this nonsense. Now, yes or no?"

"Yes." Bhima glares at Parvati, defying her to contradict her. "Please, doctor sahib. Whatever you can do to make her well."

"Okay. No drama." He scribbles on his notepad and tears off the sheet. "Here. You hand this at the admissions window. But remember, they will ask for a cash deposit before they will admit her."

"Tear it up," Parvati grumbles as they walk down the hallway. "Tear it up and let's go back to our work. I'm telling you sister, you throw me in here, these wolves will return my dead body to you."

Bhima remembers the funeral pyres, first Raju's and then Pooja's. The hospital in Delhi had taken in her daughter and her son-in-law and returned their ashes. Maybe Parvati is right. Why should they court death if there is no need?

"One night only," she says without conviction. "Let's do this test he wants to do. Then we ask for some medicine and treatment as outpatient. Accha?"

Parvati smiles a strange, distant smile. "Whatever you wish, sister."

They have to wait for seven hours before a bed is available. Everybody at this hospital seems to move slowly, as if they are underwater. The slightest request is taken as an affront, and Bhima wonders if they are being punished because of Parvati's caustic queries. But then she looks around and sees that the other patients are treated with the same indifference.

As the day goes on, Parvati gets more and more quiet. When a nurse finally approaches and tells them they will be admitted in fifteen minutes, the old woman automatically clenches Bhima's hand. She's scared, Bhima thinks with wonder. This woman who had stood stone-faced in the middle of a riot is scared at the thought of spending the night in the hospital. "I'll stay with you," she finds herself saying.

"Don't be stupid. What about Maya?"

"I will make arrangements." She pauses, half hoping that Parvati will put up a fight, but the woman simply stares at her feet. Bhima gets up with a sigh and calls Chitra baby. Before she can even frame her request, Chitra has offered to go pick up Maya and have her spend the night at her house. In fact, she will leave immediately and let Maya know herself. "I am so indebted to you, baby," Bhima begins, but Chitra cuts her off. "Please. Maya is like my own niece."

Bhima cradles the receiver of the phone after she hangs up. How nonchalantly Chitra had referred to Maya as her niece. Could this be a sign that finally, after decades of drought, their luck may be turning? Her heart stops at another thought: If Amit has children of his own, then Maya herself is an aunt. More than anything, this is what rankles her—that through no fault of the girl's, Maya is alone in the world. It is bad enough that the poor child is an orphan. But Maya has also missed out on the love of her family because of her grandmother's recklessness. If only she had allowed Gopal to live out his days in a state of drunkenness, accepting that this was the price she would pay for signing that fatal piece of paper. If only she had not followed him to the bootlegger's and embarrassed him in public. She would still have a husband. She would still have her son. And Maya would've had a family beyond her desiccated, humorless grandmother.

No wonder Maya was forever asking her to smile. How hard it must be for a young girl to spend her evenings with a woman with a face as sour as a guava.

When Parvati lifts her face to her, Bhima sees the fear lurking in those eyes and knows that she has made the right decision to stay the night. Unable to say anything that will chase that fear away, she takes Parvati's hand in hers and holds it there, until the nurse comes back for them.

This hospital's general ward is different from the AIDS ward where Pooja had died. But some things are painfully familiar—the sharp smell of the pesticide they spray to keep the mosquitoes away; the quiet moans and rustlings of the other patients; the thump of the bare-footed ward boys as they race from bed to bed, clearing bedpans.

"Lost in your thoughts, sister?" Parvati inquires, those milky eyes still sharp, missing nothing.

Bhima shakes her head. "Just remembering my daughter. She was in the AIDS ward. In Delhi, not here. But it, too, was a big, open room like this one."

"Did your husband leave before or after her death?" Parvati's voice is gentle.

"Before. I raised her, married her off, all on my own." Bhima hears her voice, thick with the tears she is trying not to shed.

"It sounds like you have fulfilled your obligations to everyone, sister. There will be no more births for you to take after this one. You have earned eternal rest."

"I wish to rest my bones *now,*" Bhima says. "Not after I'm dead." Her eyes widen at her own insolence. "Listen to me. God forgive me, I am sounding like you."

Parvati lets out a cackle. "Principal always used to say I was a bad influence on the other girls."

"Principal? At school?"

"At the Old Place. The only school I ever go to. She was the madam there. She owned all of us."

"Why do you call her Principal?"

Parvati shrugs. "Why not? She gave us the best education—showed us how the world really works. What could a school teach me that was more important?"

Bhima feels an unbearable heaviness in her heart. "Do you think the world is really such a dark place?" she whispers.

Parvati's lips curl downward. "This is what I believe: There is only one true evil. And it is being poor. With money, a sinner can be worshipped as a saint. A murderer can be elected chief minister. A rapist can become a respectable family man. And the owner of a brothel can be a Principal. Understand?"

"Did you hate her?"

"Hate her? I cried like a baby when I left her. She was the only person in my life who never lied to me. My own father sold me like a bag of onions. My husband lied to me when he said he wanted a wife when all he was wanting was a servant he didn't have to pay. All the men who crawl over my body and say 'I love you'? They wouldn't have recognized me if I passed them in the market. But Principal say, 'This is what you're worth.' And when Rajesh want to marry me, she say, 'Your market is down because of that thing defacing you. Plus you're getting old.' She was the only one who ever told me the truth."

Parvati's voice is low, her tone matter-of-fact, but Bhima feels each of the older woman's words as a scratch to her face. How little she knows of the world in which Parvati has lived. She remembers how her own father used to smile fondly upon her no matter what she did, how doggedly Gopal had wooed her after the first time he'd set eyes on her, how tenderly he had held her on their wedding night, and all the nights after. Her own life seems so rich compared to Parvati's. "Did you—have you ever really loved a man?" she asks timidly.

Parvati hesitates for a fraction of a second before shaking her head. "I can't believe in something that doesn't exist."

"How you can say this?" Bhima says. "People love each other, no?"

Parvati raises her hand to cut her off. "It's not love. It's need. People just mix up the two."

Bhima opens her mouth to protest, but again, Parvati stops her. "A new mother thinks her baby loves her." She shrugs. "But he just needs her milk. A husband thinks his wife loves him. But she just needs his money. And we all know what the menfolk need. Principal teach me this, Bhima."

How can she win against this clever, sharp, bitter woman? Bhima wonders. How to prove to her she is wrong, that her brain is twisted, too cynical? Bhima feels like weeping; there is a darkness in Parvati that terrifies her. In her own basti, there is a woman with no legs. There is a child who is blind. Another woman with burns all over her body. But in the basti, one thing sizzles from hovel to hovel, much like the illegal, overhead electric wires that some of the residents have connected to their homes. It is hope. Even in the depth of their despair, hope runs like electricity throughout the basti. It is what makes the woman with no legs weave wicker baskets that she sells to a fancy shop. What makes the blind boy's mother spend her days picking rags to pay his school fees. What makes the burn victim look for a good match for her daughter.

And then it comes to her, the answer, and she sits up a little straighter. "You don't believe in love?" she says loudly. "You should."

Parvati waves her away. "Why should I?"

"Why?" Bhima taps her own chest with her index finger. "Because I'm sitting here with you in this wretched hospital. Because I'm *here*."

29

"Good," Parvati says, shaking her head vigorously. "God is great."

The doctor looks at her curiously. "Did you not follow what I said? I said it is cancer. For sure."

"I heard, doctor sahib," Parvati says, a gleam in her eyes. "I will distribute sweets in my neighborhood this evening."

The man pulls at a hair on his chin as he considers her. "If you had the money, we could've done a brain scan. Looks like the cancer is affecting your brain."

Parvati smiles broadly. "I've spent the last twenty years praying for my death, ji," she says. "Finally I have the good news. How soon before I pop off?"

At last he seems to understand, and a melancholy look comes across his face. The next second, it is replaced by fury. "I see. Then what for are you wasting my time? Wasting government money on this-and-that test?"

Parvati looks chastened. "What to do, sahib? My friend dragged me here, only." Her face collapses. "Also, this thing growing on my backside pains me a lot. If you have some medicine for that, I will be grateful."

For a moment he looks as if he's about to refuse, but then he nods. "I can give some tablets," he says. "But they will make you sleepy and maybe give you nausea. You understand?" He reaches for his writing pad and then rises.

"Will it—will the pain be bad? At the end?"

He looks at her, and this time, his eyes are filled with pity. "It will be unbearable." His face softens. "Get someone to bring you some daru when the time comes. And stay drunk."

"How much longer?"

He shrugs. "Until God is ready for you."

She manages a half smile. "In which case it may be a long time."

But the doctor doesn't smile back. "No, it won't. Your wish will be granted sooner than you think."

It is only after she is out of the gates that her knees buckle and she grips the low wall of the hospital for support. She stands there hyperventilating, attempts to reassure herself she is not upset, that she has known for some time that this new lump was vicious, different from the old, benign one. She tries hard to capture the nonchalance she had exhibited in the doctor's office, to relish the memory of his confusion at her reaction. But her brain is racing, zigzagging, thinking too many thoughts at one time, and she is unable to hold on to that memory. She takes a few deep breaths, but this only serves to make her aware of how hard her heart beats against her chest.

If she fears death at all, it is only because it will mean rejoining the people she despises. Whereas all the people she is fond of—Bhima, Maya, Rajeev, and even that ungrateful nephew of hers, Praful—are still here, living. Parvati realizes that she has been lying to herself. She doesn't really want to die. For the first time, there is something worth living for—that humble stall in the marketplace where she is an indispensable part of Bhima's business. The hand-to-mouth existence, the years spent selling bruised cauliflowers are now thankfully behind her, and every day, there is some surplus money—to take the bus instead of walking everywhere, to buy some bread and butter to eat in her room when she feels like it, to once in a while afford a Pepsi or a Limca on a hot day.

She hears a sob and looks around, bewildered, before realizing that it has come from her. Then, there is another, a helpless sound that escapes from her and lingers in the air. She smacks herself, embarrassed by her own vulgarity. How selfish, how unseemly it is for a woman who is at least fifty and a score years old to cry about dying. What claim does she have to even one more cup of water, one more morsel of food, one more gulp of air, in a city where babies die moments after birth, where children walk around with bellies bloated from hunger? Hasn't she lived enough? Hasn't luck shined upon her of late, first with the extra money that Bhima has sent her way, and now, with something even more precious? What had Bhima said to her the other night in the hospital? *Because I'm here.* That is how she'd said it, and she had silenced Parvati with three words, slayed her rubbish talk about love being a fairy tale. Ever since that night, Bhima has insisted that she go to her home and eat dinner with them. And truth to tell, more than the home-cooked food, she has begun to enjoy the simple pleasure of sharing a meal with two others. Of hearing Maya tell what she has learned at college that day. Of watching Bhima's face shine with pride as Maya says the big-big words her grandmother has never heard. Watching those two, Parvati's mind hiccups to the past, the past that she had believed could never be resurrected. She remembers her life as a little girl, when her mother was more than a cough and a pile of bones, when her father was her protector and not her merchant. Once, she, too, had had a family—poor, yes, uneducated, yes, but loving. Close-knit. Huddled together in their little house, bearing life's many beatings together. Why hadn't her father given her the choice? Between being sold and starving together, she knows what she would've chosen. Every night, she scoops a ball of rice and daal in her hand and listens to Bhima and Maya's banter and realizes how terribly alone she has been these past several years.

Tell the truth, she says to herself as she begins to walk back to the marketplace. She was lonely even while Rajesh was alive, wasn't she? Maybe not the last two years of his life, when her days were a blur of chores—sponge-bathing him in the mornings, feeding him, turning him on his side several times a night, cleaning the bedpan, washing the soiled sheets. Strange, but she was less alone after he stopped speaking. The true, piercing loneliness had begun soon after his son's visit. It was as if when Rahul left that day, he took with him his father's affection for his new wife. Rajesh had begun to view her differently after that visit, as if he blamed her for his estrangement from his son. And as time went by, he compared her more and more to his dead wife and found her lacking in every area but one. Usha kept a clean house. Usha knew how to iron his pants just so. Usha knew just how he liked his Horlicks every morning. It took all of Parvati's self-control to not tell the man that these comparisons mattered not one bit to her, because she never saw herself in competition with a dead woman.

During the day, Rajesh would spend hours in front of the television set while she sat in the kitchen or in the bedroom, trying to sew a button on his shirt or iron his clothes. This was something nobody had ever told her about being a housewife—it was boring. It dawned on her slowly—she had committed to a life with an uninteresting, older man. A man who, in retirement, had no hobbies or interests, whose idea of a good day was to sleep in until noon instead of ten a.m.

The first time he'd struck her was after they'd been married about a year. One of his old colleagues was being transferred, and they had been invited to his going-away party at a restaurant. Rajesh bought her a red sari for the occasion and even presented her with a gold necklace that had belonged to Usha. It was one of the few pieces of jewelry that his daughter-in-law had not claimed. He was lighting a cigarette when Parvati stepped out of the bedroom and he stopped, his eyes widening. "Wah," he breathed. "Those men will not be able to keep their eyes off you." She smiled, thankful that her husband was not repulsed by the deformity that everybody else noticed immediately.

It was a humid day, and Rajesh hailed a cab to the restaurant, to ensure that they wouldn't arrive drenched in sweat. "Restaurant is first-class," he told her. "Totally AC."

"How can they afford such an expensive place?"

He winked. "This is in my old precinct," he said. "Best for the owner to remain in the good graces of the police, no?"

At the restaurant, they are escorted to a private party room. The first thing Parvati notices is that there are no other women present. "Nobody else brought their wives?" she whispers, but Rajesh is distracted. "Arre, Rajesh, how are you, yaar? Enjoying your retirement?" someone says, while someone else thrusts a glass of Scotch into his hands. After a moment of backslapping and shaking hands, Rajesh reaches for her. "Friends," he says grandly. "Let me introduce my missus."

"Your missus?" someone yells. "I thought this was your daughter."

"No, yaar," someone else says. "That's his granddaughter."

Rajesh grins, unconsciously squeezing Parvati's hand tighter. She looks down at the floor, grateful for the dim light in the room, which perhaps has kept them from noticing the growth under her chin. One of the older men comes up to them and smiles at her in an avuncular fashion. "Ignore these idiots, child," he says. "Would you like a soft drink? Coca-Cola? Pepsi?"

"Pepsi is fine," she says, although she would've liked a cold beer. She keeps her eyes downcast, enjoying playing this role of demure housewife. She turns to her husband. "Jao, ji," she says. "Go enjoy your old friends."

"And leave you to these vultures?" Rajesh says with a guffaw. "Do I look like I'm mad?" Despite his joviality, she hears the insecurity in his voice, and this makes her squeeze his hand back.

There is a commotion at the door, and Parvati turns her head to see a tall, well-dressed man with salt-and-pepper hair. A murmur goes through the room, and there is a palpable, electric shift in the atmosphere. Several people rush up to greet the newcomer, who towers over most of them. He greets a few of them and ignores the others as he walks toward the bar. Even in middle age, there is a coiled strength in the way he moves that reminds Parvati of a panther in the jungle. And as if he's sensed her presence in the room, he suddenly notices her, stops midstride for just a second, smiles as their eyes meet, and then resumes walking. It happens so quickly that she is unsure if anyone else has noticed. She feels a tug of recognition, but before she can dig into her memory bank, Rajesh speaks, a breathless quality in his voice. "Kamal hai," he said. "It's unbelievable. That's chief of police Verma. Hard to believe such an important man would attend this party." He tugs at her hand. "Come. Let us go pay our respects."

"You go, ji," Parvati says, suddenly queasy. "This is between you menfolk. I'm okay standing here."

She watches as Rajesh elbows his way through the throng of men currying favor with Verma, and there is something so pathetic and needy about her retired husband still angling for an audience with his former boss that her eyes sting with tears. She sees Verma bend his head down to hear something Rajesh says, then follow her husband's finger, which is pointing to where she is standing. Verma slaps Rajesh heartily on the back, and then, to Parvati's mortification, makes his way through the crowd toward her. "Namaste-ji," he says to her in a loud, deep voice, bowing his head in a show of deference that somehow makes her feel as if he's mocking her. "I had to come say hello to the only member of the fair sex present at our humble party. May I ask your good name?"

"Parvati," she says shortly, and now, an unmistakable look of recognition crosses Verma's face.

"Ah, I thought so," he murmurs.

"Pardon?" Rajesh says, confused.

Verma puts his arm around the man. "Arre, yaar, isn't your missus named after the goddess of devotion? And fertility? And . . . love?" This time, his insolence is unmistakable, although Parvati is unsure of whether he's mocking her or her husband. "The name obviously suits your . . ." he lingers for a beat, "wife."

"Sir, I'm not understanding . . ."

"Jaane do, jaane do. Forget it." Verma flicks his wrist, a big, benevolent smile on his face, as if he is forgiving Rajesh for some insult. He looks at one of his acolytes. "Bloody hell, is this a party or a funeral? What must a man do to get a double peg of Scotch?"

"Right away, sir," the man says, scuttling away.

Verma looks down at Parvati, a sad smile on his face. "Sorry to leave your delightful company, bhabhi," he says. "But kya karu? Duty calls." And with a wink, he heads toward the buffet table.

They wait until he is a safe distance away and then Rajesh hisses, "What was he saying to you?"

"You were next to me the whole time. You heard what I heard."

"But why did he talk to you like this? In so familiar a manner?"

Parvati tamps down the queasiness in her belly. "Why you asking me? These are your friends. I would've been happy alone at home."

Rajesh shakes his head. "Everybody always says he's a strange man. But until today, I hadn't seen that myself."

As soon as Rajesh says the word *strange*, a pin drops, and Parvati remembers. Of course. This is the same man who used to come to the Old Place fifteen years ago. She remembers him now—his reputation for sadism, how the girls he called upon feared him, how their faces used to twist when they talked about his proclivities. Had she ever bedded him? She must have, given how easily he had recognized her, even though he was not one of her regulars. Principal must have protected her from him. There were a few customers whose desires were so dark, who thought so little of the girls they abused, their perversions used to shake up even Principal. Parvati can see him now: striding down the wraparound balcony in a dark safari suit, hair parted differently than today, sunglasses masking whatever perversity lay in those eyes, lips darkened by the Dunhills he smoked continually.

In order to cover up her apprehension, she excuses herself and goes to the bathroom, lingering for as long as she can. Please let the man be gone by the time I go back, she prays. Almost as soon as she rejoins the party, a waiter comes up to her and says, "Madam, please to go to the buffet line." She nods but doesn't move, waiting for her husband. A few moments later, Rajesh heads toward her, and one look tells her that he is drunk. "Control yourself, ji," she scolds softly. "Just because the daru is free . . ."

"The daru may be free. But nothing else in this life is," he replies. She stares at him puzzled, confused by the unmistakable hostility in his voice.

"What?" she begins, but is cut off by the noise on the other side of the room. Her stomach muscles tense as a familiar voice calls out, "Bhabhiji. Please, you inaugurate the buffet line. I will not allow any of these pigs to eat until you do."

"Wah. Our police chief is an expert at line maroing, yaar," someone snickers within their earshot, and she feels Rajesh tense beside her.

"Stop drawing attention," Rajesh whispers. "Go give the man what he wants."

"You come with me," she says, taking his hand and dragging him across the room.

But Rajesh gets pulled to the back of the line by Verma's entourage, so that the other inspectors get to witness the spectacle of the chief insisting that Parvati go ahead of him, then rubbing her shoulders as she desultorily fills her plate. He puts an extra pakora on her plate, then familiarly takes a bite out of it before putting it back. The first time he lightly touches her bare waist, she ignores him, but the second time, she turns around and fixes him a look. He smiles, but his eyes are hollow, contemptuous, and she feels a stab of fear. This is a man who enjoys humiliating others, but why he has targeted her, she does not know. "Come bhabhiji," he says to her in that same, humble voice, and the fact that he calls her sister-in-law grates on her nerves. "Come sit at our table. Your husband will join us in a few moments." And she has no choice but to follow.

"How is Principal?" he whispers to her as he makes a show of pulling out a chair for her. "You must be missing the action of the old days, no?"

Parvati flushes, unsure of how to respond. She looks around for Rajesh, but he is far away, in the company of Verma's men, who have clearly been given orders to detain him.

"Arre, sister, why this false modesty? We both know what you are, right?"

"I am nothing that you are not."

The handsome face darkens. "Meaning what?"

"Meaning that I look around this room and I am not seeing a single saint." She fixes her eyes on him. "All I see is a roomful of fallen men."

Verma's nostrils flare with anger and his hand curls around

the fork. Parvati closes her eyes, bracing herself for violence. Instead, he bursts into laughter. "This is not a woman," he says loudly, to no one in particular. "This is a firecracker. A fatakra. Pfooom." He lowers his voice again. "You can thank God for this lump of shit growing under your face, sweetheart. Otherwise, I would've made you forget your husband's name tonight."

"In which case, I pray to God to give me two more of these," she says.

A muscle twitches in his jaw as he absorbs the insult. He stares at her for a long moment, until his eyes lose their smolder and go flat. He turns around abruptly, yells, "Ae. Rajesh. Come look after your bride." Then he strides to the bar, where someone immediately hands him a Scotch. And Parvati feels like a fish that has been yanked out of the water and then released again.

During the trip home, she tries to reason with herself that Rajesh is not responsible for her humiliation. She has forgiven her husband for his timid passivity by the time they reach their apartment, but she has been so absorbed in her own thoughts that she has not noticed that Rajesh is furious. At *her*. And when she realizes this, all her good intentions go out the window. "You left me alone with that vile man," she cries. "Bas, a few glasses of free liquor and you would've . . ."

"Woman. I'm trying to watch TV. Can't you see? Shut your mouth."

"You talk to me like this? With such disrespect, you dare to . . . ?"

He rises heavily from the sofa, grunts his way toward her. "You are a common whore, Parvati. I knows it, you knows it, everybody at the party knew it. They were all laughing at me. My mother always used to say, why pay for the cow when you can get the milk for free? Tonight, the whole world laughed at the stupid man who bought the used cow."

She stares at him, her lower lip quivering, aware of the vileness that they have let into their little flat, like a smell that has followed them in. "If this is what you believe . . ."

"What I believe?" he bellows. "Tell the truth. Have you fucked every single man who was at that party? How did you even know that dog Verma? I offer you respectability, a decent life, but there you were, all flirty-flirty with him." He spits. "Today I learn my lesson—once a whore, always a whore."

She takes a step forward to slap his face, but he grabs her blouse near its neckline, rips it down, and then shoves her back. She stumbles and falls onto the sofa and he picks her up roughly by her arm, then punches her. Her nose bleeds immediately, but he keeps holding her, so that she can feel his stale, drunken breath hot on her face. "From this day on, you will know your place. *Wife.*" He lets go of her arm, and she drops onto the couch.

She has just received a death sentence, but somehow the doctor's words have not destroyed her the way Rajesh's words had on that day. Parvati shakes her head in amazement as she walks. How is this possible? An ancient memory that stings more than a fresh wound from an hour ago? Rajesh has been dead for years, and still she can feel his hand as he'd clawed at her blouse and ripped it. The beating itself, the first of many, had long ago lost its power, had tumbled into a spin cycle of violence. But his words, for which he had apologized the next day, had lingered precisely because they were true. Her husband had indeed made an error in marrying her, and the stench of his regret had infiltrated the rest of their life together.

Two days after the party, he had approached her. "No need for dinner tonight. I am taking the evening train to Pune."

"Pune. What for?" she had said without thinking.

His eyes glittered with malice. "What for? To see my only son. In case you've forgotten, I am not childless, like you are."

She pretended to focus on the stainless-steel pot she was scrubbing so that he wouldn't see the tears that sprang to her eyes. Her four aborted children sat like heavy stones within her, making their presence known at unlikely times. "I thought Rahul was . . . angry with you?" she ventured at last.

He sighed heavily. "That's why only I'm going. To ask his forgiveness."

She stiffened. "For what?" she asked, her back to him. "For marrying me?" She waited, half hoping that he would deny this, that he would come up to her from behind and place his hands on her shoulders and kiss her nape as he used to. But Rajesh was silent. And just when the silence felt unbearable, he said, "For desecrating the memory of his mother."

She had screamed, grabbed a plate, spun around, and thrown it toward him. But he deftly moved out of its way as it hit the wall and fell to the floor without shattering. He was upon her in two quick strides, and before she could move, he slapped her. "You will not act like a lowlife woman in this house," he said through gritted teeth. "You will not. If you do, I will grab you by the ear and drop you off at Principal's door."

"That will be fine," she spat back. "I was treated with more respect there than here."

He laughed. "More respect? You will starve to death within a week. Let's see how many men want to touch a woman with a coconut growing under her face. Have you looked at yourself in the mirror?"

She had fallen quiet, knowing he was right. Besides, the only thing she missed about the Old Place was the hustle-bustle. Everything else—the arrival of the new young girls, their dazed expressions after the first time they had been let out to a client, the bruises, and broken teeth that were becoming increasingly common as porn videos from abroad flooded the market and more clients wanted to enact what they saw there, the endless visits to the VD clinics, the addiction to drugs that almost all the girls succumbed to—she despised and was afraid of returning to.

He was gone for three days. When he returned, he came armed with smiles and sweetmeats. From this, she inferred that the visit had gone well, that Rahul had accepted his apology. She told herself that she was glad, happy for him. She was not the kind of woman who wanted to stand between her husband and his son. It was only right that there be a reconciliation. She would not allow herself to think what Rajesh had to say in order to appease Rahul.

And it was just as well that she hadn't known what he had to do in order to win his son back. It wasn't until later, much later, when it was far too late, that she'd find out the real terms of their reunion.

Parvati stops walking. The world around her has gone white as she stares unseeingly at the city. She has no idea where she is or where she is trying to go. She fights a rising panic, trying to tamp it down, to get her brain to right itself so she can focus, get a sense of where she is. Or who she is. She looks down at her arms, brown twigs, and suddenly she has no idea to whom those arms belong. Standing there in the middle of the street, a blur of people walking past her, she is acutely aware of her physical body, feels the soles of her feet press against the leather sandals, can hear the rush of her blood, the sun on her skin. But what is her name? Who does this body belong to? The knowledge hovers just beyond her reach, like a speck of dust floating in the air that she can see out of the corner of her eye. Of its own volition, her hand rises and her fingers and thumb come together like tweezers, as she tries to grab this thing that hovers in the air, just beyond her reach.

But this is not a city for a lone woman to stand still in the middle of a churning sea of people. A fast-moving teenager runs into her from behind, knocking hard against her shoulder. Parvati staggers forward, and in that motion, the confusion ebbs and her name comes to her, as fast as a coin dropped into a slot machine. Parvati. This thin brown body belongs to her, Parvati. And she has just left the government hospital where the doctor has given her the best news and the worst news she has received in a while.

She gives her head a good shake and begins to walk toward the market.

Bhima stops midconversation with an old Parsi customer and turns to her as soon as she sees Parvati. "Kya hua? What did doctor sahib say?"

"Nothing. Sab theek hai." Everything is fine.

She can see that Bhima is not convinced. But before she can question her further, the old man speaks up. "Oi, bai. Did you hear me? Do you accept my offer or not?"

"Go. Take it," Bhima waves in a distracted manner. "But next time I charging you full price."

"Next time is next time," the man says with a grin. "My wifey always says, 'Tomorrow never comes.'"

They wait until the man shuffles away with his pineapple, and then Bhima turns toward Parvati. "Tell me the truth. What did he say?"

"Arre, do you have wax in your ears or what? I told you, na? Everything is fine."

"I should've gone with you . . ."

"Why? So that we go bankrupt spending our days in the hospital instead of the market?"

"You come for dinner tonight . . ."

"Sister. You will have to excuse me for tonight. I am tired from all this walking. Tonight, I will go home directly from here and get some rest."

Bhima gives her a long, assessing look before turning away. "Your wish," she says. "But tomorrow you must come. Exams start in a month and Maya is going to be very busy, soon."

30

She misses Maya. Their little hut feels empty without the girl's presence. Bhima suppresses the unwelcome thought that rises in her mind—this is how it will be permanently, in a few years, after she finds a suitable boy for Maya and marries her off. Then, it will be only her in this hovel, and the evenings will be long and solitary.

Still, it is only two more days. Maya will take the last of her final exams on Friday and will return home from Chitra baby's on that day. What will it be like for the girl to return to this one-room place after having spent two weeks in their clean, sunlit apartment? Bhima wonders how she will ever repay Sunitabai and Chitra for suggesting that Maya move in with them while she studies for her exams. She would gladly offer to work without wages for a few months, but she knows they will not agree.

Parvati had looked at her curiously when she'd told her about the arrangement. "You're not afraid?" she'd said.

"Afraid of what?"

"That they'll try some of their tricks on her? She's a nice, good-looking girl, your granddaughter."

Bhima had flushed. "My Maya's not like that," she'd said. "And Chitra baby would never do anything . . ."

"Good," Parvati had said, turning away. "Good you have such faith in them. But you yourself have said a thousand times that you trust nobody."

Bhima had bitten down on the angry response that sprang to her lips: I did. I used to. Until I got to know you. It is you who taught me something, you bitter, old woman. That a life without trust is not worth living.

Instead, she said, "I trust them. They are good people. And they have helped me and asked for nothing in return."

"Good," Parvati said again. And this time, Bhima heard the unmistakable note of envy in her voice.

She sees Maya daily, of course. The girl is there when she gets to the apartment each afternoon, her nose buried in a book. The women have given her one of the two bedrooms, and Bhima's heart twists with pleasure as she sweeps around the books that are piled onto the floor and on the small writing desk. Chitra has explained to her that just passing in first class will not be enough; Maya has to be in the top of her class to gain entry into law college. "The competition is cutthroat," Chitra said, and Bhima had smiled. "Like at the vegetable market." But Chitra had shaken her head. "A lot, lot tougher than that," she'd said, which made no sense because Bhima knew how hard she had to work to compete against the other vendors.

Every evening, they eat the dinner Bhima prepares, the four of them at the dining table together. The first few times Bhima had felt awkward, as if she were sitting inside an airplane, but Maya had told her with her eyes how embarrassed she would be if her grandmother squatted on the floor while they ate. Now, she understands the purpose of the chairs, how it helps to eat in this manner instead of crouching on the floor like an animal. Maya, she notices, eats with a spoon instead of her hands, and the sight of this makes Bhima happy, but in a sad way.

"I like this," Chitra had said earlier today in the middle of dinner. "It feels like family."

Bhima had immediately looked at Sunitabai, expecting to see

the usual bemusement on her face, but the other woman had merely nodded. "It does." Sunita had smiled. "We are so lucky to have you cook for us, Bhima. There's nothing like coming home to a delicious meal. Thank you."

"It is my honor, bai," Bhima murmured, embarrassed by this unexpected compliment. Chitra baby she could dismiss; that silly girl was always effusive in her praise. But Sunitabai was more measured, which made a kind word from her worth even more.

"How is Parvati mausi, Ma-ma?" Maya had asked, making Bhima flush with guilt. She has been unable to invite Parvati to their house while she eats her dinner here each night.

"Who can say? Who knows what is going on inside that beehive of hers?"

Maya sighed. "I worry about her." She sighed again. "I miss her."

"No worry-forry. You just pay attention to your studies. You'll see her soon enough."

"Bhima." Sunita's voice was amused. "If poor Maya studies any harder, her head will explode."

"Thanks, Su," Maya said casually, and the sheer casualness of it, the way Maya spoke to her mistress as an equal, took Bhima's breath away. "See, Ma-ma? You don't need to tell me what to do."

They had all chuckled, and then Chitra said, "So what are we going to do on Friday when Maya gets done? To celebrate, I mean?"

All of them had instinctively turned toward Sunita, who looked taken aback. "What? You want me to decide?"

"We could go to the seaside," Maya suggested tentatively.

"I know. Let's take everybody to the club," Chitra said. "We can eat at the Chinese restaurant there."

Bhima tensed. "Radio Club?" she asked, knowing that Viraf and Dinaz were members.

Chitra shook her head. "No. This is the Breach Candy club."

"It's exclusive," Sunita said in a teasing tone. "Meant only for foreign nationals like our friend here."

"Oh, shut up. You like using the pool well enough."

Bhima looked from one to the other. "You all go," she said. "Take Maya if you like. But please . . ." She falls silent, unable to express the terror she feels at the thought of visiting such a place.

"Don't be silly, Bhima," Chitra said. "Of course we can't celebrate without you there." She let out a sudden howl. "Ow. What'd you kick me for?" She glared at Sunita.

Sunita turned scarlet. "Pagal hai. Crackpot," she said in an apologetic tone. She looked at Bhima. "It's okay. I myself don't feel very comfortable in that place. We will celebrate elsewhere."

Now, sitting on the mattress in her silent room, Bhima rolls her eyes. That Chitra baby. A grown woman's body but a child's heart. What adult woman doesn't know that if someone kicks you under the table you're not supposed to announce it to the world? As for inviting her to the club. What business does someone like her have going to a posh place with swimming pools and fancy restaurants? The chowkidar probably will not even let her pass through the front gate.

Bhima sighs. She has not been alone like this in many a year. Tonight, she aches for all those family members she has lost. Does Gopal ever think about her? Miss her? And Amit, her sweet boy, quick as lightning, whose moods could go from thunderstorms to sunshine in an instant? He is a grown man now, a middle-aged man, but all she can remember is that boy in half pants running around the corridors of their old apartment building, or begging her to buy him a new cricket bat. She had loved Pooja, of course, her quiet, docile daughter, but Amit was her heartbeat, her son, whose education she had chosen over Pooja's, the favored child who always got the last piece of halva, the extra helping of milk.

Is this why she had been punished, for valuing her son more than her daughter? These days it is different, she knows, with all the government campaigns about the value of girls. But in those days . . . Every mother she knew had made similar calculations, favoring the boys over the girls. Why then was *she* singled out to lose not one, but both her children? And which death was worse? The death she had witnessed? Or the death that is simply an absence, a hole in her heart that she cannot reach but feels constantly?

She settles down on her mattress, but sleep eludes her tonight. Finally, she gets up again and heads toward the trunk. She riffles through the chest until she finds the worn, blue aerogram. Even though she cannot read the words she had dictated to the professional letter writer who lives one lane away from them in the slum, she still recalls its content. She holds the letter to her body, smoothing its creases with her hand. It is the letter she had dictated to Gopal after Pooja's death. At Pooja's angry insistence, they had not informed him of her marriage. The girl had felt the sting of Gopal's absconding even more deeply than she had and had never forgiven her father for his abandonment of them. But the day after she had returned home from Delhi, Bhima had gone to the letter writer and dictated the letter that informed Gopal that their sweet Pooja was no more. She had kept the letter short, both because the man charged her by the word and because she did not want the news to get around in the basti that little Maya's parents had died of the AIDS. She had walked with the letter to the mailbox, but when the moment came to send it, found that she could not. She imagined Gopal opening the letter and asking Amit to read it to him. She imagined both of them, stricken, rendered mute by this news. Gopal would blame himself. She knew this as sure as she knew anything.

For years she had believed that she would never be able to

forgive Gopal for his cowardice, that her love for him had hardened into contempt. But as her hand hovered over the letter box, Bhima knew better. She did not blame Gopal for leaving them, after all; she blamed herself for being the reason why he had no choice but to leave. And without a desire for vengeance, there was no way to mail a letter containing such damning news, especially since it would be her Amit who would most likely read it first.

Would it have changed anything, she now wonders, if she had? Gopal would have caught the first train back to the city. But then what? Could they have learned to be a family again, after all those years? He would've doted upon Maya, of that she is sure. But what if he was still drinking? Could she have borne it better, the second time around? Or had the nurturing soil of his village nursed him back to health? She doesn't know.

As she puts the letter back in the trunk, Bhima sighs. It will be morning in a few hours and here she is, trying to fan the flames of a dead past. "What use?" she says out loud. "What use?"

She lowers herself onto her mattress again and closes her eyes. A melody plays in her head, a song Gopal used to sing to her a lifetime ago. She falls asleep to the song, once so alive and romantic, now mocking her in her dreams as it echoes through the years.

31

Maya is too exhausted after her last exam to celebrate. She staggers into Chitra's house around four in the evening, and by the time Bhima arrives a half hour later, the girl has climbed into bed and is fast asleep. Chitra greets her at the door, holding a cautionary finger to her lips. "She's sleeping," she says. "The poor thing is dead tired. She was up half the night studying." Bhima's heart swells with gratitude at this thoughtfulness, this interest in Maya's well-being.

The girl is still sleeping when Sunita lets herself in a few hours later. "Hi," she says, giving Chitra a light peck on the cheek. She smiles at Bhima as she lifts the lid of the pot simmering on the stove. "Papdi," she smiles, sniffing the vegetable. "Yum. My favorite."

"And some Parsi-style pallao-daal," Chitra says.

Bhima grins self-consciously. "What to do? After so many years working for Serabai, I am used to making pallao on happy occasions."

"Oh, God, Bhima. Don't apologize. We are lucky to benefit from your expertise."

They debate whether to let the sleeping girl lie, but Sunita insists that Maya eat something. "I've never seen anyone study around the clock as she has, Bhima," she says. "I think she should get really top marks."

"Sugar in your mouth, baby," Bhima intones. "I've already

promised myself that I will buy two kilos of ghee for the temple if she gets good marks." She catches the look that passes between the two women. "What is it?"

"Nothing, Bhima. It's just that . . . you know that the temple custodians just sell all the offerings and pocket the money, right?"

Bhima stays silent.

"Maybe, if you must make an offering, you can feed some beggars outside the temple?" Sunita suggests. "So much need in this city of ours."

"The need is always there," Bhima says fiercely. "More poor people than flies. But to feed the Gods, there is real power in that."

There is a short, awkward silence, and then Chitra exhales. "Well. Let's eat, shall we?" She turns to Su. "Sweetie, can you wake her up? I'll set the table."

They toast the half-awake girl as she sits at the table, cupping her chin in her hand. Maya smiles weakly, trying to blink the sleep out of her eyes. "How'd you do?" Sunita asks.

"I don't know. I don't know anything. Everything is jumbled in my head." And with this, Maya bursts into tears.

Bhima is stricken; instinctively, she looks to Chitra for help. "What is it? What's wrong, beti?" she asks, rising to cradle Maya's head.

But Chitra gestures to her to sit back down. "It's all right. It's just the tension of the past week." She looks at Maya. "You know, I was the same way after each exam. I always thought I'd done poorly. But I was always wrong."

Maya smiles weakly as she wipes away her tears. "Thanks," she says. "I wish I could find out today how I did. This waiting will kill me."

"Nonsense," Chitra says. "You're going to sit for me this summer, yes? And Binny said you can help at the law office. We're going to keep you busy."

Bhima looks from one to the other, not comprehending their conversation. "Sit? She is already sitting."

Chitra leans over and gives Bhima a quick hug. "You are so cute. I mean, Maya has agreed to pose for me. I'll pay her, of course."

The heat rises in Bhima's face. "You will be making the picture of her?"

"Yes." Chitra takes a sip of her wine. "I'm doing a series of portraits." She pokes Bhima in the arm. "You're going to be next."

Bhima scratches her head, thoroughly confused. She throws her granddaughter a helpless look, but Maya is not paying attention. They will have to talk when they get home. "Chokri," she says sternly, rapping her knuckles on the table. "Are you all packed-pooked? Do you have all your things ready for home?"

Maya looks at her shyly. "Ma-ma. Can I stay here one more night? I'm so tired. I just need to sleep. And the basti is so . . . noisy."

Bhima feels the words like a long, lingering cut of a knife. She has been counting the days for when Maya will fill up their little home again with her presence. Still, who can blame the girl for choosing this beautiful place with its plastered walls and high ceilings over a broken-down hut? She tries to hide her disappointment. "If Sunitabai allows," she says, hoping none of them can hear the tremor in her voice.

"Oh, we don't care," Sunita says with a shrug. "We love having Maya here."

The girl is wide awake now. "Thanks, Su," she says.

Bhima has always felt as if Maya is an extension of her body; now, watching the three of them chatting away, she experiences a new sensation—that Maya belongs with the other two women more than she does with her. It is not exactly jealousy that she feels. Rather, it's the feeling of being the outsider, akin to what she used to feel when she and Gopal used to go to the seaside in the old days and they'd walk by the expensive bakeries and restaurants they knew they couldn't afford. She has never felt as old as she does right this minute, listening to the three of them. How young Maya is. In this festive room, there is not a hint of the quiet girl who dwells with her in their silent hovel. Bhima has a sudden premonition—she will not choose a husband for Maya as she'd always supposed. Maya will forge her own path and select her own partner. Her role in the girl's life is drawing to a close; all she now needs to do is keep earning enough money to allow Maya to grow wings, wings that will undoubtedly take her to places Bhima herself will never visit. Bhima has never known until now that joy can feel so much like pain.

"Let's go have ice cream at Chowpatty Beach," Chitra says after they're done with dinner, and without looking at her, Bhima can sense the tension in Maya's body. They have not been back to the beach since the fateful day that they had run into Viraf there. In order to protect the girl from having to respond, she fakes a yawn. "Not tonight, baby," she says. "I am too tired." She is gratified by the look of thanks Maya casts her way. Maya may share her future with others, but their shared past will always glue them together.

"You should go home, Ma-ma," Maya says. "It's getting late."

"I'll drive you home," Chitra says immediately, but Bhima shakes her head. "No, baby. I am needing to walk." She rises and reaches for the dirty plates, but Chitra places her hand on her wrist. "We'll clean up," she says. "If you're walking, you better get going."

There is a faint light in the sky as Bhima leaves the apartment building. She walks slowly, lingering in the crowded, busy streets. She wonders if she should've insisted that Maya come home with her tonight but knows that she cannot begrudge the girl one more night of cooled air, the soft, clean bed, the hot water shower. Most of all, she cannot deny her what Maya desperately needs—the company of young people. Maya deserves to enjoy this unexpected gift of Chitra and Sunitabai's friendship. Bhima knows she was lucky to have had as kind and generous a mistress as Serabai; but what Serabai had given them was charity. What the two younger women have offered her and Maya is friendship.

Bhima hopes she is not slandering poor Serabai with these ungenerous thoughts. An image of the Parsi woman from their chance encounter at the mall rises before her eyes. How Serabai had aged. What must it have been like for her during the last few months of Dinaz's pregnancy, knowing that she herself had escorted Maya to the abortion clinic and presided over the killing of Darius's half sibling? Bhima knows that Serabai has had two confidants—Dinaz and herself. The bitter irony was that during what should've been the happiest time in her life, she couldn't turn to either one of them. And so the biggest secret of all—of Viraf's perfidy—she had to carry inside her, even as its stench grew, like slowly rotting fruit.

Is it the special curse of women, to keep other people's secrets and carry their shame? What would happen, she wonders, if all of them—Parvati, Serabai, Sunitabai—simply put down their loads one day and refused to pick them up again? She remembers what Parvati had once said to her—it is our secrets that define us. Is she right? Bhima longs for this to not be true.

Parvati is lying about her health. Every day, Bhima can see a change—in the way her eyes widen with pain more frequently, in the sweat that forms on her brow as she bends to pick up a basket of fruit, in the increasingly impatient manner in which she treats

Rajeev. And yet. How fiercely she had fought yesterday when Malik's nephew's henchman had tried collecting their weekly hafta from them. All the other shopkeepers and vendors knew to pay the collection money each week to the nephew's gang, in addition to the bribes they paid to the local police. No one else argued, and Bhima herself was willing to pay the amount, now that they could afford it. But Parvati had sprung up like a tiger, almost spitting in the man's face. "I've known that boy since he was wetting his underpants," she yelled. "You tell him his uncle had promised me lifelong protection."

"That was for when you sold less produce than a cockroach," the man snarled. "Now, you're having a big business . . ."

"And what, it's poking in your eye? You listen to me. Not only will we not pay a single rupee while I'm alive, but if you harass this woman even after I'm dead, I will come back as a bhoot and haunt you. And I will curse six generations of your offspring. You understand?"

"Why unnecessarily you're talking about cursing and all?" the man said uneasily. "This is a simple business matter."

"You go suck someone else's blood," Parvati replied. "Your boss has enough wealth that he can ignore two poor widows trying to earn an honest living."

The man had stared at her for a moment, then shook his head and gave up. "Jaane do," he said to no one in particular. "You can't argue with a pagal woman."

"Hah. And unless you wish your children's children to be pagal, also, you don't show your face here again. Saala chootia."

Bhima had blanched at Parvati's use of an obscene word she had only heard men use. For a moment she saw Parvati in her old life—crude, bawdy, vulgar—and the image made her shudder. Age had whitewashed Parvati's past. But occasionally, the Parvati that Bhima had come to like vanished and a stranger took her place. Without meaning to, she smiled at the goonda who stood glowering before them. "Maaf karo, bhaiya," she said. "She doesn't mean it." The next second, she felt a sharp pain on her shoulder where Parvati had smacked her. "Arre, wah," the older woman glared. "Who are you to say what I am meaning and not meaning?" She continued glaring at Bhima until the man muttered under his breath and departed. Then, she broke into a wide grin. "Sorry," she said. "I hit you harder than I meant to. But this is good. This way, the ruffian will remember this moment when I am no longer here to protect you. It will make him feel more kindly toward you."

"And where are you going?" Bhima had said, even though she'd known at once what Parvati was insinuating.

Parvati busied herself rearranging the tomatoes. "Who knows where any of us are going, sister?" she'd said cryptically.

Now, Bhima feels anew the uneasy feeling she'd felt at that time. Just how sick is Parvati? Surely she would not cover up some serious illness? Is her sickness a lingering effect of her past in that ugly place? Bhima has heard that such places of disrepute harbor shameful, unmentionable diseases. Hai Ram, is that what is causing that pain in the lower back? She feels her face flush at the thought.

Then, another thought: If something were to happen to Parvati, if she were to die, who would help keep the books? Rajeev is as dumb as a cabbage and illiterate like her. She could ask Maya's help, but Chitra baby has already told her that studying the law will keep the girl very busy. Perhaps she has learned enough by now to deal with Jafferbhai at one end and her customers at the other? Will she be able to manage on her own? Or, will her illiteracy again ruin her life, at a time when Maya will need financial help?

Bhima slows down her walking, pulling on her lower lip as she turns the corner into the slum. If I could remove fear from my life, uproot it, who would I be? she wonders. What would it feel like to live for today and let the future remain in the future? How much lighter her burdens would seem. The thought puts a lift in her step. She thinks of the dabbawalas of Mumbai, the army of men who deliver thousands of lunch boxes to offices and schools across the city every single day. Serabai had read an article about them to her one time as they sipped their afternoon tea together. It appeared that their failure rate of delivering to the wrong address was so low that men from a big college in America had come to study their system. But the part that had made Bhima's mouth fall open with wonder was this: These deliverymen were illiterate like her. They had simply devised a system to compensate for their illiteracy. Perhaps that's what she could do, Bhima thinks, as she enters the slum. If she ever needed to. Which she hoped she wouldn't. Because she needs Parvati's companionship as much as she needs her business sense. She has grown to care about the crazy, foul-mouthed, irascible woman who brightens her days at the market with her sharp-eyed observations and bawdy comments. As she lets herself into the dark and empty hut, Bhima resolves to question Parvati more thoroughly about the nature of her ailment. This time, she will not let the old woman slip out like an eel from under her questioning.

III

III

32

Maya has passed with the highest marks in her college. Her friend Kajal had looked up the results on the computer and called with the great news. Bhima is home early today, since Chitra and Sunita are out of town in Lonavala, and so she is there when Maya screams on the cell phone that Chitra had gifted her as an early graduation present. For a moment, the girl cannot speak, and the expression on her face is such that Bhima cannot tell if the news is good or bad. Oh God, Oh God, the girl breathes, and just as Bhima is about to panic, Maya breaks into a smile. "Ma-ma," she squeals. "I passed. At the top of my class."

Bhima crosses the floor to hug her granddaughter. "Ae, Bhagwan," she mutters. "At last You have heard my prayers. I will put two kilos of ghee at Your feet tomorrow." She hardly knows how to react to such enormous news, given how rarely she has had reason to celebrate. Maya, however, is young, and the girl jumps up and down in excitement, even while she's still on the phone. When she finally hangs up, she spins toward Bhima, her face shiny. As she embraces her grandmother, Bhima senses a shift, as if Maya is already moving out of this wretched room, gliding along a new expanse of sky. Even two years ago, Bhima knows, Maya would've bent down and touched Bhima's feet to ask for her blessings. But Maya has changed. It is a change Bhima can sense but not define. All she knows is that this change is rampant in the whole city. There is a loosening of mores and an old way of life—that of respecting your elders, knowing your station in life, knowing that women had to behave in a certain way—is coming to a close. This very education that Bhima has paid for with every drop of sweat, every tired and straining muscle in her body, will be the knife that someday will sever the ties between her and Maya. For a split second, Bhima sees this as clearly as she sees her own fingernails; the next minute, all she sees before her is an almost-grown girl jumping up and down with excitement.

"Chitra," Maya gasps. "I've got to call Chitra in Lonavala. She's dying to know."

Now, Bhima can move. "Later," she says, stopping the girl from making the call. "But the first phone call has to be to someone else."

Maya pauses, looks at her with a puzzled frown on her face. "Who?"

It is all there, in that "Who?" The ingratitude, the moving on, the not looking back. She is not yet ready for this Maya, the Maya who has taken to dressing better, who has spent the past three months of her break poring over law books, who now chats on the phone with her friends almost exclusively in English. It is all Chitra baby's fault, turning her head like this with big dreams. The uncharitable thought pops into Bhima's head before she kills it. God forgive you, she chastises herself. What kind of demon grandmother begrudges her granddaughter's success, especially at the moment of her greatest triumph?

"Ma-ma," Maya says impatiently. "Answer me. Who do you want me to call? Gopal Dada?"

Bhima blinks. "No," she says, shocked.

Maya sucks her teeth. "Then who?"

"Arre, wah. How soon you've forgotten the woman whose salt

we've eaten all these days. The woman who paid for your college in the first place. First call has to be to Serabai."

Maya's reaction is immediate. "Stop saying that," she yells. "It's a lie. She didn't pay for my schooling. You did. With your hard work, you paid."

"Chokri," Bhima says. "Keep your voice down. Do you want the whole basti to hear us?" She waits until Maya has calmed down before she says, "Serabai already paid my salary, no? So your college fees were extra. Out of charity."

Maya shakes her head. "Oh, Ma-ma. You understand so little. What charity? How much was your salary, all these years? Did she even give you a pay raise each year? Of course not. In the meantime, inflation in this country is like—" She cuts herself off. "Forget it. If you still want to think like a slave, I cannot stop you."

Bhima looks at her in incomprehension, as if Maya is speaking in a new language. Then, a slow realization dawns upon her, and she nods. "Beti. I know you're still hurting from what . . . what that snake did to you. But Serabai. She was innocent." She debates whether to tell Maya about their encounter but thinks better of it.

In any case, Maya is turning away from her. "You just don't understand," she repeats. She hands her phone to Bhima. "If you wish to call her, your wish. But I'm not going to speak to her."

Bhima dials Serabai's cell phone number, hoping that she will pick up. The phone is answered immediately, and she hears a little voice say, "Hi?" Her heart beats a little faster. It is the little boy. Darius. "'Allo? Is your . . . is Serabai home?"

There is the sound of a tussle, and then Sera says, a little breathlessly, "Sera speaking."

"Serabai?" Bhima yells into the phone as she is wont to do. "It's Bhima here."

"Bhima?" There is a silence, then, "What's wrong? Are you all right?"

Bhima laughs at the immediate concern she hears in her former mistress's voice. If only Maya could've heard it, too. "Everything is well," she yells, even though Maya is gesturing for her to lower her voice. "We are all fine here. I am calling with some good news."

"Tell me."

"It's Maya. She has passed her final exams, bai. With the grace of God, she has stood first class first."

"Bhima. This is excellent news. Oh my God. I am so happy for you." Even though she can't see her, Bhima knows that Serabai has tears in her eyes.

Now, at last she lowers her voice. "I am calling you first, only, bai," she says. "To thank you for forcing me to send Maya to college. And for paying for her schooling. May God repay you for your kindness."

There is a long silence, and after a few disconcerting moments, Bhima says, "'Allo?"

"Yes. Yes, I'm here." She can hear the huskiness in Serabai's voice. "Bhima. Believe me, I'm just as happy as I was when Dinaz passed her exams. This is a true accomplishment. And it is you who should get the credit, Bhima. I know . . . I know out of what hard clay you have built your mansion."

Bhima scratches her head with her left hand. Does Serabai think she's building a house? Before she can ask, Sera says, "Is Maya there? May I speak to her?"

She swallows the sudden fear that rises in her. "Yes, bai," she says. "Just a minute." She hands the phone to Maya, gesturing and making eyes at her. Be civil, she pantomimes, half-afraid that Maya will refuse to accept the phone and she, Bhima, will have to dig a hole and die of embarrassment. To her relief, Maya grudgingly takes the phone, sighs dramatically, and then says, "Hello."

Bhima watches Maya's face intently and is gratified when, after a few minutes, it relaxes. That Serabai, she thinks appreciatively. A tongue coated with honey. She listens as Maya says, "Sure, sure. Definitely." Then, "And how is Dinaz?" And then, "Tell her I send my love." Bhima's heart swells with pride. Her granddaughter, Pooja's daughter, has not forgotten her manners, after all.

"Serabai," Bhima says when she finally gets the phone back. "Forgive me. I didn't ask. How is Dinaz? And little Darius?"

"Fine, fine," Sera says. "Everybody is okay. But tell me, what about you? Business is good?"

"Yes," she says humbly. "By the grace of God."

"Great. So how are you celebrating today? The good news, I mean?"

Bhima freezes. She is unaccustomed to celebrating good news because she is unaccustomed to good news. She looks at Maya and wishes Chitra were in town. She would know what to do. All she can think of doing is taking the girl to the seaside for some snacks and a kulfi. And then it comes to her. "Serabai," she says. "We are going to Cream Centre tonight. We would be so honored if you would please join us." She wonders if Serabai remembers the day, decades ago, when she and her late husband, Feroz, had taken her there for lunch on their way home from a shopping trip. Bhima can still taste the chole bhature she'd eaten that day.

Behind her, she hears a growling sound. It is Maya, shaking her head no, wanting her to revoke the invitation. But it is too late because she hears Serabai's voice in her ear. "Bhima. I was supposed to go with the children to a movie. But to be honest, I'd rather join you. And they can probably use the privacy, too. What time?"

Bhima sets up a time, her stomach muscles knotting already at the thought of facing Maya's recriminations. She hangs up, turns around, bracing herself for Maya's wrath. And when it doesn't come, she says in a rush, "You don't have to understand. But this woman has saved our family more times than I can count. You're too young to understand. Why she do to me what she do. When you're a mother . . ."

"Ma-ma." Maya gives an embarrassed laugh. "It's okay. If this is so important to you, we'll go. Accha? And now, I must give the news to Su and Chitra."

"Yes, yes," she says eagerly. "Call them, beti. We are in their debt, also."

Maya frowns. "I'm calling them because they're my *friends*," she says, and as she hears her granddaughter squeal her news to them, Bhima can only marvel at this magician called education, which allows a girl from the slums to refer to the women who employ her grandmother as her friends. Let this be true, she prays. Let Maya always remain as confident as she is today. Let her not suffer the blows and betrayals that I have.

On the way to Cream Centre, they stop the taxi at the market where Parvati is finishing up. She looks up to see Bhima approaching and guesses the news immediately. "She passed?"

Bhima feels her face cracking from the breadth of her smile. "First class first. Chitra baby says she will definitely get into the law college."

Parvati closes her eyes. "Praise God," she says. Then she opens her eyes and frowns. "Why are you all dressed up?"

"Because we are going to a good restaurant. To celebrate. And you are coming with us."

Parvati lets out a cackle. "Sister, I smell like a week-old jackfruit."

"So what?" Bhima's eyes suddenly turn misty. "Your brains are what has allowed all this to be possible." She sweeps her hand, encompassing their fruit and vegetable stand.

"Rubbish," Parvati says, dismissing the compliment. But she is smiling. "Okay, I will not displease you on such an auspicious day."

Parvati and Maya chat the whole way to the restaurant, as if they are old friends. Bhima marvels at how much her life has changed. For years, she worried endlessly about what would happen to her grandchild if she were to die suddenly. Now, Maya has new people in her life—Parvati, who, Bhima knows, will watch over Maya like an old guard dog for as long as she's alive, and Sunita and Chitra, who, in their own, unassuming way, will pave a path forward for the girl. A treacherous thought enters her mind: Perhaps it is so that being let go by Serabai was a good thing. She stares out the window at the streets rushing by, transfixed by this thought. The words of an old film song that Gopal used to sing come to her: *Zindagi ek safar hai suhana / Yahan kal kya ho kisne jaana*. Life is a journey that's beautiful / Who knows what will happen here tomorrow?

"Look, look," Parvati is saying to Maya. "Have you ever heard your grandmother sing to herself before?"

Bhima gives an embarrassed cough and then laughs along with the other two at her own foolishness.

As the three of them enter the restaurant, Bhima wishes she could've warned Maya to behave well around Serabai; to not let success turn her into an ungrateful girl. Having Parvati with them has constrained her, and she can only hope that the girl's upbringing will turn her bitterness into generosity.

Serabai arrives five minutes after the three of them are seated at a booth. Maya has already ordered a soft drink for herself, but Bhima has asked only for water, because even though coming here was her idea, she knows that her circumstances do not allow her to spend money foolishly. Maya is facing the door and so she spots Serabai first and waves to her. The girl slips out of the booth and stands as Sera approaches them. "Congrats, Maya," Sera says to the standing girl, and before Bhima's astonished eyes, Maya, unprompted, bends down to touch Sera's feet. Unaccustomed to this, Sera takes a step back, then reaches for Maya, who is still bending forward, and gathers her in her arms instead. "Oh, Maya," she says. "There's no need." As Bhima watches, Maya stays in that embrace but with her hands hanging stiffly by her sides, and then, as the seconds tick by and it is obvious that Sera is not letting go, the girl wraps her arms around Sera, also. Sera must've whispered something soft into Maya's ears as she rocks the girl a little bit, and then Maya sniffs and Bhima watches openmouthed as tears roll down the girl's cheeks. And still, in the middle of a crowded, noisy restaurant with waiters flitting past them, the two stay in that rocking embrace. "I'm sorry, I'm sorry." Sera's voice is muffled against Maya's shoulder. "I'm so proud of you. You have overcome so much."

And Bhima is astonished at her own obtuseness—she has been so busy congratulating herself for her sacrifices that she has taken for granted the hurdles Maya has overcome. Less than three years ago, Maya was sitting at home dejected, listless, a shell of a girl, her unborn child scooped out of her.

Sera finally releases Maya and turns to Bhima with a big smile, extending both her hands. "Congratulations, Bhima," she says. "This is such a great day. Look at what our Maya has accomplished."

Our Maya. The two words are a rose bouquet that Serabai has presented her. Bhima takes Sera's hands in her own and raises them to her own forehead. "Serabai," she says, too overcome to say more. She keeps holding Sera's hand and reaches for Parvati's as she introduces them, so that she is holding both their hands against her heart. "I will remain in your debt for the rest of my life," she says. "Together, we have done this. Together."

"Baap re," Maya says. "I must've been a real duffer that it took three old women to get me to finish college." There is an uncertain moment, but they all see the twinkle in the girl's eye and burst into laughter. And just like that, Maya lightens the mood at the table.

After they order, Sera reaches into her handbag and pulls out a small box. "This is a little present for you, Maya," she says.

It is a pair of jade earrings. "Thank you," Maya says.

"Do you like them?" Sera asks anxiously.

"Very much."

After dinner Bhima excuses herself to go to the bathroom. When she finishes her business and steps outside, Sera is waiting outside the door. "Ah, Bhima," she says. "This is for you." She presses an envelope into Bhima's hand. "What is this, bai?" she says.

"Shh. It's a check. For law college. This—this should cover both years. No, don't argue, Bhima. You never know when the money will come in handy. Just keep it safely in the bank."

"But Serabai. Already you have given so much . . ."

"Bhima. Please. Allow me to do this." Sera smiles wanly. "Hey, look. Who knows when I'll need a lawyer? It will be good to have one in the family."

The word *family* burrows into Bhima's heart. She bows her head in submission and folds and tucks the envelope in her blouse. "You were the first person she met. I had brought her straight to your house," she says wistfully. "From the train station."

"I remember. She was such a skinny little thing. And so quiet. Wouldn't even look at me. Naturally, after what she'd gone through. Losing both parents like that." Sera shudders, then smiles suddenly. "You remember how I finally won her over?"

They both say it at the same time: "By giving her one piece of chocolate every day."

The two women fall silent, lost in their memories, and then Bhima says, "Our families go back a long ways, Serabai." There is so much more she wants to say, but she can't. Her love for this woman is real, she knows. But so are the circumstances that have driven them apart.

"So true." Sera pauses, then clears her throat. "We should go back. The others will wonder." She takes a step and stops. "Thank you for inviting me. I—it means a lot. I don't know if you'll believe me, but there's not a day that I don't think of you. You know, we Parsis have a prayer called *Tandorosti*. It asks for good health for our loved ones. When I pray the names of all my family members, I include yours and Maya's. Every morning. I've done so for years."

"Thank you, Serabai," Bhima whispers. "I . . ."

"I know," Sera says, looking deep into Bhima's eyes. "I know. Me, too."

33

It is only after she has been at the market for two hours that Bhima's unease turns to fear. Parvati has not shown up to work and Bhima is getting killed by the rush of customers. But the real source of her fear is that she doesn't know where exactly the woman lives. How can this be? she berates herself between customers. They have worked side-by-side for this long and she doesn't have an address for Parvati? Given how sick the woman has looked the past few weeks, why had she not asked? But she knows the answer—she has not bothered finding out because she couldn't see herself setting foot into that house of illicit goings-on no matter what the circumstances.

So what keeps Parvati away today? Bhima looks all around her, growing more worried by the minute. Car accident? Fainting? Something serious must have happened, especially since Parvati knows that Rajeev has taken a rare day off today. As the sun climbs in the sky, with no sign of Parvati, her alarm grows. It is now almost noon. Where is she? A customer stops by, a young man with powerfully bad breath and a nasally voice that grates on Bhima today. "Ae, baba, listen," she says, cutting off his bargaining. "This is the price. You take or leave." The man looks at her, offended, then marches off, but Bhima doesn't care. "Kanjoos," she mutters. "Miser."

If Parvati were here, they would have enjoyed a quick laugh over the expression on the man's face. Bhima pictures her on the side of the road somewhere with a broken leg, hit by a BEST bus or a taxi, and her stomach turns. No. She will make inquiries. Someone in the market must know where she resides.

"Oi, mausi," Vishnu's young assistant calls. "Phone call for you."

"Is it my chokri?"

"No. Not Maya."

"Khon hai?" she asks, puzzled.

The boy shrugs as he holds out the phone to her. "How would I know?"

"'Allo?" Bhima hollers.

The male voice is unfamiliar. "Is this Bhima?"

"Haan."

"I'm calling for Parvati. She had given this number as contact number."

Bhima can barely get the words out, her body gripped by a sudden fear. "Is . . . is she dead?"

She hears the man's chuckle. "Nahi. Not yet. But she won't get out of bed. Tell me, is she acting or what?"

The icy fear heats into anger. "If she can't get out of bed, she's sick, no?"

"Yes, yes, that's well and good, auntie. But I am needing my room. She is supposed to clear out in the morning. Saala, I'm losing business because of her. You please come just now and take her. If not, I will carry her out to the roadside."

"You don't lay a hand on her. You hear me? If you touch her, I'll bring the police." Bhima scarcely knows what she is saying, only dimly realizes that she is channeling Parvati's fierceness.

"Don't threaten me, yaar. As it is, I'm calling you out of courtesy, only. I even called her nephew, but he said he's too busy at work to come. Now tell me. Are you too busy, also?"

"I'm coming," Bhima yells into the phone. "I will leave everything and come. You please give the address to my friend here."

She hands the phone back to Vishnu's assistant, who scribbles on a piece of paper. When he hangs up, the boy's eyes are embarrassed. "This is no-good area," he says. "You must not go."

Bhima feels the heat rise in her cheeks. "If I don't go, what happens to her? Those animals will feed on her carcass. You do me a kindness, chotu. Go get me a taxi. Go now."

The boy hesitates. "What about the shop? Vishnu is not coming back for another half hour."

"I'm here, na?" she yells. "Nothing will happen to your precious shop. I won't budge until you bring the taxi."

The boy looks at her, stunned by her hysteria, and Bhima catches herself—"Don't worry," she says more softly. "You will only be gone a few minutes, correct?"

When she stands at the entrance of the dilapidated Tejpal Mahal, the white-hot fever that has gripped her since the phone call, breaks. As she clutches the piece of paper in her hand, her courage ebbs. She thinks of what her father, or Gopal, or even Amit, would've said about her entering such a building. But then, she thinks of what Sunita and Chitra and Maya would require her to do, and feels their encouragement. A man is coming out of the building, and she lurches toward him and asks, "Forgive me. But this is Tejpal Mahal?"

The man leers at her. "Yes, it is. You looking for a job here? Go talk to Mohan."

She flushes at the insult, her right hand buzzing with the urge to slap the leer off this boy's face. She settles for spitting on the ground. "I'm old enough to be your grandmother. Show some respect."

But he is unchastened. "This isn't a place for grandmothers," he says before walking away.

This isn't a place for grandmothers. The words ring in her ears as she climbs the steps into the building and enters hell.

She sees clusters of women standing on the balcony, their

saris low-slung on their hips. She sees men walking around with their flies unzipped. She hears gales of laughter that sound false in their merriment, hears the notes of desperation and carelessness they hide. But what makes her stomach turn is the smell of the place—hot, fetid, musky. This is no place for an old woman to die. The words enter her mind as a fully formed sentence, and that is how she knows: Parvati isn't just sick. She is dying. How did she not know this sooner? Her eyes burn with tears and a wild, trapped bird called grief flutters in her chest. She marches down the balcony, stops the first woman she sees. "Where can I find this Mohan? I need to see him straightaway."

She is surprised at how young-looking Mohan is and how handsome. The sweet face of Krishna, the dark heart of Ravan, she thinks. "I have come for Parvati," she says, without preamble, and he looks up, as if surprised by the contempt in her voice. "This way," he says, leading her.

Her heart sinks again when she enters the tiny room. Only the high ceilings of the old building and the tiny quarter that she assumes is the bathroom distinguish it from her own hovel. The only furniture in the room is a narrow bed upon which lies a corpse. "Parvati," Bhima says loudly. "Do you hear me?"

There is a faint groan.

"Sister." Fear makes Bhima shake her harder than she intends. "Wake up."

Parvati's eyes flutter open, and for a long moment they are terrifyingly blank. Bhima knows the old woman is struggling to place her. Then, as she comes to awareness, Parvati gives a weak smile. "Are you really here?"

"Yes. How are you? What is wrong?" Bhima sniffs suspiciously in the air. Is this daru that she is smelling on Parvati? Mohan seems to have arrived at the same conclusion because he says, "So that's the problem. The old boodhi is hung over."

"Chup re," Bhima scolds, although the revelation that Parvati drinks has shaken her. Mohan's eyes harden. "This tamasha has cost me enough. Chalo, get her out of here."

Bhima looks at the handsome young man with the soul of the devil who stands beside her. "You must've had a mother, na, beta?" she says. "Is this how you would want someone to treat her?"

"You want to see my mother?" Mohan sneers. "Go to the third floor. She's the whore with the hashish pipe." He laughs, but there is something hollow in it.

"Maaf karo," Bhima says, not knowing what she is sorry for. "At least help me get Parvati off the bed, beta. And then, if you can fetch me a taxi, I will be grateful."

Mohan goes to the door and yells to someone down the hallway to get a taxi. Then he comes back and says impatiently, "Chalo. Get up." He bends and lifts Parvati up from both shoulders until her feet are dangling on the floor. The woman sits gripping the edge of the bed, her chin touching the grapefruit on her throat. A string of spittle runs down the corner of her mouth. Bhima is gripped by a spasm of fear. Where will she take Parvati in this state? How will she manage? She winces as Mohan grabs her roughly from the armpits and begins walking her to the door, but she is in no position to plead for gentleness. She looks around the room and grabs Parvati's white cloth bag.

"Where to?" the cabdriver says, and Bhima has no choice but to say, "Gharib Nagar." But during the cab ride she looks at the dozing woman and is furious at the thought of Maya seeing Parvati drunk. First, two women who love each other like menfolk. And now, a drunk, foul-mouthed business partner with a past. She is a bad grandmother to be bringing Maya in contact with such people.

The cabdriver parks his taxi illegally to help her half carry, half drag Parvati into the slum. Bhima shuts her ears to the screams and laughter of the slum children, steels herself to the snickers and open stares of her neighbors. When at last they reach her front door, she pays the driver and gives him a tip. "You behave, accha?" she whispers to Parvati, who is thankfully looking a little less drunk. "Don't scare my Maya."

But Maya is not home, Bhima remembers. The girl is away at Chitra's house for a sitting. She is relieved. She gently lowers Parvati onto her mattress and then immediately starts the stove to make her a cup of tea.

"Sorry, sorry," Parvati is mumbling. "I am a bother to you. You should've just left me."

"I should have." Bhima doesn't try to hide her anger. "Next time you drink, you wicked woman, I will leave you in the gutter."

"Kya karu, sister?" Parvati says, in a weak, submissive voice Bhima has never heard before. "The pain was unbearable last night. One of the girls took pity on me."

Bhima's heart stops. "The pain?"

"Yes. From this chikoo fruit growing on my backside. The doctor sahib had warned me. But I didn't think . . ."

Bhima turns off the stove abruptly. She walks to the mattress and lowers herself. Without asking for permission, she pulls down Parvati's sari until she sees it. She gasps loudly, feeling her insides give way. The thing is the size of a child's fist. And even though there's no pus or blood or reddened area, it looks hostile. Angry. Evil. Not at all like a sweet chikoo fruit.

"What did the doctor say?" she asks carefully, wanting to get the information from Parvati before she has fully awakened from her drunken state.

But like the words to an old song, she knows what Parvati says before she says it: "He said it won't be too much longer now, sister. And that the pain will be terrible."

❋

They take turns staying at home with Parvati. Bhima gets up and goes to work as early as she can. In the afternoon, Maya relieves her. It is not what Bhima wants, having Maya selling produce at the marketplace, where her beauty attracts the unwanted stares of the young men who suddenly decide to walk past Vishnu's shop twelve times a day. But Maya has time before she begins law college, and Bhima needs someone she can trust at the stall. There are a few terrible days when Maya makes mistakes that cost Bhima money she cannot afford to lose, but Maya is a quick study. People, especially the young men, don't argue and bargain with her as they did with her grandmother. Bhima has stopped going to Chitra baby's home in the afternoon. Any other mistress would have let her go on the spot, but Chitra only says, "I'm so sad, Bhima. How can we help you?" and Bhima bows her head, unable to speak.

Instead, she goes home each afternoon. There is usually only a half hour gap when Parvati is alone, between the time Maya leaves for the market and Bhima leaves the girl in charge and heads home. Afternoons are a good time of the day for Parvati, and she might eat a little piece of bread, dipping it into the tea that Bhima makes as soon as she gets home.

"How was business this morning?" Parvati asks as they sip their tea.

"Good." Bhima takes a big gulp of tea. "One of the boys came around and asked for Maya. But he called her Eve. Said she sold him an apple yesterday." She pauses. "This is a joke?"

Parvati smiles faintly. "It's from the Bible. The holy book the Christians follow." She tells Bhima the story, but Bhima is not really listening, aware as she is of how exhausted Parvati looks.

"You rest now," she says gently. "Shut your eyes for a while."

Parvati nods. "Tomorrow I'm going to the market with you," she says. "I'm tired of being a weight on your head. I am used to earning my own keep."

Bhima places her hand on the woman's shoulder. "Theek hai," she says. "That's fine. Tomorrow you come with me. Accha?"

They have been having the same conversation for a week.

34

Sometimes, she smells things, foul, putrid smells. Dying things. Then, she knows she's smelling herself. Other times, she hears things. The flapping of the wings of a fly. The bored sound the stale air makes in the room. The rasp of her own breath. The growl of her stomach, the tick-tock of her heart, the strum of her bones. The swoosh of her blood. Always, always, there are sounds from beyond this closed door—children playing outside, a woman's scream, a loud curse, the tring-tring of a bicycle bell—and these merge with the sound of her memories, the hot, urgent murmurs of strangers making love to her, the drone of Principal's voice as she taught her the alphabet, the almost-forgotten sound of her mother's voice telling her to sweep their little room, the smack of Rajesh's open palm against her face, which sounded so different from the thud of his fists on her arm or shoulders. Above all, she hears the ticking of the clock, although there is no clock in this room. Still she hears it, relentless, steady, cruel, like the marching of an enemy army that draws closer and closer. Other times, she hears the stretching of trees toward the sky, the blades of grass straining toward the sun, the growing of the bones of children, the turmoil of the soil as the dead toss and turn in it. Or, she hears the incessant breathing of the oceans, the howling of the winds, the swell and shrink of the moon, the acrid burning of the sun that has tormented her for twenty years but whose heat she now craves.

Between her own exhaustion and the medicine that Bhima has purchased to diminish her pain, the hours swell and ebb and as she drifts in and out of sleep, there is always the sound of time slipping away.

Sometimes, a voice pierces through the fog and startles her awake. Today, the voice says, angrily, "Get out." She has a vision of herself scrambling to her feet, rising from this mattress and hurrying out. But when she tries to do so, all she succeeds in doing is flexing her feet three times before she drifts off to sleep.

Get out.

The voice again.

It is Rahul, Rajesh's son. Five days after Parvati had watched unblinkingly as her husband's skull had exploded in the flames of the funeral pyre, five days after she had returned to their apartment and scrubbed every wall and floor to get rid of the smells of Rajesh's bedridden last years, five days after she had begun wearing her widow's white and resolved to live out the rest of her days in this quiet, tranquil flat, a free woman at last, not owing anyone anything and not being owned by anybody, five days after she could touch her own skin, her own hair, her own genitals and believe that they belonged to her and no one else, five days after she had settled every claim that the world had made on her, Rahul had appeared at her door. He had been by her side during the last two, terrible days when Rajesh had struggled for breath, and she felt for him the closeness that springs up between those who have kept a deathbed vigil together. The boy had stood beside her as the fire consumed his father's body, not shedding a tear, but she had not thought to wonder at this. And then, he had disappeared for five days, until he appeared, pale and withdrawn, at her door.

"Rahul," she said. "Come in, beta."

He walked in, looking around the flat as he did. He allowed

her to open a bottle of Duke's lemonade for him and set down a plate with a few Parle biscuits. Then he withdrew an envelope from his pocket and handed it to her. She took it, suddenly embarrassed. Did Rahul think that she, a new widow, needed his financial help? She did not. Rajesh had a pension and some savings, she knew. She would manage on that amount.

It was a will. And it said that the flat in which she was living, the very chair that she sat in, the ground below her feet, the walls that were closing in, all belonged to Rahul. That Rajesh had disinherited her completely, that all his earthly possessions, he had bequeathed to his son. That her compensation for her devoted service, of cooking, cleaning, fucking, wiping his butt, spooning food into his mouth, was zero. When she could finally control the burning in her eyes and look up, she said, "I . . . I don't understand . . ."

"What you don't understand? It's simple. You are illegally occupying my house. And you need to get out." Rahul's left eye was twitching, but he did not look away.

"Rahul. Be reasonable, beta. I'm an old widow. I have no one. Where do I go?"

He stood up. "That is not my affair. I just want you out of my house immediately. Otherwise I call the police. Understand?"

Parvati closed her eyes. Maybe Rahul would not be towering over her when she opened them again. But there he was. "I will be out on the streets," she tried again. "At my age . . ."

She had not known what fury was until she looked into his face. "Then go back where you came from before you decided to pollute this family. Go back to live among your own kind."

She flinched. Still, she put out an appeasing hand. "Beta. Show some mercy. I left that life behind me long ago."

He spat on the floor. "Well, that life never left you."

She was out of the apartment two days later, still reeling from the shock of the revelation that Rajesh had turned the apartment and pension over to Rahul during his trip to Pune decades ago. That this was the condition of Rahul allowing his father to remain in his life. And when Parvati went to the bank, she was told that Rahul had withdrawn every last paisa. Years ago, she herself had insisted that Rajesh add his son's name on their joint account. She stood outside the bank and laughed mirthlessly at the irony.

There was one person who could have reversed this reversal of fortune—Principal. A few slaps and threats from her goondas, a night spent in the police station on trumped-up charges, and Rahul would have begged her to take possession of the flat. This, she knew. And Principal would have done this for her, readily. But Parvati knew that she could never seek help from the one person who could help. She had left behind that life, forever. Instead, she had trudged to Praful. And Malik. The two boys, both sons of whores, had managed to have a semblance of a childhood because of her kindness toward them. And with their help she had knitted together a threadbare life for herself all these years. Until the God she refused to acknowledge had brought an angel called Bhima into her life.

"Parvati," Bhima yells, shaking her by the shoulders. "Wake up. You are having a bad sapana."

The older woman opens her eyes, sees Bhima, and blinks as she tries to fight off her hallucinations. "Bhima." Her smile is unexpectedly bright. "You save me."

She sees Bhima looking at her cautiously. "I'm okay," she struggles to reassure her. "I . . ." But it is all gone, the dream, like a thief slipping behind a wooden partition. Her mouth feels swollen, as if she has mothballs in it. "I must . . ." What must she do? Something urgent. Something she must tell. What? Who is looking at her with such frightened eyes? Is it her mother? "Ma," she cries. "Help me, Ma."

"Parvati," Bhima yells. "You are very sick. You hold on, sister. I am coming right back. I bring the doctor for you."

Don't leave me, she wants to say, but Principal leaves her anyway. They are at the train station and her father is standing still, like a stake planted in the ground. Why didn't the rains come? If only the rains had come. Saala badmash, she curses the rain. May your children's children suffer. Is she itching? Where is she itching? Or is it paining? What's paining? "Who is there?" she says loudly. "Kaun hai? Khabardar. Don't you dare enter."

The doctor sahib talks mostly to Chitra. "She's getting the wrong pain medicine," he says. "Too strong. It's making her hallucinate. We can try controlling the pain with something different."

"And if it doesn't help?"

He shrugs. "We can always go back to this." He turns to Bhima, speaks to her in a low, respectful voice. "I want you to be prepared," he says. "It will not be very long now. But I can try and make it so that she is more alert. Without suffering too much pain, of course."

"There's nothing more to be done?" Chitra asks.

"I spoke to the doctor at the government hospital. He says she would not even hear of chemo." He hesitates. "How old is she? In her seventies? You have to ask yourself, we prolong her life to what end?"

Hunched in a corner, almost tucked into herself, Maya lets out a sob, and Bhima looks at her sharply, placing a warning finger on her lip. The doctor looks at Bhima again. "As her sister, you have to decide. If you want aggressive treatment, I can shift her to the hospital."

Bhima opens her mouth to correct him, then stops. Let him think that Parvati is her sister. She realizes they are all looking at her for a decision, and she is paralyzed. But then she thinks of the miserable government hospital and an image comes to her: Parvati is a bright yellow kite with a cut string, stranded on earth. When she belongs to the sky. "I don't care how long she lives," she replies. "I just want her to go with honor." And as soon as the words escape her mouth, she knows she has made the right decision.

The doctor nods. "Good. Let's try a dose of this tonight. And someone can call my clinic tomorrow and let me know if she's a little less sleepy and confused." He stoops a bit as he touches Bhima's shoulder. "Don't worry. I will be able to control the pain."

She folds her hands and bows her head. "Thank you, doctor sahib," she says. "I am so grateful."

He gives an embarrassed grin. "No mention, no mention. You have a good advocate in Chitra." He packs his bag, then says to Chitra, "Do you want to go with me to pick up the prescription?"

"Definitely."

After they leave, Maya gets up and puts her arms around Bhima. They stand there, looking down at the restless, agitated woman. "Ma-ma, I'm scared," Maya says. "I've never seen someone die before." She catches herself. "I mean, of course I saw my parents. But I wasn't there when . . ."

"I know," Bhima says. She struggles to capture the clarity she had had just a few minutes ago. "Parvati is a kite," she says. "She belongs to the sky. When the time comes, it will be up to us to release her and let her fly. You understand?"

Maya looks at her wide-eyed. "I think so," she says. But she is sobbing.

35

Three days later, Parvati is looking so much better that Bhima briefly entertains the thought that maybe the woman can return to the market after all. "Today I will make the tea," Parvati announces as soon as she walks in. "You've worked all morning."

"Accha," Bhima says, more to preserve the woman's dignity. She pretends not to notice the wave of pain that makes Parvati's face go rigid as she gets to her feet. But instead of the Primus stove, Parvati heads to where Bhima has set her white canvas bag. She digs to the bottom of the bag and pulls out a wad of money. "Take," she says simply.

Bhima frowns. "Kya hai?"

"What's it look like? It's our money. From the business. Whatever I could save from what you pay me. I have no use for it, sister. You take it to pay for my dava-daru."

"No need," says Bhima, offended. "You call me sister, but still you offer me money?"

Parvati gives her a meaningful look. "What am I going to do with it? Carry it to my pyre? Take it. Where I am going, I won't need money."

Bhima fights the lump in her throat, struggles to maintain eye contact. "You going somewhere?"

"The devil has reserved a seat in hell for me, sister. And he doesn't need money. It's only the devils that walk on earth who will kill their own mothers for money."

"You're an old woman but still talking rubbish," Bhima says, turning away, and Parvati lets her. The bills, held together by a rubber band, lie on the floor, until Bhima finally picks them up and returns them to the white bag. Parvati watches but doesn't protest.

Maya is out this evening, has plans to go to a movie with her college friends. Bhima had been anxious to get the girl out of the hut, which has taken on the smell of disease and medication. As evening falls, she is wondering what she should prepare for dinner, maybe some broth for Parvati, when the old woman sighs and says, "These four walls are closing in on me. I am longing for some fresh air."

Bhima looks at her sharply because this desire to leave the house is proof that the new medicine is working. "You wanting to go somewhere?"

Parvati looks self-conscious. "Where to go? In this shape?" she says, glancing at herself. But there is a quiver in her voice, a question.

"We can go sit at the seaside," Bhima says, only half believing her own words. But the hope that the words ignite in Parvati's face strengthens her.

"Do you think we can, sister?" There's that tremor in Parvati's voice again. "I would love that. It doesn't have to be for long."

"Then we shall go." Bhima gets to her feet with a grunt, opens the door, and steps outside. She will need help getting Parvati out of the lane, but if living in this wretched slum has any advantages, this is one of them—she will never lack for someone willing to help, whether it be out of idle curiosity or kindness. She spots her neighbor Shyam, lounging outdoors as he always does. Bhima has never liked Shyam, but now, she lunges toward him. "Ae, babu. I need to take the old lady to the seaside to get some air. Can you help me walk her out? I can pay you a few rupees."

Shyam looks offended. "If you wish to pay, mausi, the answer is no. But if you ask as a neighbor, I am willing. Among neighbors there should be no money, na?"

Bhima looks chastised. Perhaps she has judged the man wrongly. "Thank you, ji," she says. "We will be ready in five-ten minutes."

"Taxi needed?" Shyam asks.

"Yes. We will get one from the main road."

Shyam clicks his tongue. "Nahi. At this hour, impossible. Also, if they see you with an old lady, no one will stop." He chews on his lower lip. "You get ready," he says. "Taxi will be waiting when you come out."

"What—?"

"Don't worry. That Abdul fellow? Two lanes down only, he lives. He drives a taxi. Should be home by now. But don't worry. He will take you, as favor to me." He lifts his hand to squash her protest. "That way, he can help you. At the other end. And then bring you home, safeum-safe."

Abdul pulls up illegally beside a row of parked cars at the seaside and comes around to help Bhima get Parvati out of the taxi. He waits until they are comfortably seated on a bench overlooking the water. "All right?" he says. "I am going to find a parking space, accha? But I come back, faata-faat, no worry."

They both turn their heads to watch him hurry back to his vehicle. "He's a kind boy. Goes to show there is still some humanity left in this world," Parvati says, and Bhima nods. "Are you comfortable?" she asks, and in response, Parvati takes Bhima's hand, squeezes it, and holds it in her lap.

"I am so grateful I got to see the sea one more time," she says.

"Why one more time? Many-many more times, God willing," Bhima says. But she hears the lie in her own voice, and Parvati doesn't even bother contradicting her.

"The village where I was born, there was no sea," Parvati says. "I didn't know it existed until I come to Mumbai. Can you imagine?" Her face looks unimaginably old as she stares straight ahead. "First time I see it, I screamed. I thought it was some demon moving on its stomach, coming toward me to eat me. Principal laugh and laugh. Years later, he used to bring me here. It was the only thing that made life bearable."

"Who?"

"Rajesh. The man who became my husband. While I was still at the Old Place, we used to come." Parvati's lips twist bitterly. "Once we were married, all that stopped. After the first year, I'd say. Then I was just his servant."

Bhima strokes Parvati's hand. "Forget these memories, sister," she says. "That's half your illness—these sad memories."

And then, to Bhima's great shock, Parvati begins to cry. "I can't," she whispers. "I can't forget. Every man in my life has used me. Like I was a newspaper to collect trash in and then discard." She lifts a finger and points to the churning sea. "This. This was the only one who stayed with me. My brother. That's what I used to call the sea. My strong, reliable brother. The only one who swallowed my pain and made it his. You see how he moves? Those waves? Only someone who understands suffering tosses like this."

Bhima looks at Parvati out of the corner of her eye. It is hard to know if this is the drug talking. She looks around discreetly for Abdul, in case they need to rush Parvati home. She spots him sitting on the sea face wall diagonally across from them, and he raises his hand, to let her know of his presence. Somehow, that simple gesture comforts her, reminds her she is not alone.

"My Maya was raped," Bhima says suddenly. It is the first time she has ever said this out loud, and she is so stunned that she looks around quickly, as if someone else has said those words. "By Serabai's son-in-law. A boy I loved like my own."

Parvati nods. "I know."

"You know?"

"Maya told me. One day, when you were at work."

A numb, hollow ache grows in Bhima's chest. "That's why she let me go. Because she had to defend that badmash's honor. Over my own." She shakes her head angrily. "Over my own."

"Sister . . ."

They sit on the bench together, two old women, while an entire city parades past them—the old Parsi gentlemen in their faded suits and bowler hats, the college students who move in shouting, laughing clusters, the young Romeos who wolf-whistle compulsively at every attractive woman they pass, the ragged beggars who thump their dented bowls at passersby, the male residents of nearby buildings in their T-shirts and shorts. Occasionally, the ocean emits a furious roar and sprays them with its spittle. When this happens, Parvati licks the salt on her lips greedily, while Bhima wipes her face with her sari.

"I have a favor to ask," Parvati says at last.

"Bolo." Say it.

"When I am gone—no, wait. Listen. What use pretending, sister? I know my days are numbered." Parvati waits until Bhima finally nods her assent. "After I am gone, I want you to sprinkle some of my ashes here. Into the sea."

"Of course," Bhima says, relieved at the smallness of Parvati's request. "Of course."

"And then, carry the rest of them back."

"Back where?"

"To my home village. To the land of my ancestors. It is not too far from here. Maybe five or six hours by train."

"What for?" Bhima asks, calculating the cost of lost business days. "Why you wanting to go back there?"

Parvati fidgets with the lump under her chin. "Because it's

where I should've lived my life. If my kismet had been better. I want to go home."

"Are you having family there?"

Parvati shakes her head vigorously. "No. That is, I don't know. But I don't wish to find out." She half turns her head to look at Bhima. "No. My family is here. With you and Maya. Understand?"

Bhima nods, too overcome to speak. "Do you understand?" Parvati says again, and this time she replies, "Yes. Yes, I do." She attempts a laugh and then cries, "But what I will do without you, I don't even know."

Parvati gives a cackle that makes her sound like her old self. "Don't worry. The devil and I, we will take care of you."

"You don't believe in God, but you believe in the devil?"

"Sister. I have never seen the face of God. But the devil—I have seen him a thousand times. Isn't that so?"

"Baap re," Bhima says. "What blasphemy you speak."

Parvati ignores her. "There's a river," she says, as if speaking to herself. "In my village. The year I left, it was dry as a bone. But this year, the monsoons were good. Take my ashes there. That's what I ask. My savings will buy two train tickets, for you and Maya. Good for the girl to get out of this city for a day or so. Hai, na?"

"What is it called? Your home country?"

"Lodpur."

Bhima frowns. "I have heard that name."

"Lot of chikoo farms there."

"No. I don't know. But I am knowing that name."

"Will you grant me this last wish, sister?"

"Of course."

Parvati exhales, leans back her head to gaze at the sky. "You promise?"

"I promise."

36

Bhima is relieved to find out how much of the business she can manage, even without Parvati there to help her. But she has to admit that there has been an unexpected source of help, from Rajeev's son, Mukesh, who still has a year of college left but is glad to help during his summer vacation. The boy is as hardworking as his father and has also inherited his good nature. But unlike Rajeev, Mukesh is sharp, able to think for himself, and can add and multiply at lightning speed.

She has been spending more and more time at home. At first she told herself that it was for Parvati's sake, but now she knows the truth—it is for her own. Already, even with Parvati alive, a persistent ache has lodged itself in Bhima's heart. The sense of loss she feels is as concrete as a physical object. In a life marked by a succession of losses, Parvati's passing will be one more.

Bhima watches from the corner of her room as Maya takes the bedpan outside. Even a month ago, it would've been unthinkable for her to let Maya step out of the house and into the basti alone in the late evening, much less to perform such an odious task. But tending to the dying—and yes, Parvati is dying—changes the living. Old rules and mores give way to hasty, new arrangements. Bhima, unaccustomed to taking physical care of an elderly woman, is feeling the terrible weight of her own age. Every joint in her body aches, mostly from the sporadic, restless sleep they are all getting—a sleep increasingly punctured by Parvati's moans and mutterings and nocturnal bodily accidents. The old woman is up at odd hours, then sleeps out of sheer exhaustion. Bhima and Maya are both bleary-eyed. But to Bhima's great surprise, Maya has not complained once. In fact, the girl has come into her own, tending to Parvati with a tenderness that Bhima had not imagined she was capable of.

She is startled by a loud groan. Parvati has turned over on her side and is staring at her with unblinking eyes. Bhima mutters an oath but rises and scoots down the tiled floor to the poor woman's mattress. She sits on her haunches and takes Parvati's hand in hers and is startled by how hot it feels. "You are having a fever?" she cries, now noticing the sweat on her brow. "I give you a Crocin?"

Parvati shakes her head. "No more tablets," she rasps. Since the last two days, her voice has changed. "I will take a sip of water, though."

Bhima lifts the old woman's head so that she can take a sip. "Thank you," Parvati says. "What a burden I have become to you."

"I told you. No burden." Bhima's tone is curt. She wants Maya to return so that they can all get a few hours of sleep.

"Something I have to say," Parvati continues, as if she's not heard. "I want you to listen."

"What?" Bhima is still eyeing the door, not paying attention.

"I have left a note for you. It is kept in my bag. Have Maya read it after you sprinkle my ashes in my home village. But read it while you are still there, at the riverbank. You understand me? Don't open it now."

On her deathbed and still this woman is plotting and planning, Bhima marvels. She's always up to some tingle-tangle. "Why the secrecy, sister?"

Parvati's dry lips crease into a smile. "You'll see."

"Okay." Bhima is suddenly furious, the sleeplessness of the

past few weeks catching up with her. I have no time for these games, she fumes to herself. "Chalo, try to sleep."

"One more thing." Parvati raises her bony hand and grabs Bhima's wrist. Her hand burns against Bhima's skin. "One time you ask me, do I hate all the menfolk? I say yes. I lied to you, my sister. There is one man I love more than life itself."

Curiosity battles with impatience. "Who?"

"My father," Parvati says and begins to cry. "My father."

It is the fever talking, Bhima thinks. "Your father sold you to that degenerate place," she says. "You only said."

"I know," Parvati cries. "And I was angry. But I always understood why. Deep in my heart I understood why he must do what he did. He sold me to save everyone else. This is why I hated him—because I couldn't blame him. If I could have just blamed him, I could've stopped hating him. But I was so close to him, Bhima, that even at the train station, I could understand his reasons."

"I don't follow," Bhima says, but just then Maya walks in with the clean bedpan and Bhima signals to her with her eyes to go to her corner. Maya does not need to hear this conversation.

"He used to sing to me," Parvati says, but her voice has gone so soft that Bhima is not sure if she is awake or talking in her sleep. "When I was little, before the boys were born, he would occasionally take me to the fields with him. I would lie under the banyan tree and watch while he broke up that hard soil. I would beg him to let me help. He never did. Called me his rani, his queen. One time, I remember . . ." Parvati drifts off to sleep. And then suddenly, her eyes fly open and she says, clearly, "It is that motherfucker cow that I hated. The one he sold me to keep."

Bhima flinches at the crudeness of the word, then watches as the woman's eyes close again. She sits stroking her hair as Parvati falls into a restless slumber. Is it the lot of women, she wonders, to love the men who destroy them?

It is Maya who notices that Parvati's breathing has changed. The older woman is also drenched in sweat. "Dip some rags in cold water and put on her forehead," Bhima commands, but in a half hour, the fever hasn't come down. The two look at each other. "Shall I phone the doctor?" Maya asks, her voice fearful. Bhima considers, then says no. "No doctor can help her now, beti." Her voice is steady, and she looks directly at Maya, who is crying. Bhima doesn't cry. But a monsoon rages within her.

Death, when it comes, is merciful. Peaceful. Parvati's eyes flutter open a few times. Once, she grips Bhima's hand hard, before letting it fall away. The groaning ceases. Then, there is only the sound of deep, raspy breathing. A few times, the breaths stop and Bhima and Maya look at each other, bewildered. Then, there is a loud snort and it starts again. But slowly, like a train chugging to a stop, the breathing slows down.

And then Parvati becomes a yellow kite and flies to her home in the sky.

A day after Parvati is cremated, Bhima returns to the site and is handed the ashes. She spends that evening sitting cross-legged on the floor, occasionally lifting the urn that contains the ashes, marveling each time at how little the human body actually weighs. It is hard enough to accept that this is what the physical body amounts to. But what about a person's anger? What about her voice? Her laughter? Her arrogance? Her irreverence? Her humor, her ego, her honor, her character? Do these fingerprints of an individual life simply evaporate and disappear with the last exhale? And if that is so, what use all this struggle, misery, and strife? What difference whether a woman ever lived or not? Whether she was loved or unloved, educated or illiterate, wanted or unwanted by her parents, whether or not she suffered hurt and betrayal, or whether she still managed to retain her humanity and nobility? In the end, Bhima thinks, it doesn't matter. It is all ash and dust. This is what it means to be human, she thinks: grains of dust arranged in human form—some dark, some light, some tall, some short, some male, some female. And in the end, the same gust of wind breaks them all down.

37

For two weeks, Parvati's ashes sit in the urn in the corner of the room. Next to the urn lies the white canvas bag, which, Bhima knows, holds the mystery letter. A few times she has wondered whether to get Maya to read that letter, but she has refrained, out of respect for the promise she'd made to her friend. Also, she is afraid that reading Parvati's words will open the stitches that are holding in her grief. Not to mention the anger that she feels, although it is an unfocused anger, one that darts this way and that, unsure of its target. Should she be angry at Parvati for keeping her illness a secret from her until it was too late? Or angry at the government hospital where conditions are so bad that people who go there choose to die rather than live? Or at the Gods, who created a woman as proud and strong as Parvati and then did everything in their power to break that pride and strength? Bhima's lips curl in bitterness at that last thought. In her time, she has known the evil that men do. But nothing matches with the evil of the Gods, who, having created humanity, now spend their days teasing and testing it.

Stop it, she chides herself. You are sounding as blasphemous as Parvati herself. Parvati, who is dead but whose absence feels as tangible as her presence once did. In the marketplace, customers still ask where the caustic old lady has gone, the woman who sold them oranges and bananas wrapped in an insult or a killer funny observation. They like Mukesh, his good humor and the glitter of his youth, but they miss the bawdy comment, the scowl, the casual cuss word, not to mention the occasional concern, startling in its rarity and sincerity, about a sick child or a bad-tempered boss.

But it is at home where Bhima truly misses Parvati. Without Parvati to tend to, she has assumed her normal responsibilities at Chitra's home—Mukesh will continue to relieve her in the afternoons even after his college starts again—and so she doesn't get home until at least seven. As the shadows of the evening lengthen in their silent hovel, again, it is just Maya and her alone together, making desultory conversation. To their surprise, they both miss the intensity of caring for an ailing woman, even recall with nostalgia their bleary-eyed state, the sleepless nights punctured by Parvati's moans. They are, both, traumatized by their memories of the woman's suffering, and enriched by knowing that they had used every fiber of their beings to alleviate it.

Tonight, Bhima gestures toward the urn and the bag. "We should go to her muluk," she says, as she tears a piece of chapati and uses it to scoop up the spinach from her plate. "Sprinkle the ashes, like she ask. Before you begin college again."

Maya stretches. "It would be nice to get out of this city for a few days," she says. "We never go anywhere."

Bhima feels the pinpricks of shame at what she hears as Maya's criticism of her. "All these years there was no money," she says defensively. "And now, when there's some money, there's no time."

"I know. But Mukesh can manage for a few days. You trust him, correct?"

"That I do. He's a good boy. Serious."

"Handsome, too," Maya says dreamily, and Bhima is shocked. "Shameless," she scolds. "You keep your eyes on your books, understand?"

But Maya is unfazed. "Whatever you say, Ma-ma," she grins. "But don't you think he . . ."

"Bas," Bhima says. "Enough." But there is a smile in her voice. It is as if the spirit of Parvati has infected them both.

"I can go to the station tomorrow and make the booking for the train," Maya says. "When should we go?"

There was a time when Bhima would have never allowed Maya to go to the station by herself and talk to strangers. But that time, she knows, has passed. "We can go Saturday and Sunday," she says. "Parvati said it's a beautiful place. Perhaps we can stay and return on Monday."

The light in Maya's eyes tells her it's the right decision. For a moment she ponders how much nicer the trip could be for Maya if she had some young companions that she could laugh and joke with on the train, anyone other than her old grandmother. But she wants to be alone with Maya when they sprinkle the ashes. "She was here only for a short time, but I miss her," she hears herself say out loud. A memory rises of Parvati's deathbed confession about loving her father, but she snuffs it out. It is too painful, too confusing to think of love as being that complicated. It would require her to reassess everything she thinks she knows of Parvati, every defiant, designed-to-shock utterance, and Bhima knows that this she cannot do. To believe that Parvati, in the depths of her degradation, had continued to love her father would require her to reassess her own life and marriage to Gopal, to acknowledge that her own deceiving heart has continued to love her husband, even after his betrayal. Despite his betrayal. It would require her to hear again that song he used to sing to her—*"Mere Sapno Ki Rani"*—"The Queen of My Dreams"—not as the mocking taunt that she has turned it into but as she had originally heard it, a love song rendered by a man who was head over heels in love with his wife.

Bhima gets up abruptly and picks up the two plates to take them outside to rinse. Even though it is dark, the crows on the overhead wires still caw, and their sound makes her head throb. She looks at the ragged, bleak assortment of makeshift huts all around her and her stomach turns. Trees. She longs to see trees. And hills. To hear the sound of birds other than the predatory crows who now darken Mumbai's skies. To see a parakeet, maybe, or a bulbul. In the Mumbai of her youth, such sightings were common. But like the goondas and ruffians who now rule the city's streets, the unruly crows rule the skies, having chased off the more timid birds.

They will go, she and Maya. Stand before a riverbank in Parvati's home village and watch the river gurgle past them. It will do them good, to get out of this place. And it is doubly good that it is Parvati who is leading them out.

38

It is the green that confuses them, shocks them, that makes bubbles of delighted laughter spurt involuntarily from their mouths. It is its lushness, its promiscuity, like a woman sitting with her legs splayed, that makes their city eyes blink in astonishment, as they contrast the browns and blacks of their lives with this lavish, fertile green. Bhima, especially, is stunned, because she has to reconcile the image of the parched, broken land of Parvati's description with the extravagant spread before her. And there is also a knot of sadness in her heart because if this green earth was Parvati's patrimony, the unjustness of her banishment is even more apparent. As if she's read her mind, Maya turns from the train window to ask, "Why did Parvati mausi leave this paradise for our dirty Mumbai?"

Bhima smiles. "It's not dirty when you want to go to a cinema hall, hah?" she teases. "Or to Fashion Street." She watches as Maya's face flushes. "Chitra baby tell me. How the two of you go shopping, when you say you're going to get the law books. I may be old, but I'm still your grandmother, don't forget."

The railway platform at Lodpur is bigger, more crowded than Bhima has imagined. She suddenly is nervous about being here alone with Maya and is glad that she has not purchased a return ticket for Monday like Maya had wanted. "Perhaps we should perform our duty and return home tonight only, beti," she mumbles as they walk down the station.

Maya sets her suitcase down and puts her hand on her hip. "Now what's the matter, Ma-ma?" she says. "Our train is still in the station and you're thinking of going home."

"This is not our desh," Bhima mutters. "We don't know any of these people, their manner or ways."

"Oof, Ma-ma. You are a pucca Mumbaikar. Half a day out of the city and already you are missing it." Maya picks up the suitcase and resumes walking. "No, we are going to stay. You need a holiday, no? Much too hard, you have been working."

"If someone is looking at us, they will think you are the grandmother and I am the grandchild," Bhima grumbles as they walk.

Maya looks at her sharply, eyes gleaming. "Look around you, Ma-ma. No one is paying any attention to us."

Before they exit the station, Maya approaches a couple of well-dressed women and asks for a hotel recommendation. She comes back with a couple of names. "See?" she says. "How easy?"

The girl continues to take charge, giving the auto rickshaw walla the name of the hotel. "Good choice, madam," he says approvingly. "Brand-new hotel. One year old, only."

"Is it too expensive, bhai?" Bhima asks immediately. "We are poor people." She turns a bewildered face toward Maya, who has just pinched her arm.

"It's okay, bhaiya," the girl says. "You take us there only, acha?" She looks at her grandmother. "I have money," she says quietly. "She—Parvati mausi leave me all her savings. She told me to spend it on this trip."

Bhima's face darkens with anger. "And you took it? This was her hard-earned money," she says. "She could've used it on her medicine. Instead, we are going to waste it on . . ."

"Ma-ma, it's settled. These were her wishes. She left the money to *me*." Bhima hears the self-importance in Maya's voice and doesn't have the heart to tell her that Parvati had first offered it to her. Let the girl believe that she was the favored one.

The hotel room is good enough for them to delight in but not ostentatious enough to make them feel uncomfortable. They eat the lunch Bhima had insisted on packing perched at the edge of the bed, then take a nap on a mattress so soft that Bhima has a hard time sleeping. She doesn't mind, because the cool, clean, white sheets are compensation enough. Even though the room temperature is comfortable, Maya turns on the air-conditioning because they are paying for it and she wants to get her paisa vasool. After they wake up, Bhima wishes to freshen up at the bathroom sink, but Maya works the shower and demands that her grandmother get under it. The first few minutes, the flow of water assails her body like small pebbles and Bhima hates the sensation, but then her entire body sighs and softens under the heat and she thinks that she would sell a kidney to be able to experience such luxury every day.

"How do you feel?" Maya asks when she steps back into the room, but Bhima doesn't have to reply. She feels clean in a way that she hasn't for years, as if she has washed the grime of the slum itself off her skin. Even the constant pain in her hip has been helped by the pressure of the water.

"See?" Maya says. She crosses the room and stands before Bhima, placing a hand on each of her shoulders. "Don't worry, Ma-ma. Once I become a lawyer, I will buy you a big house where you can take a shower every day. Accha?"

"Accha," Bhima says casually, as if Maya has promised to buy her a chocolate bar later today. She doesn't say what she thinks: That as nice as this shower is, what matters more to her is the fierce love that shines in Maya's eyes. But that is a lesson that Maya will learn for herself, as she gets older.

"You go clean up, beti," she now says. "I would like to fulfill our obligation to Parvati as soon as possible."

The hotel is situated at the outskirts of the village, and as they leave, Bhima wonders if anyone here knows the whereabouts of Parvati's brothers. She sends Maya to ask the manager, but he is a nonlocal himself and directs them to speak to Karim dada, the old man who is the security guard.

Bhima's heart leaps when Karim dada shuffles up to them, because he is of an age to remember Parvati's family. Perhaps the brothers still till the land that their father paid for with his own blood; perhaps they would like to keep some of their sister's remains. But Karim dada's runny, yellow eyes turn cloudy at the mention of the family name.

"Are you she?" he whispers. "The girl? The one the father sent away?"

Bhima takes an involuntary step back. "Nahi," she says. "She's dead. I am her friend. Come to find her family."

The old man sighs. "You have come too late, sister. Much too late." He pauses, chews the wad of tobacco in his mouth. "They are all dead. He kill them all."

"Who killed them all?" Bhima asks sharply, wondering if this old man is pagal, gone in the head.

"He did. The father. Two years after he send away the girl. He put poison in all their food. It was terrible. Terrible." The old man shudders. "I was only thirteen at the time. My mother bought me a sweet that day. I remember. All the mothers held their children close after it happen. That poor man. What he suppose to do? We were all starving. No rains for two years. But he the only one who do this sin. God forgive his soul."

Bhima stands there, numb with shock, not even remembering to protect Maya from hearing such evil. She remembers what Parvati had once told her—that she was her father's favorite. Could it be that he had sent her away to save her? That she was the only one he chose to keep alive? Even if it meant . . . But here, she stops, nauseous at what she has heard, wishing she'd never asked.

"I am sorry to give such bad news. Forgive me," Karim dada says softly. He waits for another minute, his head bent in respect, and when it is clear that Bhima has no more questions, he says, "Accha. I will take your leave."

He has shuffled away from them when Bhima calls out, "They all died? All of them?"

He turns back slowly. "All of them," he nods. "Except the family cow. He spared her."

The cow. Bhima remembers what Parvati had said—it was the cow she had hated because the cow was her rival, competing for her father's affection. A sob gathers in her throat. "What happened to it?"

Karim dada smiles a bitter smile. "The moneylender took it, of course. Seems the family owed him money."

Below them, the river gurgles like a baby. The two women hold on to each other as they descend the short clearing and step into it, its cool waters a blessing against their feet. All around them, the trees bend toward each other and whisper their daily gossip. There is a family picnicking across from them on the opposite bank, their dress and manner branding them as city folk, and despite the sound of the river as it breaks over rocks and rushes past them, they can hear the shouts and screams of children wading into the water, the cautioning voices of their mothers. "I wish there was no one else here," Maya says. "I wish it was just the three of us here."

"Three?"

Maya gives her a quizzical look. "Yes. You, me, and Parvati."

And then Bhima feels her, feels her with an intensity that takes her breath away. She hears the querulous voice, the cackling laugh, the witty quip. She sees the scowl, the defiant glare, and then, the softening gaze when Parvati knows she has gone too far and that Bhima is upset at her. The wheedling into Bhima's good graces. But what she is experiencing here, in the woods, is more than memory. It is feeling, sensation. She feels Parvati in the tranquility of the blue sky. She feels her in the dancing treetops. In each of the submerged stones. In the mud under her feet. In her mind's eye, she sees her—Parvati floating in this river, hands behind her back, eyes closed, feet drawn in together, a smile on her face. Parvati racing through these woods with her brothers, and shimming up these trees, laughing at their pet dog barking helplessly on the ground. Parvati sitting by herself at the riverbank, imagining the boy she will someday marry, the home they will build. Unaware of her pending execution, unaware of her executioner.

"We should say something, Ma-ma." Bhima hears Maya's voice as if from a distance. "Say a prayer, before we sprinkle her ashes."

Bhima nods, snapping back into the present. She is about to start chanting when a queasy feeling rises in her stomach. "There is no need," she says. "We . . . this place. It is enough. We—" She stops, unable to proceed. Instead, she reaches for the urn. With the waters still lapping at their feet, they turn, so that the ashes will not blow back into their faces. "Rest in peace, sister," Bhima says out loud. "Here, in the birthplace of your ancestors." She fights the memory of what Karim dada has told them a mere hour ago. "May you find the peace that escaped you in this life. Now all your suffering has ended. And may—may your father find his peace, also."

She turns to Maya, and hands the remainder of the ashes to her. "Thank you, Parvati mausi," the girl cries as she lowers the urn into the water. "I will never forget you."

And so they are done. They stand staring at the river for a few minutes, then look at one another. Maya nods. "Chalo, Ma-ma. Let's go."

They climb back up the embankment and are about to walk toward the main road when Bhima remembers the letter. "Wait," she says. "Parvati was wanting us to read her letter after we sprinkle her ashes. While we are here."

Maya reads the letter out loud. When she is finished, she raises her head up to the sky, a look of incredulity on her face. Then she begins to laugh. "That Parvati mausi," she says. "Such a trickster, she is."

At that moment, the transistor radio on the opposite bank begins to play.

39

No.

What Parvati is asking of her is impossible. No.

This woman was too much, conniving and plotting even on her sickbed. Bhima is not even sure how much to believe the whole natak of wanting her ashes scattered in her home village. Was it all a ploy to get them here? And how did she even know how close Lodpur was to Tipubag, when she, Bhima, herself hadn't made the connection?

Tipubag.

Gopal's home muluk. Where his brother ran the family farm. The village Gopal had escaped to decades ago, taking Amit with him. Where, as far as she knew, they still lived. If Gopal was still alive.

And now, Parvati has declared her last wish: that Bhima and Maya get back on the train that had brought them here and travel two more stations. Just two more stations. To Tipubag. To visit her estranged husband and son. This woman, who proudly waved her lack of family entanglements like a flag, was now urging them to make the trip. Bhima feels her skin prickle with anger. What business was it of Parvati's? Directing her affairs even from the other world. Let her mind her own business. The old woman's skill was in numbers and figures, and for this, Bhima would always be indebted. But why must she poke her nose in their private affairs? What if Gopal was still angry with her? What if he rejected her a second time? What if—ae Bhagwan!—he was dead and she'd find out that she had continued to wear the red sindoor in the parting of her hair, not knowing she was a widow? What lies had he fed Amit about her throughout the boy's childhood? Otherwise, what would explain a son not inviting his own mother to his wedding? No. It had taken her years, but she had finally laid the past to rest, lined up all her memories like corpses in a morgue. She would not disturb the past again, letter or no letter.

"I didn't realize Tipubag was so nearby," Maya is saying. "Shall we find out the train schedule?"

"Chokri," Bhima says sternly. "Don't be stupid. We are not going."

"Oh, but Ma-ma, we are so close. We may not get this chance again. And once I start college . . ."

"Bas." Bhima covers her ears with her palms. "Bas. No more talking. We are not going to let a letter by a dead woman change our plans. You want to go to the village fair tomorrow, na? We will do so. Then, on Monday, we will catch the train home."

"I don't want to go back home."

"Arre, wah. You're supposed to sit for Chitra next week, correct? Who will do this? And I have a business to run, hai na? How long can I trust that Mukesh?"

"Mukesh will do fine. He's brilliant."

Bhima loses her temper. "Again, you're talking about Mukesh. I'm warning you, chokri, if I hear his name on your lips another time, I'll . . ."

Just then, the wind dies down. In the silence, the music from the radio on the other bank wafts over to them and they hear the song clearly.

"Mere Sapno Ki Rani," Kishore Kumar sings. The Queen of My Dreams.

It was Gopal's song.

It was their song.

Bhima's shoulders begin to tremble. And then she is crying.

40

Bhima looks out of the train window as the years of her life seem to fly past, bringing her to this moment, when against her better judgment she is about to show up uninvited at Gopal's home. Beside her, Maya seems impervious to the agitation that she feels; how she is bracing herself for rejection, the blank stare, the turning away of the head, the thinning of the lips, the indifference of the shrug.

Why is she on this train at all? Because of a letter from a meddlesome old woman who had plotted her way out of this dreadful life cycle. Because of Maya's tearful, incessant entreaties at wanting to meet her grandfather and uncle. But mostly because of the song.

It is a popular song from an old movie and part of the fabric of India. She has heard it a million times since Gopal first sang it to her, in the mad, heady days of their courtship and when he had whispered it to her on their wedding night. The fact that it had played from a portable transistor radio of the people picnicking across the river where they had just scattered Parvati's ashes was coincidence, pure and simple.

But perhaps this is her karma. To touch her husband's feet one last time and ask his forgiveness for humiliating him all those years ago. How many times has she wished she could walk back her angry, heedless march into the bootlegger's shop, where she had berated and struck her drunken husband in front of the other, snickering customers? As if Gopal's drinking had meant that he had no dignity left? As if his unemployment had given her permission to strip him of his manhood? The wife of every poor man learns this lesson early—when a man is destitute and has nothing, he must be allowed to retain his pride. She had forgotten that valuable lesson for one reckless moment and she'd paid for it with the rest of her life. Yes, this much she owed Gopal, this begging for forgiveness.

She glances at Maya, but the girl is chatting happily with another passenger, as if this were an ordinary trip, as if Bhima's insides are not already twisting with embarrassment at the rejection and humiliation that awaits them. Could Gopal have taken another bride in all these years? Surely she would've heard if such was the case. As for Amit, who had her son grown up to become? Was any of that bright-eyed boy still alive in the man? And what did his wife think of her, the unfortunate mother who gave up her only son without a fight?

"Ma-ma, look," Maya says, pointing. "There's a sign that says Tipubag. We must almost be there. Parvati mausi was right. It's not very far, at all."

Parvati. If there is a hell, Bhima thinks, she's sitting there, cackling and gloating over the predicament she has created for Bhima. She remembers that it was Parvati who had asked her to include Maya on this trip to scatter her ashes. If Maya had not accompanied her, if the girl had not read the contents of Parvati's letter herself, she never would have found the courage to visit Tipubag, song or no song. It is Maya's claim on her grandfather's ancestral village that has brought them here.

After they disembark, they look around the almost-empty station. Tipubag is much smaller than Lodpur. Bhima regrets not having sent a telegram ahead, but how could she? She doesn't remember Gopal's address. But if they could've alerted them ahead of arriving, she and Maya could've waited here at the station for the family to greet them, then caught the train going in the opposite direction if no one came. It would've been cleaner that way, less hurtful.

She has been to Tipubag once before, in the early years of their marriage. She remembers the shock of joy that had run through her the first time Gopal's mother had called her bahu—daughter-in-law—the newness of her married state still having the power to thrill, like the unexpected perfume from a jasmine bush at night. She remembers riding from the station in the family's bullock cart, recalls the profile of Gopal's older brother, looking so much like Gopal but more serious, as he drove the cart. She had almost yelled the first time he whipped the poor animal, but Gopal had made stern eyes at her and she had bit down on her tongue.

There is no one to pick them up at Tipubag station this time. A lonely feeling wraps itself around Bhima, and when the train begins to chug away from the platform, she has to fight the urge to run after it. She takes Maya's hand in hers, unaware that her palm is sweating until Maya comments on it. Already, she is cursing herself for not having taken the earlier train. As it is, there is the intimation of the encroaching evening in the clamoring of the birds even as they leave the station and step into the red dust of the parking lot. At this rate, it will be late evening, almost dark, before they reach their destination.

"Where is the farm?" Maya asks again, and Bhima shakes her head. "I don't know. We will have to find out."

There is a small cluster of auto rickshaws outside the station, and Bhima approaches one of the drivers who is standing next to his vehicle smoking a bidi. "Are you knowing Arun Phedke?" she asks, giving the name of Gopal's older brother.

The man squints his eyes as he thinks. "Phedke? No."

Bhima looks around uneasily. "He has a kheti in Tipubag. Whole family is from here. Surely . . ."

"Arre, baba, I said no. Must I know every person who lives here?"

"No need to be rude," Maya says, before Bhima can stop her.

The driver smiles. "Sorry, memsahib," he says. "For you, I will find out." He places his thumb and index finger into his mouth and lets out a loud whistle to get the attention of the other drivers who are milling around. "Arre, listen up," he calls. "Anyone here knows Arjun Phedke?"

"Arun. Not Arjun."

"Hahn. Arun," he yells, nodding his head.

The other drivers murmur between themselves, and then one middle-aged man steps forward. "Phedke? I know him," he says. "He does his shopping at my father's provision store. You are wishing to go to his place?"

Maya and Bhima look at each other in surprise. "Yes," Maya says. "Can you take us? Is it far?"

The man smiles as he motions for them to get into the back seat of the small three-wheeler. "Nothing too far in Tipubag, memsahib. This is a small place." He glances at them. "Where you people from? Dilli? Mumbai?"

"Mumbai," Bhima says shortly, in a tone that makes it clear that she is not in the mood for idle chatter. She peers out of the rickshaw as it splutters down the road, taking in the vivid green of the trees against the red earth. The queasiness in her stomach grows more intense with each passing kilometer. This is a mistake, to come here uninvited, unannounced, unwelcomed. Parvati is dead. Easy for her to suggest this trip. But she and Maya will have to live with the consequences of Gopal's rejection the rest of their days.

Just as she is about to tell the driver to pull over so that she can control the nausea fueled in part by the exhaust from the vehicle, the auto comes to an abrupt halt at the edge of a field. "You please walk it up from here," the man says. "Too much rain here the last few weeks. The road to the house is all muddy due to the flooding. At this hour, big problem if my auto gets stuck."

"Arre, bhai, show some mercy," Bhima argues. "How are we to walk? Evening is approaching and we are strangers here. We don't even know where to go."

But the man is already out of the vehicle and is setting their suitcase on the ground. "Very simple," he says. "You go straight through the middle here, until you reach the house." When they look unconvinced, he turns around and spots a young boy in shorts and a sleeveless shirt hanging from one of the many trees that dot the farm. "Ae, beta," he yells. "Hurry up and go tell your folks that they are having visitors."

The boy stares at them and then, before Bhima can get a close look, jumps off the lowest branch and races down a path cut in the middle of the field. He is yelling something that Bhima, busy with paying the fare, can't make out.

"Will you wait here?" she asks the driver. "Until we are finished with our business? We may need a ride back to the train station tonight."

The man looks at her curiously. "No train for Mumbai stopping again tonight, madam," he says. "Next train not till tomorrow." He turns toward Maya. "You need auto rickshaw tomorrow, you call my mobile phone," he says. "I will write number down for you." And he does.

They wait until he reverses and drives away, until they cannot hear the phut-phut of his vehicle anymore. The silence that follows is deafening, a pastoral silence that their citified ears are unaccustomed to hearing, pierced occasionally only by the calls of the birds returning home to their trees. Maya picks up their suitcase and with her other hand takes hold of her grandmother. "Don't be scared, Ma-ma," she says.

Bhima looks at Maya, her old eyes searching Maya's youthful face. "But what if they don't want us here? What if they've forgotten us?"

Maya looks shocked. "Have you forgotten Gopal baba?" And when Bhima doesn't reply, "Ma-ma. Have you?"

Bhima shakes her head. "Not for a day. Not for a minute of a day." She stares into the distance for a moment, then says, "He is the first man I gave my heart to. For safekeeping. And he never gave it back. Not even when he left."

"Then why do you think he's forgotten you?" Maya squeezes her hand. "Come on, Ma-ma. Let's go find our family."

They walk for several long minutes before they are close enough to see the distant house. With each step, Bhima's fear grows. Above them, the sky has gone from a fiery red to a soft violet and the birds are home now, quiet and at rest. The setting sun flares in the tips of the old trees, and against the backdrop of the sky, Bhima sees the silhouettes of a few men working in the fields, their sickles raised as they hack at the crops. She sees one of the figures straighten up as he spots the strangers in the distance, and then she notices the young boy from earlier, almost hidden by the tall stalks, pointing in their direction. The man appears to say something to the others, then begins to walk toward her and Maya. He walks slowly but resolutely at first and then picks up his pace so that he is trotting as he bridges the distance between them. Finally they are face-to-face.

"Hanh, ji?" he says politely. "Are you looking for someone?"

But Bhima cannot speak. Because it is Gopal who is standing before her, her young, beautiful Gopal, with his dark, shiny hair and that face that is always on the verge of melting into a smile. She waits for recognition to come flooding into his face, but instead of smiling he is frowning, not in anger but puzzlement. And then she thinks, How is it that her Gopi is so much taller than she remembers? So much more muscular and broad-chested? Her Gopal was slender and slight, one of the things she'd loved about him.

"Gopal?" she says cautiously, her eyes already flooding with tears because she knows that something is amiss, that this is another one of life's cruel jokes being played on her, that she will leave here even more brokenhearted and empty-handed than before.

The man bends his head to look at her in the fading light of the day. He blinks, looks away, then stares again. "Ma?" he says. "Ma? Is it you?" His face breaks out in a smile and he beats on his chest with his fist. "It's me. Amit."

"Amit?"

Bhima wishes they were anywhere except in the middle of a field. She wishes there was a chair for her to sit on, to wait out the pounding of the blood in her head, that makes it hard to hear, to believe, to understand. She looks blankly at Maya for help, but the girl looks as helpless as she feels. "Are you my Amit uncle?" she says.

He turns toward her sharply. "You are Pooja's daughter?"

Maya nods. And does what Bhima is incapable of doing. She takes one step toward him, just a single step, but suddenly she is in her uncle's arms, her teary face resting against his chest. "Child," he murmurs. "My child." But his eyes are still on his mother, transfixed.

"Hey," Amit yells suddenly. "Chotu. Where are you?" and just like that, the boy appears again from the stalks that are taller than he is. "Ma," Amit says. "This is Krishna. Your grandson."

A grandson named Krishna? Bhima remembers all the years she has prayed at the shrine of Lord Krishna. She curses the tears that are curtaining her eyes, making it hard to clearly see her grandson for the first time. "I have a grandson?" she whispers.

"Ha. You have four. He's the youngest." Amit laughs. He looks at her shyly. "I named him this because Dada always said that Lord Krishna was your favorite God."

"You don't remember?" she asks, and before he can answer, she shakes her head ruefully. "How can you? You were so young when he—when you left."

"But I never forgot you," Amit says fiercely. "Believe or don't believe."

"You still play cricket?"

Amit lets out a laugh. "Me? Look at me, Ma. I'm an old man. But my sons do." He picks up their suitcase as effortlessly as a toothbrush. "Chalo. It will be dark soon. Let's take you home, Ma. You city folks will not be able to see your own hand once the night falls."

"And you?" Maya asks boldly.

He laughs again, easily. There is none of the rancor that Bhima had been dreading. "Arre, munni," he says, "I can walk these fields with my eyes closed. These are my father's fields, after all."

And even as Bhima glows from the nickname—Little One—that Amit has so effortlessly bestowed upon Maya, as if they are already family, her heart twists at Amit's casual mention of his father. "Is your dada . . ." she begins, but Amit cuts her off, turning toward his son. "Ae, chotu," he yells. "Go inform Gopal dada that we have visitors."

They walk toward the house, Amit leading the way down the narrow clearing, and now Bhima can see the concrete house with the tiled roof. It is a solid house, and she is both grateful for the fact that Amit has grown up in comfort and resentful of the years she and Maya have spent in squalor.

There is a large courtyard that separates the fields from the house, and as they step toward it, the door opens and an old man walks outdoors. "Ae, Dada, come look at who has arrived," Amit calls. His voice is casual, his manner at ease, as if a million years have not divided them, as if this reunion is not a miracle, as if fate has not taken Bhima by the hand and brought her here. As if—Bhima stops walking as the thought hits her—Amit has been expecting them all along. As if he knew that someday his mother would come looking for him. She has spent so many bitter years wondering why her grown son and her husband have not come for her. Now she wonders why she waited for them to make the first move.

"Kaun hai?" The old man's voice has a tremor in it, but it is unmistakably Gopal's. And even though they are now only a little more than an arm's length away from each other, he shades his eyes with his hand, as if he's staring into the sun. That gesture, in its frailty, its tenuousness, is new, and Bhima feels it in the tug of her heart. The years have aged both of them, but in her mind, she now realizes, Gopal never got older. No wonder she had mistaken Amit for his father.

Gopal is staring into her face, as if he is trying to recollect something, and she sees her own confusion reflected in his eyes, the difficulty of reconciling the images in their heads with the flawed, bent bodies standing before one another. The moment stretches until finally Gopal looks away to consider Maya. But the next second, he is staring at Bhima again. The sky is indigo now, its ink dropping on all their skins, shading the world around them. She smells the loamy earth, hears the last twitter of the birds. The evening breeze tugs at her scant hair, loosening a few strands. It is so quiet that she can hear Maya's tense breathing, hears the sound of water running inside the house. Still, the silence stretches between her and Gopal. Beside her, she feels both Amit and Maya shift nervously.

And then, the tears come to her eyes again. Perhaps this is the rejection she couldn't have imagined—not the deliberate turning away she has been dreading, but the simple yet deadly act of unrecognition. The acknowledgment that too many years have gone by, that the past is a murder that cannot be undone. She blinks, feels the acidic shame burning in her stomach, and starts to turn away, when . . .

When.

"Bibi?" The voice is soft, low, meant for just the two of them. She hears the tentativeness in it but also something else. Tenderness. And a tendril of hope.

Mere sapno ki rani kab aayegi tu? That's the song he used to sing to her, the one that has delivered her to his doorstep. The queen of my dreams, when will you arrive?

She has arrived.

She is here, home with her family. With her husband. If he will have her.

"Gopal," she whispers, and this time he says it louder, with conviction. "My Bibi? Is it you? Is it really you?"

She bends down to touch his feet, to beg his forgiveness, but he reaches to prevent her, grabs her by her upper arms, and pulls her toward him. "Nahi," he says. "It is I who. It is I who should. Who needs to . . ." They stand like this for a moment, looking into each other's eyes in the fading light of the day, and then he lets go of her and turns to Maya. "And you are my Pooja's child?"

"Dada." Maya moves toward her grandfather, but he does not embrace her as Amit had done. Instead, he looks deeply into her face, and then, as if he's satisfied by what he has seen, he nods. There is a faint smile on his face. "It is good that you have come." He faces his fields and then sweeps his hand in an arc, to include all that stands before him. "This kheti belongs to you and your mother, child. This is your inheritance. It is good you have come to claim it."

Maya opens her mouth to explain, then looks at her grandmother, and closes it. Bhima gives her a small nod of approval. There is so much to learn, so much to know, so much to tell. She looks toward the house and sees the shadows of people flitting around. Her heart quickens at the thought of meeting Amit's wife. Perhaps she will have another daughter after all. She glances up toward the sky to offer her gratitude when Amit speaks.

"Arre, bhai, chalo, let's go in the house," her son is saying. "We have to feed our guests, na?"

"Not guests," Gopal says, resting his arm on Maya's shoulder, as he escorts her into his house. "Blood."

He looks at Bhima, cocks one eyebrow, and for a split second, he is the exuberant young man on the bicycle chasing the bus she rode to work every morning. He smiles. "Shall we enter, my bride?"

For a moment she is unable to reply, unable to take his offered hand. She stands on the threshold of his house, *their* house, and feels Parvati's presence sure as if her friend is poised to cross the threshold along with her. She feels Parvati urging her forward and then imagines a hard thump on her back as Parvati tires of her hesitation.

Bhima nods. "Yes," she whispers. And then, a little louder, "Yes."

Although it is dusk, in Bhima's heart it is dawn.

About the author

About the book

Read on

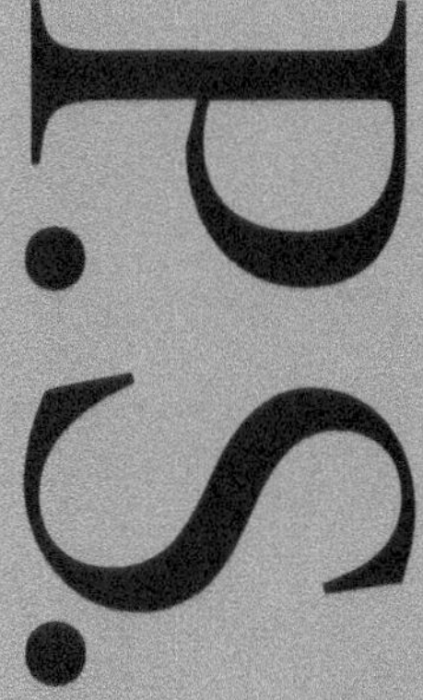

Insights, Interviews & More . . .

Meet Thrity Umrigar

Robert Muller

THRITY UMRIGAR IS THE AUTHOR OF eight novels, *The Secrets Between Us*, *Everybody's Son*, *The Story Hour*, *The World We Found*, *The Weight of Heaven*, *The Space Between Us*, *If Today Be Sweet*, and *Bombay Time*; a memoir, *First Darling of the Morning*; and a children's picture book, *When I Carried You in My Belly*. A former journalist, she has written for the *New York Times*, the *Washington Post*, and the *Boston Globe*. She is a recipient of a Nieman Fellowship to Harvard, the Cleveland Arts Prize, and was a finalist for the PEN Open Book Award, formerly the Beyond Margins Award. A professor of English at Case Western Reserve University, she lives in Cleveland, Ohio. ~

The Story Behind *The Secrets Between Us*

Ever since the publication of *The Space Between Us* in 2006, readers have asked for a sequel. At book talks, many have expressed concern and worry about Bhima's future in such emotional terms that I have occasionally jokingly reminded them that Bhima is, after all, a fictional character about whom they need not worry so much. I have also batted away their requests for a sequel because I felt that I had said everything I wanted to say about the peculiar institution that is the employment of domestic servants in India in *Space*. And I was not interested in telling the same story twice.

But over the years, I've often wondered about a minor character who nobody has ever asked about—Parvati, the disfigured vegetable vendor, who Bhima treats with horror and contempt. The novel tells us that Parvati earns her living selling six heads of cauliflower a day. And this has always aroused my curiosity. How on earth does one survive on such a meager income? And what life circumstances have reduced this poor woman, barely mentioned in *Space*, to her threadbare existence? Who was Parvati and what was her life story?

I didn't know the answers to these questions. Until, one day, I did.

Once I knew Parvati's background, I was interested in exploring her story more and seeing if it would intersect with Bhima's. It occurred to me that the time period of the novel—around 2006 or 2007—was exactly when globalization had taken root in India and the country was buoyant with hope and giddy with economic prosperity. For the first time, class mobility seemed possible and young people were at the vanguard of the shifts in cultural mores.

But what about two rickety, marginalized old women? Could this new India have room for them to prosper and grow? Or would these new currents of change simply sweep past them? I found myself excited to test these questions by placing Bhima and Parvati against the background of a changing country and to capture some of its optimism and daring.

Thus, the new novel was born.

Sera, Bhima's former employer, has a smaller role in *The Secrets Between Us.* ▸

When readers would express sympathy for Bhima, I'd ask them to also consider Sera, who had to choose between her friendship with Bhima and her loyalty to her family. Sera is as much a victim as Bhima, I would remind my readers, and her psychological entrapment is every bit as terrible as Bhima's economic prison. I hope that readers of *Secrets* will see the price Sera has paid for her choice.

If *Space* was a book that described the outward manifestations of poverty—Bhima's life in the slum, her economic anxiety, her illiteracy and the terrible cost it exacts from her—I see *Secrets* as a book that describes the internal manifestations of poverty—the social isolation and loneliness that marginalized people experience, the shame and secrecy they feel about their conditions, the daily injuries to their self-esteem.

Indeed, as I've grown older, I've come to better understand the complexity of poverty and the toll it takes on the human spirit. The new novel also engages with the fact that people need more than money to feel fully human. They need family. They need community and friendship. The introduction of a young gay couple who befriend Bhima's granddaughter, Maya, provides Bhima with an opportunity to confront her own prejudices and also to expand her definition of family. If Bhima and Parvati are to make it, it is this sorority of sisterhood that they will need to rely upon to combat all of life's injustices and betrayals.

Read on

Reading Group Guide: Discussion Questions for *The Secrets Between Us*

1. Parvati is a gruff and bitter character. At what point in the novel did you feel sympathetic toward her?

2. Sera Dubash plays a minor role in *Secrets*, compared to the first book. Do you feel as if her appearance helps you understand her decision in the first novel a little better?

3. Do you feel as if Sunita and Chitra are important to this novel? Why? What role do they play?

4. The novel claims that it is the secrets that we harbor that define us. What does this mean? Do you agree?

5. Thrity Umrigar has said that she was interested in exploring the internal manifestations of poverty. What are some examples of this in the novel and how did they increase your understanding of poverty?

6. In any good friendship, each person learns something from the other. What do Bhima and Parvati teach one another?

7. Do you see a hopeful future for Maya? Will she make it out of the slums? What gives you hope and why?

8. What is your favorite line or quote in this novel? What did it mean to you?

9. *Secrets* is also a portrait of a city and country undergoing rapid changes. List some of those changes. Are they for the better or worse?

10. Parvati's story hinges on the fact that she is sold into prostitution by her father. Do you understand his motivations, or did you find yourself judging him? What else could he have done instead of this shocking act?

11. Many readers have expressed a desire for a companion book to *The Space Between Us* for years. Did *Secrets* meet your expectations ▶

for a companion or sequel? Why or why not?

12. *Secrets* is set during the years 2006–2007 in India. What differences in the characters and narratives might you expect to see if their stories were taking place today?

13. Parvati has a minor role in *Space* and a major role in *Secrets*. Are there any other minor characters from either book whose stories you would like to know? Who are they? What do you imagine their stories might be?

14. If you were to write an additional last chapter to this book, what would it say?

15. Should there be a third book? If so, where would you take Bhima's story?

An Excerpt from *The Space Between Us*

ALTHOUGH IT IS DAWN, INSIDE BHIMA'S heart it is dusk.

Rolling onto her left side on the thin cotton mattress on the floor, she sits up abruptly, as she does every morning. She lifts one bony hand over her head in a yawn and a stretch, and a strong, mildewy smell wafts from her armpit and assails her nostrils. For an idle moment she sits at the edge of the mattress with her callused feet flat on the mud floor, her knees bent, and her head resting on her folded arms. In that time she is almost at rest, her mind thankfully blank and empty of the trials that await her today and the next day and the next . . . To prolong this state of mindless grace, she reaches absently for the tin of chewing tobacco that she keeps by her bedside. She pushes a wad into her mouth, so that it protrudes out of her fleshless face like a cricket ball.

Bhima's idyll is short-lived. In the faint, delicate light of a new day, she makes out Maya's silhouette as she stirs on the mattress on the far left side of their hut. The girl is mumbling in her sleep, making soft, whimpering sounds, and despite herself, Bhima feels her heart soften and dissolve, the way it used to when she breastfed Maya's mother, Pooja, all those years ago. Propelled by Maya's puppylike sounds, Bhima gets up with a grunt from the mattress and makes her way to where her granddaughter lies asleep. But in the second that it takes to cross the small hut, something shifts in Bhima's heart, so that the milky, maternal feeling from a moment ago is replaced by that hard, merciless feeling of rage that has lived within her since several weeks ago. She stands towering over the sleeping girl, who is now snoring softly, blissfully unaware of the pinpoint anger in her grandmother's eyes as she stares at the slight swell of Maya's belly.

One swift kick, Bhima says to herself, one swift kick to the belly, followed by another and another, and it will all be over. Look at her sleeping there, like a shameless whore, as if she has not a care in the world. As if she has not turned my life upside down. Bhima's right foot twitches with anticipation; the muscles in her calf tense as she lifts her foot a few inches off the ground. It would be so easy. And compared to what some other grandmother might do to Maya—a quick shove down an open well, a kerosene can and a match, a sale to a brothel—this would be so humane. This way, Maya would live, would continue going to college and choose a life different from what Bhima had always known. That was how it was supposed to be, how it had been, until this dumb cow of a girl, this girl with the big heart and, now, a big belly, went and got herself pregnant.

Maya lets out a sudden loud snort, and Bhima's poised foot drops to the floor. She crouches down next to the sleeping girl to shake her by the shoulders and wake her up. When Maya was still going to college, Bhima allowed her to sleep in as late as possible, made gaajar halwa for her every Sunday, gave her the biggest portions of dinner every night. If Serabai ever gave Bhima a treat—a Cadbury's chocolate, say, or that white candy with pistachios that came from Iran—she'd save it to bring it home for Maya, though, truth to tell, Serabai usually gave her a portion for Maya anyway. But ever since Bhima has learned of her granddaughter's shame, ▸

she has been waking the girl up early. For the last several Sundays there has been no gaajar halwa, and Maya has not asked for her favorite dessert. Earlier this week, Bhima even ordered the girl to stand in line to fill their two pots at the communal tap. Maya had protested at that, her hand unconsciously rubbing her belly, but Bhima had looked away and said the people in the basti would soon enough find out about her dishonor anyway, so why hide it?

Maya rolls over in her sleep, so that her face is inches away from where Bhima is squatting. Her young, fat hand finds Bhima's thin, crumpled one, and she nestles against it, holding it between her chin and her chest. A single strand of drool falls on Bhima's captive hand. The older woman feels herself soften. Maya has been like this from the time she was a baby—needy, affectionate, trusting. Despite all the sorrow she has experienced in her young life, Maya has not lost her softness and innocence. With her other free hand, Bhima strokes the girl's lush, silky hair, so different from her own scanty hair.

The sound of a transistor radio playing faintly invades the room, and

Bhima swears under her breath. Usually, by the time Jaiprakash turns his radio on, she is already in line at the water tap. That means she is late this morning. Serabai will be livid. This stupid, lazy girl has delayed her. Bhima pulls her hand brusquely away from Maya, not caring whether the movement wakes her up. But the girl sleeps on. Bhima jumps to her feet, and as she does, her left hip lets out a loud pop. She stands still for a moment, waiting for the wave of pain that follows the pop, but today is a good day. No pain.

Bhima picks up the two copper pots and opens the front door. She bends so that she can exit from the low door and then shuts it behind her. She does not want the lewd young men who live in the slum to leer at her sleeping granddaughter as they pass by. One of them is probably the father of the baby . . . She shakes her head to clear the dark, snakelike thoughts that invade it.

Bhima's bowels move and she clucks her tongue. Now she'll have to make her way to the communal bathroom before she goes to the tap, and the line will be even longer. Usually, she tries to control her bowels until she gets to Serabai's ▸

house, with its real toilets. Still, it's early enough that the conditions shouldn't be too bad. A few hours later and there will hardly be room to walk between the tidy piles of shit that the residents of the slum leave on the mud floor of the communal toilet. After all these years, the flies and the stink still make Bhima's stomach turn. The slum residents have taken to paying the Harijan woman who lives at the far end of the slum colony to collect their piles each night. Bhima sees her sometimes, crouching on the floor as she sweeps the pancakes of shit with her broom into a wicker basket that's lined with newspaper. Occasionally, their eyes meet, and Bhima makes it a point to smile at her. Unlike most of the residents of the slums, Bhima does not consider herself superior to the poor woman.

Bhima finishes her business and makes her way to the tap. She groans as she sees the long line, winding its way past the black, disheveled-looking huts with their patched tin roofs. The morning light makes the squalor of the slum colony even more noticeable. The open drains with their dank, pungent smell, the dark rows of slanting hutments, the gaunt, openmouthed men who lounge around in drunken stupors—all of it looks worse in the clear light of the new day. Despite herself, Bhima's mind goes back to the old days when she lived with her husband, Gopal, and their two children in a chawl, where water gurgled through the tap in her kitchen and they shared the toilet with only two other families.

Bhima is about to join the end of the water tap line when Bibi spots her. "Ae, Bhima mausi," she says. "Come over here, na. For you only I've been holding a reservation here."

Bhima smiles in gratitude. Bibi is a fat, asthmatic woman who moved into the slum two years ago and immediately adopted Bhima as her older aunt. Whereas Bhima is silent and reserved, Bibi is loud and flashy. Nobody can stay angry at Bibi for too long—her willingness to help, her good-natured ribbing of old and young, have made her one of the slum colony's most popular residents.

Now Bhima makes her way to where Bibi is standing. "Here," Bibi says, taking one of Bhima's pots from her, despite the fact that she's carrying two of her own. "Get in here." ▸

The man behind them feels compelled to protest. "Ho, Bibi, this is not the Deccan Express, where you have reservations for a first-class bogey," he grumbles. "Nobody is allowed to jump the queue like this."

Bhima feels her face flush, but Bibi holds out a restraining hand and whirls around to face her detractor. "Wah, wah," she says loudly. "Mr. Deccan Express here is worried about people jumping the line. But in one-two hours straight, while Bhima mausi is hard at work, he'll be headed for the local bootlegger's joint. And if there's a shortage of liquor today, God forbid, let's see then whether he jumps the line or not." The crowd around them snickers.

The man shuffles his feet. "Okay, now, Bibi, no need for personal attacks," he mumbles.

Bibi's voice gets even louder. "Arre, bhaisahib, who's attacking you personally? All I'm saying is, you are obviously a man of leisure, a man of great personal wealth. If you wish to spend your days at the bootlegger's shop, that's your concern. But poor Bhima here, she doesn't have a fine husband like you to support her. We all know how well you support your wife. So anyway, Bhima mausi has to go to work on time. And I didn't think a gentleman like you would mind if she filled her pots before you did."

The crowd is whooping with delight now. "Ae, Bibi, you are too much, yaar. Tops, just tops," a young layabout says.

"Who needs nuclear weapons?" someone else says. "I tell you, yaar, they should just unleash Bibi in Kashmir. The snows will melt from the fire in her tongue."

"Wait, wait, I have it," says Mohan, the seventeen-year-old who lives in the hut diagonally across from Bibi's. "A perfect song for the occasion. Here it is:

"Forget the atom bomb, India said
Our new weapon leaves Pakistan dead
Just like she did Mr. Deccan Express
Bibi will leave you an utter mess."

Another man, whom Bhima doesn't know, slaps Mohan on the back. "Arre, ustad, you are too much. Our slum's own court poet. With your movie star ▸

looks, you should be writing and singing your own songs. Imagine, the physique of a Sanjay Dutt and the voice of a Mohammad Rafi. On Filmfare awards night, there would be no other winners, I tell you."

Despite herself, Bhima smiles. "Okay, you altoo-faltoos," Bibi says with a grin. "Leave us alone now."

By the time Bhima reaches her hut, Maya is up and has tea brewing on the Primus stove. As the girl adds the mint leaves to the boiling water, Bhima's stomach growls. The two stand outside their hut and quickly brush their teeth. Maya uses a toothbrush, but Bhima simply takes the tooth powder on her index finger and rubs vigorously on her remaining teeth. They spit into the open drain that rolls past their home. Quickly, efficiently, Bhima dips a plastic cup into one of the copper pots and washes herself through her clothes. Her face burns as she notices the man in the opposite hut staring at her as she puts a hand under her blouse to wash her armpits. Shameless badmaash, she mutters to herself. Acting as if he has no mother or sister.

When Bhima reenters the hut, Maya pours the tea into two glasses. They sit on their haunches, facing each other, blowing on the hot tea and dipping a loaf of bread into the brew. "Good tea," Bhima says. It is the first she has spoken to Maya this morning. Then, as if the girl's look of gratitude is too much for her to bear, she adds, "Seems like at least something I've taught you has stayed with you."

Maya flinches, and the guarded, wary look returns to her face. Noticing the look makes Bhima feel repentant but strangely satisfied. She is gripped by the need to draw more blood.

"So what will you do all day today?"

Maya shrugs.

The shrug infuriates Bhima. "Oh, that's right, memsahib is no longer going to college, I forgot," she says, addressing the walls. "No, now she will just sit around like a queen all day, feeding herself and her—her bastard baby, while her poor grandmother slaves in someone's home. All so that she can feed the demon that's growing in her granddaughter's belly."

If it's blood she wanted, she has it. Maya moans as she pulls herself up ▸

from the floor and moves to the farthest corner of the small room. She leans lightly on the tin wall, her hands around her belly, and sobs to herself.

Bhima wants to take the sobbing girl to her bosom, to hold and caress her the way she used to when Maya was a child, to forgive her and to ask for her forgiveness. But she can't. If it were just anger that she was feeling, she could've scaled that wall and reached out to her grandchild. But the anger is only the beginning of it. Behind the anger is fear, fear as endless and vast and gray as the Arabian Sea, fear for this stupid, innocent, pregnant girl who stands sobbing before her, and for this unborn baby who will come into the world to a mother who is a child herself and to a grandmother who is old and tired to her very bones, a grandmother who is tired of loss, of loving and losing, who cannot bear the thought of one more loss and of one more person to love.

So she stares numbly at the weeping girl, willing her heart not to take in the arrows of her sobbing. "Even tears are a luxury," she says, but she is unsure if she's spoken out loud or to herself. "I envy you your tears."

When she next speaks, she does so consciously. "If you feel well enough, stop by Serabai's house later. She keeps asking about you."

But even through her tears, Maya shakes her head no. "I told you, Ma-ma," she says. "I don't leave the house all day while you are gone."

Bhima gives up. "Okay, then, sit at home while your old grandmother works all day," she says, as she rises to her feet. "Fatten your baby with my blood."

"Ma-ma, please," Maya sobs, placing her hands over her ears, the way she used to when she was little.

Bhima pulls the door shut behind her. She wants to slam it but controls herself. No need for anyone in the basti to know their family problems. They will know about the disgrace Maya has brought upon herself soon enough, and then they will attack her like vultures. No point in hastening that day.

As she begins her walk toward Serabai's house, a cool morning breeze leans into Bhima, and she shivers against it. She can tell from the angle of the sun that she's late. Serabai will be anxious to know what transpired yesterday. She picks up her pace.

ALSO BY THRITY UMRIGAR

THE SPACE BETWEEN US
A NOVEL

Available in Paperback, Digital audio, Large Print, and eBook

"This is a story intimately and compassionately told against the sensuous background of everyday life in Bombay."
—Washington Post Book World

THE SECRETS BETWEEN US
A NOVEL

Available in Paperback, Digital audio, Large Print, and eBook

"The women at the heart of this novel inhabit the harsh world of the urban Indian poor, and struggle separately and together for dignity and survival. Thrity Umrigar has written a moving human tale that vividly brings to life both the women and the city of Mumbai."
—Salman Rushdie

IF TODAY BE SWEET
A NOVEL

Available in Paperback, Digital audio, and eBook

"A convincing testament to the enduring power of place."
—Kirkus Reviews

THE WEIGHT OF HEAVEN
A NOVEL

Available in Paperback, Digital audio, Large Print, and eBook

"*The Weight of Heaven* packs a wallop on both a literary and emotional level. . . . Umrigar is a descriptive master."
—Christian Science Monitor

ALSO BY THRITY UMRIGAR

THE WORLD WE FOUND
A NOVEL

Available in Paperback, Digital audio, Large Print, and eBook

"*The World We Found* is stunning in its credibility and nuance . . . . This is a novel that rewards reading, and even re-reading. *The World We Found* is a powerful meditation."
—*Boston Globe*

THE STORY HOUR
A NOVEL

Available in Paperback, Digital audio, and eBook

"With grace, wisdom and incredible compassion, Thrity Umrigar has woven together the lives of two seemingly dissimilar women who must learn—against teep odds—to forgive each other and themselves."
—Paula McLain, author of *The Paris Wife*

EVERYBODY'S SON
A NOVEL

Available in Paperback, Digital audio, and eBook

"*Everybody's Son* probes directly into the tender spots of race and privilege in America... With assured prose and deep insight into the human heart, Umrigar explores the moral gray zone of what parents, no matter their race, will do for love."
—Celeste Ng, author of *Everything I Never Told You*

FIRST DARLING OF THE MORNING
SELECTED MEMORIES OF AN INDIAN CHILDHOOD

Available in Paperback, Digital audio, and eBook

"Bracingly honest and bittersweet."
—*Booklist* (starred review)